A

TORTOISE

IN THE

ROAD

A

TORTOISE

IN THE

ROAD

WARREN DRIGGS

NORTH LOOP BOOKS | MINNEAPOLIS, MN

NORTHLOOP
BOOKS

North Loop Books
322 First Avenue N, 5th floor
Minneapolis, MN 55401
612.455.2294
www.NorthLoopBooks.com

ISBN-13: 978-1-63413-857-4
LCCN: 2016902414

Distributed by Itasca Books

Printed in the United States of America

TO MY AMAZING PARENTS,
WHEREVER THEY MIGHT BE

PROLOGUE

The sunburned stretch of tar between Sun City and Phoenix is mostly irrelevant, its significance known only to sleepy truck drivers, desert creatures, and the victims of June 2, 2002. There is the faint hum from electrical wires that droop from poles stuck in the ground mile after mile, like velvet theatre rope guarding the road. Otherwise the desert is silent.

It was dusk, that time of day when headlights were a luxury. A faded red pickup truck was stopped in the middle of the southbound lane to allow a large desert tortoise to cross the road. An attractive young woman driving a Honda Civic had come to a stop behind the red pickup, and behind her was a late-model Lexus driven by an elderly woman. The driver of the pickup truck drummed his calloused fingers on the steering wheel and looked over at his dog riding shotgun. "It's one of them goddamned turtles, Wrigley." Behind him, the young woman craned her neck to look around the pickup to whatever it was that had caused him to stop, fidgeting in her seat and rubbing her taut stomach. She was anxious to find a bathroom. The elderly woman at the back of the line leaned her head against the headrest, closed her eyes, and exhaled, for she had nowhere else to be.

A commercial semi-truck hardly slowed at all. It slammed into the rear of the Lexus with brutal force, collapsing the car like a wad of tin foil. The sedan was violently propelled into the rear of the Civic, causing it to slam into the back of the red pickup. The horrific sound was compressed into two seconds, two cruel ticks that could not be taken back. The noise of metal bending, scraping, and breaking all at once roared as if God in his fury had ripped open a tin can with his bare hands.

And then it was silent again.

The dog jumped from the cab of the pickup truck, yelping and running in circles as if it had gone completely mad. The driver of the pickup threw his shoulder against the buckled door, pried it open, and then climbed out. His dirty jeans hung low on his thin waist. He wore neither shirt nor shoes. If he was injured he did not show it. He yelled into the empty desert for help and then began to chase his frightened dog that darted around the mangled wreckage.

The driver of the semi-truck staggered down from the perch of his cab. He was an ample man who wore a long-sleeved gray shirt that was stretched tight across his middle. There were dark stains under his arms and on his back. He was red and fleshy and his jowls jiggled when he cried out, "Oh my God! Oh my God! Oh my God!"

He lumbered over to the Lexus in front of him and looked inside at the elderly woman, then vomited on the side of the road. He wiped his mouth with a dirty sleeve and continued to scream for help and for mercy, any mercy at all. Then he made his way forward to the Civic and saw the young woman inside. Her head was slumped at an unnatural angle, but she was alive, for he could hear her moaning. There were blue balloons and unwrapped gifts crammed into her car. A deflated airbag hung limp before her and the seatbelt stretched over her pregnant belly.

"Oh my God! Somebody help us! Please!"

He ran back to his cab and called for emergency help, his stubby fingers jabbing at the numbers on his cell. He then sat in the driver's seat with the door open, trying to breathe. How had this happened? What had he done? His pale face was shiny from tears and sweat. It was also smeared with the pain of knowing he had done something so awful and permanent that it could never be undone; the sort of pain that would register on his face forevermore, if you knew what to look for.

The shirtless young man was frantic. He, too, had dared look into the Lexus and Civic and then stood on the side of the road and inexplicably screamed to the smattering of cacti and sagebrush for help. By that time he had lost complete control of his dog that had run into the desert to flee its fear. He ran over to the semi-truck, yelling obscenities at the poor man who was begging an unseen source for an answer to what he had done, and why he had done it. He kept striking his forehead with the palm of his hand, as if to shake the nightmare away. The young man, seeing the sincere repentance of the driver, then sought only to console him.

Soon other drivers arrived on the scene. They would later report on the horror they had seen, and they would do so with somber satisfaction, as if it had been their duty to properly record the tragedy for the benefit of their family and friends. They made way for the police and ambulances whose red lights turned round and round in the dark like lopsided tops. The lead officer at the scene was a muscled man with a military style crew cut. His starched uniform was smartly tucked without bend or wrinkle. He lorded over the mess with no visible emotion. "Load it to the ambulance," he commanded, as if the "it" was a thing instead of an elderly woman whose head had nearly been severed from the rest of her body. This man, who wore the nametag "Howard," was not to be trifled with.

"Stay away from my scene," he snapped at the reporter who had nearly beaten them to the carnage. "No photos and all witnesses are off limits until I've interviewed them. You got that? Now clear the scene so I can do my job."

The reporter was a slightly disheveled man who wore khakis that had since lost their permanent press and an out-of-style denim shirt with a tail untucked. He was a handsome man, or at least there were telltale signs of previous handsomeness. He had deep set blue eyes and a strong jaw. His thick brown hair swept back from his forehead and was untamed, as if he combed it with his fingers. He was over six feet tall with broad shoulders and still moved like the athlete he once was, but he had "let himself go," according to his ex-wife, a staple of her weekly nag when he'd come to pick up his son.

Those few precious seconds that brought together the truck driver, the elderly woman, the pregnant woman, the shirtless man and his dog, the cop, and the reporter would conspire to change lives in unimagined ways. The chance collision of these people, the arbitrary and capricious nature of their misfortune, would not end with the final period in Officer Howard's official investigative traffic accident report. For that was only the beginning.

PART I

Darkling I listen; and, for many a time
I have been half in love with easeful Death,
Call'd him soft names in many a musèd rhyme,
To take into the air my quiet breath;
Now more than ever seems it rich to die,
To cease upon the midnight with no pain . . .

—John Keats, "Ode to a Nightingale"

1

The cubicle on the third floor of the *Arizona Republic* was cluttered. A boxy computer screen was wedged into the corner of his workspace, leaving hardly any room for the collection of used Styrofoam coffee cups, overflowing in-basket, photo of a boy in a soccer uniform, and a lunch menu from Triple Play, a local sports bar. He was partial to Triple Play because it displayed a framed photo of him from his glory years, years that hadn't been all that glorious. A pair of smelly tennis shoes and gym shorts was thrown into a corner next to a coat rack where a wrinkled sports coat and tie hung, untouched for months. He was hunched over the keyboard lamenting his fantasy football standings when he heard approaching footsteps. He minimized the page to a small icon on the bottom of the computer screen, along with a partially completed game of solitaire.

"Hey, Blake, you got a minute?"

"Sure, Hal, what's up?"

"Listen, I know you're bored, and I want you to be happy here."

"I just don't know how much more of this shit I can cover, Hal. It seems like I'm writing the same story every day. I need a change."

"I'd like to keep you on the sports desk because it makes

sense to have you cover the Diamondbacks, but maybe there's something else you want to do."

"Like what? Want me to start a gossip column?"

Blake had been hired several years earlier as a guest columnist for the newspaper's sports section after he'd been cut from the Arizona Diamondbacks major league baseball team. That stint led to a full-time position with the paper. Blake covered most sports, but also some local and regional news. This reporter business had been a booby prize, for his father's sole ambition had been to make his son a baseball star. From as early as Blake could remember, his father had lived his unfulfilled dream through his toddler, like the obsessive mother who drags her six-year-old daughter to every beauty pageant in the tri-state area, dousing her with perfume, makeup, and a tiara. And so it had been with Blake, the constant pressure to perform for his father.

Neither of his parents graduated from high school. They dropped out before their senior year and were married shortly thereafter. Blake had done the math and knew his conception was responsible for their shotgun nuptials. He wasn't sure how he felt about it, either. He didn't think his parents held it against him, but there were times he still felt guilty about the whole thing. This was something that was never spoken of, because his parents, and especially his mom, were religious conservatives.

Blake had always been big for his age, the only eight-year-old who could throw a pitch all the way to home plate without at least one bounce. He loomed over panic stricken kids from the pitcher's mound while they cowered at the plate, grateful not to have been struck in the rump by a 30-mph fastball, even if it meant striking out.

Blake was the best Little Leaguer in Phoenix. He was pampered at home and school, all because he could throw a devilish curve ball better than the kids who preferred looking through a microscope, dissecting a frog, or reading a book. So, while his friends had paper routes and helped their dads around the yard, Blake rested up lest he pull a muscle doing a chore.

He remained humble through it all, probably the result of his mom, who thought the fawning was quite unnecessary. Blake was a reluctant beneficiary of his good looks and athletic prowess. He was popular but didn't place undue significance on it. This was also because of his mom, who had trained him to believe he was no better than the stocky, pimple-faced girl from down the street who had invited him to the school dance. His mom insisted he immediately say yes, and be happy about it, even though he knew the hottest girl at school planned to invite him the next day. When he became the Homecoming King, an inevitability reserved for people like Blake, he shrugged his shoulders and said, "I'd lots rather pitch a shutout." He had an easy confidence about him, as if he should be welcomed, even admired, perhaps, wherever he went.

The dream of his father was realized when Blake made the big leagues. But then his father died unexpectedly and Blake's ambition seemed to die with him. The cruel hand of misfortune intervened again when he suffered a career-ending knee injury. His fall was swift. His savings had been spent carelessly on cars, bar tabs, and women who slipped quietly away to players with guaranteed contracts. He was twenty-seven years old and already used up. But he was still handsome with some acclaim, albeit the ebbing kind—for what kind doesn't ebb?

So, he siphoned off his leftover fame and became a local celebrity pitch man. He hocked tires, furniture, used cars, and mufflers. (*"Hi, Blake Morgan here to tell you about the importance of good tires. As a ballplayer, I relied on my tires to get me safely to the ballpark. At Wickenburg Tires they care about your safety, and that's why they're the only ones I trust!"*)

He was rescued by Hal Crawford, the venerable editor for the Arizona Republic. This had been a charitable gesture at the request of the Diamondback's owner to assuage his guilt for cutting Blake from the team. Crawford was cranky, lording over the newsroom with Captain Ahab-like obsession. And now he stood at the threshold of Blake's cubicle. He pulled an unfiltered Camel from the pack, lit it, and then tossed the match into Blake's trashcan. He inhaled deeply, leaned his head back, and exhaled a contrail of smoke to the ceiling. There was a no-smoking provision at the paper but Hal blatantly ignored it. He rocked professorially between his heels and toes while Blake leaned back in his chair, looking up at him.

"What about a human interest story?"

"A human interest story? Come on, Hal, I'm no fluff writer. You know that. I can't think of one that would appeal to me, anyway."

"How about following up on a story you've covered before? You could do a 'Where are they now?' type of deal."

Blake caught Crawford looking at his scuffed shoes, and when Crawford turned his head to bark at another reporter who was late with a story, Blake slid his feet under his chair.

"Thanks, Hal, but all the people I've covered are either dead or in jail."

"Didn't you cover that crash out there on Highway 60 a few years back, the one where the truck driver fell asleep at the wheel? You could do a follow-up story on that one. That might be interesting."

"Can I think about it?"

"Sure, and if there's something else that piques your interest, let me know." He walked away grumbling something about the "goddamned copy machine for chrissakes" and was gone.

Blake finished his starting lineup for the weekend's fantasy football league and then pulled a copy of the story he'd filed five years earlier.

FIERY COLLISION KILLS ONE, SERIOUSLY INJURES ANOTHER

Investigation >> Responsible Driver may have violated maximum driving hours limit. Charges pending.

By Blake Morgan

Arizona Republic

Sun City, AZ >> June 2, 2002. A multiple vehicle collision took the life of one Arizona driver and seriously injured another on Highway 60, just south of Sun City, AZ. The collision occurred Tuesday, shortly before 9:00 p.m., when a southbound semi-truck struck a line of cars also heading south. According to witnesses, the cars were stopped to allow a large desert tortoise to cross the two-lane highway, when the large commercial vehicle, being operated by Don Weeks of Interwest Trucking, Inc., failed to stop, and rear-ended the line of three cars that were stopped in the roadway.

Fern Morris, 74, of Scottsdale, AZ, was killed instantly. Jenny Lawson, 24, of Mesa, AZ, suffered serious spinal cord injuries. She was transported by Life Flight to a nearby hospital in Phoenix, where doctors have described her condition as serious. Ben West, 40, of Glendale, AZ, suffered only minor injuries.

Officer Gene Howard of the Maricopa County Sheriff's Department stated the accident was still under investigation but the driver of the semi-truck, who did not appear to be injured, may have exceeded the number of hours he was allowed to drive under current law and may have been drowsy. "Mr. Weeks stated his trip originated that morning in Sacramento, CA, with stops in Los Angeles and Las Vegas. His final destination was Phoenix." According to Officer Howard, the length of the trip, taken over a period of one day, violated the maximum driving hours regulation mandated for all interstate commercial carriers.

Officer Howard noted that Weeks was distraught at the scene and mentioned he was fatigued at the time of the collision. Neither weather nor poor visibility was a contributing factor in causing the collision, according to Howard.

It took medical personnel at the scene more than an hour to extract Morris's body from the late model sedan she was driving. Her vehicle was propelled into the small Honda Civic being operated by Jenny

Lawson, which also sustained extensive damage. Medical personnel at the scene noted Ms. Lawson was conscious and appeared to be in the late stages of pregnancy. The condition of the unborn child is unknown at this time.

A small pickup truck being operated by Ben West suffered only moderate damage. Witnesses at the scene stated Mr. West was able to move about freely at the accident scene and did not appear to be injured. West expressed concern over potential injuries to his dog, which was apparently thrown from the pickup truck.

Officer Howard stated the investigation was ongoing and would not comment on potential charges at this time.

Blake read it over again. He remembered the scene well. What *had* happened to them? he wondered. He stood and lifted his right shoe, buffing it on the back of his left pant leg, and then repeated the task for his left shoe. He walked to the break room for another cup of coffee, feeling guilty about draining the pot without starting a new one. This was something his co-workers claimed to be fastidious about, but he knew he wasn't the only slacker.

He returned to his desk and found an archived copy of the police report online. His pen was out of ink, so he put it back into the ceramic coffee mug next to his computer and selected another one. He jotted down the names of the investigative officer and the drivers, then checked his watch. It was after five and his mother would be expecting his call. Ever since his father died, Blake's mother had become reliant on her only son. His father had been a good enough husband, but it had always been about *his* life, and not hers. And now she had attached her life to Blake, a loving son who knew how much he meant to her.

Blake's mom was a fretter, and fretted that her only son didn't practice her faith with enough enthusiasm (in truth, he didn't practice it at all, but pretended to for her sake). He assured her, as he did nearly every day, that he was fine, that he would settle down and find a good girl, that he was eating well, that he wasn't working too hard, and that he was getting enough sleep. He also assured her that his ex-wife, the tramp who had run off with her personal trainer, was a good mother and the divorce had not been totally her fault. He said this to be charitable, for he knew his ex-wife was an awful woman.

He pulled up to the curb in front of his house (he insisted on claiming it was his, because he had paid for it). His eight-year-old son, Alex, came running out with his baseball mitt. She followed him out.

"You're late."

"I said I'd be here by seven."

"And it's nearly ten minutes after."

"Can we do this another time, Laura?"

"Just have him home by ten," she said and turned for the house.

"Mom's mad, huh?" Alex said as they pulled away.

"Oh, don't worry. She's just jealous she can't go to the game with us."

2

Blake met with Don Weeks, the drowsy semi-truck driver, at the coffee shop of the Flying J Truck Stop on the outskirts of Phoenix. Don had been reluctant to discuss the accident initially, as if an unpleasant memory had been banished and then remembered. In fact, when he hung up the phone, Don considered calling back to tell the newspaper reporter that he was too busy, a casual lie that would have spared him the misery of retelling his story. But Don's nature was to be pleasant— jovial, even—and he would retell it as an act of further penance.

Don was already sitting at the booth when Blake slid into the bench across from him. His slide was arrested by a tear in the red Naugahyde that had been patched with fraying duct tape that was sticky at the edges. The tabletop was sticky in spots, too, and held the usual greasy spoon staples, including a small vase with plastic flowers whose petals needed dusting. The walls of the coffee shop were adorned with colorful prints of cartoon cowboys playing golf in pastures and deserts, the golf ball lying in a pile of manure, or in the prickly crotch of a cactus.

Don hadn't slid as gracefully into the booth. He had squeezed. His belly pulled the buttons on his shirt and his belt was cinched to the most recent homemade hole near the end of the leather, so that the final two inches didn't quite reach the first loop of his trousers. Once snugly in place, he spilled a few inches onto the tabletop. Don was large everywhere, a giant of a man. He was ruddy faced and seemed jolly in the way some heavy-set people do. His jowls sagged and his lips were stacked one on top of the other like two down pillows. He wore over-sized eyeglasses with thick frames that were too large even for his enormous head. His hair was gray and thinning on top; the few remaining stragglers combed straight back from his meaty forehead. Still more stragglers poured forth from his ears as if they'd completely forgotten where they were supposed to grow, or how they were to behave.

The server was a hard-looking woman who hurried from table to table with a pot of coffee and sensible white tennis shoes. When she asked if they were ready to order, Don said, "You bet your bottom dollar, darlin'!" It was only ten o'clock in the morning and Blake had vowed to get in shape, so he ordered only a slice of rubbery pecan pie from the laminated menu. After Don had mopped up the puddle of gravy from his chicken fried steak with the last dry roll from the basket, he asked Blake if he was going to finish his pie. When Blake said no, he reached over and stabbed it with a fork.

Don rested his huge hands on the table. He wore a wedding band that looked like a thin gold tourniquet. The ring slid on and off with relative ease on his wedding day thirty years earlier, but only a surgeon could remove it now. He wore a white short-sleeved shirt with a "D & D Trucking" logo plastered to the back. *"Dale"* was sewn in neat cursive above the breast pocket.

"Thanks again for meeting with me," Blake said.

"The pleasure's all mine, son. Now, I know you got yourself

a bunch of questions. I probably don't need to come right out and say it, but that wreck went and sent my life into a real tizzy spin. I've been through an awful lot since then and I've tried to take responsibility for what I done. I guess you could say it was the worst day of my life, that's for sure."

"I'm sorry. It must have been tough."

"I'll say it was."

"Do you go by *Dale*?"

"No, son, the name's Don."

"That's what I thought," Blake said, "but I couldn't help noticing that your shirt says *Dale*."

Don stuck his fleshy chin to his chest and looked down at his shirt. "Well I'll be a monkey's uncle! I didn't even notice," he said with a hearty laugh. "This here's my brother's shirt. He's my partner. The wife and I took him in when he hit a rough patch awhile back. It was gonna be for a few weeks, is all. But I'll be doggoned if that wasn't more'n a year ago!" Another hearty laugh. "It was mostly the wife's idea, that's Donna—now, she's as good as gold. Give ya the shirt right off her back, Donna would. Course it'd never fit Dale or me!" He laughed again. "Yeah, my Donna, she's real people. Never once complained about Dale livin' there with us. And you know how these women like their houses just so and what not. And Dale, why Dale eats even more'n I do!" Don put his head down and smiled at the thought.

"I see your shirt has a D&D logo. Is that where you work?"

"Yeah, me and Dale do. We own us Don and Dale Trucking. She's not a big outfit, mind you. Just the two of us is all. We each have us a truck and lease out to bigger outfits. I love drivin'—it's all I've ever known. I guess I just love the freedom of the open road, as they say."

"I'd like to hear your story," Blake said. "As I mentioned on the phone, I'm doing a follow-up article for the *Arizona Republic*, sort of a retrospective human interest piece on the people involved in the crash."

"Well, I guess you could say I've got a story all right. It's not too pretty a one either. Like I says, I hit rock bottom after that wreck, but I think I climbed out pretty good, considering everything. Least I hope I have."

Blake pulled a small tape recorder from his pocket and set it on the table. "Do you mind telling me what you remember about the accident?"

Don nodded at the tape recorder. "Awful formal, ain't it?"

"Oh, I'm sorry. If you're uncomfortable at all we can just . . ."

"Nah, it's okay, son. I'm just joshin' you, is all. What's done is done, I suppose. No sense in runnin' from it."

"So, what do you remember about the accident?"

"I'm afraid I remember all of it, Blake. Mind if I call you Blake?" He continued before Blake could respond. "Can't forget it, either, but Lord knows I've tried."

"You were working for Interwest Trucking, if I remember," Blake said.

"Yeah, say, you've done your homework, son!"

"I've only read the police report. You're the only one I've interviewed so far."

"I see. Well, I'd been runnin' truck with Interwest for what, six, seven years at the time. We were haulin' produce and what not from Sacramento to Phoenix, with stops in LA and Vegas. That Vegas is some place, isn't it? I keep tellin'

Donna I'll take her there some time. Course, she says she's happy where she is, but don't kid yourself, son, them women like to get dolled up from time to time. So, anyways, on this deal I got held up in Vegas on account of an unloader who was a dimwitted knucklehead, if you ask me. Anyhow, that really slowed me up good. Course I'm not blamin' him for the accident or anything, but it got me set back. You know what I mean?"

Blake nodded as if he knew what he meant.

"See, I could usually make the trip in a day, but that really put me behind the eight ball. Maybe I shoulda just stopped and slept in Vegas, but I was anxious to get home to Phoenix and musta pushed it too hard."

"Were you sleepy?"

"Yeah, I guess I was. The truth is I got a little too cocky. I had me almost a million accident free miles. I was a safe driver, doggone it. I had all sorts of tricks and what not to keep me awake, too. I'd sing a little and that'd keep anybody awake, just ask my Donna!" Another chuckle. "Or maybe I'd talk on the CB, or get out and walk around the truck a few times. Sometimes I'd even roll down the window and hold a hundred dollar bill out of it. And lemme tell you, son, that'll usually do the trick!"

"Do many drivers exceed the driving regulations?"

"You want the gospel truth, son? 'Course they do. I've seen guys' log books where a guy'll go to sleep in Memphis and wake up in St. Louis! I can't say as I haven't fudged a time or two on my logs, either."

"What do you remember about the accident?"

Don's body sagged, the way one does after a long exhale. He closed his eyes and then raised his eyelids with difficulty,

like they were weighted. He took a deep breath and again became the man who would not shirk his duty, would not flinch
from the truth. "That thing still on?" he nodded at the tape
recorder.

"Yes, but if you're more comfortable . . . "

"I was comin' south on 60, not a lot of traffic. It was about
dusk, I'd say. I was tired but I thought I'd be okay, I really did.
I seen the car stopped ahead of me, seen the brake lights and
what not. But it didn't register on me that they were stopped
in the middle of the blasted road. I just didn't expect traffic to
be stopped like that, not out in the middle of nowhere. You
know what I mean?"

Blake nodded.

"I musta been in a fog or one of them trances you hear
about, sorta like them moths that'll fly straight into a flame.
Anyways, when I was about a hundred yards away it went and
registered with me. I jumped on the brakes just as hard as I
could, but it was too late. I just plowed into the back of 'em.
The rest's a nightmare I can't wake up from."

"What happened next?"

"Well, I jumped out of the truck and run to the Lexus.
The lady inside, Mrs. Morris's her name, she was dead. That
was clear as day to me. I'd never seen a dead person in all my
life. Well, unless they were in a casket, I suppose. But I knew it
the second I seen her. Her car got shoved into the car in front
of her and just got royally squished. That's about the best way
I could put it, just squished as all get out. I remember gettin'
sick to my stomach there on the side of the road. They said I
was screaming for help, but I can't really remember."

Blake nodded as if he was aware of that.

"They got that in the report, do they?"

"I believe so," Blake said.

"I couldn't believe what'd happened. It seemed like a dream. Still does. It all happened so fast. There was a young gal in the car in front of Mrs. Morris, and I ran to her car. She—her name's Jenny by the way—'course, you probably already know that. Anyways, she was alive but in real tough shape. She was just moanin'. There was a young man, too, about your age, I'd guess, in a pickup truck. He had a dog that was running around, probably scared outta its wits. I do remember that."

"Were you hurt?"

"Turns out I was; hurt my back, slipped disc and what have you, but I didn't feel anything at the time. I musta been in shock. I didn't know what to do. I'm not even sure how the cops got there. Maybe I called 'em, for all I know. I just can't remember. It was a bad deal and parts of it are a real blur."

"What happened to you? Were you given a ticket?"

"Oh, they went and threw the book at me, all right. But I can't say as I blamed them, because it was my fault and all. 'Course it was. So I'm not gonna sit here and try and dodge on that. But it was an *accident*. That's what I kept tellin' people. I got careless, that's all. I didn't want any of this to happen. I lost everything on account of it."

"What do you mean?"

"Well, for starters, I got fired straight off. Interwest had my job the next day. But, listen, I don't mean to complain or anything. Like I said, it was my fault and all, but they made it seem like I *wanted* to hurt those people. I was sick to my stomach about it. Every single day since then, I've been sick inside. It's like I got an ugly taste in my whole body and I can't rinse it out."

Blake nodded like he understood, when really he didn't, for no one could know the pain Don had suffered.

"You ever made a mistake, son, one you wished you could take back? Ever said somethin' or done somethin' that you wished you'd never? Well, in one split second I made a mistake that ruined lives. Lots of lives. Just like that," he snapped his thick fingers. "And I'll tell you something else. There's nuthin' I wouldn't a given to take it all back. Why, if I'd died that woulda been bad I suppose, but this . . . this is worse. I'll tell you, son: the worst is when your mistake kills somebody else, and makes a pretty young gal paralyzed."

Blake dropped his eyes in recognition of the fact that this would be bad, indeed.

"For three years, I wished it'd been me," Don continued. "I couldn't watch the news. I couldn't answer the phone. It seemed like I didn't have a friend in the world, except for my Donna. Even my buddies at work disowned me, like they never drove too long or drove a tad sleepy. I heard them sayin' they couldn't believe I could be so reckless and what not. 'Course they knew better—they were just trying to save their own skin on my account."

"That must have been difficult."

"Hell yes, it was! I couldn't even open the mail, what with all the hate mail I got. How could I've done such a thing? What if it'd been *my* wife who got paralyzed? Things like that. They acted like I *wanted* it to happen. But I just wanted to get home to my own family that night. That's all. I didn't want to ruin my life or anybody else's. Of course I didn't. Like I says, I'd give anything to take it all back."

He removed his large glasses and dropped his immense head into the cradle of his hands. "How many times can you say you're sorry?" Don's chin twitched and Blake thought he would cry. But his eyes were dry, and Blake wondered if maybe he'd become permanently dehydrated from all his tears.

3

"This is the Howard residence."

"Is Gene available, please?"

"Oh, I'm sorry, but he's . . . well, he's indisposed for the moment. But this is his wife, Lila. May I take a message for him?"

"Yes, my name is Blake Morgan, and I work for the *Arizona Republic* newspaper."

"I see."

"I met your husband a few years ago, very briefly, when I covered a story on a fatal traffic accident where he was the lead officer." Blake knew they had met because he'd quoted him in the article, but now he had no memory of him.

"Oh, I see."

"Anyway, I'm doing a follow-up article on the accident and I wanted to catch up with Gene—perhaps make him part of the story, too."

"Oh, that's nice."

"Is he still with the County Sheriff's Department?"

"No, I'm afraid not," she said. "But perhaps I can leave a message for him. Mr. Blake, did you say?"

"Actually it's Morgan. Blake Morgan. I'd like to meet with him as part of the story. Would you please let him know I called?"

"If you'd like, Mr. Morgan, I can put the phone down and go talk to him now. Just give me a few minutes."

"Yeah, sure, I'd appreciate that," Blake said. This was odd. He was unavailable and now she would go fetch him? He pulled up a game of solitaire while he waited with the phone cocked at his ear. Even though it annoyed him, he was accustomed to groveling for comment on a story. But they should respect the fact that his time was valuable, he thought, as he clicked through the deck searching for a red queen.

"I'm sorry to have kept you waiting, Mr. Morgan. Gene has agreed to meet with you, but you'll need to come to our home."

Blake would have been willing to meet Gene on his terms in any event, but he was put off by this. Who did Gene Howard think he was? There was something about cops that just rubbed him the wrong way. Whenever he saw one, he bore a momentary sense of panic, certain that he must be guilty of *something*. So, he blamed this suffering on law enforcement in general.

Blake collected Gene's home address and made an appointment with Lila for the following afternoon. He then drove to the county sheriff's office and flirted with the records custodian there, a sixty-five-year-old woman who desperately tried to look forty. She wore a blond wig and fake eyelashes that looked like they'd come from a Barbie costume. A cheap Eau to Something surrounded her like an aromatic moat, but Blake endured it in good cheer until he could sweet-talk a complete copy of the police report, including the photographs and witness statements.

That evening Blake sat alone in his condo, a too-expensive-for-his-budget affair decorated by the taste of a girl he'd been dating who hadn't been invited to stay (to her elaborate and showy disappointment). The swamp cooler did triple time and still it was hot. He wore gym shorts and no shirt. There was still evidence of abdominal muscles, but one had to look closely. A bottle of Corona was perched between his legs and the accident photos were spread around him.

The accident had been a horrible one and the photos memorialized the carnage. There was a photo of a short skid mark, then a photo of the pick-up truck, then a photo of the entire scene from a distance, then *BAM!*, a gruesome photo of Fern Morris's elderly corpse. And then another. Blake was shocked. How could they take such photos? What if her family saw them? He wasn't used to the business of death, especially not the gory kind. An antiseptic photo of a heart attack victim might be appropriate, but not this.

Another photo caught his eye. It showed the back end of the large semi-truck. A sign on the back door of the trailer read: *How's my driving? Interwest Trucking promotes safe and courteous driving. Please report any of my unsafe driving. 1-800-272-2930.*

Blake drove to Officer Howard's home the next day, still with a lingering resentment that he hadn't bothered coming to the phone, bossing his wife around like a captain of the night shift. There was a makeshift wooden ramp leading to the front door that seemed out of place. The paint on the ramp had begun to peel and it was badly warped, causing it to list at a dangerous angle. The handrail was crooked and one of the sections was missing. The yard had not been tended and weeds grew to the height of the dead annuals from the previous year.

Blake rang the doorbell and a sad-looking woman answered the door. She had the look of someone who was afraid of a scolding—someone who was used to taking orders without complaint. Blake introduced himself and reached out his hand, causing her to flinch. She offered him a limp grip and invited him in. This was Gene's wife, Lila, long-time wife and apparent doormat.

Lila left Blake waiting in the living room and went to summon her husband. Blake expected Gene to march into the room erect, firm, and with a military bearing. Instead, he silently rolled in on an electric wheelchair. He could not speak. He could not move. He was able to maneuver his wheelchair only with the limited use of one small finger, as if he was navigating the curser on a laptop. His head was bent grotesquely to one side. He communicated by the use of his eyes to a computer screen mounted to the front of his wheelchair. His eyeballs and left index finger were the only moving parts on his twisted, emaciated body. Gene Howard, 56, ex-cop, was in the end stages of ALS, Lou Gehrig's disease, perhaps the unkindest illness on earth.

It was Gehrig's dreadful fate to be immortalized by his name. He was born a robust fourteen pounds to a sore German immigrant mother and poor but hardworking father. Gehrig is known for many things, including his strength and durability. He never missed a game during the New York Yankees heydays of the 1920s and 30s. As his streak of consecutive games grew beyond record levels, there were a few close calls that threatened to sideline him. There was the time he was hit in the head with a fastball, and the time he had the stomach flu and his manager cancelled the game on account of rain, even though there were only a few clouds.

But Gehrig was Gehrig, so no one complained. He was a living legend and was revered for his humility and gigantic athletic talent. But he is mostly known for the thing that finally forced him to the bench, when a few sinister cells inside his body silently began running amuck.

During his sixteenth season, at thirty-five years old, his coordination and speed mysteriously began to deteriorate. One day he could hit a baseball over the centerfield fence 400 feet away, and the next day he seemingly swung the bat just as hard only to hit a lazy fly ball to the centerfielder. He inexplicably stumbled while running the bases, too. A month later, on his thirty-sixth birthday, his diagnosis of amyotrophic lateral sclerosis was confirmed.

When Blake returned to his cubicle, he Googled ALS. He learned the nerve cells that control muscle movement deteriorate for inexplicable reasons. When the neurons stop sending messages to the muscles, the poor victim loses the ability to control his movement. The symptoms are usually subtle in the beginning. Perhaps one leg weakens and walking or running becomes awkward, causing a trip or stumble. Lou Gehrig, one of the most gifted athletes who ever lived, would trip on the dugout steps. Or maybe it's a hand that doesn't work quite right, so buttoning a shirt or turning a key becomes difficult. Soon the disease attacks other muscles. Patients lose tongue mobility and have trouble swallowing, or they experience bouts of uncontrollable laughter, or smiling (even though there isn't much to laugh about at a time like that). Those bizarre, counterintuitive expressions are caused by deteriorating motor neurons of emotion.

Most ALS patients are men, and diagnosis of the disease

can be tricky because it looks like other diseases that *are* treatable, like MS or syphilis. It's rare that a man roots for a diagnosis of syphilis, but this is one of those times. Modern medicine doesn't know the cause of ALS, but has its hunches. It could be caused by a virus, or exposure to certain metals. Or maybe it's exposure to toxic chemicals, or extreme stress. So why are Italian soccer players five times as likely to get it? Maybe there's a link between the disease and the use of pesticides on their soccer fields, but doctors don't really know. And why are military veterans sixty percent more likely to get it? It might be the result of exposure to all the bombs (and there's the stress of being shot at). So maybe that's it.

Patients are totally aware of their progressive fate and can do nothing about it. Their brains work just fine. They can see, hear, taste, smell, and feel normally. They just can't move. And by the time it's over, the only thing they *can* move is their eyes. That's it—only their eyeballs. Death usually ends the suffering within two to five years, when the lungs become paralyzed and the patient cannot breathe. This is Lou Gehrig's disease.

Gene Howard was not as famous or as talented, but his diagnosis three years earlier was just as devastating. As a baseball fan, Gene knew all about Lou Gehrig; how he lived and how he died. Like Gehrig, Gene had been dealt an awful hand. But unlike Gehrig, he wasn't adored. Gene's life was a scrapbook of intolerance and impatience. Indeed, he'd been a man of dubious integrity.

He was at the peak of his career when he was called to investigate the semi-truck fatality on Highway 60. He had investigated a thousand accidents, many involving personal catastrophe. So while this accident was noteworthy, he'd seen worse. He felt pity for Fern and Jenny; of course he did, for he wasn't a monster. But the emotion was temporary and hadn't affected his appetite that evening.

Gene had always wanted to be a cop. When he played cops and robbers as a kid, he was always the cop. This wasn't because he wanted to be the good guy—he wanted to be the one with authority. When he'd catch his friends he'd tie them to a tree, or padlock them in the backyard tool shed. His meanness was probably the result of DNA. The pattern had been set by his father who ruled the unhappy roost like an ornery drill sergeant who detested slouching. There were no weekend furloughs and few "at eases." He'd sit in his leather recliner like a boiler in the living room. The steam would build and the boiler would sweat, eventually erupting into irregular and unpredictable outbursts of scorn. His mother tried to show Gene affection, but was court marshaled whenever she did. "You keep up that lovey dovey horseshit around the boy and he'll be nuthin' but a sissy! You hear me!"

These were the waning days of the Vietnam War and Gene enrolled in the ROTC so as not to displease his father. He roamed the college campus with his rigid posture and short crew-cut, one of the few without long hair and bell bottoms—all those pansy-waist peace-niks who wanted to give peace a chance. *Give peace a chance my ass*, he thought.

He met Lila his senior year in college. She was quiet, and if she had a mind of her own, she kept it to herself. Gene was livid when she became pregnant. She'd gotten herself knocked up to trap him! He would have left her but his father intervened. The Steam Boiler agreed that Lila was indeed a conniving gold digger like most women were, but there was a code of honor, too, and his son would marry the goddamned tramp.

So they married. And, to be fair, Gene almost loved her a few times over the years. But Lila had compounded her weakness by delivering a baby girl. Gene didn't care what they named her, so Lila chose Rebecca. Gene felt victimized again when Lila bore him a second daughter, Susan. His daughters were messy and Lila did a poor job of keeping them quiet. When Lila's third baby was a boy, Gene finally showed some interest. For names, he quickly eliminated Pat, Kelly, Terry, and any other name with even a whiff of femininity. He declared the boy would be named Robert, and dared anyone to call him Bobby.

Gene treated Robert differently than the girls, who were an untidy extension of their mother who he tolerated less with every pound she gained (which wasn't much, for she was a small woman). "You're eating *that*? Aren't you fat enough already?" So Lila allowed him to monitor her diet of leafy greens so as not to "gross him out." Lila didn't live life, she endured it.

There were times, however, that Gene was kind. But his meanness would strike and then vanish, like the shark's fin that slips under the water. They knew it was lurking there, just under the surface, and would reveal itself in cruel moments. They just didn't know when. He offered uninspiring criticism to his daughters. "How do you expect to get a boyfriend if you look like that?" or "Stop eating or you'll look like your mother, for God's sake." But he doted on Robert and tried to brand him with that special Howard *thing*. It did not appear to take root, however, for Robert was a kind and sensitive boy.

When Robert dressed in Lila's heels and jewelry, Gene became alarmed. Gene could tolerate a Superman cape, or perhaps a soldier's outfit, but not this. And when Robert forsook his tiny baseball mitt for a pair of ice skates, Gene was apoplectic. "Are you trying to turn my son into a queer, for God's sake! Let me tell you something: no son of mine is going to be a faggot! You hear me!" Gene also made it perfectly clear that any inclination toward gayness came from Lila's side of the family.

It was a wonder, then, that Lila stood by him, and had even begun to love him by the time he was reduced to the man who silently rolled into the living room where Blake stood.

4

George Morris, Fern's widower, was not well. He had never fully recovered from Fern's death nearly four years earlier, which seemed to have leached the life out of him. They had been together for fifty-seven years and suddenly he was alone. He had always assumed she would be there to take care of him when he became old, and now she was gone. It had happened so suddenly, and had been so *permanent*. He had no time to prepare for his loneliness. She was irretrievably gone in the space of one brief phone call from a stranger.

When the reporter from the *Arizona Republic* called, George was reluctant to talk. This had been his private affair, and he had no interest in reopening his wounds with casual readers between a check of the local sports scores or the daily Sudoku. No, his loss was personal and profound, no matter the size of font that was assigned to it.

George was a contemplative man, one prone to mull from time to time. He was well read and educated, an intellectual of sorts, but not a snobby one. He craved intellectual discourse, and had grown weary of listening to the women at bridge discuss their medications (he was outnumbered three to one by women at every event attended by people his age). So, after mulling it over, he decided to invite the reporter to his home.

George lived in the wealthiest part of town, a gated

neighborhood that swarmed with Mexican yard care workers. The median age of those fortunate few who lived in Eldorado Springs was seventy. This was the Glen Miller Band crowd, many of them migrating from their other homes in the winter months like geese. Everyone qualified for Medicare based solely on their age and not their need. They all required medical care at their ages, and lots of it, they just didn't need the government to pay for it.

Each of the homes had its own never-used swimming pool, for no one there actually swam. There were collections of pink flamingos and expensive cars, none of them driven more than forty-five miles per hour, even in the fast lane. The Morris home was typical, if typical meant five thousand square feet, large circular driveway, two yard statues, and five decorative cactuses. It was built in the desert Southwest style, an impressively stretched earth-toned rambler with a red bar-tile roof.

George, now eighty years old and frail, was dressed in an expensive silk shirt that was buttoned to the neck and smartly tucked into heavily starched slacks that were pulled up high, nearly to the bottom of his rib cage, in the fashion of older men. His once erect posture was now stooped. But he still had the look of affluence that is difficult to hide, even for the sick, old, and tired.

He led Blake through the spacious foyer with terracotta floor tiles and collectable modern artwork. Blake assumed the art must have been expensive because it looked like it had been drawn by a fourth grader. There were books, vases, and objects d'art—symbols of the cultivated. They settled in to the generously furnished living room.

"Can I offer you a drink, Mr. Morgan? Perhaps some iced tea or a soda?"

"Water would be great, thank you," Blake replied when he would have preferred a Bloody Mary (thick on the Mary), for it was still early enough in the morning to justify it.

George returned and delivered the glass of water with a trembling hand. This was not a sign of nervousness, for George was self-assured, but rather the singular result of longevity.

"Thank you, Mr. Morris, for agreeing to visit with me."

"Please, call me George."

"Thanks, George. As I mentioned on the phone, I covered your wife's accident four years ago."

"You know, Mr. Morgan," his speech was deliberate but firm, "it seems like only yesterday, and yet, at the same time, it seems like a lifetime ago."

"With your permission, we'd like to write about what has happened to you and all the other victims since the accident."

"I prefer not to consider myself a victim. An unlucky beneficiary of an accident perhaps, but not a victim."

Blake simply nodded and reached for his notepad.

"After you called I thought back to that evening. I cannot tell you, Mr. Morgan, what it feels like to get a call from the police late at night when your loved one is not home. You never think you will get that call; you always assume it will be someone else. I am afraid there is no training that can prepare you for that kind of call."

"I'm very sorry."

"I distinctly recall the officer said that Fern had been involved in an automobile accident and that her body had been taken to St. Joseph's hospital here in Phoenix. I remember asking him, pleading really, for more information on her condition. Would she be all right? Could I talk to her? Was she badly hurt? That sort of thing. He told me again that her body had been taken to the hospital. I will never forget the feeling when his message finally became clear to me."

"That must have been tough."

"Indeed it was. When I asked him if Fern was alive, he said 'I'm afraid she may not have responded,' which was the gentlest way he could have delivered such devastating news to me, I suppose.

George looked down and appeared to study the finger-laced hands in his lap.

"I wish I could adequately express how special Fern was. But unfortunately I have neither the skill nor the eloquence to do so. She was my high school sweetheart. She is the only one I have ever given a Valentine to. She was my wife for fifty-seven years and the mother of our six children. She was the love of my life, and the only love of my life. It must sound old fashioned to you young people nowadays, but she is the only woman I was ever intimate with."

Blake felt the ache, but only briefly, for this was George's pain. He remembered when his father died, the initial disbelief that he would never see him again, and then gradually the certainty of it. His friends had expressed genuine sympathy, but it was inevitability superficial, for the pain Blake felt had been his alone to bear. And so it was that Blake felt sympathy for George, but he wouldn't be walloped every few hours by a reminder that Fern Morris was gone forever. This was George's cross.

"I am embarrassed to say that I had never done a load of laundry, if you can imagine it."

"You didn't miss much," said Blake.

George had rarely cooked a meal either, and had only a vague idea which closet the vacuum was in. Grocery shopping was as foreign to him as a recipe book. He called his daughters for advice ranging from detergent to produce. This had been an unforeseen blessing in his life, becoming closer to his children. Fern had always been the one to call the kids, and when she had quenched her interest in the minutia of their lives, she would pass the phone off to George and say, "Your dad wants to say hello."

Blake scanned the living room, now a virtual shrine honoring Fern and their fifty-seven-year marriage. Photos hung on nearly every wall, and were propped on every table. Every ounce of wall space not devoted to Fern was claimed by Jesus himself. There were paintings of Jesus, charcoals of Jesus, drawings of Jesus, and woodcarvings of Jesus. This looked to be a dead heat between Fern and The Redeemer, with a slight edge to Fern.

And the sheer number of crosses was striking. There were handsomely carved crosses complete with a desperately pained Jesus, and empty ones without Him. There were wood ones, metal ones, ceramic ones, and ivory ones. Some dramatically dripped with fake blood and others were polished clean.

"It looks like your faith is important to you," said Blake.

"Perhaps I should mention that we are Catholic. But that was mostly Fern. We were married in the church and considered ourselves to be devout, especially Fern. But I soon became absorbed in my career and my commitment wavered. Even though I still consider myself to be Catholic and have no desire to renounce my faith, I have never enjoyed Fern's level of devotion."

"What did you do for a living?"

"I was a plastic surgeon in Los Angeles for thirty years. After I retired, Fern and I moved here where we lived for several years until Fern passed away. After she died I considered moving to Denver where one of our daughters lives, but eventually decided to stay."

"Did Fern work outside the home?"

"She did volunteer work from time to time, but mostly she had her hands full with our six children. We had a traditional arrangement where I was the breadwinner and she did everything else. I must tell you, Mr. Morgan, my job was stressful and time consuming, but it could not compare with raising that many children and keeping such a lovely home for us. I don't know how she did it."

"I'm sure you must miss her."

"Oh my goodness, yes. And now, since my diagnosis, I need her more than ever."

"I'm sorry, I didn't realize you were ill."

"Six months ago I was diagnosed with pancreatic cancer. So far, my symptoms have been manageable, but now I face an unpleasant death. I prefer to speak about it frankly. I will not live much longer, perhaps five or six months according to my oncologist. Unfortunately, my remaining time will be unusually painful."

"I am so sorry."

"I've had remarkable good fortune in my life, but I will admit to episodes of self-pity, especially since Fern died. I have been lonely, and now I face a daunting six months with no possibility for recovery. I have been able to manage with pain medication, but soon I will be forced to undergo a morphine regimen. And I won't be able to care for myself, even my basic bodily functions."

"Have the doctors given you any hope?"

"No. They have been gracious and competent but there is nothing they can do. We all must die, Mr. Morgan. I consider myself to be fortunate because I have been given more time than most. My goodness, no one lived to be eighty until recently. At any other time in human history I would have died long ago. So, how can I feel cheated? I have a healthy perspective on my mortality. I wish it were different, but it has always been inevitable that I would die, and now it is my time."

Blake wanted to say that he, too, had a healthy perspective on his mortality, but he hadn't really thought about it much. He was young and the reality of his death didn't haunt him.

"There have been times in my life that I have wished this life would never end, and if it did, that I would continue to live beyond my death. The temptation has been great to believe this to be true, but I have come to believe it is a fraudulent wish."

"Why?"

"This elusive quest for immortality is fueled by our natural desire to keep living, even though our rational brains know this is quite impossible. You see, all living things seek first to stay alive. But we humans know this will not happen, so we have invented this narrative of an afterlife because we cannot imagine ceasing to exist. Of course, that is only my belief, but I believe it is a rational one."

"So you don't believe in an afterlife? You think this is all there is?"

"Of course, Mr. Morgan, I do not know the answer to that question, and I am suspicious of anyone who maintains they do. I am persuaded, however, that it doesn't really matter at this stage what I believe, now does it?"

"Why do you say that?"

"What will be, will be. And my belief will not change it. I could believe the earth's surface was flat with every fiber of my being, but that would not make it so."

"But no one knows. Maybe there really is life after death."

"Perhaps there is, but that might not be desirable in any event."

"Why not?"

"I believe it would be a nightmare, to be trapped in your existence for eternity with no way out—to be like the troglo-dytes in the City of the Immortals that Borges wrote about, desperately searching for a way out of their immortality. What a terrible curse that would be."

Blake didn't know what he was talking about, but he un-derstood the gist of the problem. "But at least there would be no fear of dying," he finally said.

"Only the fear of *not* dying. No, I believe Achilles in the Iliad understood the dilemma. He could have chosen to live forever but without purpose or remembrance, or he could die heroically on the battlefield and live forever in the memory of his friends and family. I will not die heroically, but I hope to be remembered by my loved ones long after I die. And in that way, I hope to achieve some semblance of immortality."

"Are you afraid to die?"

"I believe it is natural to be afraid of death. There is no cowardice in it. However, I believe that fear is irrational."

"Why?"

"The process of dying might be considered a life event, but death is not. We perceive everything from the perspective of a living being. The instant one dies, by definition, he can no longer experience a life event. He would no longer even be able to perceive it. Therefore, to fear death with our mortal understanding is quite irrational. There would be nothing to fear because we could not even perceive it."

"But if you *could* stay alive, if that were an option, wouldn't you want it?"

"I suppose I would, but not forever. Most of us are not allowed to choose exactly when, or how, we die. That inevitability is usually beyond our control. But I intend to make the choice for myself."

"What do you mean?"

"After much thought, and even some prayer, I have chosen to take my own life, while I still can and while I retain some dignity. I have not shared this decision with my children, but I intend to do so shortly. I want them to know my decision is not made lightly, or impulsively. However, I am firm in my resolve, for I do not wish to be a further burden on my children, not when my lot is already cast. I do not want others to take care of my basic bodily functions. If you will forgive my blunt honesty, Mr. Morgan, I prefer to wipe my own ass."

5

Blake had no trouble tracking down Ben West, the driver of the red pickup truck who was first in the line of vehicles waiting for the tortoise to cross the road. He was still at the same address listed on the four-year-old police report, a rather indistinguishable two-story apartment building in Glendale, a suburb of Phoenix.

Blake drove out to see him late in the day, after filing yet another car-jacking story. The human-interest piece on the Highway 60 accident wasn't a full-time job. Hal Crawford constantly nagged his reporters to produce more stories, trying to fill the paper on a shrinking budget with plummeting readership. Did they think the paper wrote itself, goddammit?

Blake pulled into the parking lot of the apartment complex, a lot that hadn't seen new pavement since the complex was built—about the time Pancho Villa roamed the territory. He parked beneath a sagging carport roof next to a faded pickup. The truck had tools in its dirty bed: shovels, rakes, and a few bags of smelly fertilizer. The rear bumper was bent and hung down on one side. The passenger side window was covered by a filthy mix of muddy paw prints and what Blake assumed was dried dog saliva. The doors had been branded with lettering that was made with a stencil and can of white spray paint:

BEN WEST LANDSCAPING & DESIGN

Free Estimates

"No job is too small!"

602-705-7667

He climbed the crumbling cement steps to the second floor and rang the bell at 16B. A dog barked on the other side of the door. It was the sort of bark that required effort, for it started slowly and then picked up momentum. However, it petered out early as if the dog wasn't interested after all, or was too tired to give it his full effort. He heard a man yell, "Calm down buddy, you'll scare him away!"

The door flung open and Ben West stood before Blake. He wore dirty jeans that were worn and hung low on his lean frame. He wore no shirt and his torso was tanned the color of milk chocolate. His face was tanned too, except for around his blue eyes and the bridge of his nose which gave him the appearance of a raccoon. His blond hair curled tight around his face like a lamb's fleece. He was in his late thirties but looked younger; the only telltale sign of age was a receding hairline in the power alleys. His right arm was covered by a sleeve tattoo that made him look partially lopsided.

He held out his hand for a calloused shake. "You must be the guy from the newspaper."

"Yeah, my name's Blake Morgan. We talked briefly on the phone." Blake saw a flicker of recognition in Ben's face, something Blake saw from time to time, as if people thought they should know him but couldn't quite put a finger on it.

"So, yeah, come on in."

Blake crossed the threshold and inhaled the faint smell of weed. A pair of work boots stood next to the door. They were caked with dried mud.

"Sorry about my dog here. He's pretty protective of me." The dog, who hadn't moved from his spot by the front door, ambled to his feet. He was a beautiful black lab with a graying muzzle. He stood on wobbly legs, like he wanted to lie back down as soon as possible. He was obliged to sniff Blake in the awkward places and then folded himself back down with difficulty to his favorite spot. Blake recalled that Ben had a dog with him at the scene of the accident.

"Hey, don't worry about it. I'm a dog guy, too."

The apartment was cluttered with the mess of a hoarder. There were stacks of magazines, newspapers, tools, strewn clothes, boxes, and dog toys. There were rows of empty beer bottles, shot glasses, dirty dishes, a boom box, and an older boxy television on the floor next to a wall-mounted big screen. Propped on the mantle, there was a 5x7 photo of the dog gripping the handle of a shovel with its mouth.

Ben scooted a pizza box with a lone slice of cold pepperoni toward Blake. "You can have that, if you want. It's probably still good."

"No thanks, I'm fine."

"Sorry it's sorta messy around here. I've just been busy with stuff."

"Yeah, no problem. Like I said on the phone, I was the one who covered the accident, but I don't think we actually met then."

"So, like, am I going to be in the newspaper?"

"Well, I'm just doing some background research for now.

But, yeah, I think it'll be published in the paper fairly soon."

"That's awesome. I'm surprised, you know, on account of it's been so long and all. It was a big deal back then, I guess, but nobody's asked me squat about it for a long time."

"I believe it's been four years."

"Yeah, I'd say that's about right. I was the lucky one on that deal, too. I mean, I wasn't even hurt. 'Course I probably shouldn't tell you that, on account of the settlement I got."

"Uh huh."

"Well, see, on that deal I had some whiplash in my neck. Sorta stiff for a while and I went to one of them choirpractors and that pretty much fixed me up. I got me a settlement 'cause the trucking company didn't want to take it to court. Had a lawyer and everything; one of those ya see on TV. I probably should've got more, but I think my lawyer was in cahoots with the insurance gal. That's all I can figure, anyway."

"But I thought you said you weren't very hurt."

"Well, yeah, that's true. But I could've died in the deal, you know, if it'd worked out different."

The dog, which had been lying with his head resting on his paws, struggled to its feet and wandered over to Ben, and sat down again.

"This here's Wrigley," Ben said, motioning toward his dog.

"Wrigley?"

"Yeah, see I'm originally from Chicago. I came out here to get as far away from the ex as I could. She's a total bitch, by the way, and I wish you'd go ahead and put that in the newspaper too, so long as you're at it."

"I've got one, too."

"Yeah, so anyway, I'm a Cubs fan. I used to go to Wrigley

Field all the time with my dad when I was a kid. I got Wrigley there, about ten years ago, just after my dad died. Now the poor guy has hip dysplasia and hurts like a son of a bitch. He can't hardly even walk."

"I was a Cubs fan, too," said Blake, "until I joined the D-Backs. I played ball for a few years before I became a reporter."

"Dude! I knew it! I knew you looked familiar!"

"Yeah, I played a few years back." Blake was more flattered that Ben had remembered him than he let on. "I still follow the game—still got some buddies playing. And I still do some radio color for the D-Backs."

"Dude, that's awesome! Could you score me a couple tickets?"

"I'll see what I can do," Blake lied. "If I remember right, your dog was with you at the time of the accident."

"Yeah, Wrigley's always with me. I was more freaked out about Wrigley when the wreck happened than anything else. He was sittin' in the cab with me and the crash was loud, dude. Loudest thing I've ever heard. Anyway, when I opened my door, he goes and jumps out and hides in the sagebrush. I think it just plain scared the shit outta him. Scared the shit outta me, too. I finally found him, shakin' from all the commotion of the cop cars and people yellin' and the helicopter and all that."

"What's your memory of how it happened?"

"Well, let's see. Hey, you gonna tape this thing, or take any photos or anything for the paper?"

"I thought I'd just take some notes for now, if that's okay."

"Yeah, sure, it's okay. I mean, it's your deal and all. I was just wondering if we should take some photos. Maybe something out by my truck. Get me a little free advertising outta the deal, you know what I mean?"

"Maybe later," said Blake. "For now though, I don't think I'll need photos." Blake knew this would disappoint him, but photos of the guy grinning by his pickup truck?

"I've been wondering about what happened to that girl in the car behind me. How's she doing anyway?"

"I've only talked to her on the phone for a few minutes so far. But you probably know she's paralyzed. She's a quad."

"Shit, dude, that's gotta be the worst. I hate to say it, but I'm just glad as shit it wasn't me, you know what I mean? I know that sounds bad and all, but I just don't think I could handle that."

"Yeah, me neither. So, you were about to tell me how it happened."

"Well, we were comin' home from a landscape job, me and Wrigley, up near Sun City. It was late, but not dark or anything, sort of like dusk, I'd say. Anyway, we were coming south, you know, and there's this goddamned turtle in the road. It was one of those tortoises that's on the endangered list. At first, I thought to myself 'What's that big rock doing in the middle of the road?' and I slowed down. Then I saw it move, and that's when I knew it was a turtle, or a tortoise, or whatever. So, anyway, I'm sittin' there stopped and the girl pulls up behind me, and then somebody, I guess the lady that got killed, pulls up behind her.

"So we were there, what, maybe ten seconds at the most and I was about to get out and lift the goddamned thing off the road when *BAM!* Probably the loudest thing you ever heard. Then a split second later another *BAM!* and I got shoved forward and damned near run over that fuckin' turtle."

"Then what happened?"

"Well, like I said, I opened the door and Wrigley jumps clean over me and takes off. I got out and saw the wreckage behind me. It was god-awful. It really was. A huge semi'd ass-ended a Lexus and it was shoved into the girl's car behind me. That Lexus looked like a pancake. My pickup was hardly even wrecked, just my bumper was hanging down and the tailgate got bent in. Oh, and the frame might've been bent in some too, 'cause it's never drove the same since. 'Course, I'm not complaining—I could've died."

"Who called the police?"

"I think the truck driver must've called them. I was trying to help the girl behind me who was sittin' in her car. I could tell she was in bad shape and all so I didn't want to touch her because they say that's the worst thing you can do. So, I just told her she'd be okay, you know—just reassured her some until the cops showed."

"Did you talk to the truck driver?"

"Oh, I tried, you know. But he was a fuckin' basket case, that guy. He was just walkin' around in a daze. He was like, 'Oh my God, Oh my God, what have I done?' and just saying shit like that. I tried to calm him down, but there was no use. The dude kept saying how sorry he was, and all that. I felt sorry for him, even though it was totally his fault."

"What happened once the police came?"

"I just let them do their thing, you know? I was just looking for Wrigley after that. You gotta remember I was pretty upset, too."

"How long did you stay at the scene?"

"Oh, gosh, I'm gonna say we were there the better part of two hours. I found Wrigley about two hundred yards away, hiding behind a bush. He was shaking, the poor guy. Anyway, they took my statement and all that. Then they finally let me go home. My pickup was drivable, so I just drove home. That's about it."

"Have you talked to anybody since about this?"

"I gave a statement over the phone to some insurance guy. And then the lawyers took my disposition or whatever you call it when the lawyers ask you a bunch of the same questions over and over. That was a few years ago. But I haven't heard anything since then, until you called me."

"I'm sorry about your dog. It looks like he's really struggling."

"Yeah, I'm pretty sick about it. I've took him everywhere I go now for coming on ten years. But now he's so old and sick I don't know how much longer I got with the ol' guy. The vet says I'll have to put him down soon, seeing as how he can hardly walk. I keep hoping he'll get better, but I know he won't." He looked down at Wrigley and then patted him on the rump. "I care about him more than anybody in the world, don't I, buddy?"

"Yeah, that's tough."

"Anyway, you sure on the photos? Because I was just thinkin' a couple of me and Wrigley standing by the pickup that was all banged up would be good, you know? Like, maybe I could be pointing at the bumper or something. Because I haven't fixed it; it still looks just like it did after the wreck. 'Course I'm not telling you how to do your job."

Despite his good looks, Ben had struggled socially. His best friend had always been his dad, who had been patient with Ben's ADD (or perhaps it was something else entirely, for nothing had ever been formally diagnosed). His dad had never made much money, but he taught Ben how to work, and helped him buy a lawnmower. They worked Saturdays and Sundays, side by side, mowing lawns in the neighborhood. Ben followed his dad wherever he went, even to the machine shop where he worked. He'd sit on the metal stool in the corner, ogling the machines and listening to the men talk. His dad passed on lunch with the guys to spend time with Ben over a tuna fish sandwich in the break room. It was always, "Here comes Earl and his goddamned kid."

Ben was twenty-nine when his dad died of congestive heart failure. That loss overshadowed the loss of his marriage and even the loss of his daughter, who was a casualty of his ex-wife's hysterical crusade to ruin him. But it was the way in which his dad died that made the loss so painful to watch, suffering as he did through small gasps of breath for nearly six months before he died. His dad said it was like trying to breathe through a straw. So many times during that drawn-out torture, with no hope of a cure, Ben sat by his dad's bed wishing he could do something, anything. He rooted for his dad to hang on for a few more breaths, and at the same time rooted for him to die so his misery would end.

Ben was still haunted by the look in his dad's cloudy eyes. He'd even thought about grabbing a pillow when his dad drifted off for a few minutes of sleep, his only refuge from the distress. Ben knew he could make that refuge permanent in less than one minute. He remembered pleading with the nurses to give his dad more pain medication. But that could be dangerous, they'd said. It could kill him, they'd said. Precisely,

Ben thought. It seemed so unnecessary and so unkind—this compulsory agony.

Now, Ben thought of Wrigley who looked up from the floor with cloudy eyes, too. He wagged his tail, about the only body part he could move without pain. This time Ben *could* end the suffering. And rather than go to jail for doing so, he would be applauded for doing the "humane" thing. The contradiction was startling.

Ben found Wrigley at the humane society ten years earlier. His father had just passed away, and his four-year marriage was dying, too. His marriage had been destined to fail from the beginning, something his former in-laws were determined that he know. She was white collar and Ben was blue. She'd been pampered since her first trimester, bred to financial ambition and high fashion. Why couldn't Ben be a doctor, a lawyer, or an architect? Why couldn't he be something that would look better, and spend better, than a simple landscape worker? Her parents hinted that their lovely daughter should upgrade to someone who would be allowed *inside* the country club, and not just paid to drive around it on a lawn mower.

Ben first spotted Wrigley at animal shelter. There he was: frisky, happy, and energetic. And all this despite his solitary confinement in a small wire cage, without a lawyer, and with time running out. How could this dog be happy? Didn't he know he'd been rejected? Didn't he know he was a few days away from the needle?

Ben plucked Wrigley from the cage—commuting his sentence to life with a man who needed him. Perhaps Wrigley knew, deep down, that he'd won the canine lottery, the mother lode for dogs on death row. But there was no gloating to his former cellmates as he was carried out in the arms of the curly-haired man who smelled of cut grass and the pungent, blessed, smell of fertilizer. Wrigley was humble, and there would be no showboating.

Wrigley's new co-owner, however, was upset with his homecoming. "What in the hell have you brought home now?"

"It's Wrigley, our new dog. That's what I've named him. I found him at the Humane Society."

"Well, you can take him back! I won't allow that . . . that . . . *animal* in my house! What makes you think you can waltz in here with some goddamned dog and not even discuss it with me?"

"Hey, sorry. Relax. I was just thinking, maybe . . ."

"That's what you get for thinking. What makes you think you can take care of that animal when you can't even take care of us? You have an old truck and you mow lawns. And now you have a stray mutt to play with. My God, Ben, when are you going to grow up?"

"I'll take him with me to work."

"You're damned right you will! I want nothing to do with it!"

Wrigley looked at both of them, his tail wagging as if they were showering him with compliments. Ben scooped him up and put him back in the cab of the pickup for another drive to burn off some steam. Wrigley assumed he was being rewarded for being such a good dog.

Over the next two years, as the marriage unraveled, Wrigley had come to believe that "Rita" and "bitch" were synonyms. Ben felt a bit guilty about complaining to Wrigley about his adopted mother, because it is never in good taste to trash someone's mother. But Wrigley seemed to agree with him.

He'd blink and wag his tail, which was all the confirmation Ben needed that he had, indeed, married the biggest bitch in all of Illinois.

When she left Ben for a stockbroker with clean finger-nails (that she'd been banging on the side), she took every-thing he owned except the truck, some lawn care tools, and Wrigley. Ben needed a new start. He'd heard about the build-ing boom in Arizona. The place was exploding with new con-struction, which would inevitably lead to new landscaping. So, he packed what few possessions he had into his truck and, with Wrigley riding shotgun, put Illinois in his rearview mir-ror and headed for Phoenix.

6

"But, Rich, can we really afford it? My goodness, it costs more than our car!"

"I know, but think of the investment we'd be making in our daughters."

"That's awfully sweet of you, Rich, but let's be serious. Jenny is only eight and Liz is barely five. How could they possibly tell the difference between this one and that upright over there that's less than fifteen hundred dollars?"

"You said so yourself, Joanne," Rich countered. "Jenny has a gift. Her teachers say the same thing."

"She might be better than the other kids in the neighborhood. But a Steinway grand? Don't you think that's going a bit overboard? I mean, really."

"Just keep thinking of it as an investment, Jo. And besides, you like to play the piano, too."

"I can play chopsticks and a few Sunday School hymns, all of which sound perfectly fine on a used upright. The eight-year-olds in my class don't know the difference between a Steinway and a Fisher-Price. And where on earth would we even put the thing? It's as big as our living room!"

"It'll fit. Come on. Let's just do something crazy for a change."

And so it went—the marital wrestling match over priorities. Joanne always put up a good fight, making all the sensible arguments, but Rich usually got his way in the end. Besides, in this case it really was an investment in their daughters, both having shown uncommon musical talent. Especially Jenny, who could read music by the age of four and could hear a song and replay it on the piano, by ear, when she was seven. People were already whispering "prodigy." Neither Rich nor Joanne Kimball had a clue where this talent came from.

Like other good Mormon newlyweds, they'd planned to have a large family. But health problems intervened and Joanne could have no more children after Liz was born. She and Rich prayed for another miracle egg that was never fertilized. So, with unshaken faith, they committed to do all they could for the two girls God *had* given them. There were dance and swimming lessons, tee ball and soccer. And there was the piano.

Rich Kimball an insurance agent. He insured just about everyone in their Mormon congregation and extended family, despite the promise he'd made to Joanne that he wouldn't solicit them. Joanne had been mortified when he first became an agent to see friends and family scatter when they saw him coming, afraid he'd shake them down for another life insurance policy they didn't want. But Rich was Rich; friendly, gregarious, likeable, and warm. He was hard to say no to.

Joanne was also friendly and outgoing. But where Rich was persuasive, she was pushy. Rich was a charmer, and Joanne was a bulldog. He finessed his way into your lap to cuddle, whereas she stood at your feet and barked.

The Kimballs were an attractive couple. Rich was tall and slender with thinning hair. He was handsome, too, except perhaps for his nose that, in profile, looked like a ship's sail. He looked nearly the same as he had on his wedding day, a fact that perturbed Joanne because he never exercised or watched his diet. Even the graying on his temples looked distinguished. Joanne did more to earn it. She'd run the gamut of diets, but was currently on an organic-gluten-free-low-dairy something or other. She highlighted her dark hair to hide the gray roots and white streaks, for while it may have looked distinguished on Rich, she didn't want to look like a common skunk. She wore spandex most days because there was always an aerobics class, and the sheer amount of product she used on her face was impressive. She didn't consider herself to be vain of course, she was merely trying to "maintain." But, despite all the maintenance, there was still the inevitable aging. It was so depressing.

Both their daughters were pretty, their genes having conspired to create tall hourglass offspring (without Rich's sailboat nose). But, to be blunt, Jenny was prettier. Both were athletic, too. Jenny moved gracefully, as if she were gliding across the soccer field, delightfully unaware of her beauty. Liz, on the other hand, was all movement; limbs flying every which way. She spent as much time rolling on the ground as standing upright. By the end of a game, Jenny would have scored three goals without a stain or a smudge. Liz would have scored at least as many, but looked like she'd earned it.

Jenny was a tow-headed child with large blue eyes. She had thick blond hair until she was in high school. At that point she remained a blond, but with help. Liz had darker hair and was less obsessive about it, for she cared little for fashion. Despite their differences, Jenny and Liz adored each other, tolerating the other's monopoly of the bathroom they shared and swapping clothes without keeping track.

There was much for a teenage boy to worship about Jenny. She ran for cheerleader. Of course, she won. She entered piano competitions. Of course, she won. She was always the first one picked when choosing sides for anything. She was invited to every school dance several times over. And despite it all, she didn't act too cool for the other kids. Naturally, this made her even more attractive. So it was no wonder that Clay Lawson fell so hard for her. And, as fate would have it, he was a Mormon, too.

They began dating as soon as Jenny turned sixteen and immediately became inseparable. Clay never missed a piano concert or one of Jenny's games. He adored her. She was a tomboy who looked elegant in her prom dress and up-do. She was full of life and game for anything. Well, anything that allowed her to be fully clothed, for she was a conservative girl and even Clay Lawson, just about the coolest boy in all of Mesa, would not taste the fruit until the marriage certificate was properly filed with the county clerk. But he tried. He was a conservative boy, too, but he was driven by his loins. Regrettably, none of his well-rehearsed speeches caused her to budge. So he'd repackage his motley collection of arguments and resubmit them, but with the same unfortunate result.

When Clay turned nineteen he was urged to go on a two-year Mormon mission. He didn't want to go, for what able-bodied nineteen year old wants to go to Uzbekistan for two years? But the thought of not going would have broken his parents' heart. So, he would do his duty to God. Every day for two years he woke early and tried to find pleasure in reading the Bible (because, really, what sane boy wants to read the Bible?). All day long he knocked on doors of people who pretended they weren't home, and then returned to his dumpy apartment with his nineteen-year-old companion from Provo, Utah, who was a total nerd. He wasn't allowed contact with his family or friends, except for a weekly letter. He wasn't allowed to watch TV or listen to his music, either. And he wasn't paid.

The final indignity, Clay knew, was that Jenny roamed the campus of the University of Arizona carrying a textbook for her course on Human Sexuality, while he lugged around copies of the Book of Mormon. She joined a sorority and date-dashed the months away while he pedaled his rusty bike dressed in a suit and tie, trying to persuade people in a foreign language that he had the truth and they did not. He vowed that when he returned he would never let her go. He counted the days with one single obsessive desire: Jenny.

Liz was sixteen and felt stifled by her controlling parents who didn't understand what it was like to be cool. Without Jenny around as a buffer, they butted heads. Rich and Joanne fought with Liz and they fought with each other, the strain of raising a teenager ruffling the otherwise smooth fabric of their relationship. Liz heard it all. "When Jenny was your age, blah blah blah." Or, "Why can't you blah blah blah like Jenny?" Or, "You'll never get anywhere unless you blah blah blah the way Jenny does."

The more Liz pulled away, the harder her parents pushed back. Joanne blamed Rich for being too lenient and Rich blamed Joanne for being too strict. When they found an empty beer can in the back seat of Liz's car they went berserk, threatening a wilderness boot camp for wayward teens and the Betty Ford Clinic. The beer can hadn't even belonged to Liz, but they didn't believe her. *Do we look stupid?* they'd asked. Liz successfully avoided the gutter over the following weeks and Rich and Joanne relaxed once more. But Liz knew she would never be Jenny.

Jenny became pregnant. But before that she was married. And before that she was engaged. The engagement was a foregone conclusion. As soon as Clay returned from his Mormon mission he proposed to her in the conventional way; one knee, 1/8 carat, and a promise to never leave her. In sickness and in health. This had been an easy promise to make at the time.

Clay wanted to be a lawyer like his father, who managed a successful law firm in Phoenix. However, his parents vowed they wouldn't spoil him, so the newlyweds tied the knot with $1,135 in the bank, between them. This would not ordinarily portend a successful partnership, but they knew their love was one for the ages. Jenny transferred to Arizona State where Clay enrolled as a freshman. Their parents agreed to pay their tuition. This was almost *too* easy, they thought. His plan was to graduate with perfect grades and then attend law school at either Harvard or Stanford, a decision they would make down the road. Perhaps it would come down to climate. And all this before he enrolled for his first semester of college.

The outdoor garden wedding was perfect except for the downpour and the one and only zit Jenny ever had in her life. The bride and groom were radiant. And why not? Whereas before they'd been threatened with eternal damnation if they slept together, now they were encouraged to do so. Wedding gifts swamped their small apartment. Blenders, salad spin-ners, crockpots, and oven mitts. There were tool sets, place-mats, and a mop.

Clay lay on the bed and watched Jenny dress for the day, fascinated by all the primping. After fussing with her hair for an hour, the small apartment smelled like burnt plastic. Clay was savvy, however, even for a newlywed, and had the good judgment not to say her hair looked about the same. He had no idea women required so many products—so much that they wouldn't fit in the impossibly small bathroom, even if the plunger and spare rolls of toilet paper were removed from the cabinet under the sink. There were cleansers, shampoos, conditioners, and lotions. And the makeup! Tools to put it on and tools to take it off. The tangle of cords from hair straighteners, curling irons, and blow dryers looked like an orgy of delirious snakes making love without so much as a courtesy nod to monogamy. And how many hairbrushes could one woman need? There was only one electrical outlet, so two adapters were necessary for the hair equipment alone. Their tiny closet accommodated only a third of Jenny's gear. So Clay's was shoved under the bed. What didn't fit there was stored in the kitchen drawer beneath the oven, next to the pots and pans.

Jenny and Clay were poor, but they were happy. Jenny brought in spare change teaching piano to kids who didn't practice and Clay worked nights at a Chinese restaurant that served pizza and French fries. They studied hard and ordered from the right side of the menu.

Two years later, Jenny had graduated, Clay was earning respectable grades, and Jenny was pregnant. For seven months, she listened to other women wax on about their pregnancies. This one had an epidural and that one required a caesarean section. This one delivered a week late and that one's water broke at the movie theatre. These were riveting details that she bore in good cheer. She had been thrilled to become pregnant initially, and then wondered what she had been so thrilled about. Her romantic illusions of motherhood caused her to question the ways of nature, and then revolt against them. There was the nausea, swollen veins, back pain, lethargy, tender breasts, and the urgency to pee. And her emotions were completely out of whack. She plodded around with a watermelon strapped to her belly, and dreamed about delivering a litter of puppies.

An aunt who lived in Sun City agreed to throw a baby shower for her. Jenny marked the calendar with swollen fingers: June 2, 2002.

She made a haul at the shower—all the accoutrements of parenthood that would somehow be squeezed into the apartment along with the crib, strollers (she informed Clay they needed two), playpen, car seat, diaper bags, high chair, and toys.

After the party, the gifts were loaded into Jenny's Honda Civic, along with the blue balloons. It was 8:35 p.m. She headed south on Highway 60, anxious to be home. She called Clay from her cell and then took her shoes off because her feet were swollen. She was exhausted, but happy. Her life was nearly perfect.

A few miles outside of Sun City, the faded red pickup truck that she'd been following slowed and then came to a stop in the middle of the road. Jenny slowed and stopped a safe distance behind it. She was impatient because she needed to pee, again. She craned her neck to look around the pickup to see why it had stopped. She rubbed her taut stomach and felt the baby turn, pressing on her bladder. She noticed in her rear-view mirror a sedan slow and stop behind her.

The violence of the collision a moment later was horrific. She had the sensation that her car had been lifted up and then dropped again. There was thick smoke in the air and she couldn't breathe. She had the vague impression that she'd been hit from behind and catapulted into the red truck, but it was all confusing. A man without a shirt came to her window. A dog barked, the only sound in the desert stillness. She was in and out of consciousness. The baby! She reached for her stomach but couldn't move. She was out again. The *whosh whosh whosh*. Was it a helicopter? On the road?

She lost consciousness again.

7

Steve Olson was Blake's best friend and would be his best man, should the urge to marry return. They'd been friends since grade school. Steve was unusually tall, a gawky back-row kid in all the school photos who fit somewhere between handsome and average-looking. He had soft features and tended to lurch, the type of boy who might be teased for being dumb when really he wasn't. Some described him simply as "the big oaf that Blake Morgan hangs out with," a description that was neither fair nor accurate. He was quiet and stood in the wings, like a spectator at a play, looking on with interest but never taking the stage himself. So, while Blake had been the school president, Steve had been his campaign manager, and while Blake had been captain of the football team, Steve had been his blocker.

Steve's expectations in life were modest—he only wanted to take over his father's appliance repair business. He drove a minivan and bought regular gasoline. He wore out-of-style jeans, a braided belt, and white tennis shoes. He hadn't changed his hairstyle since the seventh grade. He didn't know which fork to use, or whether to pour a cab or a chardonnay. But he was the finest man Blake had ever known. There was even admiration when he annoyed Blake. Like the time they were driving to pick up their dates for the Sr. Prom and saw a stranded car on the side of the road. "Don't stop, Steve. Seriously, we'll be late," Blake had said, because Steve always stopped. He crawled under the car to help plug an oil leak, brushed off his tuxedo, and got back in the car like nothing had happened. Blake just stared at him. "What?" Steve said, as if that had been the most natural thing in the world to have done.

Steve treated Blake exactly the same both before and after Blake's bout with fame, for he was unimpressed with shallow achievement. As far as Steve was concerned, Blake had been just Blake, whether he had a large sports contract, or not. So when Blake's star fell, Steve remained. He hardly even mentioned it, other than to say, "Sorry, man. That sucks. But it's not that big a deal. Alison doesn't even know you played. Nothing personal."

Alison was Steve's wife, and if anyone was worthy of Steve, it was her. She was an attractive woman with green eyes, high cheekbones, and hair the color of wheat. She could have been even more beautiful had she invested in her appearance, but she didn't fuss with it, content instead to yank her hair into a pony tail and dress in modest apparel from the discount rack, for she was a devout Christian. And so was Steve.

They saved enough money for a wedding in Alison's parents' backyard and a trip to London for their honeymoon. Actually, Alison won the London trip in a raffle at work. It was supposed to have been an all-expense trip, but they soon learned that all-expense meant two seats in coach and a two-star hotel for five nights. For Steve, who'd never been on an airplane before that trip, his experience was something he never forgot. They cobbled their money to see Rent, the Broadway hit, and Seasons of Love became their song. Over the years whenever they fought, one of them usually sang the first few lyrics as a sign of contrition. Hurt feelings were soothed by "five hundred twenty-five thousand six hundred minutes."

When they married, some people privately wondered what such a natural beauty was doing with a man like Steve. But Alison could see beyond the surface and loved Steve unflinchingly. She had abandoned her career when their son was still about the size of a pecan, hanging onto the wall of her uterus for dear life. From that time forth, she had a singular purpose; to be the best wife and mother she could be. And she had done so without a single regret. Twelve years later, she was fulfilled, despite the protestations of her dwindling core of sorority friends who privately whispered that Alison only *thought* she was fulfilled, because all she did was chase her children around the house all day. And who can find fulfillment in *that*?

Alison liked Blake well enough, because Blake was likeable. But she didn't understand his reluctance to settle down. It was a bit unsettling that her husband's best friend "carried on" the way he did, enjoying a string of serial relationships with attractive women. Even though she didn't feel threatened by it, there was still the potential influence on her husband who had navigated the seven-year itch but was still human. But Blake was in no hurry to remarry, having been burned once before by a woman he thought he knew. Then she'd run off with the handsome personal trainer (who Blake's mother didn't think was all that handsome), and revealed herself to be an incorrigible bitch.

So Blake dated a lot, going through relationships at the

approximate rate of full moons. His first girlfriend after the divorce had a hoarding problem (he'd counted forty-two turtlenecks in her closet, but he never saw her wear anything that didn't expose her ample cleavage). His next girlfriend talked too much, a curse for a simple man who only wished to eat pizza and watch ESPN. She spoke to herself, too, as if she couldn't stand a moment of silence. *"Let's see, I've got my umbrella and I've fed the cat. Wait, have I fed the cat? Where is that silly cat anyway? Oh, there you are, you naughty thing. And I'll pick up some milk on the way home, and, oh those plants need watering. Hmmm . . . this coat has a smudge. I wonder where that came from . . . ."* On and on she'd go. Blake could only imagine her threading a needle. *"Okay, good, good, good. Oops. There we go. You're a tricky little devil, aren't you? Careful, watch it, watch it, good, careful, careful, almost got it, good, good, aha!"*

He'd almost married once before, until his fiancé, in a maudlin display of remorse worthy of an Academy Award, tearfully confessed a series of affairs over her fourth glass of pinot noir. Of course, these affairs apparently meant nothing to her, but they did to Blake.

Blake and Steve shared history and a few secrets too. Like the time Steve loaned Blake $15,000 from his modest retirement savings, to cover one of Blake's boneheaded moves (Alison would have flipped out). Or the time they'd gone to Vegas. They shared identical interests too, except where religion and politics were concerned. Steve and Alison were staunch in their religious devotion, the spirit pulling them heavenward like a Great Dane on a leash. Steve would pass up a ballgame on Sunday if it overlapped the church service, something that would've been anathema to Blake. When Blake looked deep within himself he could see no flame of faith, not even a flicker, for the pilot light was out.

Blake's latest girlfriend was to be his last. Naomi was a clinical psychologist with a stunning figure and skin as soft as smoke, the type other women are wont to dislike. But Naomi was self-effacing. She knew she was beautiful and could pass her reflection without tilting her head or touching her hair. She was olive skinned; a blend of exotic far-flung ethnicities—the most delicious of all merlots. Blake knew there was risk in dating a psychologist ("Why did I say *that*?"). And he was guarded in what he said about his mother, lest he inadvertently expose a latent Oedipus complex. Naomi had assured him he wasn't on the clock, and he believed her, but still he kept his opinions about his mother to himself.

The two couples spent time together and generally got along. Naomi, however, didn't share Alison's devotion to God, for she hadn't even gone to first base with Him. After their first double date, Alison asked Steve, "So do you think Naomi is pretty?" Steve, who had nearly choked when Naomi walked into the restaurant, said "Uh, sort of. I didn't really look at her that close, but yeah, she was okay, I guess."

Blake and Steve threatened to get back in shape from time to time. This they had usually done over a meat-lovers pizza and pitcher of beer. But then, in an uncharacteristic moment of bravado, they had solemnly vowed to run a marathon, a vow each of them began to rue from the moment it was made.

Blake sat in his cubicle looking at the mildewy pile of running clothes and shoes heaped into the corner. Just one more game of Solitaire and, if he won, it would be a sign that he should go for a run. Three wins later, he changed into his running clothes and pulled on his shoes. He walked into the break room hoping to be seen in exercise gear and then out to the street. He decided to run to Steve's appliance store because it was a perfect six miles away, and he wanted Steve to see that he had, indeed, been diligent with his training vow.

The first mile was difficult, as it always was, but then he found his pace and became lost in thoughts of George Morris. Would he end his *own* life? This was a wistful thought because death was as distant as the Milky Way, so he treated it the way he'd treat the question of what he'd do with the money if he won the lottery. And what about Gene Howard, that poor bastard with ALS? Ugh, the thought was too depressing, so he focused on his breathing and the rhythmic slap of his soles to the pavement. Soon he approached the hard-luck stretch of town, just west of Lincoln Street, the side of the tracks that tax dollars seemed to forget.

Olson & Sons Appliance and Service (there was only one son) was located on a street occupied by marginal rent payers who somehow managed to stay in business selling old record albums, radios, alternative clothes on chipped mannequins, and not-old-enough-or-European-enough antiques. The sidewalk squares were lined with weeds and weary-looking trees that had once promised shade for strolling shoppers. Their trunks were coated with exhaust fumes and their stunted branches bravely rose above the blight below them.

He pushed open the glass door and a bell jingled to let the shop employees know someone had entered. The lobby was cluttered with boxes and spare appliance parts. It smelled like metal, grease, and burnt coffee, the culprit being a Mr. Coffee that held an inch of black sludge. Next to it were two stacks of Styrofoam cups and a handwritten sign that said, "For Customer Use Only," as if there'd been a run of non-customers sneaking in to drink it.

"Gimme a minute," Steve hollered from the back.

"It's me. Blake."

"I'll be out in a second."

Blake stretched like runners do, pulling each leg up behind his back like a stork, then sat on a plastic chair in front of a coffee table. He thumbed through the selection of tattered and swollen magazines whose subscriptions had long since expired.

Steve emerged from the back wearing an Olson Appliance golf shirt (Blake had one too, swag from the annual Olson Appliance Golf Tournament where Blake was always the celebrity ringer). He also wore his trademark jeans and sensible white tennis shoes in a size fourteen. Blake, who was six feet tall, rarely looked upward to people but he did to Steve, who was at least six-foot-four.

"Seriously? You *ran* here?"

"Yeah, I told you I was going to do it. And I'm not letting you off the hook. If I have to suffer through this, so do you."

"I don't know if my knees will hold up."

"You having knee pain?"

"Not yet, but I might. How's Naomi?"

"It's all good." He then leaned into the counter to stretch his calves.

"Dude, I get it. You ran here."

"Hey, this is random, but I was wondering something. Would you ever kill yourself?"

"If I had to smell you any longer, I might. You need a

shower, dude."

"No, seriously, if you were on death's door, would you consider speeding up the process?"

"If I were on death's door?"

"Yeah, let's say you had a terminal illness and were going to die anyway. Would you kill yourself to end the misery?"

"No way, dude. I don't believe in suicide. That's God's business."

8

Don Weeks, the drowsy semi-truck driver, didn't wish to dwell on the accident. So when the "handsome young man from the newspaper" called, he was conflicted. But Don was so kind that he didn't wish to disappoint. He agreed to meet Blake after work at his home in Maricopa, a small suburb of Phoenix. The neighborhood was called "The Estates," a title the developer came up with in a fit of optimism when "The Tracts" would have been more apropos. The houses were basically stationary mobile homes. Each of them was well cared for, and there was a satellite dish on every roof. Evidently, they watched a lot of television at The Estates.

The yard had no trees or grass, just gravel. There were several decorative yard objects strategically placed around the property; an antique wheelbarrow, a saguaro cactus made of metal, and a rusty life-size silhouette of a cowboy near the chain link fence. The iron cowboy leaned back on his spurs with one boot and tilted his hat with a hand. In the other hand he held a sign that read, "Howdy Partner." There was also a lonely wrought iron bench stuck in the corner of the yard, amidst the gravel. Blake wondered what it was doing there, baking in the Phoenix sun with only a view of the neighbor's carport where an old Ford 150 pickup with flat tires was permanently parked.

Blake parked in the driveway and climbed three weathered redwood steps to the porch. There was an elaborately scrolled "W" welded into the screen door about waist high, something in an Old English font. He knocked and heard a woman's voice inside say "He's here, Don!" The door opened.

"Well, my goodness, you must be Blake, from the paper! Honey," she turned and hollered into the house, "it's Blake from the paper!" She turned again to Blake. "Well come on in before you roast to death!"

"Thank you. You must be Don's wife."

"Sure as shootin! The name's Donna." She stuck out a soft, pudgy hand. She wore a sleeveless top and pink shorts that were probably too short to flatter her round figure, for she was squatty, like a keg. "Don, for Pete's sake, hurry up, we've got company!" To Blake she said, "He'll be out in a jiffy. He's just changing into something presentable for company."

Donna wore flip-flops and there were cotton balls wedged between each toe. She saw Blake look at them. "Oh, just had me a pedicure. It was *heavenly*. I keep telling Don to go and get him one but he's too embarrassed. Thinks it's a girlie thing. But, truthfully," she looked around conspiratorially and lowered her voice, "he needs one." And then she laughed. "But I'll keep him, big old ugly toes and all!"

The paneled walls in the living room were covered with portrait-style photos of family that were slightly crooked. In each photo, there was the sense that Don was uncomfortable in his polyester suit and couldn't wait to loosen his tie. The carpet was a brownish cultured shag that was laid when the home was built in the 1970s, about the only time cultured shag was ever laid. The carpet abutted the kitchen linoleum that was lumpy in spots, like it'd been inadvertently laid on top of a few small mice.

Don entered the room wearing a pair of ironed Wrangler jeans with a good stiff crease. They were rolled at the cuff and held up by suspenders and a belt with a large brass buckle. He wore a shirt with the D & D logo, only this time "Don" had been sewn above the breast pocket. He took Blake's hand in both of his huge hands that were nearly the size of catcher's mitts.

"Sorry to keep you waiting. Just wanted to gussie up a bit, is all."

"No problem," said Blake. "It's a pleasure to see you again and to meet your lovely wife, Donna."

"I told you she was good as gold, didn't I?" Don still stood awkwardly, although there was nothing uncomfortable about him.

"Well, for Pete's sake," Donna said, "what kind of hosts are we! You must be parched, what with all this heat. Just have a sit right there, young man," she said and pointed to a large leather recliner that dominated the room. It was covered with a homemade afghan made from six different colors of yarn. "I'll be back in a jiffy with some iced tea."

Don sat on the crushed velvet sofa and stretched his large legs well beyond the coffee table; a huge slice of tree trunk that had been the product of their son's high school woodworking class many years earlier. He leaned back with a satisfied sigh and laced his fingers together over his stomach.

"So, how's your project coming along?" he asked.

"It's going well," Blake said. "You've all been through a lot."

Donna returned with the iced tea and produced knitted doilies for coasters. There was a proliferation of homemade knitted, crotched, and needlepointed objects within sight. Blake told her the knitting was nice. This he said to be kind, for his interest in doilies was low.

"Oh, these little things are nothing special," she blushed.

"Tell me, Don, what happened legally after the accident?" asked Blake once the iced tea was poured and properly commented on.

"Well, can't say as I'm too fond of the legal system after that whole hullabaloo. We were sued every which way, weren't we, Donna. Course, the insurance people paid the tab on it and what not, but we were on the hook too, it seemed like."

"Tell him about the lawyer, Hon," Donna prodded.

"Well, my lawyer, he told me to go ahead and tell the truth, about my driving logs and what not. So that's what I did and then they were furious with me. Musta cost 'em a bundle."

"They were mad because you told the truth in court?"

"Damned straight they were, if you'll excuse the French with the lady present."

"Oh, Hon," she said with an exaggerated frown, "I've heard swear words before."

"Well, when you're in the truckin' business you hear all sorts of cussin'. And Donna's right; she's lived with me all these years and heard a few doozies I suppose."

"Damned straight I have!" They both put their heads back and laughed, sitting next to each other on the sofa, holding hands like teenagers.

"Do you know what the judge said?" Donna asked. "Tell him Don. The judge came right out and said Don was one of the most honest witnesses he'd seen. Didn't he, Hon."

"Well, I guess he . . . "

"He said Don was the best thing they had going for them. Didn't he."

"Well, he said . . . "

"Go on, tell him. That's what he's here for, Hon." She patted him with her free hand to lend encouragement.

"Oh, well, on that, we were hauled in to meet with the judge. This was about three weeks before the trial where we got sued by Jenny, the paralyzed girl. Don't get me wrong, the poor thing oughta get plenty, God bless her. Anyways, the insurance company for Interwest was being cheap . . . "

"Now, Don," Donna interrupted, "you don't know that as a fact."

"Yeah, I guess you're right. But anyhow, the judge wanted to get the case settled up and he made no bones about it. So he ordered us to sit in that blasted courtroom until we agreed on an amount. So we sat there like bumps on a log for hours— me, Jenny, and her husband, Clay, I think his name was. We just sat there twiddlin' our thumbs while the lawyers went back and forth to talk to the judge. My lawyers wouldn't even let me talk to her, sittin' over there in tears on the other side of the courtroom like she was; said it wouldn't be proper. Don't even know why I was even there, for cryin' out loud. Anyways, they finally agreed on a figure to settle 'er all up."

"And that's when the judge said Don was such a good witness," Donna said.

"Oh, it was nothing, really." He took off his huge glasses and wiped them with the tail of his shirt and then put them back on. "It's just that the judge said they oughta settle because I was gonna make a good witness on account of my honesty on the deal."

"Did you admit it was your fault?" asked Blake.

"Well, yes, I suppose. The only time I give my testimony was at the lawyer's office at the disposition, or whatever they call those things. That's when my lawyer got mad at me because I told them all it was my fault. But it was just the plain truth, so I don't know why they got their hackles up like they did."

"So there wasn't a trial?"

"Nope, got it all settled outta court."

"Other than the traffic ticket, did you have any other fines or anything?"

"No, just got fired and lost all my benefits. Nobody would hire me after that. They wouldn't touch me with a ten-foot pole."

"Tell him that's why you went in with Dale," said Donna.

"Well, she's right. That's why me and Dale started our own company, you know. But that wasn't for about three years and during that time I didn't work."

"Bless his heart," said Donna. "He beat the bushes looking for work. My Don's not a slacker. He'd work circles around most men."

"Oh, Donna, you're just being prejudiced."

"You mean biased, Hon, and you're darned right I am. But when Don's back started acting up, well, that's when it got pretty tough on us. But we're fighters, aren't we Don?"

"We come out of it all right, I suppose," said Don. "But I hit rock bottom after a couple years. I was depressed—taking lots of pills and what not. My back hurt like a son of a gun and

I couldn't find me a job. It got me pretty low."

Donna leaned over and kissed him on the cheek. "Poor Don had nightmares about it." She glanced at him to be sure he wasn't upset with her for divulging this. "Why, I'd wake up to him flopping in bed like a fish out of water. Poor thing'd be covered in sweat when I'd bring him out of it. But he's better now, aren't you, Hon?"

"I suppose so."

"I'd like to hear about what you went through," said Blake, "if you're comfortable sharing it with me."

"Oh, I don't suppose I have too many secrets any more. But it seems like we're doin' all the talkin' here. We wanna hear more about you, son."

"You're right, Hon. Listen to us yammerin' on and on and we don't know the first thing about you, Blake. I'm going to put on some dinner and you're going to tell us all about yourself."

Blake knew they wouldn't take no for an answer. So he sat back and told them about his life while they peppered him with questions, Donna hollering from the kitchen, "I'm listening," about every two minutes. She returned with bowls of cream soup and thick slices of homemade bread. She put a ceramic bowl in front of Blake and then switched it with Don's when she saw it was chipped.

When they were settled she said, "We'd like to say grace, if you don't mind." Before Blake could respond, she'd reached over and taken his hand and Don's hand, too, and thanked God for their abundance. When she finished, she said, "Now, where were we?" An hour turned into two (for they knew nothing about baseball). They walked Blake to his car and Donna hugged him. Blake went in for a handshake with Don just as

Don went in for a hug. So Blake compensated by holding the hug an extra count to show he felt good about a man-hug all along. But it was still awkward.

As Blake drove away he saw them in his rear view mirror, hand in hand, heading straight for the wrought iron bench.

9

J enny was confused when she awoke two days later from her drug-induced coma. Her head hurt and she couldn't speak. She was strapped to a bed, but the bed was tilted at a forty-five-degree angle, like she had been lashed to the steps of an opened stepladder. The bed was slowly spinning from near horizontal where she could only stare at the ceiling, to near vertical where she could only see the door to her hospital room. Her arms were extended and her legs were spread, each limb tethered to the bed. She looked like Da Vinci's Vitruvian Man, or like she was being crucified on a gyroscope.

Her head was bound to the bed. She was unable to wiggle it even an inch because of the bolts that had been drilled into the sides of her skull. A ventilator tube had been shoved down her throat. She could not have known at that moment that the breadth and magnitude of her paralysis extended even to her lungs.

Clay was in the room and so were her parents and sister. They orbited around her like she was the sun. Everything they thought was so important in their lives; the meetings, hair appointments, and birthday parties, was forgotten without another thought. There was only one thing that mattered now as Jenny spun like a pig on a barbeque rotisserie.

Jenny looked at them for an explanation. Why was she

tied up like this? They were all crying for some reason. It was a man she didn't know who finally spoke.

"Jenny, my name is Doctor Sanders. I know you can't speak because we had to place a ventilator down your throat to help you breathe. I know it's uncomfortable but I'm afraid we'll need to leave it there for a few more days. I know you must have many questions, so let me explain what has happened to you."

She tried to focus.

"Two days ago you were in a serious automobile accident. You were brought here in a helicopter with life-threatening injuries to your neck. You've been in surgery, where we stabilized your cervical spine. We attached a metal brace to your head to keep it immobilized while we hope for some recovery to your spinal column. The trauma was so significant that it severed most of the nerves in your neck. Those nerves control your ability to move."

Her mom buried her head into a wad of tissues. Clay stood to her left with his hand on her arm, but she could not feel it. Her dad had his arm around her sister, Liz, who sobbed uncontrollably.

"Unfortunately," continued the doctor, "there was profound damage to your spinal cord. We always hope for some nerve regeneration, but the damage in your case was extensive. I'm afraid, Jenny, that you are paralyzed. Because the injury to the spinal cord was in your neck, at the C2-3 level, you are a quadriplegic."

So there it was. This could not be real. She searched the faces of her family where the true size and scope of the situation was impossible to hide. When the doctor officially pronounced the word "quadriplegic," Joanne and Liz cried out and then tried to stifle it so the sheer awfulness might stay hidden.

"You also suffered a significant concussion. We are working to evaluate any potential injury to your brain so we can give you the best treatment possible. I am hopeful your head injury will clear with little, if any, residual loss."

Her parents nodded their agreement that the head injury would indeed clear up, and Rich even smiled to chase away the tears.

"I promise you, Jenny; we will do all we can in the coming days and months to provide you with the best care in the world. We have a fine team of neurosurgeons, psychologists, and therapists who will do everything in their power for you." There was little more the doctor could say. He knew there was a fine line between life and death in cases like this. It could have gone either way. When he saw her there, lashed to the table, a beautiful young woman not yet in the prime of her life, he thought about his own daughter. He wondered if the miraculous modern ability to save her had been a good thing, or bad.

"Jen, it's me. Clay. We're all here for you, babe," he said as he dragged the sleeve of his shirt across his face. He wore the shell-shocked look of a private stumbling back from the battlefield.

"Oh, Jenny honey, we love you so much." This time it was Joanne. "We were afraid we'd lost you. Everyone is praying for you. You're strong and you'll pull through this." This hopefulness was betrayed by their wet, red faces.

"They say," said Rich, "that we might see some progress

in the next few days." Every muscle in his face was at work trying to hold back his tears. His chin quivered, his jaw flexed, and there was subtle rapid movement all about his eyes. He wanted to be strong for his daughter. "Mom's right, you know. You are strong, and no matter what happens, we're all here for you." There was no more effort to control his tears now as he bent over her bed and held her. She had never seen her dad in so much pain and tried to put her arms around him to comfort him, but they wouldn't respond.

Jenny did not cry. She was still confused. Her head hurt and her throat was sore. Her mom brushed a few strands of hair from her face.

"I love you, Jen," said Liz. "You're my hero." It was all her younger sister could do to say it, and she needed to say it quickly, in one breath, practically blurting it all out at once.

There was no blood, no cuts, and no bruises. There were no broken bones either, except for an unseen skull fracture, one that required no treatment and would heal without a cast or brace. Aside from the contraption that held her, and the fact that she wore no makeup and her greasy hair was pulled back from her face, Jenny looked normal.

"Jenny, honey, you have a beautiful baby boy." Joanne tried to smile, and for a moment she was happily reminded of the good news.

"Yeah, babe, we have a little boy!" said Clay with exaggerated excitement. "He looks just like you. You had a C-section right after the accident. He's almost five pounds and the doctors say he's a fighter."

Her baby. She was pregnant. The baby shower. A boy. All the Lamaze classes, the breathing exercises, the anticipation of the delivery, and yet she had been unconscious through it all. She wanted to be happy; she wanted to concentrate on this good news, but she kept drifting off.

She awoke a few hours later. She was still on the rotating spit. The only pain she felt was in her temples where the bolts ran into her head, like Frankenstein. She also had pain in her throat from the tubes, but otherwise she felt nothing at all.

"Babe, it's me. I have our little boy. Look." Clay stood in front of Jenny and held the bundle in his arms. The baby's head was covered by a tiny white beanie that peeked out of the blue blanket, like a morning glory.

Clay took a few steps to the bed where Jenny was splayed out, now at a forty-five degree angle to the floor while the mechanical bed rotated counter-clockwise. He laid the baby on her chest, just under her chin so she could smell the scent of her newborn. He then lifted the tiny body to her face and laid its soft cheek onto hers. She could not kiss him because of the clumsy respirator in her mouth. She could not hold him. She could not even touch him. It was only then that she became visibly emotional. Clay used the baby's blanket to wipe her tears. Jenny had now rotated on the spit so that she was nearly perpendicular to the floor, and Clay lifted the baby from her cheek and held him a few feet directly in front of her face. Her vision was blurred by tears that she could not wipe away. But the smell—she would never forget the newborn smell.

When Jenny woke again there were people crammed into the hospital room. Her friends were there and so were extended family members. Her sorority sisters came in twos and threes because they could not face her alone. They tried to be cheerful, but turned away to wipe a tear or to stifle a sob.

There were Get Well cards and cheery home-made posters. There were balloons and flowers and stuffed animals. And always, there was Clay.

When Jenny awoke again (*How long had it been?* she wondered) something had changed. There was grief that was new. The only sounds were the steady rhythmic hissing of the accordion ventilator and an occasional sniff. She searched Clay's bloodshot eyes for understanding.

"Jenny, it's our baby." Clay was sobbing now. "We lost him. The doctors did all they could, but he didn't make it. His lungs were just too small." Clay's despair passed to Jenny, but didn't leave him. It just expanded to claim another victim.

Gone were the empty pep talks. There were no more "It'll be okays," or "We'll get through this just fines." All that was left was the crushing recognition that it would not be okay; the acknowledgment that some things were not, and would never be, okay.

Their world seemed to have lost its edges. They walked through the days that followed only out of habit and later on could not recall how they had survived. But somehow they had. The ventilator was removed and Jenny could speak. But what could she say? Well-wishers continued to pour in and out of her hospital room, extending their genuine sympathy. However, they were eager to leave, because even though the room was artificially decorated with cheerfulness, it had no cheer at all. Before leaving they said the obligatory things like "Let me know if I can help," and "We're there for you."

Countless prayers were said on her behalf; sincere and urgent prayers. Rich prayed like he had never prayed before, from the very bottom of his soul. He did so without all the pomp and ceremony of the "Thees" and "Thous" and "Thys" and "Halloweds." These prayers were real. "Please, God," he pleaded, "I will do *anything* and I will give *anything*. Please, I'm begging you, let my Jen get better." There was no price he would not have paid, no concession he would not have made. He was bargaining with God who held all the trump cards, as He always does.

Joanne laid out her nighttime prayers like a lawyer presenting the closing argument in the biggest case of her career. She outlined the illnesses, the troubling family finances, and her own sterility. She marshaled all the evidence she could think of that might now justify a blessing on her daughter's behalf. She, too, would have made any deal that was offered.

Visitors said it would turn out all right. They said it was God's plan and that He worked in mysterious ways. Some said it was a test from God; a trial that would make them stronger, as if her quadriplegia had been a blessing in disguise. But this was a blessing the well-wishers wanted nothing to do with. They said God had been with her in the car that evening, for without His loving protection, Jenny could have been killed. Jenny was unmoved by this nonsensical rhetoric. She wanted someone to tell her the truth, that this was awful and unfair.

Did these well-meaning friends honestly believe God had protected her? And, if so, protected her from *what?* Did it not choke them to say such things, when God had been asleep at the wheel just like the drowsy semi-truck driver? Could not the awesome power of God have braced her neck, she wondered, or awakened the driver in time? She wanted to believe that God loved her, but was she expected to praise Him for saving her life? Was that it?

As the weeks passed, the number of visitors slowed from a torrential stream to a small brook, and then to a trickle. Initially there had been such excitement over the terrible news. (*"Did you hear about Jenny Lawson?" "Oh my gosh, isn't it awful?"*) Jenny hadn't been forgotten, but what more could the well-wishers do? And how much sadness could they take? They had their own lives to live, their own crosses to lug about.

None of the nerves regenerated despite so many earnest prayers. Prayers that had boldly demanded recovery had now become meek requests for strength to bear it all. Fingers that had been crossed for days were gradually uncrossed without comment. All that was left was the sad reality, the resignation that this cross was a heavy one. None of them fully recovered, of course, for how was that possible? And what did recovery look like, anyway? But there was partial recovery, not in a direct linear fashion, but a general upward trend as each of them compensated for the new reality.

Jenny was generously tended to. Her limbs were diligently moved by therapists and family members to prevent bedsores and frozen joints. Liz wondered out loud why they even bothered.

"I mean, what's the point? She can't move anyway, so why does it matter that her joints work?"

"Of course it matters!" Joanne said. "She's your *sister!*"

"I know she's my sister, but it seems like we aren't helping, that's all."

"Well, if you don't want to help, then you don't have to. But I promised to do all I can, and I intend to keep that promise."

Liz secretly wished, more than once, that Jenny had died. This wish wasn't a selfish one, and it was never expressed publically, but she believed Jenny's sentence was worse than death.

Jenny began to lose weight. She went from a strongly muscled athlete to a shrunken shell of her former self within a few weeks. The weight of the steel halo brace bolted to her cranium was designed to rest on her shoulders. But when she lost weight, and lost the layer of muscles on the top of her shoulders, the heavy brace no longer quite reached her shoulders. So instead of resting there, gravity pulled it down and the entire weight of it hung from the bolts, causing severe pain in her temples. They considered drilling new holes in her head to reposition the brace but she was too weak to undergo such a significant surgery. The cruel irony was that she suffered pain in the one and only place on her body where she had feeling.

After weeks cooped up inside, she was taken outside to see the sun and breathe fresh air. She was loaded onto a gurney, taken down the elevator, and out to the hospital's courtyard. The walkway was made of cobblestone and the bouncing gurney caused sharp pain in her head. They parked her in the sunshine and propped her up so she could see the gardens. She was thrilled to be outside! She smiled and mouthed the word "Hello" to every passerby. Most passersby smiled larger than usual to compensate for the tragedy somehow, while others pretended not to see her, checking their wristwatches instead, or looking into their purses, because it was awkward for them.

After two months in the hospital, they removed the brace. This was a happy day, for everything was now measured by a new reality. She was also moved from the hospital to a rehabilitation center where she would spend two more months. This was another milestone of sorts. It took Clay three separate trips to transfer all her flowers, cards, posters, and balloons to the new facility.

One day Jenny yawned and her right arm jumped a bit. Quite by chance, they discovered a limited amount of muscle contraction in her right bicep muscle when she yawned, so over time she learned to lift her right arm to her mouth in an uncoordinated way. She learned to drop it with the help of gravity, but this was awkward because it required an assist from her useless tricep.

Her fingers curled inward, like a partial fist, bent at the second knuckle of each finger. She spent hours with a spoon wedged into her curled fingers, trying again and again to lift it to her mouth before dropping it again. Her discipline and determination were an inspiration to the staff. She demanded a manual wheelchair to prove to herself that she was not completely powerless. She'd sit for hours in the vain attempt to move her right hand toward the wheel to see if she could move it, even fractionally.

She was moved from the chair to the bed or exercise table by a hydraulic hoist with a large cloth "sling", similar to the image of a stork delivering a new baby. This hoist was particularly humiliating because she couldn't even pretend to have any power, flopping around like a small bird with broken wings. At least with her manual wheelchair she could imagine that she had some independence, even if this imagery was counterfeit.

She was taken to watch other spinal cord patients play basketball at the rehab center. This was done to inspire her, but it backfired. It depressed her to see these superstars of rehab, pushing the basketball with the foot pegs of a motorized wheelchair, nudging it along like a dog with its snout.

She was finally allowed to go home, but not to her second story apartment which she would never see again. Never again would she use her blow dryer or hair straightener. Never again would she be able to apply makeup or put on her shoes. If she tossed away all the things in her closet that she'd never wear again, there would've been one hundred empty hangers. Those tall leather boots and her favorite sequin belt? Her high heels and cute black sundress? All she needed was a comfortable pair of slippers. And why, she thought, would they even need to be comfortable?

Her parents lived in a rambler with extra room. Jenny and Clay would live there until other arrangements were made. Carpenters expanded the door widths, lowered the sinks and mirrors, and removed the carpet for easy rolling. Liz helped her dad paint the room a cheery yellow color. They put motivational posters on the walls. On one wall there was *Life is what you make it!* On another wall there was *Tough times NEVER LAST but tough people do!* In the bathroom there was a quote by Helen Keller. Rich initially resisted putting it up for reasons he couldn't articulate; there was just the sense that he didn't want to foist the association of Helen Keller onto his daughter. But Clay put it up anyway, and it read: *Keep your face to the sunshine and you can never see the shadow.* And, finally, above the bed: *Once you choose HOPE, anything is POSSIBLE.*

A Welcome Home party awaited Jenny's arrival. Clay and Rich lifted her from the car to her wheelchair (she only weighed ninety pounds, but it was dead weight and unmanageably floppy). They left her alone on the driveway and hurried inside to make sure all was ready. When they opened the front door she heard laughter from the guests inside and heard her piano being played. The piano.

The Kimballs' driveway had a slight grade running to a busy street. She had the sudden thought to end it all. She lowered her arm to release the wheel brake so she could roll down into the road, but she didn't have the strength to flip the lever. She was not even able to kill herself. Clay returned a few moments later with exaggerated cheerfulness and wheeled her up the ramp into her new home where the party was underway.

The merriment immediately became more subdued, even awkward. The *Welcome Home Jenny!* banner even seemed to sag. When a kind neighbor, in a moment of forced celebration, raised a glass to toast Jenny, her inability to participate in the toast was uncomfortable for everyone. One by one, the well-wishers bent over to give her a unilateral hug and then left to resume their own lives.

Jenny was at a crossroads. The list was long of all the things she couldn't do, all the ways she'd been robbed. It was tempting to wallow in self-pity, to luxuriate in her sorry mess, for what a sorry mess it was. Day after day, she sat staring out the picture window to the street where drivers cruised past, absorbed in their own dramas. They could freely move their arms and legs but that hardly guaranteed contentment. Combing their hair and brushing their own teeth didn't make them happy—it was even something of a burden. They fretted over the small stain on their blouse, or their son's B- in algebra. Jenny realized that, however trite the cliché, happiness really was a state of mind. This epiphany did not happen overnight, but over a series of nights.

This realization that she could *choose* to be sad or happy was powerful. She gradually climbed from denial to resignation, and then from resignation to acceptance. Of course, she wasn't happy about it. Who would be? But instead of focusing on her limitations, she began to consider what she *could* do.

Her mind was sharp and she could control it. So a few months later she enrolled for spring semester at the local community college. She'd already earned her degree in Music, but that wouldn't do her much good now. Forget Beethoven's Fifth; she couldn't even play chopsticks. She decided to earn a degree in counseling physically handicapped children.

The first day of class was a disaster. She'd been determined to go it alone, so Clay dropped her off in the parking lot with her motorized wheelchair. She drove across the parking lot and up the wheelchair ramp to the door where a handicap button would automatically open the door. She pawed at the button with her right hand, but with so little pressure it wouldn't open. She couldn't use the weight of her head because it was strapped with Velcro to the wheelchair's headrest. There she was, not even able to enter the building the way handicapped people do. She wanted to laugh. She wanted to cry.

A young man saw her. With kindness and ease that was wholly taken for granted, he pushed the button and the door opened. She maneuvered the wheelchair down the hall to the room where her first class was held. She was now running a few minutes late and the crowded class of students had begun without her. She turned the wheelchair with herky-jerky starts and stops through the open doorway, but crashed into a garbage can at the front of the room, knocking its contents to the ground. There was silence as the teacher and other students stared at her. She was pitied.

10

They sat in the front row, their hands held high above their heads, as the old roller coaster climbed with a clickety clack. They reached the flag at the top of the hill, one hundred feet above the midway where kids squealed and teenage boys threw balls at stacks of heavy milk bottles, spending a day's wages to win a cheap stuffed animal for their girl. The car gave way to gravity and they hurtled down the track, the backs of their heads smashed to the headrest, arms still raised, but not quite as high. They careened through the first hairpin turn and down again. Fern screamed and George hollered as the car screeched to the finish.

George was a gangly seventeen year old with pimples who towered over sixteen-year-old Fern, barely five feet tall, as they walked the midway holding hands. His thick hair was slicked back with his dad's Brillcreme and Fern bounced alongside him in her poodle skirt, saddle shoes, and his high school letter jacket that hung on her like a cape. There was energy and enthusiasm in their light steps. The thought of old age was foreign to them, and so was the inevitability of their deaths, a vague concept for their grandparents to worry about.

These were heady days following the war and George dreamed of becoming a doctor. They married as teenagers and began having children like the good Catholics they were.

After three children he was accepted to medical school at UCLA and the family moved to Los Angeles. They had three more children by the time he finished his residency in plastic surgery. The pill had yet to be invented and, for all its promise, the rhythm method had proven to be quite unreliable. Fern believed this was God's will. Upon the gentle coaxing of her doctor, and her exhausted husband, Fern was persuaded that she had honored the papacy enough times.

George began his career as a plastic surgeon in the early 1960s, before the boom in cosmetic surgery. Breast implants and tummy tucks were rare, even in Los Angeles. Plastic surgeons worked on people who were injured, not on those who followed the steps of Ponce de Leon's futile search.

Cosmetic surgery took root a hundred years before Christ. The Romans liked to get naked in front of each other and any abnormality was viewed with either amusement or suspicion. Penises in particular were prime targets for improvement, so circumcision became popular, because no one wanted to parade around a public Roman bath with a funny looking penis. But the Middle Ages stopped the cosmetic surgery craze in its tracks. If the good Lord wanted your nose to have a big hook in it, then you had to live with it. Power to heal the body was considered magic, and magic was wicked. If someone was caught practicing magic he would've been tied to a stake, surrounded by townsfolk with dreadfully small breasts holding pitchforks and yelling terrible things at him through their crooked teeth and thin lips while he burned.

It was the Renaissance that allowed for better dental care and a good rhinoplasty. War helped, too. When noses were blown off and ears were severed, doctors found a way. Skin grafts, rebuilt limbs, and better suturing techniques were the result. But still, no breast implants.

That happy discovery occurred in the 1960s, about the time young Dr. George Morris became certified. Showgirls demanded larger breasts so doctors began injecting liquid silicone directly into their moneymakers. George hit his stride by the 1970s, which coincided perfectly with attitudes about cosmetic surgery. He soon became known as the Knife of the Stars. Word spread from Santa Monica to Bel Air. If you wanted the best, and were willing to pay for it, then Dr. George Morris of Beverly Hills was the guy. Lips grew, breasts swelled, and eyes lifted all over Los Angeles County.

Fern thought the cosmetic enhancement business was silly. This had been easy for her to say because an aggressive liposuction wouldn't have extracted a thimble of fat from her tiny frame. She never sat down and never stood still. She paced and fussed like a barnyard hen, so it was no wonder she had nothing to spare on her bones. But she endured the silliness because it paid for the large house in Hancock Park with the impressive wine cellar. It also put the kids through the best private schools and paid for the country club.

George handled his success well. He didn't consider himself to be special, and at times was slightly embarrassed that he hadn't done something nobler with his skill, something beyond nurturing the vanity of his patients. He worked hard but found time to cultivate other interests in his life; poetry, art, music, and history. His greatest regret was that he hadn't spent more time with his children. And now he was dying.

It had been three weeks since Blake first met with Fern Morris's widower. George had agreed to meet with him again, but with less enthusiasm, for the disease had been unwilling to stay within the confines of his pancreas. He was racked with nausea, vomiting until nothing came out but acid flavored strings of spit. And his abdominal pain felt like his insides were on the medieval rack. Blake noticed that he had lost more weight and his skin had a yellow cast to it, common symptoms of the end stages of pancreatic cancer.

"George," Blake said, "I'm sorry to see you are not doing well."

"This is my destiny, Mr. Morgan. One I would not have chosen."

"You told me before that you had decided to kill yourself." Blake regretted his choice of words, for the way he'd said it seemed too crass.

"Yes I did, and that is still my plan. I intend to take my life shortly, while I still can and while I still have the physical strength to do it. You see, Mr. Morgan, I believe there may be dignity in suffering, but there is also grace in accepting the inevitable."

"Have you talked with your children?"

"Yes, I have and they did not take it well. Well, I should say most of them were opposed to my decision."

"Did any of them support you?"

"Well, I have a son who has been anxious to receive his inheritance for some time." He paused and smiled at the thought. "I would not be calloused enough to say that he wants his father to die, but I believe he would manage to find a silver lining in the process." He looked down at his hands that were clasped together in his lap and smiled again, but it was more forlorn than merry.

"I'm sorry to hear that."

"Oh, don't be. I understand. Ever since Fern passed away I have become something of a burden to my children. They have loved and supported me, but now it is my time to go."

George would not have been surprised to overhear the conversations that swirled in the kitchens and bedrooms of his children. He knew they loved him, but he had a pragmatic view of it. The son he spoke of was conflicted. A few days earlier this son had been discussing his father's illness with his wife. The discussion was prompted by a looming inheritance, but to speak of it frankly would expose something ugly, as if the money were more important than the father he rarely saw.

"Boy, Dad's hanging in there longer than anybody thought he would."

"Yeah," his wife said. "I thought the doctors said he only had six months and that was eight months ago."

"I just want what's best for him."

"Me too, but this is tearing the whole family apart. The cost included. If he had a better prognosis that'd be different, but . . . "

"You're right. It's not cheap. I heard he's spending something like ten grand a month on treatment. Thank God he has the money."

"I know he has it, but it seems like he's just throwing it away on fancy treatment that won't make a difference anyway."

"He still has a lot left," said the son. "But you're right, it seems like a waste."

"I don't care about the money, but I just thought he'd probably want to give as much as he can to his kids."

"I just hope his suffering ends soon."

"Me too. I just hate to see him suffer."

George would not have been angry to have heard it. He had similar conversations with Fern when his own father was dying. He had justified them at the time because he was raising a young family, and was saddled with student debt.

Blake asked George, "Is part of the decision to end your life based on a feeling that you're a burden on your kids?"

"I wish that I could say it was. But, truthfully, my reasons are more selfish. I want to end my suffering. That is, quite simply, my principal motivation."

"Have you talked to anyone else, maybe from the church or something?"

"Well, as a matter of fact, I have. Shortly after I told the children I received a visit from our local priest, a kind young man who offered his sympathy and expressed concern about my salvation. My daughter must have called him out of her worry."

George then described his meeting with the Catholic priest. This was a meeting he didn't pursue, but neither did he resent it. Earlier in his life he had sweeping certainty of an afterlife, but as he grew older, he realized there hadn't been much heft to it. He had only regurgitated what he'd been told throughout his childhood years, and then later as an altar boy. He concluded there was nothing to conclude. He hoped to see Fern again, but hope alone was an unsatisfactory basis upon which to believe. There were other beliefs he'd read about, but he found no comfort in the possibility that he might be reincarnated as a cow.

George was trained in science. He had been able to compartmentalize his views of science and religion, but he hadn't been able to find a satisfying way to meld them together without gaping holes. He marveled at his peers' ability to require scientific scrutiny in their careers, but seemingly required no evidence in matters of their faith. It was as if they had a toggle switch inside their brains that could be switched on and off depending on the circumstances, or the audience. In front of their peers, they would scoff at the scientific impossibility of bringing a patient back from the dead. However, in church they glossed over the scientific curiosity with little thought, or perhaps with no thought at all.

Even though George had seen incredible advances in modern medicine, he believed that man's wisdom hadn't kept pace with those advances. Science allowed doctors to save and prolong life, but George believed mankind didn't have the wisdom to know when to save, and when to prolong. And to do both, at all costs, simply because they could? George believed a calibration was due.

The priest, Father McClinn, was smart and compassionate, but young. He could quote scriptural chapter and verse, but George knew that youth could not buy wisdom on credit; it must be earned and paid for in advance. For the young, even young men of the cloth, lecturing wizened veterans of life is a naïve proposition, no matter the length of their academic resume.

The sympathetic priest reminded George that taking one's own life was a grave and mortal sin. He reminded George that Catholics believe humans' lives are not their own to give away—that they are gifts from God and properly belong to Him. For George to intentionally destroy that gift would be to wrongly assert dominion over something he didn't own.

In the early days of Catholicism, people who committed suicide were denied funeral rites. Church cemeteries had separate areas for those who died without the proper rites. The sinners were fenced off from the others and the grass above them was rarely mowed; basically left to seed. The weedy graves were a stark reminder to anyone that dared reject the taboo. George knew the church had since softened its position, for now they mow everywhere. The church assumes suicide is caused by mental illness, so its victims ought to be cut some slack. But what about George? He wasn't crazy.

"Father," George said. "My choice is not made thoughtlessly or impulsively. I have confidence my mind is alert and healthy. Can I be forgiven?"

"Well," said the young priest, "through the love and atonement of Christ we can all be forgiven. But have you considered that each of us has an obligation to love our neighbor?"

"What does that have to do with this?"

"Your death would inflict suffering on others, especially your children."

"But my death is inevitable. If I don't act, I will die within a few months anyway. I believe my less painful and costly death will create less suffering for my family *and* me."

"But when we interfere in God's plan we thwart His design. It is not our role to play God. It is blasphemous for us mortal men to cause untimely death."

"Father McClinn, I have played God my entire career. I have intervened as a mortal man countless times to save lives, lives that without my intervention would have been lost. Do we not play God routinely? Do we not intervene from the first tetanus shot we give a child, or the surgery to remove a ruptured appendix? Have we abrogated God's design with the discovery of antibiotics? I would have died well before now any number of times, and any number of ways, but for modern medicine that routinely plays on God's turf. Do you believe it is reasonable or logical that we can do that, but we cannot end human suffering in the final days of life?"

"The miracle of modern medicine cannot only prolong life, but it can also make end of life suffering less painful than ever before."

"Do you believe God gave me pancreatic cancer and wants me to die from it? Is that His plan?"

"I cannot say what God has in store for you, George."

"But if I choose to end my life a few months early, and God, for whatever reason, does not want that to happen, isn't He more powerful than the pills I might take, or the bullet I might use? Do you really think I can trump God's will?" George was loathe to believe he could ambush God in such brazen fashion and get away with it.

"I'm afraid we don't know the mysteries of life, or death."

"But do you believe God wants me to suffer when my lot in life is to die in a few months anyway? Whose purpose does that serve? God's? Mine? My family's?"

"We look to the word of God to answer our most trying questions. And, as you know, the Ten Commandments strictly forbid killing an innocent life."

"Father McClinn, I am no student of the Bible. However, the commandment is not restricted to killing *innocent* life. And yet the Good Book is filled with killing; righteous kills, evil kills, ambivalent kills, and convenient kills."

George had a greater knowledge of the Bible than he let

on. He knew that, despite the prohibition of Number Six, the Bible was chock full of killing. There was killing by God, killing by righteous prophets, and killing by wicked criminals. And he knew there were examples of suicide in the Bible, too. King Saul fell upon his sword to kill himself, and his loyal bodyguard followed suit. Ahitophel also committed suicide when he got on his ass, road out of town, and hanged himself. Samson was another who intentionally killed himself by knocking the pillars down, crushing all the wicked and himself, too.

"I believe your life will not end with your death. Your soul will live on, and I suspect you agree with me."

George stood with effort and walked across the living room to retrieve the Bible from the shelf. It was a family heirloom of sorts, hardbound and black as Bibles always are, for there must be something malevolent about a colorful one, or one adorned with anything more that simple words, or perhaps a cross. It was swollen to nearly twice its normal thickness, like a book left out in the rain. He sat back down and thumbed his way to Ecclesiastics. He read a verse, his voice still strong and confident, but with the gravely rust of old age:

"For the fate of the sons of men and the fate of beasts is the same. As one dies so dies the other; indeed, they all have the same breath and there is no advantage for man over beast, for all is vanity. All go to the same place. All came from the dust and all return to the dust." He closed the book and rested it on his lap.

"But, George, surely we know there is an afterlife. Those who proclaim their love for God, and are properly baptized, will live with Him again someday."

"I hope you are right. However, I am inclined to believe the scripture. It is all vanity, this notion that we will live beyond death, because we cannot imagine the concept that we will completely cease to exist. If there is life after death, I hope that a loving God will understand my predicament. He may not have had a hand in my pancreatic cancer, or perhaps He had, but I hope He will not condemn me a second time."

"Do you believe in God's love?"

"Sometimes I do, but my belief is less than certain." George had seen so much suffering in the world that it was difficult for him to reconcile the love of God. Would God punish him for a wobbly belief? And just how wobbly could it be? Was there a threshold for wobbliness? Or did God require complete conviction with no room for doubt? Sometimes George wondered.

"I believe," said the priest, "that the questions of life and death are interesting as a matter of philosophical debate, but the basic principles are simple."

"Ahh, the simplicity of it all. I do not wish to argue with you, Father, for I sincerely appreciate your kindness and concern for me. But the sticky corners of religion are many, and I'm afraid we've made it quite complicated."

Father McClinn agreed to provide the last rites to George, notwithstanding his unholy intention to kill himself. Indeed, he would provide loving counsel and support during George's final days, an act of generosity and commitment to George's soul. A soul that only God could claim.

11

Blake's mind had been piqued by the concept of euthanasia. As he shuffled through his notes, he came upon the interview with Ben West, and realized George's wasn't the only pending death. Ben's dog would die soon, too. But he would be euthanized, and presumably against his will, or at least without his consent. So how, Blake wondered, did that square with the entire article that was rattling around in his head?

The literal translation of euthanasia is "good death," the entire point of which is to make death quick and painless. A slow, painful death is something quite different; like cancer. Blake was struck with the thought that people have been giving their dogs and horses the good death for years.

But not their humans.

Humans love their pets so much they cannot bear to see them needlessly suffer. If someone required his dog to stick it out to the bitter end, others would think him cruel. Indeed, some might believe he was a monster. Why would he make his beloved dog suffer like that? Why, it makes no sense at all. So the animal is taken to the vet, or out behind the barn, for a quick and painless death. This is euthanasia.

Animal euthanasia is different from animal slaughter. Humans do a lot of that, too. And it's also distinct from pest control. Most people are saddened to learn of the death of a dog, or a cat, or maybe even a goldfish. But a rat? Or a mosquito? In the history of civilization there has never been a single tear shed for a gnat, an ant, a fly, or a buzzard.

Wrigley's vet was a middle-aged woman who wore faded jeans and a pair of crocs. She had taken an oath to honor the principles of veterinary medical ethics, which, fortunately for Wrigley, included the promise to "relieve animal suffering." There was no comparable provision for the treatment of human beings, for better or for worse, because the Hippocratic Oath was a stickler. The ancient oath included the classic provision to do no harm. Doctors also swore they wouldn't have sexual intercourse with their patients (presumably this had been a chronic problem). The oath had dire consequences, too, for it was sworn to Pagan gods and witnessed by Apollo, Asclepius, and Panacea, none of whom were to be trifled with.

The vet told Ben that Wrigley's time was up. Even though Wrigley may have been ready to die, Ben wasn't ready for him to do it. The concept needed to marinate a few more days. The vet understood, because she knew that many dog owners suffered more over the death of their dog than their elderly parents. Ben carried Wrigley out to the pickup truck and laid him on his seat.

Wrigley had been spoiled. Ben took him everywhere he went, including to work where Wrigley ran around all day sniffing smelly things. He'd introduce himself to passersby, lopping up to them without stopping, for he was an extroverted boy. After work he'd hop into the cab of the pickup with little effort and sit shotgun like an Egyptian sphinx. Ben talked to him like he was a human being, even a therapist. He reviewed his budget, talked about what they needed to pick up from the nursery, and complained about his wife. Wrigley occasionally turned his head to look at him, confirming that he understood, then he'd resume his vigilant stare to the road ahead. When it was hot he'd stick his head out the window, tongue flapping, blinking every few seconds from the wind, spittle flicking to the rear quarter panel.

He slept on Ben's bed every night for ten years, even when he had bad gas. Ben would tell him to quit farting and cover his face with the sheet while Wrigley looked at him with feigned innocence. Ben gave him a bath nearly as often as he took one himself. Wrigley would shake himself off and sprint outside to roll around and dry off. But he was no burden to Ben, even when he misbehaved, using the remote as his chew toy or dragging his bottom on the carpet for a good scratch.

Ben was not a religious person. He'd been raised Presbyterian but would be hard pressed to define what that meant. Did he believe in heaven? Would dogs be allowed? And could it be heaven without dogs? Why should he be given everlasting life and not Wrigley, too? After all, Wrigley had been a good boy. Well, except, that is, for his history of sexual deviance. Wrigley had shown uncommon disrespect for other dogs in the neighborhood. Quite frankly, he behaved badly and Ben's wife had seen enough.

"That damned dog is completely out of control, and I won't put up with it."

"How do you mean?" asked Ben.

"How do I mean? Are you serious? That dog humps everything! It's embarrassing. He has got to be fixed."

"Relax a bit, Rita. He's just doing what dogs do."

"No, Ben, you're wrong. Normal dogs don't hump the

Dudley's weeping willow, and they don't try to mount their cement angel either. It's a garden statue for God's sake. It's absolutely ridiculous!"

Ben hoped Wrigley wasn't listening. Or, come to think of it, maybe he *ought to* listen up. A cement angel? He also knew Wrigley would sexually assault any dog regardless of gender. It wasn't his place to judge Wrigley's intent, but how hard was it to determine if the Richardson's schnauzer was a boy or a girl?

"If you won't take him in, then I will. And it's coming out of your money because I'm not paying for it."

"But, Rita, you don't work, remember?"

"Just get him fixed. I don't want to debate the level of our poverty again."

Ben felt guilty on the drive over to the vet to have Wrigley "fixed." This seemed the height of cruelty because Wrigley was just a teenager at the time and his best sex was still ahead of him. He'd tried to talk it over with Wrigley; tried to reason with him. Wrigley just looked at him with a look that said he knew Ben had his back. Of course, that look only made Ben feel worse.

Wrigley took it like a champ. During recovery he was desperate to lick his stitches but he wore a white plastic cone around his head that made him look like William Shakespeare. By the time he'd healed and the cone had been removed, Wrigley was back to his old self. He jumped dogs, trees, and statues. This caused in Ben no small amount of relief.

But that was then. Wrigley was old now. He could barely walk and rarely ate. His back swayed like an old horse. He was deaf and almost blind. He lay on his pillow and stared at Ben through milky eyes, only a thump of his tail from time to time. Ben carried him outside several times a day to relieve himself. Sometimes Wrigley couldn't wait and Ben patiently cleaned up after him. There was no sense in scolding him.

12

No one expects police officers to be perfect. They speed and run yellow lights. Some drink too much. The same officer who is called out on a domestic dispute might not be above a little shove of the missus. They might ding your car door in the mall parking lot, too. Gene Howard did all these things, and more. He'd justified it because he put his life on the line every day and wasn't paid enough for the sacrifice. So he took perks where he found them. Maybe it was a favor from the hooker he'd busted in exchange for a promise not to arrest her. Or perhaps he'd grease a palm in the department to have a record expunged.

There was talk within the precinct about Howard; nothing specific, just an uncomfortable hunch that he was dirty. Female officers in particular remained wary of him. But there was a smoldering testiness about Gene which made him the sort you didn't want to confront. He had a way of walking the opposite direction down life's crowded sidewalk where family and friends parted and swerved, going every which-way to avoid him. He rarely swerved or accommodated, causing glancing blows and hurt feelings to those who just wanted to get along. He projected his inherent distrust onto others, his eyes darting about as if he expected defiance from one unknown source or another.

About six months after he investigated the semi-truck accident, Gene stumbled in his driveway. He was startled because there had been no rock or crack. He thought nothing more about it. A few days later he felt clumsy using a simple can opener. His right hand felt numb and there was an awkward gracelessness about it. It was annoying, not painful, like an itch you can't quite reach. He thought it was the early symptoms of carpal tunnel syndrome, but nothing serious.

Gene was not a hypochondriac. He rarely saw a doctor because he'd always been healthy, and because he had to wait like the other patients do. So these odd happenings were not enough to make an appointment. Besides, Gene didn't get sick, for that was the province of weak people, and Gene was not strong enough to show weakness. So instead, he simply pointed it out in others.

Within a week or two, he began having trouble getting in and out of his car. His left leg felt like it didn't belong to him, as if a sodden log had been attached to his body and he'd been forced to lug it around. His colleagues at the precinct commented on his handwriting that now looked sloppy. He felt alert in the head, and he had no pain, but his muscles acted as if they had a mind of their own, or perhaps no mind at all.

Gene had always been blessed with high energy, and was annoyed if Lila or the kids slept more than seven hours a night. He woke early and made as much noise as he could to wake his ambitionless wife and children. So when he lost his energy and began to sleep more, he panicked. His primary care physician showed concern but no obvious alarm. He ordered blood work and sent him to a neurologist. By now it had been a month since his first clumsy symptom. The neurologist withheld his diagnosis pending the results of a brain scan and still more blood work. When Gene returned for follow-up a few days later, the neurologist, with all the tact of a toddler, sat him down in a small standard examining room.

"Mr. Howard, you have amyotrophic lateral sclerosis."

"What in the hell does that mean?"

"Amyotrophic lateral sclerosis is a disease for which there is no known cause and no known cure. Perhaps you've heard it described as ALS, or it is sometimes euphemistically referred to as Lou Gehrig's disease."

Gene stared at the doctor, trying to process this horrid information. "Are you saying I have Lou Gehrig's disease?"

"I'm afraid so. You are experiencing a neurodegenerative chain reaction in which a faulty cellular structure is causing some version of cascading muscular malfunction." Gene heard nothing of this scientific explanation because all he'd heard was "Lou Gehrig's disease."

"But how do you know?"

"I am a physician trained in this area. I'm sorry."

"Well, can't you take more tests?"

"I'm afraid further tests are unnecessary. Again, I am sorry."

"But I have good insurance! I want the best specialists. What does this mean? Will I die? Can I still work?" Those were a few of the ghastly questions that came to Gene's mind all at once. And right behind them there were a dozen more.

"Mr. Howard," the doctor said in a patronizing way that was unkind under the circumstances, "I am quite certain of my diagnosis, but I am less certain about how much time you have."

"How much *time* I have? You mean before I *die*?" He had always been in control. This had to be a cruel joke.

"ALS is a degenerative disease that attacks the neurons in the brain, which affects muscle movement. Unfortunately, the disease is progressive, meaning you will gradually lose the ability to control your muscles. The disease will eventually claim the patient within two to five years." The doctor spoke as if he were presenting a lecture to his colleagues at an AMA convention in Sun Valley, or reading straight from a medical text.

"*Claim* the patient?"

"Yes. ALS is a fatal disease. I'm terribly sorry. Progress is being made, however, to make the experience less painful. And modern technology allows patients to communicate through the use of their eyes, which is the only thing that escapes the disease."

"But . . . isn't there something you can do? There must be *something.*"

"I wish there were, Mr. Howard. I can offer you hope that the time frame for demise can sometimes exceed a few years. You are undoubtedly aware of Stephen Hawking who was diagnosed years ago and has accomplished incredible things since that time. Even though he is the rare exception, there is always that hope."

So the hope would be to live like Stephen Hawking; bent, shriveled, wheelchair-bound, unable to feed himself or care for his own basic needs. And that was the hope, the "rare exception."

Gene could not recall how he got home. When he arrived, Lila was in the kitchen with a dishtowel draped over her shoulder. She had just pulled a footstool over to reach the top shelf in the pantry closet.

"Here," he said, "let me get it."

She stepped aside and searched his face as she always did when he came in, trying to decipher his mood. She assumed he must have been in a good mood because Gene rarely volunteered to help her. She thought she saw evidence that he'd been crying, because his eyes were red and shiny and there was a broken humility about him that she'd never seen.

"Are you all right?"

He sat down at the twenty-five-year-old dinette set, one of the few things Gene had ever given her. He was still in his uniform. He looked at her without speaking then put his head down to the table.

Lila came over to where he sat and tentatively rested a hand on his shoulder. "What is it Gene? What's the matter?"

"I'm going to die, Lila. I'm going to die."

"What . . . what are you talking about?"

"They got the test results back."

Lila raised her hand to her mouth and slowly sat across from him. He lifted his head and looked at her without speaking, as if lost in thought. She reached her hand across the table and rested it on top of his.

"What is it, Gene, honey?"

"I have Lou Gehrig's disease." It was the first time he had vocally confirmed his diagnosis. "It's ALS, Lila. I have ALS." He dropped his head again and began to cry. In twenty-seven years she had never seen him cry. She stood and walked behind him, then leaned over and wrapped her arms around his shoulders and smelled his cologne. He reached a hand up and laid it on top of hers. His swagger, his contemptible impatience had vanished, leaving him vulnerable and scared.

"You'll be all right, Gene. You'll see."

"No, I won't!" he said, and she flinched backward. He realized his reaction was uncalled for, and he said, "I'm sorry, I just can't believe it."

Just then their son, Robert, walked in. "What's the matter? Is everything okay?"

Gene's head was still down but Lila's look told him it wasn't okay.

"I'm sick, Robert. I'm sick and I'm going to die."

"But . . . what do you mean . . . ?"

"Your father has a very serious . . . "

"I have ALS, goddammit!" he said, as if Robert should know what this was and what it meant. It was quiet for a moment as Lila and Robert shared a common look, a look that said the ice was thin. "I'm sorry, son. I didn't mean to . . . "

"It's okay, Dad. I'm sorry. I didn't know you were . . . "

"We'll get through this, won't we, Gene?"

"No, we won't. No, we won't. There's nothing they can do."

There was no retirement party for Gene. His medical leave was sudden and unexpected, leaving no time to throw a farewell bash with a sheet cake in the precinct's break room. He hadn't cultivated enough friends within the department to generate anything but a Get Well card signed by the clerical staff. A campaign to raise donations for Gene's family petered out quickly. People meant to give, but ultimately didn't.

Word of Gene's illness spread quickly, as the misfortune of others usually does. Some were cold enough to believe he'd finally received his comeuppance. But after it had been talked about in subdued tones for an hour ("Isn't that the thing that Stephen Hawking guy has?"), it was back to the routine at the precinct.

Gene was in a wheelchair within a few months. He still had the use of his arms and legs, but his movements were grossly inelegant, like a string puppet whose puppeteer was two sheets to the wind. When family or friends came to visit and reached for a handshake, he pawed back at them like a dog. The muscles in his neck were so weak that his head lolled from one side to the other, and then upright, before falling to the side again.

He was tormented by his previous intolerance of the physically disabled. He had shamefully ignored the handicapped parking-space signs and grumbled at the cost of all the goddamned ramps. Bleeding-heart politicians threw handouts to these invalids, which was bankrupting the national treasury. It was an outrage that his taxes were going up because of this unnecessary charity. Now, he was that person.

One of Gene's heroes was Dieter Dengler, the only pilot to escape a POW camp in Laos during the Vietnam War. He'd been shot down and taken prisoner deep within the jungle. His desperate situation and incredible will to survive against overwhelming odds was legendary. His body had been tortured, but he refused to give up and die. When he was finally rescued, they found a half-eaten snake in the pocket of his ragged military uniform. Thirty years later, Dieter was diagnosed with ALS. This decorated war hero, whose body had been indestructible, was now self destructing. He said the disease was worse than his POW experience because no matter what he did, he couldn't escape it. So he rolled his wheelchair to the driveway and shot himself in the head.

Gene now faced the same inescapable disease; he'd become a dead man walking the moment his neurons started cascading out of control. He felt trapped, like he was living inside a barrel. Just like his hero, Gene decided to kill himself while he still had the ability to do it. He'd seen the aftermath of gunshot suicides as a policeman and decided he couldn't put his family through that. And besides, he wasn't sure his hand was steady enough to pull the trigger.

He figured if he took enough sleeping pills he could kill his fragile body. He decided to do it as soon as he had a few hours in the house alone, before he changed his mind. An opportunity presented itself two days after he'd made his decision. He wanted to leave a note for Lila and his children, but he couldn't write. He thought to leave them a recorded goodbye, but he could barely speak.

While Lila was out and Robert was at work, Gene swallowed an entire bottle of over-the-counter sleeping pills. His inability to swallow normally, and his uncoordinated effort, left several pills on his lap or the floor beside his wheelchair. Water, saliva, and vomit ran down the front of his shirt. But he got most of the pills down before losing consciousness. He would escape the only way he could, in the way of Dieter Dengler, for what purpose was there in allowing his disease to consume the last ounce of his dignity?

13

If Blake wanted to make phone calls to his mother brief, he would call a few minutes before the evening news because she obsessively watched it, luxuriating in the world's problems. She was convinced that the younger generation didn't know a thing about leading the world anywhere but to hell in a hand basket.

"Oh," she'd said during the daily afternoon briefing, "and can you swing by to take a look at the lawn? It seems long to me."

"Sure, Mom," he said, for he was a dutiful son and mowed her lawn every week, whether it needed mowing or not.

He finished the lawn and went inside where he found her in the kitchen removing bowls of Tupperware from the refrigerator. "I hope you're staying for dinner. I've got some of that yummy chicken tuna casserole I made last week." His mother made food so she could have leftovers. She had never thrown away a scrap of food in her life, even a bite-size piece of pork chop or potato. She kept it until it was moldy, and then she'd cut the mold off and refrigerate it again, so her fridge was packed with smallish cartons, wads of tinfoil, and zip lock bags.

"Thanks, Mom."

"Let's see, I know you like my yummy beets," she said as

she pried open lids looking for the beets. Blake had once said he liked her beets so she assumed he was addicted to them forevermore, when in truth he'd simply wanted to compliment her on the beets. That is all. But now he'd become her son who was "fond of beets."

"Sure, that'd be great," he said.

As he saw her there in the kitchen he was reminded of the time he'd seen her shortly before he left the house for college. He'd come into the kitchen unexpectedly and found her standing in front of the refrigerator with the door wide open, leaning into the fridge with her forehead resting on a carton of milk.

"Mom, what's the matter?" he'd asked.

"Oh, it's nothing," she'd said.

"What do you mean it's nothing?"

She'd sighed and closed the refrigerator door and fanned her face. "It's a female thing, Blake. I'm fine. Women my age . . . oh, it's nothing, honey. I promise."

"So," she said as she placed an entire meal of leftovers in front of him, "tell me about Naomi."

"There's nothing to tell. We're just dating."

"I just wonder where this is going. You know I don't like to pry." This was something he did not know.

"She's a great girl, mom, and maybe we'll get married sometime, but I don't want you to worry about me. I'm fine."

"But, Blake, you're nearly forty years old."

"Mom, I'm barely thirty-eight," (his mother always rounded up when she wanted to make a point).

"This might not be any of my business, but it must be hard on younger people these days without being married."

"What do you mean?"

"Well, I know I may be old fashioned, but I assume you have . . . needs," she said. "I'm sorry to be so blunt, but you asked for it." She turned her head toward the sink to hide her mortification at having broached the subject, and for having done it so brazenly.

"Mom, *seriously*? I'm fine, okay?"

"Well, I just think it's time you settled down, that's all. The way that Laura runs around, why, I think it's shameful. Alex needs a better example. I know I shouldn't say it, but it's the truth whether you want to hear it or not." It was always "that Laura" when speaking about his ex-wife, a woman she would never forgive for walking out on Blake and her grandson.

"She's a good mother, Mom."

"I've said my piece, and I won't bring it up again." This was most unlikely, for she brought it up nearly every time they spoke, and each time it came with the vow that she would not bring it up again. "Now, tell me about your work."

"Actually, I'm working on a pretty interesting article. It's about the people who were involved in an automobile accident I covered a few years ago. At first I was going to do a short follow-up story on what happened to them, but now it's evolving into an article exploring the right to die. One of them has terminal cancer and intends to commit suicide."

"My goodness, that sounds awful."

"To be honest, I'm not sure how I feel about it."

"About what? About suicide? Oh, Blake, of course you know how you feel about it. Everyone knows it's wrong to commit suicide."

"But, what if you were going to die anyway and you only

had a few months to live?"

"I don't care if you've only got a minute to live. It's wrong, plain wrong. And it's a very selfish thing to do, too. Very selfish."

"He doesn't think so. In fact, he thinks it's an unselfish thing to do."

"Well, he's wrong, and if he's a Christian he ought to know better. My Lord, what's he going to do, shoot himself?"

"I'm not sure."

14

George had thought about it a lot, and he'd never seriously considered using a gun. Too messy. Too gruesome. Too blue collar. He'd seen a few cases in medical school, however, and knew it was awfully effective. If he stuck a gun in his mouth and shot upwards into his brain it would do the trick, unless he flinched at the last split second, in which case he'd probably wind up a vegetable. The same thing could happen if he pointed at his temple with a lousy aim.

He vaguely recalled the story of Japan's Prime Minister during WWII who had ordered his doctor to draw a chalk mark on his chest where his heart was supposed to be (George wondered how he became the Prime Minister in the first place if he needed a doctor to tell him where his heart was located). When the invading army was at the doorstep he fired his pistol into the chalk mark, but somehow missed his heart and survived. Unfortunately, he was hanged for war crimes three years later, so his plan had essentially backfired. Even though George knew he could find his heart with a bullet (he was a physician), a gun wasn't an option for him.

Cyanide was probably a classier way to go. All he'd have to do is bite down on a capsule filed with potassium cyanide and, voila; he'd be dead in seconds. Barbaric Nazis used it to kill gypsies, and homosexuals, and it worked pretty well for them. But George also remembered the madman who ordered the mass suicide at Jonestown. He'd stirred potassium cyanide into the fruit punch. The adults drank it from Dixie cups and children had it squirted down their throats with syringes. But they didn't die as quickly as advertised—the few survivors reported gagging, vomiting, and screaming for several minutes. George ruled out cyanide.

George recalled a movie where a character committed suicide by injecting air into his vein. However, as a physician, he knew that this was pure Hollywood, because he'd need to inject a lot of air (more than a syringe worth), and quickly, into a big vein close to the heart. And even then it might not work. There was the risk he'd wind up permanently brain damaged, but not dead. So he scratched air injection from the list.

He simply would not, could not, hang himself. He knew it would be easy (if such a thing as climbing onto a three-legged stool with a rope around your neck is easy), but there was something creepy about it—the way he'd dangle and gasp, kicking and swinging. And he knew it would be cruel to those who discovered him, blue faced with his swollen tongue sticking out, swaying from a leather belt tied to a rafter.

George had never treated a drowning victim, but he'd heard it was painless. He was suspicious about these reports, however, because how could anyone report on their death from drowning? Every time he'd seen someone on the verge of drowning the victim appeared to be quite uncomfortable. But still people tried it, dunking their heads into sinks, tubs, and even toilets. Setting aside the issue of sanitation, he knew there would be the impossible temptation to lift his head up.

They say freezing to death is a pleasant way to go, too, but

George wondered who "they" were. And jumping is popular. People have jumped off buildings, bridges, mountains, and even silos (they're the only thing tall enough in some places). They have jumped from airplanes without a parachute, and down dark elevator shafts. They've jumped in front of cars, buses, trains, and tanks. All these jumps would take nerve. George had the nerve, but he wasn't a jumper.

Suffocation was an option, but it didn't make the short list. George knew he wouldn't be found in an abandoned refrigerator, having crawled inside and closed himself in by yanking on the condiment shelf. And the thought of tying a plastic bag around his head was repugnant.

Wrist slashing was popular for a while, but enthusiasm for it seems to have waned. George had seen too many cases where patients wound up surviving, with only temporary anemia for their trouble. Another complication of surviving wrist slashing was severed nerves and tendons. George didn't want to attempt anything that, if gone awry, would leave him in even *worse* shape. Wrist slashing seemed to fit in that category.

Every thoughtful person who wanted to end his life would at least consider exhaust fumes. This included George. Carbon monoxide would kill him painlessly if he found a small airtight garage, or if he could rig a hose directly from the exhaust pipe into the window of his Lincoln. As long as he didn't run out of gas he would die. But it was also something of a hassle and required work, and George had no desire for that.

The list was exhaustive. George had seen people stab themselves in crucial organs, intentionally drive their cars into trunks of sycamores, stick forks into electrical sockets, and drop hair dryers into their baths. He'd seen reports of desperate people who doused themselves with lighter fluid and struck a match, or starved themselves, or allowed rattlesnakes to bite them.

But George, having eliminated all those and more, chose pills. Lots of pills. Because he couldn't choke down enough Drano (and really, who could?), he had to hoard pills. This took patience and planning. His goal was a lethal combination of barbiturates and opium. He secured forty-two tablets of Seconal (a barbiturate sleeping pill) that he would take along with an equal number of Codeine tablets (the opiate derivative). He also bought an anti-nausea drug to reduce the risk of vomiting up the poison before it worked its sinister end. And there it was: a deadly cocktail of eighty-five pills that would stop his heart cold.

Finally, he would wash it all down with his finest single-malt Scotch. He would do this for three good reasons. First, he enjoyed a good Scotch when he was in a contemplative mood. Second, it made no sense to save it. Third, he knew that alcohol would enhance the pills' potency. It would make the pills that were designed to release their active ingredients gradually, more soluble, nearly doubling their lethal effect. Besides, he believed most things in life were enhanced with a little booze. Why should death be any different?

George's confused cancer cells were mutating out of control. Or maybe they weren't confused at all—just aggressively proprietary. The oncologist had now given him six more weeks to live. His abdominal pain flared like he was passing kidney stones. Each day was terminally long and he remembered every moment. The will to keep living is durable, however, whether the death sentence is imposed by law or nature. But George believed that once it was over, it was over, and there was no prize for the manner in which one dies.

The Morris family was scattered across the western United States, but they remained close in spite of the geography. George had two sons and four daughters. Catholicism had prospered in George's downline; there wasn't a black sheep in the bunch. They also eschewed widespread use of the pill and their breeding habits were impressive, even by Catholic standards—twenty-one grandchildren so far. This breeding pace was especially noteworthy in view of the fact that one daughter was gay (something that was well known but not outwardly acknowledged) and another was barren.

George and Fern had their share of parental challenges. There had been a divorce, two juvenile court appearances, a few broken bones, rattled self-esteem, and trips to the principal's office. But it was all fairly benign. George hadn't worried about the kids much, for he was practical enough to believe it made no sense for *both* of them to worry about it. So, he directed his worry to things like monthly bills, taxes, and skyrocketing malpractice rates.

George's worrying over financial matters had paid off handsomely. He and Fern enjoyed a good life, but they had also been frugal in that post-Great Depression sort of way. Fern clipped coupons and shopped at discount stores. They socked away as much as they could for a rainy day that never came. So their assets mushroomed over time and George would leave something in the neighborhood of eight million dollars to his grateful brood.

There was a time that George obsessively counted his money. He'd watch the stock ticker everyday with a financial porn-like addiction. If the market went up he was happy, and if it went down he was not. But ever since Fern died in the accident he'd lost his interest in it, and whatever interest remained vanished when he was diagnosed with cancer. There was truth in the cliché; he really *couldn't* take it with him. So he became detached from the things that had once defined him; his money, clothes, cars, furniture, paintings, and toys no longer had any value to him. Indeed, they were now a burden.

These were times of great personal reflection for George. When he felt well, his days were filled with pleasant mulling. He was slammed with a forty-nine-year-old memory. He and Fern were at the State Fair. They were young and healthy; new parents with no clouds on the horizon. They saw an elderly man in a wheelchair with an oxygen tank and hose. He must have been eighty years old, an age that seemed incomprehensibly distant to George at the time. He leaned over to Fern and whispered that if he ever got to that point she was to shoot him. Make it painless and quick, but shoot him nevertheless. The words had been so casually spoken from the safe perch of youth.

George called each of his children and asked them to come down to Scottsdale for the weekend. He had already told them about his decision to end his life, so it was implicit that this would be his farewell. There was one thing they all knew about their dad; when he put his mind to something, it was as good as done.

The six children and their spouses (those that had them) arrived one by one Saturday afternoon. There was much love and joy, but the impending loss hung heavy over the gathering too, like the shield the dentist puts over your chest when he x-rays your teeth. It was not George's way to be outwardly affectionate with his children. Not one of them doubted his love, however, each assuming he or she was dad's favorite. Saturday evening they mingled and reflected, they laughed and they cried. Long-forgotten stories were remembered and retold. It was a treasured time for George and his children, one they would never forget.

On Sunday they all went to mass—even George, who slowly and painfully took his place in the Saints Simon and Jude Cathedral for his last church service. He'd always been uncomfortable with the ritual of the service—the fancy robes, hats, and smoke. The ornateness of it all disturbed him, knowing the golden monument to God was borne off the backs of mostly poor people who were eager to pay the premium for a death insurance policy. He'd thought about making a final confession, but then decided there was insufficient data to justify it, for his recent years had been quite dull.

Sunday afternoon, they gathered once again in the living room.

"It is hard for me to imagine a better life than I've had," George began. "When I was born, my life expectancy was fewer than sixty years. And who could have dreamed I would spend fifty-seven years with your mother and have each one of you. No, it's more than I could have asked for. But now this cancer has ravaged me to the point that I have no more desire to live. I know you must understand."

"But, Dad, what did the doctors say? Did they give you a . . . timeframe?" It was Sarah, George's oldest daughter, who loved her father more than anyone else in the world.

"I'm told I have approximately six weeks. This is a mere estimate, of course. I might be able to defy the odds and live longer. Perhaps not."

"Have you made arrangements for, well, um, for your will and that kind of thing?" This time it was his son, the one who'd shown more interest in his father's estate than the others. He loved his father but was temporarily blinded by his financial self-interest. Perhaps not completely blinded, only partially so; like a man with a financial windfall stigmatism. His siblings shot him looks of barely disguised alarm, but, of course, they wanted to know the answer, too.

"Yes, I have," said George. "My affairs are in order and I hope to make the dissolution of my estate as easy as possible for you. When I die, you will hear from John Boardman, my attorney and the executor of my estate. I believe most of you know John. He will describe the distribution. I can tell you that my estate will be divided into six equal shares, one for each of you."

"Maybe, um, this isn't the time, but do you have like a rough estimate on the size of your estate? Like how much, um, we can, you know, expect?" The son had been nudged by his wife to probe for this information. This he had done to the chagrin (and well-disguised gratitude) of the others. He figured as long as he'd gone this far he might as well dig a little deeper so he could, you know, um, plan. His wife had exercised rare good judgment in allowing the actual heir to do the probing here, even pretending by her own look that the question was slightly outrageous.

"I believe each of you will receive more than a million dollars and I hope you will be charitable with that gift."

"Dad, we don't know what to say. When Mom died we were crushed, but when you die . . . ." Sarah could not finish.

"You are all so remarkable. Each one of you has inspired me in your own way. Your mother and I did the best we could, and you have rewarded us with more happiness than you will ever know. But my passing is inevitable and appropriate now. You see, every single thing that has ever lived has died, or will die. And because death is so inevitable, the challenge is not to escape it; for that is impossible. The challenge is to do it well.

"I told you last week of my decision to speed up the process, if you will. I did not make that decision lightly. I want each of you to know that my death will bring me peace. I prefer not to tell you the details of my plan because I don't want to worry you or implicate you somehow. But, I assure you, my passing will be a gentle and good one.

"I believe you've all met Maria, my primary caretaker over the past few months. She knows nothing of my intentions and I prefer to keep it that way. I will purposefully coordinate my passing so that she remains unaware. I do not want her to resist my intentions or attempt to resuscitate me. I hope you will each honor that final request."

There was plenty they wanted to say, like "Please don't leave us, Dad," and "We love you so much, Dad." But the room was silent, except for the soft sound of tears. Here was the most important figure in their lives, the indestructible giant of their youth, the dad who could fix anything—the rock solid anchor of their family, seen and touched for the last time.

George was emotionally and physically exhausted. The

next day, Monday, would be his last. Maria would leave at 6:00 p.m. and not return until eight o'clock on Tuesday morning. His life would end Monday evening, on his terms, and by his own hand.

15

Don found a dead-end lane near a low-priced subdivision. How appropriate, he thought, that he'd find himself on a dead-end road at this moment. He shifted his weight in the cab of his old pickup truck, roasting in the desert's heat. The back of his shirt was soaked. The Smith & Wesson .357 lay on the seat next to him. Its black handle was covered with small bumps for a comfortable grip. He picked it up with his meaty right hand. The weight of it surprised him. He turned it over with deliberation, as if he were inspecting it. The pawnshop owner had asked no questions about its intended purpose, which couldn't have been good.

He removed a single bullet from the box of shells and put one in the chamber. He then slid his seat back as far as it would go and leaned back to the headrest. An opened letter lay on his lap; one of several, mostly anonymous, that he'd received since the accident a year earlier.

> How do you sleep at night? All you cared about was making an extra buck. Do you even care about the lady you killed, or the pregnant girl you paralyzed? Shame on you. I hope they take everything you've got, but you'll probably get a good lawyer and get off scot-free.

Perhaps this person would have been satisfied to know that Don didn't sleep at night. His motivation hadn't been to make an extra buck and, the note writer would be pleased to know, Don had indeed learned his lesson.

He lifted the gun. His palm was sweaty, making the handle's grip slippery. The barrel was oily. He opened his mouth and put the barrel inside. There was the metallic taste, like he'd been sucking on a handful of pennies. His hand shook and the barrel clicked against his teeth. He worried that he may have chipped a front tooth. This was absurd, he knew, because the appearance of his face didn't matter now.

He didn't put his finger on the trigger. Not yet. He wanted a few more moments of self-pity. He took the gun from his mouth and laid it back down on the torn vinyl seat.

The past year had been unkind. He'd felt lost, sinking deeper into despair, like a stone sinking soundlessly to the bottom of a lake. The dread of waking each day was progressively overwhelming, for what would he awake to? Pain? Addiction? Sorrow? Self-pity? Poverty? He could have picked any one from the list, carrying them all like a heavy bag of rocks wherever he went.

Within a few days of the accident, Don developed severe back pain. It was constant and radiated down his right leg—a burning sting. There were times he relished the physical pain, the throbbing ache, as a small down payment for his crime, for at least he knew he hadn't gotten off "scot-free." He had back surgery which temporarily gave him relief from the stabbing leg pain, but his back hurt constantly. The narcotic pain medication he was given at the hospital took the edge off, and allowed the covering fog to envelop him like a thick coat of varnish. So he sought refuge there in the mist with more and more pills.

Once the unemployment and workers compensation benefits expired, Don was broke. He'd been granted disability benefits but it wasn't enough, and the small inheritance that Donna's parents left them trickled away within a few months. All his friends had fled, leaving only Donna and his brother, Dale. They encouraged him to stop taking the pills and drinking the booze. This advice was well meant, but naïve, for they were trying to reason with an addict. Don couldn't help himself, because when a craving hit he was as predictable as Pavlov's dog. He could see the wreckage but felt powerless to do anything about it. Pain passed back and forth between Donna and him like a recycled fruitcake.

As Don's addiction to narcotic pain pills increased, so did his desperate ingenuity to get them. He walked into every emergency room in the valley with an exaggerated limp. He feigned one ailment after another. Dentists were another temporary source, and so were the medicine cabinets of extended family members. There was the brief exhilaration when he'd open the mirror above the sink and find a stash of pain pills. And when he didn't, at least there was usually a swig of Robitussin.

Don was not picky. He drank anything that deadened him. He'd return from the liquor store with the cheapest stuff on the shelf, then drink himself into numbness and wash himself off to bed as predictably as the surf. He was hurtling down to his destruction and couldn't find the ripcord. The first time he broke into his neighbor's garage and stole some tools, he'd been overcome with guilt. The theft bought him another week of drugs, but at a cost that was bankrupting his soul. And then he did it again, to a neighbor farther down the street. His humiliation was now at code-red levels, for here he was, Don Weeks, a good and decent man, hawking Black and Decker power tools from his neighbor's garage. He felt evicted from his life, because it no longer seemed to be his. He was this broken-down, inebriated man in the cellar who smelled of whiskey and day-old sweat.

It was then that Don began to think Donna would be better off without him. He'd squirreled away enough money for the pawnshop where he'd purchased a permanent solution to his problems. In the days leading up to that moment in the cab of the pickup with the gun in his mouth, he had persuaded himself it was his best option. When he picked up the gun for the second time, his face was soaked in sweat. It dripped off his jowls to the front of his wrinkled tee shirt. Yes, he was ready now.

Don didn't know what to believe about fate, for he hadn't thought about it much. But he might have acknowledged the role it played in the perfectly timed ring of his cell phone that day. The gun was in his mouth and his finger was on the trigger when the ducks started quacking. This was an obnoxious ringtone according to Donna, but Don liked to hunt ducks. He kept the barrel in his mouth but looked down to the caller ID. It was Donna, the only person in the world who gave a shit if he lived or died.

He hesitated. He took the gun out of his mouth and stared at the phone. He leaned his head back and listened to the racket the ducks were making. Then he pressed the green button.

"Oh, hi, Hon," she said. "It's just little old me. I was thinking about how much you've been through, but we'll be okay. You'll see. We're gonna lick this thing, you and me. Now you get on home because I've made your favorite beef stroganoff, and I picked up that *Anchorman* movie, the one with Will Ferrell that you've been itchin' to see."

Don put the gun down a second time, and this time for good. How could he do this to Donna? She wouldn't be better off without him; she would be crushed. His death would be a tiny ripple in the big scheme of worldly things, but to Donna it would be a tsunami. She needed him, and the realization of her need saved his life.

16

"Hey, Morgan, you got a second?" It was Hal, Blake's editor. "Sure, I'll be right in."

Blake stood and made his way through the cubicles to a glass room in the middle of the maze where *Hal Crawford, Editor* was neatly stenciled on the door. Hal waved him in. Blake moved a stack of papers from the only available chair and sat.

"What's up?"

"What's going on with that story of yours? The follow-up deal." An unlit cigarette hung from Hal's lower lip and jumped with each word he spoke. He held a burgundy and gold coffee mug with ASU DAD written on it, which Blake found odd because Hal had no children.

"I swear to God they're jinxed."

"Who's jinxed?"

"Does anyone ever complain about that?"

"About what?"

"Smoking in here."

"For chrissakes, Morgan, you got a problem with this, too?"

"No, I was just curious."

"So who's jinxed?"

"The people who were in the wreck. The cop has Lou Gehrig's disease; the husband of the lady who died has pancreatic cancer, and the girl's a quad. But what's really interesting is the husband of the lady plans to kill himself rather than wait out the cancer. A Kevorkian kind of deal, I guess. He's not some loon on a crusade, either."

"Hard to blame the guy. He ought to be able to do whatever he goddamned well pleases. But you mark my words; you put that in the story and those goddamn right wing nut jobs'll go ape shit." He took a drag on his cigarette and Blake braced for another rant, because once he wound up, Hal wouldn't stop until he'd exhausted everything that irked him about the goddamned-right-wing-nut-jobs. He had no tolerance for their goddamned intolerance.

"Got a problem with me writing about it? As long as it's okay with the guy?"

"Hell no. But for chrissakes, Morgan, I thought we'd go with something lighter, like a goddamned lottery winner or something."

"I'm going to pursue it then if you're sure it's okay. Maybe get into the whole right to die issue."

"Knock your socks off. We need to stir up a little controversy around this state. I'm bored with Bush and this goddamned Iraq fiasco. People don't give a shit anymore. But be careful, I don't want a goddamned lawsuit."

"I understand. I'll let you see it first. I've already started digging around a little and I've found this whole death debate has been around forever. Some of the stuff they did back in the day was crazy."

"I'm not surprised. Bunch of religious fanatics."

"Not really. Mostly it was a practical thing. Like, when the nomadic American Indians moved to better hunting grounds, or better weather, they'd just leave the old ones behind to die. They'd just pack up and leave them. Same thing with the Eskimos. When they couldn't carry their weight anymore they'd leave their igloo, hop on an ice floe, and freeze to death. Can you believe that? I mean, that's the way it was—they knew it was their turn and it wasn't a big deal."

"Okay, I like where this is going. Keep me posted."

"Thanks, Hal." Blake got up to leave.

"Oh, and get me an article on that warehouse fire down in Glendale. I want to run that thing tomorrow morning."

Blake left early to pick up Alex and took him to the Diamondback's baseball game. After the game he stayed up late, hovered over his computer reading about Eskimos and Indians. He'd become preoccupied with the story, like a hangnail he couldn't quit pulling at. Maybe they were onto something—this notion that it made no sense to expose the whole tribe to risk on account of grandma when she was just going to die anyway. It occurred to him that it has only been a recent luxury to keep her alive without jeopardizing the tribe. And then, he thought, maybe the whole tribe *was* still at risk because of the staggering cost.

Blake found Indians and Eskimos weren't the only cultures who weren't shy of dying. Take the Vikings. They actually *wanted* to die so they could get to paradise, and a more violent death was all the better. So they lined up for battle, on the front lines. And if they weren't lucky enough to get stabbed in battle, the next best option was suicide. The gorier the better. The last thing a Viking wanted was to die peacefully in his sleep.

Ancient Romans didn't act like they were afraid of death,

either. If a Roman brought dishonor to himself or his family, he was expected to kill himself. And his family didn't try to talk him off the ledge, either. They may have even nudged him a bit, for his own good. The Japanese didn't want the oldies around anymore than the Romans did. They carried old people to desolate places and left them there to die.

Blake felt especially sorry for the oldies in Serbia once they became too much of a burden. Youngsters in the community clobbered them with sticks at a carnival until they died. The whole village was invited to attend the party. But the widows of India had it the worst. They showed their devotion to their deceased husbands by being cremated alongside them. These healthy women threw themselves onto the funeral pyres whether they'd liked their husbands or not. This was genuine marital devotion. The husbands, however, just remarried younger women when their wives died.

And, finally, Blake scribbled notes about the Greeks. An old person, or one with a terminal illness, would throw himself a bash. Friends and family would toast the soon-to-be-departed while he'd bask in the compliments at his own funeral (because what good is a flattering tribute if you aren't around to hear it?). When the party wound down they'd draw a warm bath for him. He'd slide into the bath, slit his wrists, and gradually drift off to Mount Olympus while surrounded by his loved ones. This seemed quite civilized to Blake.

Blake's first recollection of death was when he was nine years old. He'd heard of it before then, but he didn't fully realize the enormity of it until Mr. Henstrom down the street died from a brain tumor. He couldn't recall why he'd known it was a brain tumor, other than he remembered thinking Mr.

Henstrom grew two brains and it killed him. Julie Henstrom was in his third grade class. It was all quite horrible.

He remembered lying in bed thinking about the awfulness of it all. Of course, it'd frightened him that this might happen to his parents, too. He'd heard them discussing it in hushed tones in the living room. At least he assumed they'd been discussing it, for what else would they possibly have been discussing besides that? He felt better when he'd heard his mom laugh, and then he'd heard the cards shuffle and knew they were playing gin rummy as they always did when their friends came over. But still he couldn't sleep.

When his parent's friends left, he went down the hall to their bedroom. His dad was asleep but his mom's lamp was still on. She was sitting up in bed reading. Her face was covered with cold cream and her hair was in curlers. She pulled the sheet up to her neck in a fit of modesty then scooted over and patted on the bed beside her. Blake crawled in. He could still summon up the smell of his dad's Vitalis and the musty smell of her book.

"Are you and dad going to die?"

"Of course not, honey."

"But what about Mr. Henstrom?"

"It's really sad what happened to him, but that's not something that will happen to us. And it won't happen to you either, I promise."

"How do you know?"

"I just know."

"So do you think he's in heaven?"

"Of course he is, honey. We all go there when we die. So there's no reason to worry."

"But what if you're not good?"

"Then God decides where you will go. But I'm sure we'll go to heaven."

"Do you have to wait when you're underground?"

"No, honey. As soon as you die God is there to take you to heaven."

Blake didn't recall if he'd been satisfied, or even comforted that night. But he never looked at Julie Henstrom the same way because her dad died.

Blake went into the spare bedroom of his condo where Alex was sleeping. The baseball mitt he took to every game lay next to him. He sat on the edge of the bed and combed Alex's matted hair with his fingers. It was hot, even with the swamp cooler rattling so late at night. Alex was sweaty and he smelled like a boy. Blake wondered if Alex's generation would see death the same way as his own. He leaned down and kissed him on the forehead.

17

Jenny made it through the first semester of school but conked out after that. It was too difficult to navigate the classes and books. She tried not to wallow in self-pity, but she was stuck in a chair, the same chair, day after day, and had plenty of time to contemplate her predicament. And what a contemptible predicament it was.

Then there was the dilemma over Clay. She felt guilty about it. He was a young man in the prime of his life who spent most of his days and nights taking care of an invalid. Would he leave her? *Should* he leave her? Could she survive without him?

"Clay, do you ever think about divorcing me? You can tell me the truth."

"No, babe, of course not. I haven't even thought about it. Don't even think that way." This was a lie. He had thought about it, of course he had. He had no plan to do it, but he'd thought about it.

"I know it grosses you out to take care of me, you know, when I go to the bathroom and stuff."

"Jenny, I love you. You know that. And I know you'd do the same for me."

"Do you ever wish I had just died in the crash?"

"Of course not." This lie was more complicated. There

were many times he thought her death, while tragic, would have been easier for everyone. He could have moved on with his life; remarried, found a life partner who could actually move. Someone he could take to a movie, or even to church. Someone who could use the toilet. These thoughts made him feel guilty, too.

They were still living at Jenny's parents' home and had settled into something of a routine. Clay was a month away from graduating college with honors, an impressive achievement under the circumstances. The plan was to enroll in law school that fall. He'd been accepted to several schools out of state but was still wait-listed at Arizona State. What if he didn't get in? The thought of abandoning his dream was unfair, but the thought of hauling Jenny to a different city seemed impossible.

Clay and Jenny were devout Mormons who believed in the immense power of prayer. Even though it privately occurred to them that the power had, so far, been less than immense, they put their faith in God. They begged Him, they made deals with Him, they scolded Him, and they cried to Him. Even though He didn't appear to be listening, or ignored their pleas for His own mysterious reasons, they clung to their beliefs. For what else did they have but the hope that He might eventually intervene on their behalf? So they prayed harder, longer, and with more humility. Their most recent supplications were to grease the wheels of the admissions committee at the ASU law school to open a spot for him there (they'd pretty much given up asking for any more help with the quadriplegia).

They also prayed about the lawsuit. They asked God to soften the hearts of the claims committee at Great West Casualty who insured the semi-truck company. So far, at least, God had either put the request on hold or the stone-cold heart of the claims adjuster was impenetrable. Every night they put another bug in God's ear.

At last their prayers were answered, to a point. Great West offered to pay $2,750,000 to settle the case. After lawyer fees and medical expenses, they would have enough to buy a van with a motorized lift, pay ongoing medical expenses, and get a place of their own. Their lawyer told them it wasn't nearly enough, but they were not litigious people and had never felt right about dragging Don Weeks through the ringer. Besides, the ongoing litigation was taxing, and all the money in the world wouldn't reattach the bundle of nerves. They asked God for confirmation that it was wise to settle. The heavens were quiet. They finally told Him they were inclined to take the money, so, if He disagreed, He should pipe up as soon as possible with a heavenly sign. When no sign appeared, they assumed He had endorsed the settlement. So they took it.

Jenny and Clay rarely fought. But they got into a barn-burner over the sensitive issue of money, and specifically God's share of it.

"Clay, now that we're making a budget and setting money aside, aren't you forgetting the most important expense of all?"

"What expense?"

"Well, you haven't said a word about tithing."

"Jen, I don't earn much at the restaurant, but I always pay my ten percent tithing to the church. You know that."

"But what about the money from the settlement?"

"You mean the $1,500,000 we got from the case?"

"Yeah."

"But, Jen, that'd be $150,000! That's not something you tithe."

"No, Clay, I think it *is* something you tithe. And not only that, the settlement was for $2,750,000, not the $1,500,000 we got after the lawyers and everything."

"So you want to give the church $275,000! Are you serious?"

"Of course I'm serious. And it isn't going to the church, it's going to God. He's been there for us. Sure, He's given us challenges like everybody else, but tithing is a commandment."

"Jen, are you telling me you want to pay the church $275,000? Of our money?"

Jenny gave him a long, sad look of disappointment. "Yes, Clay, that's exactly what I'm saying. And Clay, it isn't 'our' money. The money belongs to me."

Her statement hung in the air between them like a stink bomb that couldn't be unlit.

"I can't believe you just said that." He looked down at her in the wheelchair and then at the ceiling to compose himself, but he wasn't composed. "I wish you would have told me you felt that way *before* I shared every dime with you. And I wish you would have told me that before I gave up my life for you, before I changed your diapers, and fed you, and carried you, and never once left you, other than to go to school or work my tail off."

Before she could retract it he was gone, door slammed. What had she been *thinking*? That wasn't how she felt at all. She would give everything she had to Clay, and more. She'd said it, but she hadn't meant it. She didn't even know where it'd come from. If she lost Clay, and over money of all things, it would be the greatest loss of all the great losses she had suffered.

Clay didn't go to a bar, because he didn't drink. Instead he drove around the city in tears. He didn't consider himself to be a martyr, but, damn it, he had been an innocent victim, too. It had been over a year since the accident and when he envisioned his future he saw . . . what *did* he see? Not the future he had expected, not the future he would choose. Could he do it? Could he remain patient and faithful for the rest of his life? But even in this moment he knew Jen was home alone and needed him, because his in-laws were out of town. He called Liz.

"Liz, can you go over and help with Jenny tonight?"

"Sure, what's up? Big night out with the boys?"

"I just can't do it tonight, Liz."

"Oh. Sorry. Is everything all right?"

"Yeah, I just need some time alone right now."

"Are you guys okay?"

"Yeah, I guess. I don't know. I just need some help to-night."

When Liz went over she found Jenny in her room sobbing. "What was I *thinking*? What if he leaves me?"

"He isn't going to leave you, Jen. Clay adores you."

"But look at me."

Liz did. She saw the same beautiful girl she'd idolized ever since she could remember. "You are an amazing woman, Jen. He'll be back. You two will work it out."

A few hours later, after Jenny had been bathed and put to bed, Clay returned. It was dark in their bedroom and he carefully crawled into bed, hoping she was asleep because he didn't want to discuss it further.

"Clay," she whispered, "I'm sorry."

"It's okay. We can talk about it tomorrow."

He rolled over and pretended to sleep, but both of them were awake and they knew it, for neither of them had the deep breath of sleep.

"Clay," she whispered again. "Will you make love to me?"

———

Their First Fight (and really the only fight they'd ever had) had been two years earlier. They had negotiated a truce over the amount of money God would extract from them. Jenny had agreed to a much lower figure as a peace gesture, and Clay had suggested they give more, both of them having swapped positions to mollify the other. Their motivation had little to do with replenishing the church's swollen coffers.

Their initial lovemaking a year after the accident was inevitably clumsy. Clay felt a twang of lechery for having had sex with her. Actually, it wasn't a lecherous feeling, for that would imply she was simply a powerless receptacle. Maybe it was selfishness he felt—an animalistic urge to relieve himself at her expense. Jenny wanted to please him, and she was partially able to assuage her guilt by providing a sexual relationship to her husband. It didn't cause her physical pain of course—she felt nothing externally. But there was a certain energy to it that she did feel, a bond that kept her close to Clay. This was something she enjoyed, and from that time forth there became a consistent rhythm to their intimacy.

Clay had been accepted to Arizona State law school and

was now in his final year. Of all the prayers that had been answered, none was more appreciated than that. They bought a modest rambler in a nice neighborhood with the settlement money and remodeled it to accommodate Jenny.

Jenny became pregnant after they'd been in their new home about a year. Despite their basic grasp of biology, it hadn't occurred to them to use birth control. Maybe they thought Jenny's uterus wouldn't function properly if her neck was broken.

This pregnancy did not generate the excitement of her first pregnancy. In fact, they didn't tell anyone for five months because they didn't know how to feel about it. They briefly flirted with an abortion, skirting around the edges of the concept without coming right out and openly discussing it, fearing God might revoke His help if they did. Because neither one of them openly advocated for it (perhaps hoping the other would), no affirmative action was taken and the fetus was allowed to grow unmolested. Eventually that option was passively rejected and treated as if they had never, nor ever would, even *think* about such a thing.

Clay was embarrassed by the pregnancy. He knew there was no legitimate reason for this feeling, because they were a married couple. But now everyone would undeniably know that he had sex with her. This feeling hadn't existed when Jenny became pregnant the first go around, this feeling that people would pause to consider *how* it had happened in a way they wouldn't otherwise do in a conventional marriage.

He fretted for other reasons, too. If they were to have a baby, he would be forevermore stuck in the relationship. This remained a private concern because Clay was not angling for a way to get out of the marriage and neither was he cold-hearted enough to publically express how trapped he felt. There was also the fundamental question of who would care for the child.

Joanne was thrilled for her daughter. Jenny deserved some overdue happiness and this pregnancy would give her a new reason to live. And it might have, but another personal growth opportunity came in the form of a late-term miscarriage. Clay was sad for Jenny, but mostly he felt immeasurable relief. Joanne was devastated. It wasn't from the loss of her embryonic grandchild—it was the effect on her fragile twenty-six-year-old daughter.

Clay spent a lot of time contemplating the vow he'd taken six years earlier. In sickness and in health. What did that *really* mean? Were there exceptions to the general rule? And if so, what were they? Would he shamelessly break that vow if he left? Or what if he led a quiet double life on the side? He and Jenny wore matching rings with the initials *WWJD*, a fashionable jewelry item for Mormons those days. He looked down at the ring. What *would* Jesus do? But, damn it, he wasn't Jesus—he was just an ordinary young man.

Clay sought guidance from his local bishop, Brother Danielson. Mormon bishops are unpaid, part-time clergy who are selected from the neighborhoods where they serve. They put out brush fires—marital discord, welfare needs, wavering belief, and sin—and are usually worn out from keeping scandalous secrets and dishing out advice for which they have little or no training. Indeed, Bishop Danielson was a plumber—a certified one with a committed clientele, but a plumber nevertheless.

He was a decent man who had enormous compassion for Jenny and Clay, a couple who never missed a Sunday church service despite their unusual hardship. Clay made an appointment to meet with him that Tuesday evening at the church house; a functional red brick building without adornment. There was no stained glass or carved gargoyles. Even the steeple was modest. The bishop sat behind a desk in his humble office beneath a framed picture of Jesus. Jesus looked like a handsome Southern California beach bum and not a blue-collar Jew from the first century. On another wall there was a photo of the serious-minded Mormon Prophet, also impressively framed.

Clay sat across the desk from the good bishop, who wore a turquoise polyester suit with white stitching around the lapels and pockets, and a red tie with a knot the size of a tomato. His crocodile-skinned cowboy boots were polished. He was humble, reverent, and smelled strongly of Old Spice.

"Welcome, Clay," he said and offered a calloused hand that spent most of its time gripping a monkey wrench. His nails had been clipped but there was still evidence of his career in them.

"Thanks for meeting with me."

"It's my privilege. I probably don't need to tell you how proud I am of you and your beautiful wife."

They chatted briefly about law school and football, safe topics before getting to the meat of the matter, because the bishop knew Clay hadn't come to discuss the Sun Devil's injury-plagued quarterback position.

"Would it be wrong, Bishop, if I thought about getting a divorce? I mean, I haven't, like, seriously thought about it, but

I was just wondering."

"Divorce is a serious thing, Clay, especially since you were married in the temple. Only you can make that choice, but I hope you'll make it with guidance from our Heavenly Father."

"I know, Bishop. And I've tried. Heck, I've worn my knees out in prayer."

"Your marriage won't end when you die, unlike marriages outside the temple. You've been sealed together for eternity. And don't forget that after we die we'll be resurrected and have perfect bodies, including Jenny."

"Yeah, I know, and I believe it. It's just that . . . "

"You've been blessed with a difficult challenge, Clay. But God will never give you a challenge you can't overcome."

"It's just that . . . it seems like I can't get any answers to my prayers."

"Heavenly Father works in mysterious ways, Clay. Maybe He's already answered your prayer but you haven't been humble enough to hear it."

"Gol, I feel like I've been humbled enough," said Clay. "And why would God answer me in a way I couldn't understand? That doesn't make any sense. I know God loves me, and I know he isn't playing games with me. But why won't He give me direction when I keep asking for it?"

"Maybe he already has."

"Maybe he already has?"

"Yes," said the bishop, "maybe he has."

Clay sat looking down at his hands. He racked his brain for evidence of divine direction that he might have overlooked. "I just don't see where God has answered me, Bishop. But maybe you're right. Maybe He has and I just don't see it."

They spoke for a few more minutes, and then ended the meeting in humble prayer, thanking the Good Lord for His bounteous blessings and for answering their prayers.

18

Ben started at first light when it was cooler, because digging trenches for the sprinkling system would've been unbearable in the midday heat. He called it quits in the early afternoon and dropped by the bank to make a meager deposit. The drive-thru was closed for repair so he parked and threw on a dirty tee shirt. He walked around to the passenger door of his truck and lifted Wrigley from the seat and carried him into the bank.

"I'm sorry sir, but pets are not allowed inside the bank." It was a young man with a perfect part in his hair who'd been impressed with his position as assistant manager at the branch bank.

"Yeah, I know. But it's too hot to leave him in my truck. Sorry."

"But, you'll have to leave him outside."

"Hey, I'll just be a second—just want to make a quick deposit."

"I'm sorry."

"Then fix your goddamned drive-thru!" Ben said and walked out with Wrigley in his arms. He'd have to ask the veterinary clinic to hold his check for another day. His appointment was at 3:00. An appointment. How surreal he thought—making an appointment to end Wrigley's life, as if it were a routine teeth cleaning.

Ben was emotionally done in. He usually went to bed early so he could wake before dawn to beat the heat. But the night before had been restless. His ex-wife had called to screech at him from several states away. A friend of hers had apparently reported that Ben had accused her of having an affair. "I went easy on you, Ben, you asshole! You're out there in Arizona or wherever the hell you are, living high on the hog. I could've got a lot more from the divorce, but I'm a decent person, Ben. And this is how you repay me?" The woman was insufferable, Ben thought, like a scratched vinyl record album with the needle stuck in one nasty groove, screeching the same tired lyric over and over.

It was the appointment the following afternoon, however, that kept him up. On Wrigley's last night, Ben had lifted him to the bed. He'd curled around the warm black bundle and listened to the shallow breathing. Ben would not carry him out that night because Wrigley was scarcely eating or drinking now. His chest slowly rose and fell; there was an occasional wheeze and then a soft snore. Two or three times during the night, Wrigley's body jerked with small spasms. Ben assumed it was another seizure, but he hoped it'd been a good dream.

The next morning Ben scooped him off the bed and carried him down the crumbling cement stairs to his truck in the pre-dawn darkness where he would ride shotgun for one more day. He wondered if Wrigley had some sense, some premonition of his fate. He had personified Wrigley with human thoughts and emotions. Wrigley must be sad, or Wrigley thinks this is funny. And he knew that Wrigley agreed with his opinion of the ex-wife, politics, and his downstairs neighbor's abysmal choice of country music. So he didn't want to alarm him with the news that he would be dead before the end of the day.

He moved Wrigley several times throughout the morning, positioning him in the shadiest spots and taking extra time to tell him what a good boy he'd been. For lunch he lay down on the grass next to his beloved dog and stroked his sweaty coat of hair. Wrigley thumped his tail a few times with effort, but otherwise just stared at him. *What was he thinking,* Ben wondered?

The veterinary clinic's waiting room smelled like dogs. Ben sat with Wrigley on his lap and rubbed his head the way he liked it. A large calendar with a cute photo of kittens in a wicker basket hung on a wall. A *Dog Fancy* magazine had been left on the empty chair next to his by a white-haired woman who looked strikingly similar to her Afghan. Another woman sat across from him holding her pug. She, regrettably, looked like her dog, too. Dogs were barking in the back.

"Ben West?"

"Uh, yeah, that's me."

"Sorry about the wait. You want to follow me back?" asked the young woman in blue scrubs.

"Sure. Come on, Wrigley, time to go."

She led them to an examining room. "You can just lay him here if you'd like," she said, motioning to the exam table with a fresh sheet of paper.

"No, it's okay. I'll just hold him on my lap if that's okay."

"Of course. Sorry about the wait. We've been swamped today but the doctor will be with you shortly."

The vet came into the room a few moments later. Again

she wore faded jeans and a pair of crocs. On top she wore green scrubs. "So how's Wrigley?"

"Not good. I think it's time I put him down."

She leaned over and stroked Wrigley's head. His eyes turned toward her but not his head. He offered a half-wag of his tail. She rolled a stool over to where they sat and faced Ben.

"Ben, I'm sorry. I know how much your dog means to you."

Ben only nodded, for his throat was too tight to speak. His eyes were shiny and full and he dragged his tattooed arm across them.

"This is the part of my job that is so difficult. I am supposed to heal the sick and relieve their suffering. I hope I am about to do just that for Wrigley."

Ben nodded again and mouthed the words: Thank you.

"I'll put a topical anesthetic near his front paw and then place a catheter. I'll make sure he's comfortable so there will be no pain. A few minutes later I'll give him a drug to induce cardiac arrest, usually within thirty seconds."

Ben wanted to say something, but if he'd opened his mouth the only sound would have been an unintelligible sob. So he just nodded his head instead.

"All right, if you'll step out of the room for a moment I'll get the catheter in. Of course then you're welcome to have as much time as you'd like with Wrigley before I inject the drug."

Ben laid Wrigley on the exam table and the paper crinkled. He left the room and walked down the hall. Despite all the barking and meowing it was a peaceful place somehow. Animals were tended to with care and respect. He leaned over the drinking fountain and wept. No one judged him, no one thought him weak or oversensitive. These were people who understand what it means to love a dog. A few minutes later Ben was back in the room and the vet excused herself so the two of them could be alone.

"I don't know what to say, Wrigley," Ben sobbed. "I'm so sorry. I'll never forget you, buddy." Ben bent down and kissed Wrigley's head. He didn't bother to wipe the tears that now ran in rivulets to the bottom of his jaw, and then dripped to Wrigley who looked at him and blinked. He wagged his tail for the final time as if to say he understood perfectly.

There was a tap on the door and it opened partway. "Are you ready, Ben?"

"Yeah, we're ready. But can I hold him?"

"Of course."

Ben lifted him off the table and sat again, draping himself over his beloved dog. The vet injected the drugs into the catheter near Wrigley's front paw. Ben no longer tried to hide his emotion. He put his face next to Wrigley's and whispered what a good boy he'd been. Wrigley's eyes closed, his breathing slowed, and then stopped.

"You can stay here as long as you'd like." She stepped outside so Ben could be alone with his dog. A few minutes later he left the room and walked to the counter to pay the bill.

"There's no charge."

"But I thought I had to pay . . . "

"Well, it's eighty dollars but the doctor came out and told me there was no fee for this one. Oh, and she wanted me to give you this," and handed over a folded piece of paper.

Ben walked out to his truck and sat down. Another wave of emotion hit him when he realized he'd never been in his truck without Wrigley. The blanket that covered the passenger seat was empty. There was a tennis ball and mangled chew toy on the floor, and he noticed the paw prints on the window.

He took the paper from his pocket and unfolded a handwritten note on the back of a prescription slip.

> I know Wrigley was special and can never be replaced. But there may come a time when you could use another friend. Call me when you're ready because I have a rescue dog that needs a home. Claire

19

There was a muted buzzing, like static after a radio dial is bumped from a station. Gene saw a light above him, like the full moon on a cloudy night. The light was becoming brighter, and the clouds were thinning. The white light was becoming brighter still, but at a distance, when all else was dark. Now the light was getting closer, round and distinct.

Was he dead? Was he going to the light? Was this Jesus? But the light did not draw nearer and looked nothing like the pictures of Jesus he'd seen. And now another light, and another—shafts of light from above him in a dark room. The murmur, the buzzing, a bit louder now. Were they voices? The heavy mist that dulled his comprehension was incrementally lifting. He was lying on his back and looking up. He was comfortable and warm. He tried to move but was met with firm resistance. A hand perhaps. Gene was emerging from the tunnel.

The bright lights above were now made clear. It was not the moon and it was definitely not the white light of Jesus. They were the lights of a hospital operating room. The muted murmurs now clearly voices, urgent but unintelligible. He tried to move again, to test the resistance.

"I think he's coming to! Gene, it's me, honey. It's Lila. You're going to be all right. Can you hear me?"

He couldn't speak. Lila?

"Mr. Howard, my name is Dr. Matsumura. You are in the hospital but you will be all right. We have given you some medication to calm you."

A doctor? A hospital? He was on a gurney. People were hovering over him. There was something in his throat, something in his mouth. More voices.

"He's coming out of it."

Nausea. Confusion.

"It's me. Lila. Can he hear me? I don't think he can hear me."

The doctor said, "You may feel some discomfort in your throat, Mr. Howard. It was necessary to place a tube to pump your stomach. You ingested numerous sleeping pills. Your son found you unconscious, but I believe the danger has passed. You may feel nauseated for a day or two, however, so we recommend you remain here at the hospital until your condition stabilizes."

"We're all here, Gene," Lila said. "Robert's here. Go ahead, Robert, you can talk to him now."

"Dad, it's me. You really scared us. If I hadn't come home when I did, you probably wouldn't have made it."

Gene looked at Lila and Robert, still groggy. He had tried to kill himself with pills. Yes, now he remembered. The ugly reality then struck him with dread. He had ALS. He was in a wheelchair. He could not speak.

"I called 911. And they got to our house as fast as they could. If we had waited, it probably would've been too late."

Too late? Too late for what? To die? Didn't they realize I was *trying* to die? What in the hell were they thinking? Why would they save me? Save me for what? To die a painfully slow and humiliating death?

"I called Mom right after I called 911. She beat the ambulance to our house. They got you to throw up and then got you here and pumped your stomach."

"Gene, honey, it's me again. The doctor said you'll feel better in a day or two. I'm so sorry I wasn't there when you needed me."

Didn't she know he didn't want her there? Had they honored his wish he'd be dead by now. All the hard work, the pain, and the fear would have been over. Instead it was just beginning. Now he would have to go through it all over again. If only they had just let him die!

"Dad, I hope you're not mad, but I had to call 911."

Here was the backward existence for Gene. He awoke not *from* a nightmare, but *to* a nightmare. His only refuge was either sleep or death, so why did they wake him from his permanent refuge? Why? This was all wrong. He wanted to drift back to unconsciousness.

Even though Gene could barely speak, he grunted and shook his head. He couldn't understand why his family would sentence him to death a second time. It was actually even worse than that. They had sentenced him to a few more years of hard labor and *then* to another death.

Lila and Robert looked at each other. They felt hurt and confused. How could he be so mean, so unappreciative when they had saved his life? Surely he had to know they hadn't been motivated by selfishness. *They* were the ones who were given a sentence. A sentence of feeding and dressing him. A sentence of bathing him and changing his diaper. They were sentenced to home arrest for as long as he lived, yet they voluntarily chose this sentence. And how did he repay them? With meanness, as he always had.

Lila, for the first time, seriously thought about leaving him. How could she continue to take care of him? Then there was the whole "in sickness and in health" vow to consider. Maybe they could put him in a care center, but the thought of dumping him at a nursing home was troubling. There was the guilt, and there was the money.

"Sorry, Mom," Robert said, as they walked across the hospital's parking lot.

"You did the right thing, Robert. He's just confused, that's all."

"No, he's right; I should have walked away and let him die. It's what he wants."

"But it would've been wrong. No, Robert, you did the right thing."

"Why does he need to be so mean all the time?"

"He's just been through so much."

"Why do you always apologize for him, Mom? He doesn't deserve you."

She took his hand and merely gave an explanatory sigh, as if she were too tired of her own story to relate it. "It's complicated."

Gene remained at the hospital a few days. He had no visitors other than Lila and Robert, who visited his father for his mom's sake. The nurses did their duty and left him, for he wasn't good company at all. There was the unspoken acknowledgment that perhaps it would've been better if they'd just let him die.

20

Blake jumped off his bike at the front door and grabbed eight folded newspapers from the large wire basket mounted to the handlebars. The glass doors were locked at night to keep the inmates in, so Blake put the newspapers under his arm and entered the code. It was 5:00 a.m. and so cold he could see his breath. "On your mark, get set, go!" He took one more gulp of fresh air, as much as his twelve-year-old lungs could hold, and pulled open the door and stepped inside. Normally he might have lingered in the heated lobby of the Haven's Rest Nursing Home. But the smell was so awful he didn't dally.

He ran down the corridor to the business administration office and dropped the newspapers in front of the door belonging to Louise Reynolds, head honcho of this smelly enterprise. Even though he'd held his breath, he could *feel* the smell; stale urine, disinfectant, despair, decay, and old age. He turned and sprinted back to the front door. He didn't make much money and it was hard work, pedaling around all morning in the cold when his friends were still asleep.

When he delivered the morning newspaper, the one and only job he had as a kid, he could not have imagined a career *writing* it. No way, he was going to be a Major League Baseball player. Any other job would have been an epic default on the scale of Richter. It's what he wanted, and it's what his dad wanted for him. Blake's dad had been a high school ballplayer himself before his arm wore out and he found work as the produce manager at a local grocery.

"I don't like it, Ruth," his dad had said. "He could throw his arm out."

"For Pete's sake, Earl, it's a paper route. He'll be fine. It's good for him."

Left unsaid was her obsession with the newspaper's circulars, because Blake's mother was a coupon nut. So Blake woke at 4:30 every morning to a bowl of Corn Flakes on the kitchen counter and a note reminding him to bring home extra coupons from any spare papers. Then he'd hop on his forty-pound Schwinn and pedal to the newspaper drop area, load the papers into his basket, and ride around the neighborhood to deliver them. And he did all that for a lousy $4.00 per hour. But the worst part of his job was collecting the money. This was before the advent of automatic billing and Blake was required to go door to door at the end of each month to collect the fare. That's where he'd met Louise Reynolds, the hard-boiled sour puss who ran the nursing home.

When he went to Haven's Rest to collect the money, he was again assaulted by the smell. Every morning it was bad, so bad it would sting his eyes. But this time he had to wait for Mrs. Reynolds. She was meeting with a pair of fifty-year-olds who were there to get the sales pitch on behalf of their ailing parent. So he had to wait in the lobby, inhaling with regularity.

After a few moments, Blake was told to wait in an adjoining guest room, where the current short-term incumbent was on a "serenity walk" with a loving CNA. This walk consisted of traversing both corridors and the parking lot. The wait was agonizing. Inmates passed by, pushing walkers, their feet in shower slippers, shuffling along while their hospital-style gowns sometimes revealed too much. Had they turned their heads to look at him he would have jumped, but they looked straight ahead without curiosity. To a twelve-year-old boy, it was like a march of the living dead.

Blake sat alone on the guest's bed that had recently been made to show the prospective clients how orderly and clean their parent's new home would be. Surely a well-made bed would help alleviate their guilt from putting their mother in this ghastly place. So he sat on the edge of the bed with his toes barely reaching the linoleum floor. After a moment, he felt his bum getting damp. He stood and felt the back pockets of his new corduroys. They were wet. He turned and looked at the spot on the bed where he'd been sitting. It was also wet. He smelled his hands and recoiled from the stench of urine. Haven's Rest, that sanctuary for the golden years, had made the bed over the urine without even changing the sheets.

He collected the money and walked down the corridor, no longer holding his breath or breathing through his mouth, resigned to the fact that the air—the decay—had completely infiltrated his body down to the very marrow of his bones. He walked past near corpses, mouths hanging open; nobody home. He rode his bike home, threw his corduroys in the laundry basket, and quit his job.

Now, thirty years later, Blake returned to the scene of the crime that had so horrified him as a kid. His story on the fatal accident on Highway 60 had evolved into something larger than a story about the survivors of the accident. He planned to write on the entire question of aging, and specifically the right to die. As part of that story, he thought it made sense to consider the cost of keeping people alive when they are well past their prime. And that's why he chose to return to the nursing home. He wanted to see the quality of life there firsthand as an adult—how these old people really lived, and what it cost to warehouse them.

Blake figured his impressionable young mind had grossly embellished the experience, for that's the way it usually is. He recalled the time Steve and he had door-bell-ditched the neighbors and then later felt bad because Mr. Rasmussen was about sixty years old and probably near death, being so old and all. How much fun was it to door-bell-ditch someone who could hardly make it to the door? Blake remembered thinking that Mr. Rasmussen might as well die and get it over with, because what was there beyond sixty, other than wrinkly skin and old-age pills?

Haven's Rest Nursing Home was still in business, and business appeared to be booming. Blake pretended to be the loving son of an elderly mother who needed full time care. Louise Reynolds was no longer there, having ungracefully slid from administration directly into the "resident" category, and then slowly dribbled away to her death. She'd been replaced by an equally humorless woman who now made the sales pitch to Blake.

The place still smelled, just like many of the other "old folks" homes he'd had the misfortune of smelling over the years. But, to be fair, it wasn't as bad as he'd remembered it. Maybe the smell was worse in the morning before all the wet beds were remade. Or maybe age had diminished his sense of smell, or his sense of shame. At least it wasn't as horrible as the poor houses they used to have—Alms Houses they called them—filthy, overcrowded asylums with rats, where the elderly were cast off to die in places Dickens might have written about.

He was given a glossy brochure to review as he waited in the lobby, the boarders carefully hidden from his view. The brochure showed a handsome older couple, civilized, with gray hair and contented smiles, secure in the knowledge that they would while away their glorious sunset years living on this cruise ship, playing backgammon and sipping martinis with other intensely interesting residents. The photo suggested they might dress in linen suits, or perhaps slacks and a nice dinner jacket. They would sip fine wine and discuss philosophy, the successes of their grandchildren, and offer important insights into the world's affairs.

But this richly contented geriatric couple with gleaming white veneers looked nothing like the residents Blake saw who were often toothless, leisure suit-less, and appeared to discuss absolutely nothing; not even the medications they took. There was not a backgammon table or a martini glass in sight, just an occasional IV bag hanging above their hydraulic beds and a bag of urine hanging below.

"Thank you for visiting us today, Mr. Morgan. As you can see, we have a beautiful facility with friendly residents and staff. I'm sure your mother would be very happy here."

"It does look lovely," Blake said.

"Would you like to take a short tour?"

"Sure, that'd be great," Blake said.

As they walked the corridor, LouAnn asked a few questions about Blake's mother. For example, did she play bridge, suggesting an intellectually competitive game of bridge might break out in the rec room at any moment. They passed a sitting area where two elderly men with thick yellow toenails were staring blankly at a game show on television. The volume on the TV was set so low they couldn't have heard it, even with much younger anvils, stirrups, and hammers. But they didn't seem to care either way.

An aide walked past holding a tray filled with small plastic cups that held a variety of old age pills. The aide stopped just long enough to hand a cup to a stooped old woman, who stood in the middle of the hall wearing a hospital gown that partially exposed her backside. Her feet were planted in a bowlegged stance. The old woman just looked at the pills and then put them in the pocket of her gown, along with the lint, as if she didn't know what else to do with them.

The dining room was festive. It was November and some of the residents had cut out silhouettes of pilgrims and turkeys and hung them on the walls. Each table was adorned with a ceramic cornucopia filled with fake squash and yams and a crepe paper turkey accordion fan. LouAnn was proud of the dining room.

They wound their way back to the office, passing the "Spa and Work Out Room." It was a small, windowless room with outdoor carpeting. There was an anatomy poster on the wall and another poster of the human skeleton that looked alarmingly like some of the residents. An older treadmill faced the wall. There was a pair of red five-pound plastic dumbbells, an exercise ball, and a jump rope. The spa was otherwise empty.

"How much does this all cost?" Blake asked. "My mom doesn't have much."

"Well, we at Haven's Rest are sensitive to the escalating cost of elder care. That's why we have several different plans to accommodate most budgets."

"I know she's on Medicare, and when my dad passed away he left her a small nest egg. Of course, we want the best for her."

"Well, certainly you do. And so do we. Our semi-private rooms are only $3,495 per month. Unfortunately, that is all some of our residents can afford."

"What about a private room?"

"Well, they are also affordable. Why, we happen to have one available now for only $4,995 per month."

"Wow, that's more than we wanted to spend. That'd be $60,000 a year."

"I know how tough it can be." LouAnn was warming up now. "Your mother worked hard her entire life." Warmer still. "You don't want to go into too much debt, but I'm sure you want the very best for her." *Too much* debt? Blake didn't want to go into any debt at all. LouAnn barely even disguised the insidious guilt, tempting Blake to challenge her assertion that his beloved mother deserved more than a cheap-ass semi-private room with a lousy view.

Blake had done his homework and found that the average cost of a private room in a nursing home was nearly $70,000 per year. A semi-private can be a real bargain in the mid $50,000's. Of course, as long as you're paying that much you ought to just skip the family vacation and spring for the private room so your mom doesn't need to hear, or smell, her roommate on the other side of the curtain.

Blake learned that the cost of elder care depends on where

you live. If grandma falls in love with Alaska in her golden years, she'd spend nearly $220,000 per year for a private room. That's over $570 per day! It'd be cheaper to put her on a good, clean, top-of-the-line Royal Caribbean Alaskan cruise ship with a midnight buffet.

If you were broke (or it was your mother-in-law who always treated you like a good-for-nothing bum), you could ship her off to Shreveport, Louisiana where the average room in a nursing home is only $36,000 per year. Maybe there was a lower thread count on the sheets in Shreveport. Blake figured the extra bells and whistles were presented for the family and not the resident, most of whom don't attend the stimulating lectures on the History of Greece or the field trips to the county library.

Blake did the math. What about the school teacher who spent forty years cramming arithmetic down the throats of bored pre-teens? If she was able to sock away $10,000 per year, she'd burn through that savings in no time. Then what? And what if she lived in Anchorage?

Blake didn't begrudge a nice little profit off the elderly, so long as it was reasonably small. He was beginning to see, however, there was an incentive to slow the dying process to keep Grandma around for one more Thanksgiving. Pump the pills! Take the serenity walks around the parking lot! After all, dead people don't take pills, or pay rent. Blake was not cynical enough to believe this was done purely for profit, but he knew the corporate board room's focus was on the bottom line. The families demanded their elders stay alive, and the capitalists were willing to oblige.

Blake had investigated the physician-assisted suicide

laws that were sprouting up around the country. The visible opposition to those laws comes from religious groups who fear mankind has lost its way where matters of life and death are concerned. Blake found, however, that opposition is also quietly funded by corporations that earn more money the longer grandma stays alive. Their mantra is "Dignity in Living," and surely there's an appeal to that, especially if it's your mom. But Blake knew there wasn't much dignity in many nursing homes where the elderly are being kept artificially alive in living graves with bedrails.

LouAnn was a darned good salesperson. She capitalized on the agonizing decision adult children face every day. That heavy conscience that weighs on the next generation who are duty bound to give their parents the best care. Do they dig into their savings to keep Dad warehoused somewhere else, or do they bring him home to live with them and wake every morning to soiled sheets and his dentures soaking in a drinking glass next to the coffee maker?

21

Gene was sick to his stomach for several days. His head thumped like it had its own heartbeat. But he eventually recovered from his self-inflicted poisoning. What was unexpected was the change in his attitude. For the first time in his life he acknowledged the sacrifices his family made for him. He'd been humbled because he realized he had so little power. He couldn't even properly kill himself. The disease was *his* unlucky journey, not Lila and Robert's, and yet they agreed to accompany him. Would he have been as patient and compassionate if the shoe were on the other foot? He was ashamed of the answer.

The disease was gaining momentum. At its current pace, however, he figured he might still have two or three years left. He could unhappily wallow in self-pity or bravely face it, doing all he could to make his remaining time count for something. He knew he wouldn't become Stephen Hawking, but he could try. For starters, he resolved to master the computer technology that allowed him to communicate.

A computer monitor was attached to his wheelchair a few feet from his face. A video camera mounted just below the monitor pointed to Gene's eye movements. Software analyzed Gene's eyeballs to determine his visual "gaze point." When his eyes fixated on a specific letter on the keyboard monitor, the system printed the letter on the screen. This was painstakingly slow going and required patience. His first word was meant to be GENE, but it came out GRMR. With a few weeks' practice, however, Gene learned to "type" fifteen words per minute using his eyeballs alone. He was thrilled with his improvement.

Lila and Robert were patient caretakers and Gene felt humbled by their service. They included him whenever possible in their conversations. And when they changed his diaper there was no revulsion on their faces. But other times they just had to laugh about it. "Geez, Dad, what in the hell did you *eat?*" Robert, in particular, spoke to his father about his struggles. He could be honest because Gene had lost his power to intimidate as he sat shrunken, diminished, and mute in his chair. There was nothing menacing about Gene Howard now.

By the time of Gene's diagnosis, neither Becky nor Susan lived at home, each having left the unhappy box at their first opportunity. Becky married young and Susan fled to college in a distant town. Robert, who was nineteen years old, lived a quiet life of desperation in the basement of his parent's home. He was going to night school at the local community college and worked days at a hair salon. He'd done all he could to help his dad after the devastating news and had even built the wheelchair ramp that led to their front door. This had been a genuine effort at love, for Robert had no familiarity with tools. When his friends built a tree hut in their back yard as kids, climbing the tree with hammers, saws, and mouthfuls of nails, Robert had been hunkered down over Lila's sewing machine, making curtains for the hut. The ramp tilted and sagged, and didn't meet a single building code provision, but his son had built it.

Robert told his dad about the friends who ridiculed him because he wasn't "one of the guys." The teasing he endured was heartbreaking. This haunted Gene because he had contributed to that pain, and he was ashamed with himself. Even though he didn't understand Robert, and even though he thought homosexuality was abhorrent, this was his son. Whatever the community thought about his "urges" was quite beside the point.

Lila's affection for her invalid husband was largely the result of pity, for it is easy to be sympathetic to a dying man. But there was something else about Gene, a sense of shame that humanized him and made him almost endearing, because everyone loves a repentant sinner. It made the full-time chore of his caretaking easier, almost enjoyable. She had finally found a loving companion, but only after he was nearly out the door.

Gene got the hang of the computer within a few trying days. His first full sentence was this:

THNK U LILA

22

The smog gradually lifted to disclose the wreckage of Don's life. His despair had been like a well-watered vine, creeping and forking into every nook of his soul, tiny capillaries of pain. A quick survey revealed no job, ill health, debt, and addiction. He'd crawled out of the crud to emerge a better man, but it hadn't been easy. And it hadn't happened overnight, or without Donna's help.

She'd come home from work and found him passed out on the sofa, like a walrus lying on a rock. He hadn't showered in three days. The mask of pain he wore had calcified so that his face had become a mask. He was too sick from chemicals to even watch television. She sat on the homemade coffee table and watched him. Her upbeat pep talks hadn't been enough. Trying to get him to apply for a job by handing him the phone and ten telephone numbers hadn't been enough.

"Don, honey," she put her hand on his meaty shoulder and shook him. "We need help with this."

"I'm fine. I just need a little time."

"You're not fine."

"It's just my back. I'll be okay once that gets better."

"No, Don, honey, you won't. It's not your back. You've got yourself addicted and you need some help."

"I just take 'em for the back pain. I'm not hooked. I'll quit taking them when I get my back straightened out."

"Don. Look at me."

He opened his eyes but didn't otherwise move. "What? I'm fine. Just let me sleep."

"I can't do this, Don."

"Can't do what?"

"I can't live like this."

"So what do you want me to do about it? Can't you see my back hurts?"

"I want you to get some professional help. Because I don't know how to help you."

"I already did and he said it's just going to take some time."

"Don, you need to get into therapy."

"I don't need some shrink. I'll be fine, okay?"

"No, you won't be. I can't do this anymore, Hon. If you won't get into some therapy I'm going to . . . " What was she going to do? Leave him? No, and she didn't even want to threaten it. But her friend at work was married to an alcoholic and she'd said the worst thing you can do if you're in a relationship with an addict is go down with the ship. And their little ship was taking on water fast.

He sat up. He'd been reluctant to acknowledge he had a problem, even to himself. It was just normal medication for back pain, that's all. But he knew twelve pills a day, washed down with whatever booze he could find, was not normal medication. And neither was it normal to chug Robitussin. He was scared.

"What do you want me to do?"

"Get help."

"Where? I don't even know where to look."

"I'll help you. I need you, Don. I need my old Don back. But I can't help you if you won't help yourself." She put her head down, completely spent, for she had worried more about him that he ever did.

Don looked around at the other addicts when he'd first arrived at the rehab clinic. What in the world was *he* doing there, he thought. I'm not one of *those*, he told himself. Those people were real addicts, but not him. He still could not, or would not, acknowledge the obvious. So, it didn't work. He was sober for two days and then relapsed. The second go-around was more difficult, because he faced the truth.

Don should have seen it coming. He should have seen the thread coming out of the spider as she methodically wove the intricate trap, but now he'd been caught in her insidious web. It was her nature to expel that sticky thread, inch by inch, ensnaring hapless people, rich and poor. He sat in the rehab building with its cinder block walls painted thick with coats of seafoam green. He could recover only by first absorbing the cold truth: he was an addict and needed help. Or, he could deny it and be eaten by the spider.

He vowed to stop and work himself loose. He'd untangle a few threads and then a trigger would strike and he'd relapse, the strands restrung. Vow to commit and then relapse, the pattern of addicts everywhere, those with backbones and those without. His problem was compounded by genuine ongoing back pain. This was no ruse to justify narcotics. This is how it'd all started in the first place. If he could reduce the pain, he might be able to resist the insatiable craving for pain medication. Gradually, through patience, hard work, and over-the-counter analgesics, he weaned himself from the hard stuff.

His therapist urged him to make amends with all those in his life that he'd hurt. There was Donna who scoffed at his sincere apologies: "That's really sweet, but don't be silly. None of us are perfect, Hon. I'm just glad I got my old Don back. That's all." There were others, including his brother, Dale, who didn't exactly know what Don was talking about. "This some sort of fancy piece a therapy goin' on here? Cause you've always been right straight with me, Don. Got no complaints at all."

And then there were the victims of June 2, 2002.

He looked up the number for Fern Morris's widower and called it.

"Hello."

"Mr. Morris?"

"Yes, who is this?"

"This is Don Weeks."

There was no immediate reply, so after another moment of silence, Don added, "I was the driver of the semi-truck." Another pause. "The one in the accident with your wife."

"I see."

"I know you must hate me, but . . . "

"I don't hate you, Mr. Weeks."

"I guess I just wanted to call, and, you know, tell you how sorry I am."

Don waited for George to say something, yet all he heard was breathing on the other end.

"So, I don't know, I just . . . I'm not sure what to say. I'm just so sorry about all of it."

"It was an accident, sir. You made a mistake."

"But it was my fault."

"That, Mr. Weeks, does not reduce your suffering. Perhaps it has enhanced it. However, I certainly hope not. There has been enough suffering, I'm sure."

This time there was silence on Don's end of the line. He was trying not to cry. He rotated the phone receiver toward the ceiling and wiped his nose and eyes with a hankie. Neither man spoke.

Finally, Don said, "I know you didn't sue me like the other ones did."

"No, I don't believe in all that suing. What's been done has been done."

"See, I wanted to thank you for that, too."

"I don't suppose that is necessary. To be frank, I did not choose to let it go for your sake, but rather for my own. I did not want to prolong the tragedy through the legal process. What benefit would that have provided—me wringing money out of the insurance company? And what on earth would I have done with the money anyway? Buy a new car? For God's sake, the mere thought of making money off Fern's death is repulsive."

"I just want you to know that I've thought about it every single day." He wiped his nose again. "I'd give anything to take it back."

George did not speak. Don squinted his eyes tight, squeezing out tears. "I wanted to call you sooner, but it's just that . . . ."

"I appreciate your call. I'm sure this wasn't an easy one to make. I hope you will be able to find some peace. I am confident that my Fern has. No, Mr. Weeks, I wish you no ill will."

Don's apology to Jenny was more difficult. He drove out to Mesa and found Jenny and Clay's home. A quick glance may not have revealed it, but Don recognized the telltale signs of a disabled person. A large van with a wheelchair lift was parked in the driveway. A ramp, not steps, led to the front door. The yard was spare and tidy.

Clay, a handsome young man in his late twenties, answered the door and led him to the sparsely furnished living room. There were none of the usual trappings found in the homes of young married couples. There was no high chair for the baby, or Legos scattered about. There was no mess at all, not even a stick figure drawing taped to the fridge. In fact, there appeared to be no life at all within the antiseptic walls, just quiet and somber desperation.

Jenny silently appeared in the wheelchair she controlled with clumsy movement in her right hand. Her hair that had been bleached blonde was now dark brown and short. It was partially covered by a red beanie. Her head was held upright with Velcro to the headrest of the wheelchair. She was very thin, maybe eighty-five pounds, and her withered limbs were atrophied, like a young woman with anorexia.

Don stood when she entered the room. Sorrow hung around his neck like a cement yolk. This had all been the result of his unintentional handiwork. He approached her and held out his massive hand. When she didn't move to take his hand he awkwardly pulled it back, embarrassed to realize she couldn't lift her tiny hand to meet his. She said nothing; she only stared at him with . . . what? Contempt? Apathy? Don could not say.

"Thanks for coming," Clay said.

Don pulled his chair up close to Jenny, so small and fragile. He looked into her eyes, searchingly, without either of them saying a word for a long time.

"Jenny," he finally said. His chin began to quiver. "I am so sorry."

He reached across and buried her tiny curled hand under his, bowed his head, and just sobbed.

23

A number of bizarre rules have developed over time concerning the killing of each other. A man is allowed to kill a kind stranger from a foreign country if his president declares war. Indeed, there is no penalty at all for such a thing. If a man has the ingenuity to kill an entire squadron of kind strangers he might even be honored with a parade. But if that man kills the same kind stranger a week after the politicians sign a peace treaty, he might be sentenced to the electric chair.

What if a perfectly sane man hides in the bushes and shoots a demented serial killer who is being led to the gallows? He will be hung next, even though his victim was a terrible human being who was about to be executed in any event. Not only that, but the executioners will be paid by the state for their labor when they kill *him*. It is all quite confusing.

There are exceptions to the rules, of course. There are always exceptions. But, generally speaking, it is wrong to kill a human being. And because a human being is a person, it is also against the rules for a person to kill himself. In fact, it's a first degree felony. When the rules were made many years ago, if a man killed himself, his corpse would have been mutilated and his property would have been automatically forfeited to the King. If he failed in his suicide attempt, the law required that he be executed for having broken the anti-suicide law. "You have been convicted of trying to kill yourself, you wretched beast! Your sentence is death! Off with his head!"

Jenny was not a student of history, legal or religious. Yet she'd been taught that suicide was a sin. According to Mormonism, her body was a gift from God and her mortal life was a "testing period" to see how she'd do—a probationary time to evaluate how she measured up on the worthiness scale. No one, according to Jenny's theology, had the right to evade these tests. Her faith, however, allowed an exception for someone who was plain crazy. But the "crazy" line is a fuzzy one, for there are many people who walk it, but aren't certifiably crazy—maybe just eccentric.

Jenny, however, was not out of her mind. So the "crazy person" loophole didn't apply to her. She could incur the wrath of God if she killed herself, sane as she was. For that reason, she considered her decision carefully before discussing it with anyone, even Clay.

Jenny knew her options were limited if she wanted to end her life. She would most likely require help. She didn't know the sad dilemma illustrated by a fellow quad named Carlos, a thirty-year-old who lived in Colorado at the time. He tried to shoot himself but couldn't lift the pistol high enough. Then he tried to drown himself by driving his motorized wheelchair into a river by his house, but he got stuck on the muddy shore. No one would help him. He lived in a small bungalow, and when the caretaker was absent, he maneuvered his wheelchair into the living room and positioned himself next to the drapes. After several clumsy attempts he was finally able to produce a small flame from a cigarette lighter. He lit the drape on fire and waited, sitting in the middle of the raging inferno.

He was not crazy, just desperate.

Jenny first shared her suicidal thoughts, not with Clay, and not with her parents, but with her Mormon bishop. This was the same compassionate plumber whom Clay had consulted with months earlier about the demerits of a potential divorce. That had been fairly straightforward (if not a bit murky, under the circumstances). But *this*? The bishop was a prayerful man of God, but he was unqualified to counsel Jenny on this sensitive issue. Give him a clogged toilet or a garden-variety sin, like shoplifting, and he'd do fine. But thoughtfully taking your own life? When you weren't crazy? Other than a quick review of his Bishop's Handbook, he was in way over his head. And the water was deep.

Jenny met with him in his office at the church building where they worshipped every Sunday. The bishop sat behind an executive desk. Two matching wingback chairs faced the desk. Many a restless sinner in the neighborhood had squirmed on those very chairs because a confession to cleanse their souls was Step Two in the repentance process (Step One was acknowledging something you've done that was bad enough to warrant Step Two). And, unlike congregants of other faiths who enjoy the luxury of a dark confessional booth, Mormons confess their sins openly to their bishops. They can't disguise their voice when coming clean about their addiction to Asian porn, or owning up to the time they'd swiped the blouse from Nordstrom. Hence the squirming.

The bishop scooted one of the wingbacks out of the way to make room for Jenny's wheelchair and then resumed his position behind the desk. This was not a power play, at least not a conscious one, for the bishop was unusually humble in his polyester suit and shiny cowboy boots.

"I don't want to live anymore, Bishop. I'm just so unhappy all the time." Jenny had both the courage and grace to speak with such simple truth. "I'm a burden on everybody. I don't have any joy. I can't do anything. I've prayed my guts out to Heavenly Father for four years. But I haven't received an answer. At least not that I know about."

The bishop leaned forward and cocked his head slightly. He wanted to help her, but he didn't know how.

"I've never told anyone this, but I wanted to kill myself the day I got home from rehab. There was a welcome-home party for me and I tried to roll my wheelchair into the road so I'd get hit by a car. But I wasn't strong enough to even do that. Since then I've thought about it a lot, and I would have already done it, but I can't. I mean, I can't do it physically. I can't take pills by myself, or shoot myself, or jump off a building, or anything."

"But, Jenny, God loves you," the bishop said. "He has given you more than your share of challenges, but He's also helped you overcome them."

"Really? Because I don't see how He's helped me very much at all. I'm sorry, but I don't. And I don't think I've overcome any challenges either. Tell me one thing I've overcome, because I can't think of anything."

"Heavenly Father tests us, Jenny. And sometimes He gives His most valiant children the toughest tests of all."

"But why would God single me out? I don't understand." Jenny practically pleaded for a reasonable answer to this vexing question.

"Because He loves you, Jenny."

"Because he *loves* me?"

"Yes, more than you can possibly know."

"So does he love His other children, too?"

"Of course, he does. He loves all His children equally."

"Then how come I'm the only one who's a quadriplegic?"

These tautological questions were fair, but difficult to answer. Why indeed was she the only one? "He loves you Jenny, just as much as any of His other children."

"Really? Don't get me wrong, I'm not blaming God. I don't think He caused the accident. I was just in the wrong place at the wrong time. But He didn't stop it from happening either. And since then I haven't seen all these blessings everyone talks about, other than I'm still alive. But that's something I never asked for, and I don't even want it." There was the smallest crack of faith in her armor; a thought that God is given too much credit and not enough blame. But the crack was not allowed to expand, for she quickly banished the thought whenever it reared its head.

"Jenny, what would be accomplished if you committed suicide?"

"I wouldn't suffer anymore, and my family wouldn't keep suffering either. Everybody could get on with their lives."

"But, Jenny, maybe God is using you to help them grow."

"What do you mean?"

"Well, God works in mysterious ways, and maybe He's made you a quadriplegic to teach others the virtue of service—Clay, your sister, your parents."

"So I'm an *object lesson?* You mean my injury is a way for God to help *them?* Couldn't He figure out a better way to teach them that lesson?"

The bishop realized the point he was trying to make was a bust. He believed it, knowing as he did that God worked in such mysterious ways, but could not articulate it well.

"It might sound like I'm losing my faith, Bishop. But it's just that I don't understand."

"God loves you, Jenny." This was a reliable phrase when a more helpful response was not forthcoming. But could anyone else come up with a better apology for God's stillness? Could anyone else have justified His failure to intervene? Or was His intervention limited to simply allowing the accident, but not the subsequent repairs? The bishop was put into an awfully tough spot.

"So you're saying God loves me so much that He made me a quad, and keeps me a quad so others will grow?"

"I don't know, Jenny. But there are other lessons, too. Your life here on earth will give you humility, patience, and empathy in the next life."

"So what happens to people who aren't quads? Are they going to be arrogant and impatient in the next life?"

"Jenny, I wish I knew the ways of God."

"I'm sorry, Bishop. I don't mean to be snotty."

"There are so many lessons each of us must learn here on earth. Maybe God is teaching you the lesson of pain and suffering."

"Well, if God wants me to suffer pain, for whatever grotesque reason He might have, wouldn't I be fouling up His plan if I take pain killers?"

"I'm not sure I understand what you mean."

"Do you think I should stop taking the pain pills? Because I wouldn't want to foul up God's plan to make me suffer."

"No, Jenny, of course not. That's not what I'm saying. I'm just saying God works in ways we can't understand. But I do know this, Jenny; God loves you and he has a plan for you."

"But I've always been taught that we have free agency and God wants us to take responsibility for our own life?"

"That's true."

"Well, if I'm supposed to have free agency to do what I think is best for my life, I think I ought to have it for my death, too. I believe God loves me; I really do. And I don't think He'll punish me anymore."

"He won't punish you anymore if you do what?"

"If I use my free agency to die."

"Jenny," he adjusted his tie. "That isn't something, I mean . . . God has told us . . . Suicide is never a good solution."

"I've thought about it a lot, and I think God will understand." She then told the bishop that she had decided to forgo food and water. She told him that if God wanted her to remain alive in her shell for whatever mysterious purpose He had in mind, then He could use His considerable power to trump the absence of food.

Jenny had decided to die this way because it was something she could actually do, alone, without help. If she starved herself to death no one else would get his hands dirty. No one else would risk the fire and brimstone of hell, or the loss of his medical license.

Foregoing food and water seemed so . . . well, so much less sinister to her. It didn't have the same immoral *feel* to it as shooting herself in the head, or hanging herself. It didn't seem like "suicide" in the way she normally thought of it. It wasn't as evil in her mind because she wouldn't be taking

194 | WARREN DRIGGS

any affirmative action; it was just an act of omission. A mere denial of the basic essentials. No mess, no fuss.

Jenny knew it wasn't against the law. No one could legally force a competent person to accept medical care against their wishes, and no one could force her to eat either.

"Have you talked to Clay about this? Or your parents?" asked the alarmed bishop.

"Not yet. I wanted to talk to you first. I have a strong testimony in God and Jesus and all that, but I think I'm ready to die. I know God loves me and I think He'll forgive me if I fail this one final test."

The good bishop was at a loss. Should he call forth the power of the law, or the church, to ban this act that threatened her salvation? Should he pull all the stops to protect her from herself? Or should he support her? Did the time-honored confidentiality between a priest and a parishioner extend to this, or should he tell someone? These questions were left to dangle in his mind as he walked across the church parking lot, climbed into his plumbing van with the extension ladder strapped to the top, and drove away.

Clay was nodding off on the sofa when Jenny came home. He was wearing pajama bottoms and only his Mormon underwear on top. A textbook on Torts was in his lap.

"Clay, can I talk to you?" Jenny asked.

"Sure, what's up?"

"I hate it that you feel like you're stuck with me. Nothing's going to change and I don't want to keep doing this."

"Jen, I know it's hard, but we'll make it through this," Clay said.

"Yeah, I guess we could. I guess we could just keep doing

this until I eventually die. But by then you'd probably be too old to have kids and raise a family."

"Don't even think that way."

"And what about me? This is torture for me, Clay. Do you remember how much I loved to play the piano? And can you remember how we used to run? Look at me now," Jenny paused. "No, *really*, look at me."

"Jenny, I decided long ago that I wouldn't leave you. I love you. I know you'd do the same for me."

"But, Clay, I can't let you keep doing this out of duty."

"It's not out of duty, Jen. I love you."

"Yeah, I know you do. But it's me more than anything else. When it comes right down to it I guess I'm selfish. I want it to end."

"What are you saying?"

"When we die we'll be resurrected into perfect beings, right? Isn't that what we believe?"

"Yeah."

"So after I die I'll be resurrected with a healthy body, right?"

"Yeah, that's what the church says."

"Can you imagine how much I want to touch the keys on the piano again, or to walk on grass and feel it tickle my feet? Do you know what I'd pay to run or dance? Do you know how much I want to feed myself or brush my own hair? It probably seems like a hassle for you to brush your teeth. But for me? I wish I could stand in front of the mirror and just brush my stupid teeth all day long. I wish I could be pretty again and put on makeup and shop for clothes."

"I still think you're pretty."

"Come on, no I'm not. We weren't meant to live like this, Clay."

He didn't know how to respond. He put a pencil in his book to mark the page and closed it.

"I've thought about this for a long time," she said. "I don't want you to think this is something that I just barely thought about."

"What?"

"I've decided I'm not going to eat or drink anything."

"Why? For how long?"

"Forever. I'm not going to eat or drink again. I don't know how long it would take, maybe a few weeks or a month, but then it'd be over."

"Are you *serious*?"

"Yeah."

"But that's suicide, Jen."

"I don't think it's the same thing. And it's my choice. We believe in free agency. The church teaches that, too."

Clay put his head down and studied his hands.

"Say something."

"What do you want me to say, Jen?"

"I don't know. Just say something."

He stared at her hard, and then he slowly shook his head back and forth, back and forth. "Jen, please don't do this for me. I'm not asking you to do this."

"I know you're not."

"I know how much you suffer, and I support you all the way. But this . . . this is different." Clay's voice was thick.

"If you love me, you won't stand in my way."

"If I loved you, I wouldn't let you do it."

"I'm not asking for your permission, Clay."

He stared down at his bare feet. There were times he wished she'd died. But he hadn't really thought this through, like what it would be like if she were really gone. "You need to think about it some more."

"I've thought about it a lot, Clay. I've thought about it for almost four years."

"Jen, I'm going to be with you to the very end no matter what. Whether you die tomorrow or live to be a hundred, I'm going to be there. If you're absolutely sure about this, then I'll support you. And if you decide not to, then I'll support that too. But, like I said, either way I'm going to be with you to the end. I promise."

Clay didn't want Jenny to die. But when he pondered his future he saw no change. There would be no children, no family, and no vacations to the beach. He was held captive by quadriplegia, too. In times of self-pity (and those times were common), he felt cheated. If Jenny died, despite the sadness, his life could begin again. There could be another woman who dressed up and wore makeup and perfume. Sometimes he'd allow his mind to wander, a simple indulgence that was becoming more frequent. Was this disloyal, and did he feel guilty about it? At times. But mostly he was defiant in his selfishness, because he didn't wish for anything extravagant.

His parents were conflicted, too. They loved Jenny, but they loved their son more. They would not actively encourage him to divorce, for they would not be found guilty of such a calloused thing. But in the privacy of their bedroom they had thought it would've been better if Jenny had died. They wanted their only son to be happy, and to have children and provide grandchildren to them. So they said equivocally safe things, like "We know you'll do what's best," and "We'll support you no matter what you decide to do."

Jenny's parents were predictably upset, especially Joanne. "How can you even *think* this way? How can you believe for one second that you are a burden to us? Who's put these thoughts in your head? Is it Clay?"

"Mom, how can you say something like that? Clay's stuck with me night and day for four years without a single complaint. So don't even say that. This is *my* decision and nobody else's. Clay will support me in whatever I choose because he loves me and knows I've thought about this for a long time. It's not just something I came up with yesterday. Give me some credit, mom."

"Jen, of course we support you." It was Rich, himself a tireless supporter. "You're an amazing girl. You've taught us how to live gracefully and with dignity. If that's your choice my heart would break. But I won't stand in your way."

"Thanks, Dad. I love you."

"This is absolutely ridiculous!" Joanne said. "You're not thinking clearly. You don't just one day up and decide you're going to kill yourself! I can't believe we're even having this discussion. Besides, I don't think you're capable of making this decision on your own anyway."

"Why not, Mom? Is there someone else who has the right to choose for me?"

"It's a *sin*, Jenny. It's a sin and you *know* it. Surely Heavenly Father would not approve, and neither do I."

"I'm not asking for your approval, mom. I'm asking for your support, because now's when I need it the most."

"Listen to you! Talking like you're deciding what kind of car to buy, or what kind of dress to wear. This is suicide! And I won't stand by while my daughter kills herself!"

"Mom, you're right. It's not like a decision to buy a car or a dress. I can't even drive a car, and I can't even wear a dress."

Joanne felt the sting of Jenny's reproach and softened her tone. "We'll take care of you, Jenny. You know we will."

"I know you will, mom. You've always been there for me. But what about when you're gone? And even if you were always there, even if that could be guaranteed, I don't want to live this way anymore. Can you blame me? And do you really think Heavenly Father would send me to hell? Honestly?"

Rich and Joanne's relationship had been tested repeatedly over Jenny. There were times the crisis had brought them together, and times it had pulled them apart, stretched to the point that one more ounce of pressure, one more cutting remark, would cause a fatal rip. Joanne was furious with Rich after their visit with Jenny. She wanted nothing to do with Jenny's thoughtless decision and believed Rich should've helped her put the kibosh on it.

"Don't you see, Richard?" she pleaded. She grabbed his arm and shook it as though to make him agree. "You agree with me Rich, don't you?" She gave it another tug. "Tell me you can see through this nonsense! Tell me!"

"I don't know what to think, Joanne."

"Yes, you do. It's simple. It's wrong and you know it."

"It's not simple, Joanne. None of this is simple."

Liz was tuned to the meter of her parents, for she was a sensitive girl and the house was small. For her part, Liz would support her sister. But could she really watch Jenny sit there and starve herself to death? Then again, would it be much different from what she'd seen the last four years? Jenny had become shriveled and pale with greasy hair. She weighed eighty pounds. No, Liz thought, the whole discussion was crazy because Jenny was already dying. And all this was happening right before their eyes.

The sadness that settled on the family like a thick layer of dust was offset by Liz's happy news. She and her husband were expecting a baby. When the pregnancy was announced, Joanne's first impulse was to look at Jenny, for her antenna was always up where her oldest daughter was concerned. But Jenny had been genuinely happy for Liz. Surely there was regret, but not the ugly, jealous kind.

Blake formally met Jenny for the first time a few days after she'd announced her intention to stop eating. She agreed to let him come to her house to discuss the accident and its heavy aftermath. He parked in the driveway and walked up the ramp to the front door. Clay answered it before Blake could knock.

"Hey, you must be Blake. I'm Clay." He was the absolute picture of health. It was 8:00 p.m. and he had just returned home from work at his new law firm. He wore a tie but had loosened it to hang around his neck like a noose. He seemed relatively happy and not as forlorn as Blake expected him to be. After all, he worked all day and then returned to a house that felt like a morgue and slept with a woman who couldn't move. "Here, have a seat," Clay said, "and I'll go get Jen."

The house was furnished with the bare necessities and there was virtually nothing on the walls. This was not a conscious design strategy but rather the product of disinterest. There were a handful of photographs, each one taken before

Jenny was confined to the chair. She was beautiful in those few photos.

A few moments later Clay returned and Jenny rode in behind him on her electric wheelchair. Blake was struck by the startling contrast between the two of them. They hardly looked like husband and wife; they could have passed for a son and his ailing mother. Blake had seen a photo of Jenny's driver's license, which was included in the police report, and she'd been a drop-dead beauty. Now she looked withered and drawn. She wore navy blue sweat pants and a matching top. A red beanie and slippers completed the unfashionable outfit. Her eyes were dull and her skin was an unhealthy shade of pale. She spent most of her time cooped up inside and it showed. There was a stale smell to her, the kind of smell you get from hair that hasn't been shampooed in a while.

Jenny was not unfriendly. She answered each of Blake's questions about the accident but without elaboration, as if she was being questioned about a crime. Clay helped fill in the blanks with good humor and warmth. He sat next to her with his hand on top of hers, the fingers curling in at the second knuckle, like a partial fist. There was no polish on her nails.

"So do you have plans to get more schooling?"

"Not anymore. I went back to school a few years ago but I didn't like it very much. Besides, it probably wouldn't make any sense now, anyway."

"Why not?"

She looked at Clay. "I guess I can tell him, right?"

"It's up to you, Jen. I doubt he'll interfere."

"Sorry," Blake said. "Interfere? Interfere with what?"

"I've decided not to eat anything."

"Is this a . . . medical thing?"

"No. I'm going to do it to die." This was said as if she dared Blake to question her right to do so.

"Oh, I'm . . . I'm sorry to hear that."

"It's all right. It's not something I just thought about. In fact, I've been thinking about it for a long time now."

"Have you already stopped eating?"

"Not yet."

"She told her mom she'd wait a few more weeks," Clay volunteered when it was clear that Jenny had no more to say on the subject. "Her mom is pretty mad about all this."

"What about your dad?" Blake asked.

"He's sad. But I don't think he'll try to stop me. I think he's worried about making my mom mad though, so he doesn't know what to do."

Blake looked at Clay. "How do you feel about this?"

Jenny's eyes turned toward her husband. And in those eyes there appeared to be genuine interest in his answer, registering emotion for the first time in the meeting.

Clay looked at Jenny and leaned into her slightly. "I want what Jenny wants." Blake waited for more, but there was no more forthcoming from either of them on the subject.

"Would it be okay," Blake asked, "if I tell about that in the article?"

"Would they try to stop me?"

"I'm not sure who 'they' are, but the paper wouldn't take any action. I would only try to tell your story as honestly as I could."

"I think that'd be okay. What do you think, Clay?"

"It's up to you."

"You know, I don't have a big speech or anything to make. I'm not trying to be a pioneer and I don't want there to be anything that would hurt my family, or my church. We're Mormons, and Mormons don't believe in suicide. So I don't want there to be anything that hurts them, that's all."

"I'd be sensitive to all that. I'll let you read it ahead of time," he motioned to Clay, "if you want."

After exchanging contact information with Clay, Blake got up to leave. Jenny lifted her folded hand a few inches from the arm of her wheelchair to shake his hand. Blake took it. It was cold and clammy.

"Do you think I'm doing a bad thing? You can tell me the truth."

"It's not for me to judge." He thought about George Morris. "I respect your right to do what you think is best." This, he thought, was the way George would have responded.

Blake left their home and immediately began to research death by starvation. He couldn't find any hard and fast rules about how long it takes to die without food and water. Most healthy, well-nourished adults can go forty days and forty nights without food before death, almost Biblically, but some die within a few weeks, especially if they are already sick or malnourished.

Most experts say it doesn't hurt. But Blake had to wonder, again, who "they" were. It is reported that the first few days are the hardest, and then the hunger pains diminish. But he came upon the case study of a man named Hector, a prison inmate who'd become paralyzed from a drug overdose. He thought his life had lost all meaning and he wanted to die, so he decided not to eat because, like Jenny, he couldn't kill himself in more conventional ways. But the state of Colorado had control over him because he was in prison, and it challenged his right to stop eating. After acrimonious debate the courts finally granted him permission to starve himself.

It took Hector fifteen days to die and he suffered excruciating pain from dehydration. He slipped in and out of a coma. The prison doctors weren't allowed to give him a fatal dose of morphine because that would have created an illegal execution (as opposed to a legal one), and there was the Hippocratic Oath to consider. So they sat in his room and watched him writhe in pain (to the extent quads can writhe) until he finally died. The prison medical staff could do nothing for the poor man. Well, they could, but they couldn't. And therein lay the rub—an ugly conundrum that appeared to serve no one, except perhaps God.

Jenny's case added an entirely new level of complexity to the issue because she didn't have a terminal illness like George did. The terminally ill don't choose to die, for that fate has already been foisted upon them, so they might only choose the time and place. But Jenny wasn't expected to die from quadriplegia per se; she might live another forty years in her chair. Should the state have the right to interfere in her conscientious choice to commit suicide by not eating? It was complicated.

Until someone could persuade him otherwise, Blake decided the tie should be broken in favor of the one whose life was on the line.

24

Blake met with Gene and Lila twice in preparation for his story. At the time Gene investigated the accident, before his cells started going haywire, he stood six feet tall and weighed 190 lbs. Now, four years later, he weighed no more than one hundred pounds. His height was impossible to measure, all bent and shriveled as he was.

Lila walked Blake out to his car after their first meeting. "You know, Mr. Morgan, Gene is a different man than before he got sick."

"How so?"

She looked toward the doorway and lowered her voice. "He was a difficult man to be married to, he really was. He was sharp with us, especially poor Robert." She paused and looked down, fingering the pleat of her dress. "We were afraid of him, because almost anything could set him off."

"Uh-huh."

"But ever since he took all those pills, he's been different."

"You mean after his suicide attempt?"

"Well, yes," she looked down again as if calling it for what it was exposed something shameful.

"How is he different?"

"Well, it's hard to describe because, you know, he can't talk, but he's been so sweet to me. I know I shouldn't say it, but I think his ALS has been a good thing in a lot of ways. I think it's been good for our whole family. Even Gene seems more at peace."

Gene's disease had indeed changed him. He'd lost all control and something had to give. What gave was Gene's unreasonable expectation that he could live forever. He'd done more than simply resign himself to his fate, however, for that would imply his attitude was only so-so, when it was actually better than that—he was nice. This change was a pleasant shock to everyone who knew him. Those around him changed, too, because they were no longer afraid of his ugly outbursts. For how intimidating could he be when he couldn't even speak?

For three years Gene sat in his wheelchair, pondering, for there wasn't much else to do. What was the meaning of his life? Did he contract ALS for a reason, or was it random bad luck? And what about his suicide attempt? He should have died, so was he saved for a reason?

He'd never been a reader, defaulting instead to a crucial ballgame on television (there was always a crucial game). But the big game lost its relevance and he began to read instead. New software allowed him to "turn the pages" with his eyes. He devoured history, philosophy, biographies, medical literature, and even an occasional romance novel. Lila couldn't wait to tell the girls that their dad was engrossed in *The Notebook* ("Dad, as in *our* dad?").

He also studied religion. He *studied* it, but he didn't *find* it. This ambivalence of belief did not trouble him. He considered a death bed conversion to hedge his bets but then surmised if God actually existed He wouldn't be easily manipulated by a bite of the wafer. He had nothing to lose by a Hail

Mary heave as time was expiring, but he assumed God might not cotton to his phoniness.

Gene's reading of philosophy was enlightening, especially thoughts on death. He read from all the famous thinkers, from the ancient Greeks to the present time. Oh, how he wished to engage others in thoughtful conversation about the big philosophical questions! He craved searching discussion about life and death without the ignorant, narrow-minded certainty and the clutter of 11th century thinking. But his disability would scarcely allow for it and most people weren't preoccupied with the subject, in any event. They were secure in their mortality with bills to pay and lives to lead.

Gene also read about advances in genetics that he'd previously not bothered with because it hadn't pertained to him. But like most people with an illness, he'd now become an expert on it. He was a strong proponent of stem cell research that might unlock the mystery behind cellular malformation. This wasn't a selfish view, for there would be no cure for him, and he knew it.

And there were the practical questions that drifted in and out. What would it actually *feel* like when he died? That remained the one thing he was afraid of. He thought about Lila too, still a relatively young woman at fifty. Did she think about remarrying after he was gone? Was she already planning for a life without him? Probably so. And how did he feel about that? How he had taken her for granted! He watched her all day—the wisp of hair that wiggled free from her clip and the way she'd absently brush it out of the way with the back of her hand, or blow it from her face with her lower lip pulled over and out. Or the way she sung old show tunes when she thought no one could hear. When she'd turn and see him listening, she'd blush and turn away when what he'd wanted was for her to sing to him.

Blake met Gene for the final time a few days before he died. His head lolled to his chest so he was forced to peer up from under his brow. His courage was remarkable in the face of his challenge; the ultimate challenge of dying well. Blake's conversations with Gene were laborious, as all of Gene's communication was. The words took shape on the screen, letter by letter. Blake could not imagine a greater curse to an impatient man.

They were sitting in Lila's kitchen that was decorated with dated fork and spoon wallpaper. The twenty-five-year-old glue had begun to give way at the seams. A cuckoo clock with an obnoxious rooster opened its door ten minutes after the hour.

THATS A LATE BIRD ISNT IT. There was the trace of a smile on Gene's face, but it was hard to see because his face had melted at a sideways angle.

"Looking back on it," Blake asked, "how do you feel now about your attempted suicide?"

Blake waited until the words began to form on the screen and then leaned over and read: THAT 3 YRS AGO. I FELT HOPLES NOTHING TO LIVE 4. ANGRY THEY RESCU ME. NOW HAPPY TO GET 2ND LIFE.

"But your condition has deteriorated since then, as you knew it would."

YES IT HAS! BUT MY PAST INCOMPLTE AND NOT EX-AMNED. NOW MORE FULL.

"Knowing all you know now, would you have done the

same thing again?"

NO. SHOLD NOT KILL SELF. GLAD GOT 3 YRS MOR. WANT TO KEEP GOING EVEN WITH ALS.

"What is the most important lesson you've learned in the past few years?"

LIFE IS RANDOM. NOT KNOWNG MAKES IT FULL. BEFOR I SAY SAME OLD EVERYTHING FINE. NOW I SEE SAME OLD IS BEST LIFE CAN OFER. SO DON'T TAKE 4 GRANTED. TOOK TRAGDY TO SEE.

"So do you believe the last few years of your life have been good ones?"

YES! BEST IN MY LIFE. IF IT TOOK ALS TO APRECATE MY LIFE AND FAMLY THEN WORTH IT.

"Do you consider yourself to be a religious person?"

YES. 4 SURE. SO I CAN BLAME THIS ON SOMEONE ELSE! HAHA!

"How do you feel about God? Do you believe in a God?"

SOMTHING BUT NOT SURE. I WILL TELL YOU SOON. HAHA.

"Do you believe in an afterlife?"

MAYB. HOPE SO BUT ??

"Lila told me you've welcomed a new addition to your family."

BEST THING 4 ME! SUSAN HAD BOY LAST YR. NAME JACK. FIRST ONE. I WATCH HIM HOURS NOT BORED. BUT HE LOOKS AT ME AND SEES OLD SHRIVL MESS! HAHA. BUT I HAD MY DAY! HAHA.

I WISH MY KIDS LIVES AWAY. SO SORRY. BIG MIS-TAK. COULDN'T WAIT TIL GROW AND OUT OF HAIR! BUT THEN IT HAPPEN. I WAS FOOL. SO LOVE JACK AND

DON'T TAKE 4 GRANTED. IF I DIE WITH SUICIDE I COULD NOT MEET HIM.

"And I heard that your son, Robert, recently celebrated a milestone too."

YES! GRADUTE COLEGE. VERY PROUD. MY GOAL WAS LIVE LONG ENOGH TO SEE HIM GET DIPOMA. NOT POSS WITH ME DEAD! SO GLAD I DIN'T DIE. I DID NOT UNDRSTND HIS LIFE. STILL DONT. BUT I WAS WRONG. BEAUTIFUL PERSON AND HOPE HE FORGVES ME.

Gene was a flawed man with failings that were significant but not uncommon. And now the pen was poised to write the epilogue on his life. His life would end prematurely at the age of fifty-four, but it would end well. Not on his own terms, of course, but it would end well, nevertheless. It took Lou Gehrig's disease and the verge of losing his life for Gene to find his soul.

Gene's final hours were spent surrounded by Lila, Robert, and Susan. His oldest daughter, Becky, was not there, for she was unable to forgive him for all his previous unkindness. This was a decision she would later come to regret and could not undo, because one's father dies but once.

Two weeks earlier he'd written his last goodbye. There'd been no sound, not even the click of a keyboard stroke. On his final day they gathered around him and he brought it to the monitor. He searched their faces as they read it.

I HAV WONDERED ABOT THE IMP QUESTIONS AT MOMENT LIKE THIS. WAS I GOOD FATHER? WAS I GOOD HUB? DID I DESERVE U? I AM ASHAMED I DIDNT.

SUSAN. I WANT U 2 KNOW U WERE MY SUNSHIN. I WISH I WOULD LUV U BETTER. U DESERVE IT. I WIL

MISS U SO MUCH.

BECKY. PLEASE TELL HER IM SORRY. ITS MY MISTAK, MORE TRAGC THAN ALS COULD EVR BE. I LUV HER AND I HOPE SHE WIL FORGIVE ME SOM DAY. SHE DESRVES BEST HAPPINESS.

ROBERT. DAY U BORN WAS HAPPIEST DAY OF MY LIFE. LUV U SO MUCH. SO PROUD OF SON LIKE U. I AD-MIR YOUR STRENGH & CORAGE. I HOPE U WIL B WHO U ARE. BEST SON EVER. PROUD TO B YOUR DAD.

LILA. I MADE MESS OF THINGS. CAN U EVER FOR-GIVE ME? U ARE MOST BEAUTIFUL PERSON EVER LIVED. I LOV U SO MUCH. MISS U ALREDY.

Gene died in his home an hour later. It was late afternoon and they were all in his bedroom. His last conscious thought was the sunlight that streamed in through the slits in the shutters—perfect vertical shafts filled with dancing specks of nearly invisible particles of dust, each one so light it scarcely bothered with the law of gravity, just orbiting its space. He was struck with the final thought: dust to dust. But, he thought, dust is matter, and will exist forever in some form.

Gene's death had not been a surprise as death so often is, and neither was it exceptional. But still it was humbling like every death that preceded it, for there is nothing more humbling than death.

Lila, Robert, and Susan hugged each other and wept. "He's gone. He's really gone, isn't he?"

"He could be so ornery," Susan said between sniffs.

"I know," Lila said, "and I will miss him so much."

Robert lifted his father's emaciated body from the wheelchair where he'd spent the final three and a half years of his life and laid him on the bed. Lila put a quilt over him as if he were merely sleeping.

The next day, Robert dismantled the ramp in the front yard and threw the scraps of wood to the side of the yard, where they began to rot.

Three days later, Gene lay naked on a cold stainless steel table. He was flanked by an older woman to his left and an even older man on his right. None of them looked well. Gene's head was shaved and the older woman was awfully pale. But they both looked better than the older man, who was missing his head.

When Gene agreed to donate his body to science he was not told what they would do with him. He assumed they'd use him for research, or perhaps display him like a shaved chicken for first-year medical students.

"Are you really sure you want to do this, Gene?" Lila asked.

I WIL B DEAD. ITS OK.

"But, they might . . . well, they might cut you. You just don't know."

HAHA. MAYBE I'LL LOOK BETTR THAN NOW.

"Are you sure that doesn't bother you?"

SUR. LEAST I CAN DO. I WONT FEEL IT ANYWAY):

It wouldn't have been okay with Lila. She couldn't bear the thought that she'd be splayed out naked on a table for anatomy students to stare at, peered upon both inside and out like a frog in eighth grade science class. There were parts of her body that she didn't want anyone else to see. But Gene didn't care. As he said, he'd be dead and they could do with him as they pleased.

And they did.

Gene eventually wound up in the morgue of the Arizona State Medical School, in the interim having been kept on ice like a fillet of cod. He actually became known as "Dennis" in the anatomy lab, because the medical students didn't know who he was and wanted to humanize him. So they'd chosen Dennis on a whim and stuck with it. They pretended not to care if he'd been a homeless person or a rock star (but, still, there's some cachet in dissecting a famous person—there just is).

He was surrounded by others in the morgue; headless, footless, heartless, brainless, eyeless, and torso-less cadavers that paid no attention to him. When his time came he was wheeled into a room that was clean and white. There were no windows and nothing on the walls. It seemed like a harmless enough place—except, that is, for the large band-saw in the center of the room. People who dressed like butchers walked in and out of the room. Some whistled while they worked while others found no particular joy in their job.

Gene was placed onto a table and then fed into the band-saw like a 2" by 12". First his legs were sawed off for study. Then an arm. Gene had previously been embalmed for the sparsely attended funeral, so there was no blood splatter or messy ooze. Each body part was wrapped in cellophane like a rump roast, tagged, and put in cold lockers for further use. The technician handled his job like a pro, only wincing when he rotated Gene's torso to cut off his head. This had always creeped him out. Seeing a lonely head there on the table was disturbing, even for someone who chopped up ca-davers for a living.

Gene's brain was an important prize. Medical researchers would use it to try to decode the mystery of ALS which, so far, has eluded them. But nothing is wasted on a donated cadaver. Podiatrists study feet, ophthalmologists learn about eyeballs, and cardiologists pick apart hearts. Heads are popular too. Budding plastic surgeons eagerly line them up on tables to practice face lifts and nose jobs, because if they botch them there's no risk of a lawsuit.

Gene deferred to the researchers (he really had no say in the matter), but if he'd had his choice he would've been used for a noble purpose, like the elimination of a stubborn disease instead of perfecting the invisible scar on a routine tummy tuck. So he would have been happy to know his body was well used. After he'd been studied, poked, and prodded, his body parts were collected and cremated.

Donating his body to science had been Gene's final act of contrition.

25

"Hey, babe, what time is it?" Naomi's voice was still groggy and a bit raspy, a shade deeper with that early morning sexiness.

"It's 6:00," Blake whispered. "Sorry, I tried to be quiet."

She propped herself onto one elbow. "But it's Saturday. Where are you going so early?"

"I promised Steve I'd meet him for a hike this morning. I'm already a little bit late."

"You're crazy. I'm going back to sleep."

Blake wondered if indeed he was crazy. He was now able to run eight miles, but it was still hard. All the talk he'd heard about a runner's high was an old wives' tale. Endorphins? Not so far. Steve was running, too, but his resolve to check a marathon off the bucket list had waned. "Listen," he'd told Blake, "let's mix it up a bit. Maybe do a hike instead. We ought to be cross-training anyway."

Steve had said this between bites of a chili dog at Triple Play, the local sports bar where Blake's autographed photo hung near the ceiling on a wall plastered with sports memorabilia. Blake had never been crazy about the photo—he thought it looked cheesy the way he'd been posing with his bat cocked for the cameraman. Four frames below the small-ish photo of Blake, and slightly to the right, was a photo of

Mickey Mantle. So Blake had made "The Wall," but one had to hunt to find him.

They met that morning at the trailhead of Camelback Mountain, a popular hike in Phoenix. Steve stood at the base of the trailhead, next to a bulletin board covered with hiking club flyers, fire safety tips, and outdated 5K's.

"Where in the hell have you been? I thought we were meeting at 6:30?"

"Yeah, sorry. I just couldn't get out of bed this morning for some reason."

"Did Some Reason spend the night at your place again?"

"Yeah."

"How's it going anyway?"

"It's good."

"So, are you thinking about making it permanent? Sorry, I have to ask because that's the first thing Alison is going to ask me."

"Yeah, maybe. Probably."

"Actually, I was a few minutes late, too. We had a pretty rough night with Chad. He was up all night with colic or something, poor kid." Chad was Steve and Alison's fourth child. Blake was his godfather, an honor that flattered him even though he didn't know what it meant, or what he was supposed to do with it. Was he supposed to buy him his first beer? Pay for his college? Attend Back-To-School nights? When Alison told him he was responsible for Chad's religious instruction, Blake thought she was kidding. "So, you mean, like, teach him stuff from the Bible?" Alison just rolled her eyes.

The hike began with a modest incline, but then became steep. After an interminable number of dusty switchbacks they reached the peak and were rewarded with a panoramic view of Maricopa County—from Glendale to Mesa, and beyond. Despite the view, Blake's mind drifted back to Naomi, probably still in bed, her dark hair fanned across the pillow.

"Not too shabby, huh?" said Steve, as he took a long pull on his water bottle.

"Yeah, it's spectacular," Blake said.

"Trail mix?"

"No, I'll save it for some real food. Maybe we can hit Triple Play later."

"Sounds good. You ready to head?"

"Yeah, let's go," Blake said. "I've still got to get in a run."

"You're kidding."

"Wanna go with?" Blake asked.

"Of course not."

"You're going to owe me. Big time."

"I'll believe it when I see it. How's work going by the way?"

"Hanging in there. I'm still working on that story about suicide I told you about."

"About the old guy with cancer?"

"Yeah, that's part of it. It's about the whole end of life and all that."

"I know it's easy for me to say, but I still think it's wrong to kill yourself. I don't care how bad it is."

"I'm not sure how I feel about it," Blake said. "You probably don't remember, but this whole thing started out as a 'Where are they now' type deal on people in a traffic accident. One lady died and it's her husband who has the cancer. Anyway, another girl in the accident is a quad. It's some pretty sad shit."

"Yeah, that would suck. I think I'd rather be dead."

"No kidding. In fact, she wants to starve herself to death."

"Who? The quad?"

"Yeah."

"So they *both* want to kill themselves?"

"Yeah."

"That's messed up."

They nodded at a group of hikers on their way up, grateful they were now going down. "Those guys started too late. It's gotta be ninety," Blake said.

"Are you trying to talk them out of it?"

"Who? The people in my story?"

"Yeah."

"Not really, but I feel sorry for them."

"Who wouldn't? But that doesn't make it right to kill yourself."

"A lot of people think it should be legal."

"What, exactly, ought to be legal?"

"Assisted suicide."

"You mean like Kevorkian?"

"Yeah, I guess. Basically it'd be the right to die when you're already screwed. And you ought to be able to get help from a doctor so it'd be safe and less painful."

"Safe?"

"Well, yeah, I guess safe isn't the right word. But at least less painful."

Steve was quiet as he scrambled down a few large boulders. "I know their lives would suck, but they'll just make it worse by killing themselves."

Blake knew that Steve would be opposed to it. Whether this was something Steve had come to on his own, or something that he'd been told to think, surely Blake couldn't say. But he wondered how Steve would feel about it if he'd had a clean slate, without the clutter of dogma. "Don't you think it ought to be their choice? It's their lives, after all. And these people aren't wackos. The old man was a big-time doctor and the girl is pretty religious."

"I don't see it. Sorry, but I just think it's wrong."

"Why?"

"*Why?* It's a sin to kill yourself. Hey, don't get me wrong; I feel sorry for those people too, and I know I shouldn't judge them, but killing yourself crosses the line."

"They obviously don't think so."

"Murder is murder. I know I probably sound hardcore, but there's no way I'd do it."

"Murder? Come on, dude, don't you think that's a little harsh?"

"Okay, maybe not murder, but anybody who's read the Bible ought to know it's wrong."

Both of them collected their thoughts on the subject as they scrambled down the mountainside, trying to compose a good retort. They rarely talked politics, or religion, because it usually ended badly. And then they'd move to something safe, and have a good laugh, to demonstrate how they could have a friendly disagreement while showing each other how reasonable they could be.

"But what if you were going to die anyway, within a few months, let's say? Don't you think that's different?"

"It's still God's job."

"It seems to me the question isn't whether they're going to die. God or nature or whoever has already decided that. It's *when* and *how*. I'm not a big religion guy, okay? But I gotta think God would show them a ton of mercy. Don't you?"

"Okay, so where would you draw the line? We're all going to die of *something*. So isn't the *when* and *how* part the whole shebang? It's a pretty slippery slope if you ask me."

"I just think it's different if you're already in the process of dying."

"The girl isn't."

"Okay, maybe not her. But, geez, it's hard to judge her."

"I think God gave us the will to live. I don't think I'd ever just give up."

"Okay, how about when you're lying there on the bathroom floor next to the throne, sicker than shit. It's just the flu or a hangover or something, so you know it's only temporary. But you're there with your head over the can making insane deals with God to feel better because you can't think of anything else. Right?"

"Yeah, I've had some of those nights."

"So what if you knew the misery wasn't ever going away—in fact, you knew it would only get worse until you finally died. And then somebody comes along and offers you a painless way out. Wouldn't you take it?"

"I don't think I would," Steve said, "because it goes against God. So in the long run, I'd be worse off."

"These people don't want to die. And they don't want to piss off God, either." This was a concise summary of the generally understood assumption that everyone wants to go to heaven, but nobody wants to die to get there.

"Then don't do anything to piss Him off."

"Okay then, how about the cost to keep all these people alive? My editor's parents are in some old-folks home and pay $12,000 per month! $12,000 a month! Their money's about gone, and they don't even know who their son is. So where's the life in that?"

"It'd suck—I'm not saying it wouldn't."

"And when there's no more money, then what? Should the government pick up the tab?"

"Well, you know me. I'm sick of the government getting into everything. Spending is already way out of control."

"Okay, then who *should* pay for it?"

"I don't know. But I can't believe killing yourself is the answer and neither are those 'death panels' I've heard about. I don't want some doctor, or a bunch of Washington, D.C. liberals telling me when I'm supposed to die. I'll let God decide that one."

And so they marched down the quarrelsome trail of politics and religion; a trail that inevitably lead nowhere, until Steve finally said, "Maybe you're right. Hell, I don't know, Blake. Let's go to Triple Play. We've earned it. All this talk about dying is making me hungry for some reason."

26

Joanne and Rich Kimball had been the rounds over Jenny's decision to end her life, but neither of them had scored a knockout. The latest round occurred in the kitchen. Joanne was carrying a basket of laundry and Rich was at the table going over a stack of bills.

"Jenny doesn't know what she's doing," Joanne said. "She obviously isn't thinking clearly."

"What do you want me to say, Joanne?" He leaned back in his chair and removed his reading glasses, bracing for another argument. "Jen has suffered for four years. She's already been through hell and back. I think we need to respect her wishes."

"How on earth do *you* know what she wants?"

"She's told us. Many times, in fact."

"So you are just going to sit there and let her go through with this, this, *suicide*? You won't even fight for her?"

"I believe I am fighting for her," said Rich.

"So you would allow our daughter, *your* daughter, to kill herself and not do everything within your power to stop her? You are her *father!* Don't you even care about her?"

"Of course I do. And you know that more than anyone." He tilted his head and looked at his wife with pity. "If I could trade places with her you know I would. But I can't."

"Well, if you loved her as much as you say you do, you'd

224 | WARREN DRIGGS

stop this nonsense, this craziness, this voluntary *suicide!*"

"This isn't a contest over who loves Jenny more, so let's not go there. We both love her, okay? But our lives go on."

"Your life may go on as if nothing happened, as if your daughter's life isn't worth saving. But my life cannot just 'go on'; not while my daughter is so confused."

"But I don't think she's confused. She's suffered for so long. It's time to let her go."

"Let her *go*? Listen to yourself! You sound just like Clay: 'Let her go so we can get on with our lives.' Shame on both of you!"

"You know me, Joanne, and you know what's in my heart. You know I would give my life for her. She deserves to have *her* choice, as awful as that choice may seem to you, or to me, or to the bishop, or to the judge, or to anyone else."

"I ended a life when I was eighteen, and that 'choice' has haunted me ever since. I won't do it again, Richard. I won't. After my so-called 'choice' I met you and converted to the church. I did it for you, Rich."

"I'm sorry, Jo. I don't know what more I can say."

"There's plenty you can say. But you won't."

"Jen has her free agency. No one should be able to take that away from her, whether we think she's making a mistake or not. God will judge her, and He'll judge her with mercy."

"When we got married we made a promise to each other that we would build a family based on the sanctity of life, not the destruction of it. And now I don't even know what you stand for anymore."

She stared hard at him a few more seconds, then picked up the basket of laundry that she'd set on the kitchen table and turned her back to him. He could not believe that her simple back could express so much anger, so much pain. He also knew that on the other side of it was the look of a devastated woman and a man soon to be punished for it.

Joanne hated the mire of Rich's arguments. All this business about "free agency" when it was their *daughter* they were talking about for God's sake, and not some hypothetical discussion about gospel principles or religious dogma. All her pleadings with God had been for not, as if she'd been negotiating with management with nothing to show for it. All the contracts she made with Him had been breached. Of course, these had all been unilateral contracts; if He would cure the quadriplegia she'd do such and such, or if He would stop Jenny's suicidal thoughts she'd do this or that.

When Blake called the Kimballs to see if they would meet with him for the story, they fought some more. Rich was reluctant to insert Jenny's personal battle into the public forum. Joanne, however, hoped the *Arizona Republic* might be an important voice to muster support for a Right to Life campaign.

"Jen, how do *you* feel about this?"

"I'm okay with it, dad."

"Are you sure? Because your mom and I won't talk to them if you don't want us to."

"Yeah, I'm sure, especially if mom wants to." Jenny knew this would spark controversy, and she wasn't a crusader. She'd come to believe, however, that this choice was hers alone to make.

Rich and Joanne's house was obscured behind a row of overgrown junipers, which mistakenly made it look like the owners were reclusive, or were hiding something. Joanne invited Blake in with a firm handshake. She was younger than Blake expected her to be. She was polite, but all business, as if there was no time for idle chit chat. Rich wore a golf shirt tucked into out-of-fashion jeans. He seemed more relaxed, but his jaw was set. He, too, was younger than Blake thought he'd be.

The walls of the living room where they sat were adorned with religious art, but without the frenzy of crucifixes, like George Morris's house. There were paintings of Jesus, but they weren't tragically sad and gory. He wasn't hanging on a cross with a towel twisted around his middle and weepers beneath him. The picture above the fireplace in the Kimball's home depicted Jesus surrounded by well-behaved children who swarmed around Him like a rugby scrum. The children appeared to be of Scandinavian descent, or the first settlers of Utah. Jesus looked alarmingly like Fabio, and He was smiling.

Blake asked how they felt about Jenny's "self-deliverance" through starvation (he'd come up with that term on the drive over, and was proud of it, because he thought it sounded less morbid than Jenny's "suicide").

"We disagree," Joanne said. "We, at least I, think she's making a terrible mistake. She has too much to live for."

Blake looked at Rich.

"I'm more conflicted than Joanne. I don't want Jenny to die, of course I don't, but I've come to believe it's her choice and we should respect it."

"I assume you've talked to Jenny about your feelings?"

"Of course we have," said Joanne. "And I think she knows it's wrong, but she's confused. She's a strong girl, but she's been through so much." Joanne dropped her head. "So much.

And I don't want her to make an irreversible decision, especially when she's not in the proper frame of mind."

"And I happen to believe," Rich said, "that she is." He reached over and put his hand on Joanne's as if to acknowledge this was simply his opinion. Joanne did not squeeze his hand, but neither did she shrug it away.

"Do you think she's trying to make a statement?" Blake asked.

"No," they both answered in unison. "That's not Jenny," Joanne said. "I don't think she'd want to force a law or anything that would make suicide legal. At least I hope she wouldn't want that."

"We're both devastated," Rich said. "Joanne is a fabulous mother and Jenny is lucky to have her." He offered the hand a squeeze. "It's a complicated thing and we just see it differently."

"I'm sorry, Rich," she said, "but I don't think it's that complicated. I think if we both tried to convince her that suicide isn't the answer maybe she'd listen to us." She looked at Rich, pleading for reason. "I know how much you love her, and I'm sorry if I've said anything to suggest otherwise." She turned to Blake. "Rich is an amazing father. It's just that . . . I wish he'd do more to stop her." She turned again to Rich and took his hand in both of hers. "I'm sorry, Rich—it's just the way I feel."

Rich looked down at the carpet. "We both want what's best for Jenny."

"I can't imagine what you're both going through," Blake said. "I'm sorry."

"It's been tough," was all Rich could say.

Rich lost his parents a few years earlier—his mom and then his dad. His mom had arrhythmia and her doctors recommended a pacemaker. Rich and his siblings had mixed feelings about that too, because she was eighty-five years old at the time and her health was only so-so. If she'd been younger it would've been an easy decision. Her mind, however, was starting to fall apart, crumbling to pieces like a dry biscuit. So the adult children resisted the procedure, but then ultimately deferred to the doctors who said her heart would give out if they didn't "do something." Rich wished they'd had the courage to tell the doctors to let it be—to let nature run its course. But they felt guilty saying that, and so did their aging father who was obliged to do all he could.

The pacemaker worked like a charm, allowing her heart to stay in perfect rhythm while the rest of her body tried to die naturally. She lived another five years in a state of marginal dementia, and at a staggering cost. Worst of all, it took a vicious toll on Rich's dad. He'd been fairly healthy when his wife was given the pacemaker. But as she kept deteriorating, and wouldn't die, he was forced to be her caretaker. The kids helped, but he'd felt it was his duty. They'd saved some money, but the nursing care was expensive and his mom's unnaturally extended life took everything they had. And for what, Rich wondered?

Even though Rich loved his mom, he'd wanted her to die. And he knew many others with aging parents privately wished for the same thing. Was that a selfish wish, he wondered? And did he feel guilty about it? He didn't think so.

He knew his parent's ordeal was different than his daughter's, so he didn't bring it up with Blake. Rather than try to further justify his position, or apologize for his wife's, he had only sighed heavily and told Blake that "It'd been tough." And indeed it had, for he was on the verge of losing his daughter, and his wife, too.

And all this for the wont of a tortoise in the road.

Blake returned to the Republic to find his editor haranguing a reporter. The editor took a drag from his cigarette and then crushed the end of it against the side of his trash can and dropped it.

"Can I talk to you when you get a second?" Blake asked.

"Just give me a second, will ya? I'm trying to run a goddamned newspaper around here with reporters who give me stories I wouldn't wipe my ass with, for chrissakes!" The young reporter stared down at her shoes.

"Don't worry about it," Blake said to her. "He gets like this." He returned to his cubicle and checked his messages. One was from his ex-wife, and another was from his mom. He called his ex first because he knew she'd badger him until he did. She was sweet because she needed him to watch Alex for the weekend. His mom hadn't heard from him in three days and was worried something terrible had happened.

"You're working too hard, Blake. My goodness, I haven't seen you in over a week. Can't you come over for dinner tonight?"

"Sure, mom, that'd be great. I'll swing by on my way home from work."

"And did you hear about your uncle Frank?"

"No, what happened?"

"Well, he had his hip replaced."

"Isn't he almost ninety?"

"He's eighty-eight, and just as crotchety as ever. For the life of me, I don't know how they put up with him."

"I thought he was in a wheelchair half the time anyway."

"I know, but they're thinking with a new hip he might be able to get up more. And seems it didn't cost anything, they thought they might as well do it."

"What do you mean it didn't cost anything?"

"It was free. Medicare paid for it."

He hung up from his mom, too weary to engage her about his uncle's free treatment. Hal buzzed him.

"What's so goddamned urgent, Morgan?"

"I just wanted to touch bases on this article I'm doing—the one about dying."

"Are we ready to run it?"

"Not yet. Sorry, but I keep running into new angles on this thing."

"Like what?"

Blake told him about Jenny, and her parents. He told him about the nursing home research and Gene's death from ALS, but only after Gene had been grateful his attempted suicide *hadn't* worked. "And then I just got off the phone with my mom and she tells me about my eighty-eight-year-old uncle who just got a hip replacement. He had it done because Medicare was picking up the tab, so they assumed it was free."

"Free my ass. What is it with these people? No wonder we're broke."

"Anyway, if you don't mind, I might need another week or two to flesh this out a bit more."

"Knock yourself out. Nobody gives me anything I can run on time anyway."

Blake leaned back in his chair and thought about his eighty-eight-year-old uncle and his new hip. It used to be when people wore out they died, but now they're kept alive. Was that God's way, Blake wondered? Or was it God's way to keep them going at all costs? He figured it couldn't be both. Had medical ethics kept pace with scientific progress? Were people being kept alive just because it was possible, without considering if it was a good thing?

Blake wasn't cynical by nature, but he couldn't help but see the perverse financial incentive to keep people alive. There is the doctor, the hospital, and the manufacturer of the device. Then there is the nursing home, where bathroom sinks are shrines to Pfizer, Johnson & Johnson, and Bayer, with the calculated understanding that the rent stops when the tenant dies. There are drugs to increase this and drugs to decrease that. Drugs that cause one side effect, and then another to counter it. Around and around it goes. And often the patients don't even know what they're taking.

Blake wondered why eighty-five year olds who were dying of chronic lung disease are given daily heart medication, or why patients with terminal cancer are given vitamins and cholesterol medicine. Pain killers made sense. But Lipitor?

The road trip to the Grand Canyon had been Rich's idea—some time to get away with the family and decompress. Jenny knew her parents would use the trip to persuade their captive daughter that she was about to make a terrible mistake. But this would likely be the last time she had with her parents and sister, so she agreed to go.

They loaded Jenny's van with the accoutrements of the disabled and headed north on I-17; Jenny, Clay, Rich, Joanne, and Liz. They had travelled thirty miles when it started.

"So, Clay," Joanne asked, "how's the house working out?"

"I think it's pretty good. We like it."

"How long do you think you'll be there before you and Jen move?"

"Uh, I think we'll stay there for a while. I don't see us moving, maybe ever."

"But when your career takes off you two will be able to afford something nicer."

"Mom, please don't do this."

"Jen," said Rich, "I think mom is just trying to be positive."

"You don't need to apologize for me, Rich. Jenny isn't dead yet."

"Mom!" Liz said. "Seriously? If you're going to do this the whole way then let me out."

"We're just taking each day at a time," Clay said.

"And that's all you can do," Rich said. "That's all any of us can do. And in the meantime, I have to tell you guys, the Grand Canyon is one of the most spectacular places you'll ever see. The river cut the . . . "

"I'm sorry, Jen," said Joanne. "I just love you so much."

"I know you do, mom. So now let's let dad give us one of his boring travel logs like he always does." And she smiled at her mom, who she knew would have traded her places.

The Grand Canyon did not disappoint. They arrived in the late afternoon on that autumn day and pulled up to the edge. It was a cavernous furrow, as if God had dragged His plow too deep across the high desert plateau of Arizona. The sun was almost down, low enough that they could look at it without hurting their eyes, resting as it was on the smooth edge of the canyon's top shelf. The scent of Bristol pine was in the breeze. The purple and lavender shadows contrasted with the sunlit sandstone walls. One large slab of rock was bright orange and looked to be on fire. The cottonwood trees shimmered yellow and the contrast with the blue sky was unlike anything they had ever seen.

They were quiet, each of them left to their own thoughts about the magnitude of this natural masterpiece. It was so vast and timeless, and they were so small and temporary. Jenny was struck with the insignificance of her little life in the grand eternal scheme of things. She would live or she would die. No, she *would* die. Whether it was tomorrow, or the next day, or the next year, or the next decade, she would die. But this canyon would endure. Her life was important only to a small group of people, all of whom would also die in the wink of time in comparison to this. This thought did not depress her, it inspired her. For as she looked out at the enormous void, Jenny realized she would be at peace. She would be at peace in the arms of God who created all this, or she would become nothing, unable even to know what suffering was.

And there was peace in that, too.

27

He awoke Monday for the final time. He called old friends and listened to their voices with an intensity he hadn't previously known. George was determined to relish each moment of this, his last day. Several times throughout the day he checked the stash of pills that he'd acquired in the preceding weeks. They hid quite conspicuously in plain sight, among the row of pill bottles that stretched across his bathroom sink. It was a comfort to know they were there, because the mere possession of them gave him a sense of control. Whether he used them or not, at least he knew they were there. And that is all he'd wanted—all anyone wants, really—to feel like they have some control.

Maria, his housekeeper, left him at 6:00 Monday evening, but only after he assured her that he was fine and would retire early. He walked out to the back patio for one more moment in the sun, one last moment to breathe fresh air. He sat on the patio swing where he and Fern had spent so much leisure time. It squeaked in rhythm with his swinging. He heard a bird and listened. He saw an ant carrying a load twice its size on its back across the patio and marveled. He concentrated on each of his senses as if hearing, seeing, and smelling for the first and only time. Nothing was taken for granted, not on this day.

He finally stood and went inside, locking the door behind him. He was locking himself into a tomb of sorts. His lifeless corpse in the end-stages of rigor mortis would be hauled out on a stretcher. Maria had prepared a light meal for him which he picked at out of obligation, for he wasn't very hungry. Besides, he wanted his stomach to be empty so the poison would absorb quicker.

He removed his clothes and drew a bath. As water filled the tub he took an inventory of his wrinkled body. How many times over the years he had looked in the mirror, at first hoping he looked older, perhaps old enough to drive, or date, or order his first beer. Then, later, as the years began to pile up, he'd looked in the mirror hoping to see the reflection of a younger man. But it was a hopeless cause. His body had done what bodies do, in all species—it had deteriorated at a steady, inevitable rate. His once young, strong, and handsome physique had gradually morphed into what he saw before him now in the mirror; a decrepit old man staring back at him.

He eased himself into the hot bath. It felt good on his tired bones. He lay motionless until the water began to cool and then he washed himself with earnest deliberation, counterintuitively, he knew, for what he was about to do. He dried off with a towel that seemed to grow in comparison to his shrinking body.

Shaving had always been a sensory experience for George. He bought the most expensive shaving creams and enjoyed the routine of lathering the cream in a wooden bowl and painting his beard with the shaving brush, breathing in the luxurious sandalwood scent. He did so a final time then meticulously dragged a new blade across his thinning beard. He could hear the blade cut the copse of whiskers. He splashed his favorite aftershave and felt the brief sting for the last time.

He selected a blue pinstripe suit and his favorite tie. With knobby fingers he tied it, but was dissatisfied with the knot so he undid it and tied it again. He recalled the time his father taught him how to tie a Windsor knot. They'd been standing in front of a cloudy mirror in the small dining room of their home off Harrison Street. Seventy-five years later and he could still smell his father's hair gel and unfiltered cigarettes. The phonograph played Fred Astaire's "Cheek to Cheek" and his father had playfully dragged his mother from the kitchen and they'd danced to the scratchy tune while he and his little sister sat on the sofa watching them, content and safe. Where had the years gone?

He put on his favorite classical music and then took several anti-nausea pills, knowing they should be taken at least thirty minutes before the pills that would kill him. He poured a large glass of water and another glass of his best single-malt scotch, neat, the way he liked it. He placed both glasses on the bed stand between a photo of his family and his pile of pills, eighty five of them in all.

The pills were white and reminded him of the arsenal of snowballs he and his cousin stockpiled to throw at passing Buicks and Hudsons. He smiled at the memory. His mind then drifted to other misdeeds, all of them minor in the grand scheme of things. Did he have any regrets? He couldn't readily think of any, for his life had been good, and full. He felt like he had as a young boy at the county fair when his favorite ride was drawing to an end. He wasn't mad. He didn't feel as though he'd been cheated—for the ride had been worth every penny. But he was sad the car was coming to a stop.

George lay on top of his king-sized bed, formally dressed in his suit and tie. The bed was grossly big and lonely ever since Fern died. He propped the pillows up so that he was comfortably reclined on the cotton polished floral duvet. He smiled to himself thinking how Fern would roll over in her grave if she saw his black polished shoes on her bedspread.

His mind drifted to her. Where was she? Did she exist? Was she watching him now? Would he see her soon, or was this really the end? And did it even matter what he believed on the subject? Surely his belief alone would not change the eternal nature of things. Believers and nonbelievers alike would share the same basic fate. The knowledge that billions of people had already crossed this threshold gave him comfort. Soon he would join them. Or he wouldn't. Soon he would experience a grand heavenly afterlife. Or he wouldn't. And he couldn't do a damned thing about it either way.

Was he a brave man to end his life this way? Or was he a coward? He wondered. And what difference did it really make, anyway? He'd made his choice and was comfortable with it. An old proverb came back to him from some unknown recess of his mind, timely and prescient: *Once the game is over, the Kings and Pawns go back into the same box.*

If he'd done his homework correctly, he would die painlessly and with a certain amount of dignity that would likely be absent in a few more months. Yes, this was his choice, a choice made easier when he was punched by another cascading wave of abdominal pain.

The order in which he took the pills was unimportant. He began taking them two at a time. After five minutes he had taken nearly half of them, six to eight pills, and then a sip of scotch. On and on it went, the pile of snowballs slowly melting. After nearly twenty minutes he had taken every pill, and the water and scotch were also gone. He put his head back on the pillow and lifted one of Fern's scarves, sprayed with her perfume, and placed it next to his head.

He closed his eyes and hoarded every last moment, every last few breaths. He began to drift in and out of consciousness for several minutes and then gave in to his overpowering desire to sleep. His hands were folded reverently across his chest as the notes from Debussy's "Claire de Lune" whispered in his ear. His breathing slowed to a crawl and finally stopped. After pumping almost two and a half billion times, his good heart beat no more.

Maria arrived at 8:00 on Tuesday morning and found him lying on his bed, immaculately dressed. He was pale—pallor mortis having begun almost instantly upon his death. He was cold—algor mortis having gradually reduced his body's heat to the ambient room temperature. And he was stiff—rigor mortis having changed the chemicals in his muscles beginning about three hours after death and reaching maximum stiffness after twelve hours.

Maria found the empty pill bottles but registered no judgment towards this gentle man who had only shown her kindness. There was even a certain degree of increased respect for Mr. Morris, in spite of her personal views of suicide. Who was she to judge him? Let God treat him with the mercy and peace he deserved. She sat on the edge of the bed and called

George's daughter, Sarah, who was relieved but heartbroken. Sarah called her siblings and then the mortuary.

Sarah arrived an hour later and sat, alone, next to her father. She looked around his room and noticed those things he surrounded himself with; photos of his family, books, paintings, and poetry. There was nothing from his career. There were no plaques, diplomas, certificates, or awards; even though she knew he had received many. George had been adorned with accolades throughout his impressive career, but he hadn't made a shrine to himself. She felt a surge of affection for him. He was first and foremost a husband, father, friend, and a man thirsty for knowledge. The fact that he was also a celebrated physician, the Knife of the Stars, seemed unimportant to him—just another candle on the cake.

Sarah found it hard to believe that he was really gone, for good, when his wallet was still on the kitchen counter and his dirty white tennis shoes that he used for gardening were still out by the back door where he'd always left them. She wanted him back, but she didn't judge him for leaving. She desperately believed in God, now more than ever, because she demanded assurance that she would see him again. She wondered what God would do with this situation. And what if her father had asked her to help him because he'd been unable to take his own life without some assistance? Would she, could she, have helped him? She was glad it hadn't been asked of her.

She noticed a worn book of poetry on his nightstand. It was a collection of poems by Dylan Thomas, dog-eared and opened easily, as if the binding was loosened from use. She opened it to one of the dog-eared pages and read:

Do not go gentle into that good night,
Old age should burn and rave at close of day:
Rage, rage against the dying of the light.

Though wise men at their end know dark is right,
Because their words had forked no lightning they
Do not go gentle into that good night.

Good men, the last wave by, crying how bright
Their frail deeds might have danced in a green bay,
Rage, rage against the dying of the light.

Wild men who caught and sang the sun in flight,
And learn, too late, they grieved it on its way,
Do not go gentle into that good night.

Grave men, near death, who see with blinding sight
Blind eyes could blaze like meteors and be gay,
Rage, rage against the dying of the light.

And you, my father, there on that sad height,
Curse, bless, me now with your fierce tears, I pray.
Do not go gentle into that good night.
Rage, rage against the dying of the light.

Sarah reached over and took her father's clammy hand.
When had he last read it, she wondered? When had he folded
the corner of the page? When had his mind changed when
there was no longer the rage, the effort to stay the night, instead of gently surrendering to it?

She walked into his closet and buried her face in his
clothes. His smell shot into her nostrils, making him come
alive again. She sobbed into the clothes, allowing herself a

long and messy cry. Oh, how she would miss him. She was struck with the thought that she was an orphan now, a surreal thought that she put away for the moment to contemplate another time.

Two young men from the mortuary arrived late in the day. They parked their brown van in the circular driveway. The van was unostentatiously decorated with the Schmidt Mortuary logo. The young men looked good in their conservative black suits, inexpensive but durable two-pant specials from Men's Warehouse. They spoke in hushed and reverent tones appropriate for the occasion.

The two of them wore practiced grief on their faces in keeping with the solemnity of the event. These were professionals who had done this so many times, and with so much feigned dignity, that they occasionally pulled it off wearing small earplugs running to iPods buried in their pockets. One of them was, at that very moment, listening to the best of Van Halen.

Sarah escorted them to the bedroom where George's body lay undisturbed. A gurney was rolled into the room without a sound. A blue padded blanket covered the top. A pillow was placed at the head of the gurney so George's corpse could ride comfortably down the hall, into the van, and to the mortuary. The pillow would be discarded once he reached the morgue, but for now it looked awfully good—a show of genuine concern.

Next, they placed a black body bag on top of the gurney and the two young men, standing side by side, lifted George's body to it. This was a routine that had been rehearsed down at the mortuary using dead bodies as part of their training, for they didn't want to strain their backs, or drop the body. There was no need to appear clumsy in front of the grieving family.

They wrapped the body bag around George and zipped it to his chin, leaving only his head exposed. Then they strapped him down using canvas belts. They cinched the belts so tightly Sarah was concerned it may have uncomfortably pinched her father, or cut off his circulation. A perfectly folded white sheet was ceremoniously unfolded and placed on top of George like an American flag onto the casket of a soldier killed in action. They wheeled George from his home to the waiting van and bolted the gurney into place. The van pulled solemnly out of the driveway and slowly down the street. It picked up speed as soon as it was out of sight of the distraught family, and the young men turned up the radio.

28

Blake was at his mom's house, just having changed her furnace filters. Now he sat at the kitchen counter while his mom fussed over Tupperware cartons in the fridge that were labeled with abbreviated scribbles on masking tape, cobbling together dinner for him and his son, Alex.

"Mom," Blake asked, "would you rather be buried like dad or cremated?"

"My goodness, Blake, it sounds like you've already got me dead and buried!" she said without looking up. She pried open a lid and stuck her nose into a small plastic carton for a good whiff and then put in on the counter. "I'm just fine."

"I know. I was just wondering."

"Well, I suppose I'd prefer to be buried like your father."

"Why?"

"I don't know. We've just always done it that way. And I don't like the thought of being burned to death. It's too barbaric. I think I'd be more comfortable being buried."

"But you'd be dead, so why would it matter?"

"It just would."

Left unspoken was her imagination that she would live forever in some bodily form, maybe a spirit or something, in the same shape as the body she was used to. In fact, she envisioned looking down on her funeral, like most people do.

She'd see her friends and family on the pews weeping and saying incredibly generous things about her. And how on earth would she be able to do that if she were a pile of ashes?

"Would you like an open casket?" Blake asked.

"I don't know. I don't even want to think about it. I'm fine."

Blake's mom did not suffer from the sin of vanity anymore than the average person. But she had misgivings about an open casket because she was afraid of how she might look. Would they do her hair right? Or would it look too poofy on the sides? She didn't trust how they'd do her make-up either. Just the other day she'd been to her aunt's funeral and knew her aunt would have been mortified at the way they'd done her make-up.

"What's a casket?" Alex asked.

"It's nothing, honey," she said, and then looked over Alex's head at Blake and opened her eyes wide in warning, as if this subject was inappropriate for such impressionable ears.

"When someone dies," Blake said, "they are put into a casket, like a box, before they're buried in the ground."

"What if they aren't really all the way dead? How would they get out?"

"Well, the doctors make sure they're really dead."

"But how can they tell for sure?"

"Here, Alex, honey, let me get you some of this yummy tuna casserole." She then stared hard at Blake as if to say, 'Now look what you've started.'

"They just can," Blake said. "You don't need to worry about it."

The topic had been on Blake's mind ever since his meet-

ing with Glen Schmidt, proud proprietor of the Schmidt
Mortuary and Funeral Home. A few days earlier he'd read
George Morris's obituary. His funeral service was to be held at
Schmidt's. Blake didn't attend the service, but he'd decided to
slightly expand his story by following George all the way to the
finish. He wanted to know what happens in the days after one
dies, and Schmidt's was a good place to start.

Glen Schmidt was a sixty-five-year-old man whose hair
had been dyed black (too black) and wore a polyester suit.
He made his living selling caskets, funeral services, and burial
plots to loved ones floundering in grief, relying upon his sin-
cerity to guide them through the final ordeal. And Glen was
sincere. When Blake called to make an appointment, Glen
calculated the windfall of free advertisement in the *Arizona
Republic*, for he'd recently cut his marketing budget. People
were no longer paying a premium for fine headstones so he'd
been forced to pull his ad in the obituary section of the newspaper and his logo from floral shop wall calendars.

"Well, hello, Mr. Morgan."

"Yes, you must be Mr. Schmidt."

"Please, call me Glen," and he offered a firm handshake,
one that said he cared. "When you called, I said it myself, 'Self,
why not give this nice young man a tour of the place.' So here
I am, at your service."

"Thanks. As I mentioned on the phone, I'm writing an
article on . . . "

"Yes, yes, on the funeral process. It can be a trying time
and there are so many decisions to make. When my parents
died years ago I said to myself, 'Glen, aren't you happy you
took care of this business when you did, so you wouldn't have

to worry about it now?' That's why we encourage people to plan ahead. It's more cost effective that way, too."

"Yeah, maybe I'll look into that some time."

"Before you leave I'll give you a few brochures. We've got several different plans to fit any budget. But listen to me; you didn't come to buy a burial plot, now did you?"

"Maybe you can take me on a short tour and explain how it works."

"Be happy to."

They entered a lamp-lit area that looked like a furniture showroom. It was decorated with thick fabrics and potted plants. "This is our Casket Display Room. As you can see, we have a large selection of caskets and all of them are competitively priced."

"So how much for the cheapest coffin you sell?"

"That would be our Burrelson, over here," and he led Blake to the far corner of the room where an ugly blue-crepe casket sat on a gurney. "As you can see, the Burrelson doesn't have a lot of bells and whistles. For example, it doesn't have a gasket to keep out the elements. But for those on a tight budget it will do nicely."

"How much is it?"

"This one is only $1,395."

"Which one is the most expensive?"

"That would be the Majestic, over here." They walked a few paces to a bronze tomb the size of a sub-zero refrigerator. "You can see the fine craftsmanship. Now, I'll warn you, it's expensive, but some people choose to honor their loved ones with the Majestic. They'll say to me, 'Glen, I'm not a rich man, but I think my Wanda deserves this one.'"

"How much is it?"

"I believe this one costs $24,400."

"Wow, that sounds like a lot for a casket."

"Well, it is, and we don't sell many of them."

"Which one is the most popular?"

"Our big seller would be this Cashmere here. It sells for $4,500. You can see it's an attractive option and comes with a gasket. Of course, these prices don't include the cost of the vault."

"The vault?"

"Yes. Once the hole is dug, our vaults are placed into the ground. The casket is then placed into the vault. All our vaults include state-of-the-art gaskets so they have an airtight seal."

"And how much is a vault?"

"Again, it depends on quality. But the average vault will run you about $1,500."

They admired the other caskets before moving on, including the Regal Gold ($10,000), the Princeton ($8,000), and the Silver Rose ($6,000). Each one had a satin pillow and looked quite comfy.

Glen then took him to the Refrigeration Room. It was a nondescript room the temperature of a grocery store's walk-in produce section. There were four corpses on a table. They were modestly covered by white sheets. Each of them was toe-tagged.

"The bodies are brought to this room first. They'll stay here until the family gives us permission to embalm."

They walked down the hall and entered a door labeled Embalming Room.

"Now, I probably shouldn't let you in here, but I think it'll be okay if you just take a quick peek."

"It's all right; I don't need to see . . . "

"It'll be fine—here, just take a quick look."

The room was brightly lit. Two corpses, covered by sheets, separately lay on trays, like dark blue enamel roasting drip pans, so the fluids could drain. An incision had been made into each of their jugulars and the blood was removed and replaced with embalming fluid.

"Are all the bodies embalmed?"

"Only those that need to be preserved for a funeral. If they're going to be cremated we don't embalm them."

"What's the percentage of people who are cremated?"

"Maybe forty percent, but the percentage keeps growing every year."

Next, Glen took Blake to the Cosmetology, Dressing, and Casketing Room. An elderly woman who was roughly the color of her sheet was having her hair done by a woman who'd been her personal hairdresser for years. A middle-aged man dressed in a gray pinstriped suit and tie was having his hair cut. In the corner another older gentleman was lathered up to be shaved. The final corpse was safely tucked into her casket. She looked radiant in a pink gown and thick coat of make-up. Blake wondered if her family would recognize her. He also noticed there was a small urn tucked into the casket near her feet.

"What's that?" Blake asked.

"That's her cat. It isn't technically allowed, but we like to honor the requests of our customers who wish to be buried with their pets. In this case, her cat died and was cremated a few years back and she asked to be buried with its cremains."

Glen checked his watch. "It looks like I have a few more minutes. Come on, I'll take you to the crematory."

"That'd be great. Thanks."

"Let's swing by the office real quick so I can get some of those brochures for you."

He rummaged through his desk. "Doggone it, Glen, I know you put them here somewhere," Glen said. Blake looked around the office. On the wall there was a Rotary certificate, an award from the Phoenix Chamber of Commerce for Best Mortuary 1996, and a framed newspaper article with a photo of Glen standing in front of the funeral Home. The headline read, "Funeral Home Celebrates Ten Years Serving Phoenix Area." Glen had a full head of hair in the photo and a hearse in the background was a 1970's vintage Cadillac.

"Oh, here they are, Glen, you scatter brain," Glen said and handed a few glossy brochures to Blake. "Might just want to take a quick look at those for the newspaper article."

"Thanks."

Glen then took him to the crematory.

"Most funeral homes don't have their own crematory. They'll just use the State's. But I said to myself, 'Glen, if you're going to have a full service mortuary, then doggone it, you ought to have a crematorium.' So here you go."

"Yeah, I've never seen one of these."

"Like I said, we're seeing more and more people choose cremation. I suppose the thought of their body decomposing underground is an unpleasant thought."

Blake recalled stories by Edgar Allan Poe about people being buried alive and he remembered being scared out of his wits when he and his friends sneaked into the graveyard at night to play Hide 'n Seek. One night he unintentionally broke Steve's nose with a right hook when Steve jumped out from behind a headstone. Steve was laughing so hard he barely felt it. It was still unsettling for Blake to walk through a cemetery at night. And now he had the image of a fat worm roaming at will into one hole of a corpse's skull and then out another.

"This here's the oven. We call it the chamber, and it's no Easy Bake Oven. It'll hit 1,900 degrees. Mind you, most industrial ovens will barely crank out a third of that heat."

The chamber wasn't as large as Blake imagined it would be. It was designed for only one body at a time, consistent with state law.

"It's not that big," Blake said.

"Yeah, it'll fit a large person. But we had one time, no make that two times, where they wouldn't fit. They were just too darned heavy. I'll bet they went a good four hundred pounds."

"So what did you do?"

"Well, we had to cut them in half. I know it's not pretty, but that's what we had to do. I would appreciate it if you wouldn't mention that in the article, of course."

"Uh, yeah, of course."

"The law forbids putting a corpse in naked—we need to put them in a box or container of some kind. So most heirs will put them in the least expensive box they can find. It makes no sense to burn a perfectly good casket after all."

Blake saw the wisdom in that, but then wondered about the logic of *burying* a perfectly good casket, too.

"We also rent caskets. If your loved one chooses to be cremated, we can put him in a nice rental for the funeral, and then go ahead and remove him and put him in a cheap container for the actual cremation."

"Really? You have rental caskets? Who'd want to be buried in a used casket? Sorry, but that's creepy."

"Our rentals have removable bed liners, so we dispose of the liner after each use. It's actually quite practical, but we don't recommend it, per se."

Blake assumed this recommendation carried a smaller price tag, and hence the reluctance to recommend it.

"Cremation is less expensive," Glen said, as if he'd read Blake's mind. "There's no need for an expensive casket and vault. And, of course, you'd save on the burial plot, too."

"Are there restrictions on what you can do with the ashes?"

"Not really. You can bury them in your backyard, or bury them on top of someone who's already in the grave. Or you can spread them wherever you like, because they present no health risk."

Blake learned that ashes can be sprinkled, poured, decanted, splashed, or sprayed however, and just about wherever, the heirs want. Loving heirs have been known to keep them in fancy urns, or in plain milk cartons. They have sprinkled them from mountains and airplanes, and spread them over flower beds. Others put them in helium balloons. Or, for the NRA buff, it might be a fun gift idea to put grandpa's ashes in a dozen shotgun shells. Still others have mixed the ashes into paint and commissioned oil portraits of the dearly departed.

George had made it clear that he'd wanted to be cremated. His daughter, Sarah, didn't like this, for cremation is a controversial choice for a practicing Catholic. It was strictly forbidden in Medieval Europe (unless there were multitudes of rotting corpses lying around after a major sword battle, in which case they were piled up and burned). Catholics are now allowed the right, but the church's position is still wishy-washy. The handwringing occurs because the body is considered to be a holy object and shouldn't be destroyed; otherwise it might impede God's ability to resurrect it to the proper form. It is not entirely clear what will happen to the victims of a hand grenade, but there remains the comfort that God will provide for them somehow.

The chamber was preheated to 1,900 degrees. George was then placed into an inexpensive carton and shoved into the chamber. His organs and soft tissues disappeared almost immediately from the intense heat. But his bones took longer. A good rule of thumb is one hour cooking time for every one hundred pounds. So, in George's case, he would be finished in about an hour and a half.

There was a viewing area for family members who wished to watch the incineration. A love seat with plaid fabric, two matching side chairs, and a coffee table faced the chamber about twenty feet away. A few informative brochures were spread over the coffee table for lighter reading. Blake was dumbfounded when Glen told him family members occasionally chose to watch their loved ones vaporized, like they were watching the Thanksgiving turkey through the glass oven door.

After ninety minutes, George's bone fragments were swept from the chamber floor and pulverized by a crushing machine into gray powder the color of moon rock. This process took another twenty minutes. The result was sand-sized granules mixed with a few larger pieces of stubborn bone bits, perhaps the size of a pea. George's ashes weighed in at six pounds.

The assistant funeral director at Schmidt's then solemnly presented Sarah with her father. In an urn.

29

Joanne was given two weeks. Two weeks to stop her daughter from killing herself. She'd used every arrow in her quiver to get that concession from Jenny, for once she'd put her mind to it she wanted it over and done with. Joanne's primary weapon was plain old fashioned guilt. She was a master, a real virtuoso. Her two daughters and husband were nearly powerless under its weight, even when they saw it coming and even when they saw it for what it was.

Did Jenny delay her starvation death march because she might change her mind? Was she not quite as certain as she thought she was? Or was she simply capitulating to the pressure from her forcible mother? She had waited this long, she decided she could wait two more weeks for her mom.

Aside from the onslaught of guilt, Joanne had other weapons, too. She would start with the most potent form of manipulation and control known to mankind: she would start with religion. For what is a more powerful disincentive to misbehave than the threat of eternal damnation? People can be persuaded to do just about anything. They will fly planes into buildings, drink cyanide Kool-Aid, perform clitoral circumcisions, and take their neighbor's fourteen-year-old daughter to the wedding bed.

When Joanne met with Jenny's Bishop (the kindhearted

plumber), she realized he didn't have the requisite fire in his belly to persuasively threaten the dire eternal consequences that were necessary here. So she went over his head to the Stake President, who was the next rung up the Mormon ladder of command. Joanne's request to meet with her daughter's Stake President was a bit unusual, but so were the circumstances, so he agreed to meet with her.

The Stake President was a distinguished man who wore his authority with airs. Unlike Jenny's plain-spoken bishop, he was a wealthy businessman who looked the part. He dressed in an expensively tailored suit and tie with a heavily starched shirt. Joanne hoped he could use his considerable ecclesiastical power of persuasion to stop this madness.

"Isn't there something you can do, President?"

"Well, Sister Kimball, the church doesn't ordinarily take a position on individual issues like this."

"But doesn't the church teach us that suicide is a sin?"

"Yes, it does. But we are also given our free agency."

"But couldn't you at least talk to her—tell her it's a serious sin? I'm sure she'd listen to you."

"And if she doesn't?"

"She will."

"But if she doesn't, what would you have me do? I can't stop her. We can only hope and pray that Heavenly Father will guide her to choose righteously."

The Stake President knew this was a potential can of worms. He was not ready to defend his position on the Eyewitness News at 10:00. And what was his position anyway? Was not eating a sin comparable to *real* suicide, the kind where you blow your brains out, or jump off a cliff? It just seemed less wicked, for some reason.

He agreed to think it over, and pray about it. Joanne had little cynicism where church leaders were concerned, because she believed they were inspired by God. However, she could feel his lukewarm-ness and knew he wouldn't wage the necessary battle for Jenny's soul against the forces of Satan. This upset her, because the Lord didn't need a weak-kneed ecclesiastical leader who weighed the political correctness before doing what was right, for evil prevails when good men do nothing.

The second stop in Joanne's three-prong attack was a lawyer. She believed Jenny was not thinking clearly. Therefore, she could not be trusted to make this irreversible decision. Joanne didn't tell Rich about her appointment with Jenny's stake president. And she didn't tell him about her meeting with the lawyer, either, because she knew he would have been upset with the meddling.

Rich had strong pro-life views, just like his wife. He voted Republican on moral grounds. He saw Jenny's situation differently, however. She was making a deeply personal choice, a choice that she alone should own; not the government, the church, or her parents. Rich believed Jenny should be allowed her "free agency" to choose and bear the consequences of that choice, for better or for worse. He ruefully acknowledged to himself that maybe he was pro-choice after all.

Joanne found her attorney. Attorney Gail Bellicose lobbied the Arizona legislature for conservative causes at every turn. She was a champion of the unborn, and enemy of illegal immigrants. She was the vanguard of the government's right to control women's bodies, but was anti-government on nearly everything else. She believed government should butt out of people's lives, except where matters of the bedroom were concerned. This paradox did not appear to trouble her.

Bellicose had written a legal article sharply criticizing the court's decision in the celebrated *Terri Schiavo* case. Schiavo suffered massive brain damage from a heart attack and was reduced to a comatose vegetable. She was unable to communicate and could not eat on her own, so a feeding tube was inserted to keep her alive. After a few years, her husband wanted to disconnect the feeding tube. But Schiavo's parents wanted no such thing. The lines were drawn and the legal battle raged for eight years.

A lower court ruled that Schiavo would not want to be kept alive in this vegetative state and allowed the husband to remove the feeding tube. Schiavo's parents appealed and the higher court ordered the tube be reinstated a few days later. After three more years the court ordered that it be removed again. This judicial whiplash at Schiavo's expense was exhausting.

Right to Lifers rallied around Schiavo's parents and vilified her husband. This was judicial murder! Politicians, eager to win the hearts and minds of God-fearing voters everywhere, rushed to the scene, vying for their fifteen minutes on one cable TV program or another. Schiavo's life and death became a frantic feeding frenzy. "For the love of God and country, this comatose vegetable must be kept alive!"

Not to be outdone, the Pro-Choicers shouted back. The moral outrage on both sides was palpable. There were marches, sit-ins, and hunger strikes (how apropos). Both sides, the left and the right, raced in on their high horses from far and wide. These galloping do-gooders rode in on Arabians, Clydesdales, and Shetlands, for even their small horses were high.

President Bush galloped into Washington, D.C. on the highest horse of them all, signing legislation specifically tailored to keep the feeding tube lodged snugly in Schiavo's throat. There was a stampede of hooves brandishing their moral values in the face of an appellate court rife with liberal debauchery. They high-stepped their way around the manure, screeching at the top of their lungs that the moral fiber of our great nation, conceived in liberty, with justice for all, would become morally bankrupt if Schiavo's feeding tube was not reinserted, post haste.

Even the Pope weighed in, proclaiming that health care providers were morally bound to provide food and water to all individuals, including human vegetables. To do otherwise was to play God. The Pope's commentary did not address whether the artificial feeding tube wasn't something straight out of God's playbook to begin with, for without it she would have been long dead.

Schiavo's parents condemned the removal of the feeding tube as illegal and immoral euthanasia. A few conservative tycoons even offered to pay Schiavo's husband one million dollars if he would cede her guardianship rights to them so they could plug her back in. The courts ordered the feeding tube to be removed for the final time and Schiavo died from starvation thirteen days later.

Joanne hoped Gail Bellicose, Esq. would passionately advocate for the government's right to intervene in Jenny's case, just as she had in *Schiavo*. Joanne met with her in an unpretentious office. There were no diplomas on the wall. There was only a photo of her family. Piles of papers and legal briefs were stacked on the desk and floor. Bellicose was a zealous advocate and handled many of her cases for free. She was unmotivated by financial remuneration or greed, for she was a true believer and not just a convenient one.

Joanne laid out the case before her. Was there anything she could do legally to force her daughter to eat? The case had many similarities to *Schiavo*, but there was a clear difference; Jenny had the capacity to articulate what she wanted.

"Has your daughter ever been declared to be mentally incompetent?"

"No."

"Could you find a doctor who would testify that she is mentally incompetent to manage her own affairs? If so, we might be able to create some good law here."

"I don't know," Joanne said. "I doubt it. Jenny is pretty sharp and handles most of the household finances. But she did have a concussion at the time of the accident. The doctors thought she might have a serious head injury. But luckily she recovered from that."

"Hmmm . . . " Bellicose tapped her pencil into the palm of her hand. "The law can't force a competent adult to undergo medical treatment, or to eat and drink for that matter," she said. "I believe life is sacred and government ought to do all it can to limit its destruction. Don't get me wrong; I support individual liberty, but sometimes we need to step on a toe or two for the greater good. And I refuse to apologize for that."

"So," Joanne asked, "unless we prove Jenny is mentally incompetent there's nothing we can do legally?"

"I'm afraid not. Liberal activists have seen to that." Bellicose was fond of lambasting "judicial activism." She believed
her judicial activism was appropriate, but the judicial activism of others was morally reprehensible.

Joanne was discouraged when she left the lawyer's office.
What good were laws that failed to protect us from ourselves?
She didn't appreciate the way government forced people to
behave, but it ought to at least force its citizens to eat.

Joanne's third prong of attack, her final hope, was Congress. Perhaps they could pass a law quickly, or bring political
pressure to bear on the situation, like they had in the *Schiavo*
case. Joanne had apparently been skipping the news or she
would have known that Congress hardly passed anything, and
especially not a bill that infringed on a personal "right." The
political parties would use the issue to further drive a wedge
between the reds and the blues, each side offering up its sanc-
timonious drivel about how the Jenny Lawson bill would spell
an end to the Republic. The right would sound the warning
cry from every church steeple in America that there was no
greater evil than the loss of life. The left would sound a similar
alarm that the Jenny Lawson bill would take away every individual right so painstakingly earned. Did all the sit-ins and
bra-burnings count for nothing?

The Kimballs had modestly donated to the perpetual
re-election campaigns of Howard Arnold, their U.S. congres-
sional representative. Arnold's district had been gerryman-
dered to ensure his continual re-election in the conservative
population of Mesa and surrounding Republican communi-
ties. His campaign staff worked tirelessly to come up with a
new slogan every two years—each one more dire in its appeal

to stop America's moral decay.

The congressman's most recent campaign, "Arnold, Now More Than Ever," generated a war chest of $2,000,000. Arnold worked hard for his war chest, personally soliciting money from every God-loving person in his district. He reminded them that without their financial support, the vast left wing conspiracy would take away their guns, jack up their taxes, allow the Mexicans to waltz in, and take God out of the classroom.

The wall along the Rio Grande grew higher with every speech he made. But he was always on the lookout for other issues to brandish his conservative credentials. When the congressman learned of Joanne's request, he immediately hired a pollster to determine how he felt about the issue. He didn't want to be seen on *Larry King Live* opposite this articulate young woman who wanted to take no life other than her own. If the poll showed the majority of his constituents favored legislation, and especially his larger donors, he would sponsor it.

But the poll results were ambivalent. There just wasn't enough public outrage over a competent adult quadriplegic choosing not to eat.

The letter came too late to pass a bill, in any event:

> I am sorry to inform you that our office is unable to sponsor legislation in this unfortunate matter. I believe strongly in a robust Right to Life platform, and I pledge my full support in favor of legislation to further those principles. I appreciate the support you and Richard have given me in the past and I look forward to your continued support in the future.
>
> Sincerely,
> Howard Arnold

The days passed and Joanne had no more arrows in her quiver. She pled with Jenny and she pled with Clay. But the support she received from Rich was tepid. And Liz had given up too, for both she and her dad had come to believe that Jenny had the exclusive right to make this decision. So they fought. Their tenuous relationship stretched to the point of snapping. Their daughter was about to take her own life, and neither one of them could prevent it.

30

"Right this way," the maître d' told Blake, Naomi, Steve, and Alison. His voice was one octave too high and his hair was spiked, so that he looked like a stegosaurus. "We only have outdoor seating available this evening, but I have a table with a view that's to die for," he said and then sashayed away carrying four leather-bound menus to a table that didn't have a view that anyone would actually die for.

"Your server will be right with you," he said, and then lightly touched Blake's arm before he shimmied away.

"I think he likes you," Steve said to Blake.

Neither Naomi nor Alison paid any attention to the maître d' because they were too busy checking each other out. Initially they did so silently, and then with both guns blazing. "I *love* those jeans! Where'd you get them? And those are the cutest shoes *ever!*" *What, they were wearing shoes?* Blake and Steve wondered.

Neither Blake nor Steve noticed what the other wore. Steve had spent a total of two minutes getting dressed. He'd grabbed the first semi-clean thing he saw, took a whiff of the pits, and declared it adequate. There was only the brief internal consternation: "Does this go with this?" Blake did roughly the same thing.

Naomi and Alison continued to talk over each other,

commenting on every item the other one wore, while Blake and Steve checked out the clientele. Guilliani's was the trend-iest meat market in town—the new place to be seen. Nearly everyone there was looking over everyone else's shoulder, pre-tending to care about what the other self-absorbed-one was yammering on about.

"Thanks for joining us last minute," said Steve.

"Hey," Blake said, "we're glad you called."

"Chad's been colicky for a week, but he's finally feeling better and we needed a break," said Alison. "We haven't been out in forever, and I could use a drink."

"I thought you had Alex this weekend," Steve said to Blake.

"My mom is babysitting," said Blake. "He loves it over there anyway because my mom lets him get away with murder."

"She's a hoot," Naomi said and smiled at Blake. "The first time I met her she asked if we'd had intercourse. I'm dead serious. I about died."

"Oh my God! What did you *say*?" asked Alison.

"I lied. But since then she's been so nice to me. She's one funny lady. And she adores Blake." She turned to Blake and kissed him on the cheek. "You're such a good son."

"How's the knee?" Blake asked Steve.

"What's the matter with your knee?" Alison asked her husband.

"He hasn't told you about his knee?"

"I've told you, Ali," Steve said. "Remember? It's been kill-ing me."

"You lying sack!" Blake said. "We're going for a run to-morrow and I don't want any excuses."

"I'll see how it feels. How's work going?"

"Seven. Before it gets too hot. I'll meet you at the corner of Scottsdale and Bell. And don't be late."

"Fine. So how's it going at the paper?"

"Well, circulations are down, and . . . "

"No, I mean with that story you're so wrapped up in."

"What story?" Alison asked.

"Blake's been working on a big story on suicide. Well, not really suicide, right? Isn't it more like killing yourself when you're sick? Hell, I can't explain it. You tell her, Blake."

"Well, I've got caught up in a story about end of life choices, I guess you'd call it. You know—the right to end your life when you can't stand the pain any longer, or when there's no hope. I got wrapped up in the issue sort of by accident."

"I'll admit I haven't really looked into it," Alison said. "All that Dr. Kevorkian stuff. I feel sorry for people like that, but I just think it's wrong. God should decide when we die."

"I think Kevorkian was onto something," Blake said. "I just think he went about it the wrong way."

"Me too," said Naomi.

"He went to prison," Alison said. "And that's where he belonged. Didn't he kill like fifteen people or something?"

"I honestly don't know much about him," said Blake, "and that's not really what I'm writing about any way. I'm talking about people who take their own life."

"And I think that's wrong. I'm sorry. That's up to God."

"But don't you believe in chemotherapy and heart bypass surgery and stuff like that?"

"Of course I do."

"Well, then, if it's totally up to God, why waste our time

with medicine? Why even bother injecting ourselves into God's business? Maybe we shouldn't cheat nature and just let them die."

"Blake," she said and shook her head. "That's totally different. We're helping them *live*, not helping them die. If we allow these Kevorkian types to get away with it, then before you know it we'll have a bunch of liberals with their death panels deciding who's worth saving and who isn't."

The handsome waiter arrived with the bottle of cabernet they'd ordered. Both Naomi and Alison touched their hair and smiled at him.

The four of them toasted each other as friends. But before Steve could change the subject to the Diamondbacks winning streak, or even to colic, Alison wanted to drive a final stake into this "right to die" business.

"I hope your story will be evenhanded."

"I really don't have an agenda here. I just think it's an important topic, and it's one we ought to be talking about."

"Well, I hope you'll point out that it's selfish to commit suicide. And if the radicals get their way it'll lead to killing more innocent people. I'm not trying to be overly dramatic here. I'm just saying."

"I'm not talking about killing people. I'm talking about someone who *wants* to die. Don't you think that person should be allowed to die peacefully and without pain if they want?"

Alison closed her eyes and smiled, but no one would mistake the wry smile for agreement.

"Yeah," said Steve, now ready to weigh in, carefully, so as not to insult Blake, but to make his wife happy. "Nobody in their right mind *wants* to die. They'll cut off an arm like that hiker guy, or they'll drink piss to stay alive."

"But," Naomi jumped in, "the issue isn't whether they're going to die, but *how* and *when* they die. Right? Isn't that the issue? I'm with Blake. I don't see what the big deal is. I think it makes sense. Nobody's coercing them."

"Yeah," Blake said. "If they have to die, they just want the least bad death."

"It all sounds good," said Alison. "But a *right* to die could become a *duty* to die, especially for old people who think they're a burden on their families. The government could just step in and say, 'Okay, time's up; you cost too much to keep alive, so now we have to kill you.' It's a slippery slope, all this killing business, and once we open that door we cheapen life."

"That's a good point," said Blake. "But there are only a couple of states that allow for physician-assisted suicide. We've had about fifteen years to see what's happened in those states. And you know what? There have only been a few hundred people who've done it. That's it. So it's not like there's been a stampede to die. And, remember, all of them *wanted* to die."

"Yeah, but we can't condone killing people," said Alison. "Our society doesn't do that. We're a Christian nation. We honor life." She looked at Steve.

"I agree with Alison," said Steve. "I just think it sends the wrong message." Alison reached over and took his hand.

The server was back for their orders. They quickly scanned the fifteen page menu. Blake and Steve ordered steak and Alison ordered salmon. When Naomi chose the vegan tofu special Alison made a thin smile and the tiniest little humph, as if to say "of *course* she would order vegan tofu."

272 | WARREN DRIGGS

When the server left, Steve shifted in his chair and racked his brain for a topic they would all agree on. Just as he was about to ask if they'd seen the latest DiCaprio movie, Blake returned to the subject.

"You just said this Christian nation doesn't accept killing, but of course we do. We do it all the time."

"How so?"

"We kill people in self-defense, and that's okay. We kill people with capital punishment, and that's apparently okay. And we kill people in war, and that's okay, too. So all this so-called 'justified' killing hasn't made us so dense that we can't distinguish one type of killing from another. And I don't mean to beat a dead horse, but all those people we kill are people who *don't want* to be killed. What *I'm* talking about is people who *do* want to die, people who are already dying.

"And, by the way," Blake continued, "it wasn't always that way with Christian nations. A few days ago I read where the earliest Christians condemned all killing, even in war. They just laid down their weapons and were killed rather than raise the sword against another human being."

"Seriously?" said Steve.

"Yeah, but then the Roman Empire started getting massacred by the whole rape and plunder crowd, so they wised up and changed the rules."

"Maybe so," said Alison, "but it's against the law and I bet most people think it should be."

"I think the more important question," Blake said, "is not whether it's against the law, but whether it *ought* to be against the law. We can't automatically say a law is "morally right" just because a majority of the people believe it is."

"Sure we can," Alison said. "That's how we decide what's morally right in the first place."

"Was slavery morally right? If we decided the morality of something by how we felt about it we'd get it wrong a lot of the time. Maybe our feelings are just irrational prejudice. We used to "feel" black people were inferior, but obviously our feelings were wrong."

"Would you want to know when you're going to die?" Steve blurted out to change the direction of the conversation.

"No way, I think that'd be creepy," said Naomi. "The only way I'd want to know is if it was a long way off; like I was over sixty-five or something."

"I think Jesus ought to answer this debate," said Alison. "And I think He already has." Alison was willing to ignore for the moment her Christian belief that Jesus presumably chose to end His life when He did.

"Let's say you have two choices," Blake said. "One is to die painlessly in your sleep. The other is to die miserably after suffering for, let's say, six months. Which would you choose? Of course you'd want to die painlessly in your sleep. So why should we oppose someone facing that choice in real life? Why should we condemn them, or prevent them, when we'd prefer the same choice?"

The meals arrived and everyone politely surveyed everyone else's and commented how good the other person's choice looked, even the tofu.

"But," Alison said, "there's always the possibility of a cure. You can defy the odds and recover. People do it all the time."

"Yeah, that's true," Blake said. "But would you *never* pull the plug on someone? Would you *never* give up on a brain dead person being kept alive by modern medicine because a cure might be just around the corner?"

"But doctors sometimes make mistakes. They label patients hopeless but then they recover."

"You're right about that," Blake said. "Sometimes it happens. But just because they are sometimes wrong doesn't mean they can never know for sure if someone is hopeless. That would be like saying that since some people mistake apricots for peaches no one can ever be certain which is which. Sometimes there's no doubt at all. But, yeah, I agree with you that we ought to err on the side of caution."

"Well, let's hope so!" Alison said.

"Wouldn't it be great," Naomi interjected, "if we could figure out a way to separate religion from science."

"Good luck with that," Blake said.

"It seems we got sidetracked a long time ago," Naomi continued, "and now I think we've got it all backwards. Humans worshipped at the altar of religion for centuries because we didn't have science. All we had was the witch doctor. So everyone worshipped Zeus or the Sun God, or whatever. But eventually science got a toehold and we figured out that Zeus wasn't real, and that the sun wasn't God. Now we look back and say those people were crazy ridiculous. But they weren't ridiculous back then."

"Yeah," Blake said. "You have to wonder what they'll say about some of the stuff we believe in now. I'm sure they'll get a kick out of what we think is cutting edge."

"All I know," said Naomi, "is science and religion have been at it ever since. They probably always will."

"And that's too bad," Steve said.

Naomi lifted her glass of wine. "To the hope they'll get it together." The others raised their glasses, including Alison.

"You know," Blake said. "It shouldn't be that complicated. Why can't religion focus on a moral code and let science do its thing rather than demonize it."

"I don't necessarily think it does," Alison said.

"Really? They hauled Galileo off to jail, and there are still a bunch of people who insist Darwin was a kook. Whether the earth is flat, or how evolution works, or when dinosaurs lived: what do those things have to do with our morality? They ought to be the province of science, not religion. I mean, the advancement of carbon dating isn't important in deciding whether to be kind or to love each other, is it?"

The others contemplated Blake's comments. Steve poured more wine for each of them.

"I like this place," Steve said. "We'd come back."

"I think God has already spoken," said Alison. "Rather than focus on the scientific mysteries maybe we'd be better off just following the advice God has already given us in the scriptures."

Blake wasn't sure if she was referring to the Bible, the Koran, the Talmud, or the writings of Zepheri, the medicine man. He didn't say anything, because what would be the point? Both of their minds appeared to have closed on the subject. But he was glad he didn't live back in the day when people lived on a flat surface under the demanding eye of Zeus.

"Well, I guess we can't solve all this tonight," Steve laughed. "But we tried!" Another hopeful chuckle.

"Yeah, I think you're right," Blake said. "I know you're all ready to talk about something more fun than death. I know I am. I just think it's an interesting subject, this concept of the good death. I'm not sure how the story will turn out, but it's something plenty of people are struggling with."

"The good death?" asked Steve.

"The term 'euthanasia' comes from ancient Greece. Literally translated it means 'The good death.' Of course, that simple fact, because I know it and because I care, doesn't make me enlightened. And it sure as hell doesn't give me immunity from death. I think it's pretty sobering that every king, ruler, prophet, scientist, rock star, monarch, pope, and pharaoh has died."

"So true," Alison said. "Let's just hope it doesn't happen for a while."

"I'll drink to that," said Steve and raised his glass. The others clinked amiably, for the topic had run its course and they were friends.

31

Jenny's fast began without ceremony or fanfare. She just stopped eating. She sipped on water occasionally throughout the day, maybe half a cup, but that was it. She also discontinued any medications; her daily multivitamins seemed counterintuitive at this point. So did seat belts, childproof safety caps, guardrails, and sunscreen.

Clay ate his meals outside the home. He didn't want to satisfy his hunger in front of her, so the kitchen was closed. Joanne and Rich were frequent guests those first few days, and so was Liz, so pregnant now that she waddled. They put on their happy faces and talked about superficial things, but the elephant in the room loomed large and clumsy. It bumped into each of them from time to time with its tail or its trunk or its huge hind legs, for it couldn't get comfortable in the small quarters of Clay and Jenny's rambler.

Blake met with Jenny again on Day Three of her fast. She was propped up in her bed. Her wheelchair had been banished to a corner of the room as if it were in forced timeout. She would never sit in it again. There were no pill bottles, medical equipment, hoses, wires, and all the other paraphernalia you might expect to see dangling from a sick person's bed. There wasn't even a jar of Vicks Vapor rub, or a cough drop.

Blake noticed that Jenny was now collapsing in on herself.

Her cheeks were sunken and there were dark rings under her once beautiful blue eyes. She no longer had the will or the strength to lift her right arm the few inches she had worked so hard to earn over four long years of therapy. Her eyes were hollow, yet there was still life in them. She mostly stared at Clay and said little.

"Jenny, is it still okay if I tell your story in the newspaper, or in a book?" Blake was now flirting with the idea of writing something more than a simple newspaper article.

Jenny simply nodded, as if speaking would require too much physical effort on her part.

"Are you sure about that, Jen?" asked her mom, now resigned to her daughter's decision but fiercely protective of her.

"Yeah, thanks mom, but I'm sure." It was faint.

"Do you ever have doubt about your decision to, uh, move on to the next life?"

"It's okay," Jenny whispered, "you can say 'die.'"

"Do you have any doubts or regrets about choosing to die now?"

"No."

"You must have a lot of strength and courage."

"Not really. But I have a lot of faith. Both Clay and I do." She turned her eyes to Clay but not her head.

Joanne left the room to take a call on her cell.

"Have you made peace with your mom? I know she disagreed with this."

"My mom loves me and I never doubted it. Ever. Nobody cares more about me than my mom. My mom and Clay." She spoke so softly, as if she were just breathing the words.

"Are you afraid?"

"Not too much. I just hope I can sleep the last few days. I don't want to take any drugs, but maybe I will if the pain gets too bad," she whispered.

Blake was touched by Jenny's grace and courage. She was making an unpopular and painful choice with honesty and conviction. Clay held a child's sippy cup with a small spout to her mouth. She took just a sip. Rather than sooth her it appeared to cause her pain when she swallowed. Clay then held an ice cube and gently rubbed it over her dry and cracking lips. Her eyes never left him.

Joanne returned to the room with Liz as Blake was leaving. Blake hovered in the doorway, like a voyeur, hoping to see the interaction between mother and daughter. Even though Joanne disagreed with Jenny's decision there was no more pleading and no more guilt. Just love, and a lot of it.

Joanne lay down next to Jenny on one side of the bed and Liz lay down on the other side. Liz's huge belly nestled next to Jenny's tiny frame. One sister was the picture of radiant health, new life ready to spring forth from her, and the other sister the picture of death and decay. They took turns touching Jenny's stringy hair and stroking her cheeks and forehead. Between their tears, they told Jenny how strong she was and how proud they were of her.

A week earlier, Liz had come over to Jenny and Clay's house. Jenny was in a funny mood, the type of mood that comes from a good buzz, even though she'd been sober. The burden of decision had been lifted and Jenny felt free, as free as she'd felt since before her accident.

"You can take my clothes," she'd said to Liz.

"Your clothes are stupid," Liz said.

"What? You don't want this beanie? You don't want these slippers?"

"No, they're hideous!"

"I'm shocked. At least tell me you want these sweats."

"No way, but I'll take some of your jewelry."

"What's your favorite?" Jen asked.

"I love that pearl necklace."

"That's my favorite, too. I want you to have it."

Just as suddenly the mood changed. Somehow they'd hit a nerve, the reality of the situation, and they didn't know how, or why. Liz burst into tears.

"I don't want it, Jen. I want you to have it. I want you to be here."

"I love you, Liz. I'm sorry I can't be here for you."

Liz hugged her sister hard, like she wouldn't let her go. All the talk had been cheap to that point. Yeah, Jenny was going to stop eating. Sure. Whatever. We'll cross that bridge when, and if, it actually gets here. Well, it had arrived and the reality of it was awful.

"I'll miss you so much," Liz cried. "I'll wear that stupid necklace every day, and every day I'll think about you."

"I'll be watching you, sis."

"Well, you won't see me wearing that ugly beanie. No way," she laughed through her tears. But it wasn't a funny laugh, it was a tragic one. For Liz knew she would cherish that beanie for as long as she lived.

Now, a week later, with Jenny weakening, Liz told her about the baby. It was due in two months. Jenny wanted to feel the baby kick, but she couldn't. So Liz scooted up in the bed and rested her belly against Jenny's cheek. Jenny smiled when she felt the baby move.

Liz told Jenny of her favorite childhood memories; the huts they made with blankets in the family room, stacks of encyclopedias pinning the blanket to the coffee table, and how they almost burned down the garage, and the time they cut a piece of fabric from the curtains in the living room to make a skirt for their doll, convinced their mom would never notice because it had been a small piece of fabric at the bottom of the curtain. Jenny said little, she just rested between the two women in her life who would have traded her places if they could.

Over the next several days, visitors came to say their last goodbyes. Hardly any of them actually acknowledged they were there to see her for that reason. It was obvious. They tiptoed in, saying little to Jenny—they mostly just whispered to others in the room. They whispered things like, "How's she doing?" or "Has she changed her mind at all?" or "How's Clay holding up?" They were uncomfortable visitors who were there because they could not imagine not going.

And what *do* you say in those circumstances? "Hope you die soon?" or "So, do you think Clay will remarry right away?" or "So, are you hungry yet?" Some of them tried to be happy, and even crack a joke or two. But it was so forced that it just made it even more awkward.

By the ten-day mark, Jenny was only taking a sip or two of water. She weighed no more than seventy pounds. Despite the vigilance of her family she developed ugly bed sores that would have been horribly painful if she could have felt them. Mostly she slept. Her doctor came every day to take her vital signs and estimated she could last another week, at the most, before she "passed." Her doctor was a compassionate woman who struggled with the meaning of her oath where Jenny was concerned. She'd taken the Hippocratic Oath that forbade her from doing harm to her patient. But what did that mean? What if her patient *asked* her to help end her suffering? Would that be a violation of her oath? Or would it be a violation *not* to intervene and help her end her suffering? She wondered.

This caring doctor knew that modern society assumes death is rare and can be indefinitely postponed. Join the gym, take a multivitamin, get a good colonoscopy and mammogram every few years, and you should be good to go! There is death and disease, but it is well hidden. When a tsunami or earthquake kills thousands of people in a foreign land, or when a friend of a friend dies of cancer, it is brushed off as an unfortunate aberration. But when the Reaper strikes close to home there is surprise, even outrage, for modern American society forgets just how common death really is. Human dying, especially in the western world, is done behind closed doors. So when someone personally knows a child that dies, he sees the process as more exceptional than it really is.

By Day Fifteen, Jenny was mostly incoherent. The only visitors now were her parents. Clay guarded her privacy and met other well-wishers at the front door with a friendly but firm request that she not be disturbed. "Well, please tell her that we stopped by," they said. "Oh, of course I will," he promised them, as if she were awake and coherent. These were charitable win-win visits. The visitors got credit for visiting and Jenny was left undisturbed.

The last time Jenny was awake was Day Sixteen. Rich

knelt next to her bed and held her tiny stiff hand in his.

"Jen, I know you can hear me. I hope you can feel what is in my heart." This was more difficult and heartbreaking than he could ever have imagined. "You have been, and always will be, the sunshine of my life. I remember when you first learned to ride a bike. You said, 'I'll show you how to do it, Dad. It's cinchy.' You have been showing me how to live ever since. And now you are showing me how to die; with grace, courage, and dignity. I am so proud of you."

Rich didn't even try to hold back his tears. "When I walked you down the aisle I cried tears of joy because I knew you were going to be with someone who loved you. And now I'm doing it again. God is waiting for you, Jen. I know He is. I just know it. You will walk to Him, Jen. No, sweetheart, you will *run* to Him." Rich could not finish. He buried his head on the pillow next to her. Tears slid down the sides of her face. She knew how much her dad loved her.

Joanne, always in control, had little of it now. "Jenny, it's me . . . Mom." The words came out slowly between sobs. "If I could be half the woman you are . . . if only I could have half your strength and courage . . . I didn't want you to do this because I was selfish . . . I didn't want to lose you . . . I'm so sorry.

"We might be separated for a time . . . but I will see you again. I know I will. Until then I'll carry you in my heart wherever I go. I won't forget you, Jen, not for a minute. I'm so proud to be your mom. Now you are free to go. We'll be okay. We have each other. We'll be strong and so will you. You will play beautiful music again and I will count the hours . . . until I can see . . . my baby . . . girl again."

Clay bent down and lifted his bride off the bed. He cradled her, rocking her as if she were a child. He said nothing. He just stood with her in his arms, swaying back and forth. Jenny opened her eyes and stared at him. He kissed her dry rough lips. He laid her back down on the bed and stroked her hair. She closed her eyes for the final time.

Jenny was now unconscious, finally free from her pain. Her breathing was steady and strong for two hours. And then it changed. She began to breathe rapidly, like she was hiking a steep hill, her mouth agape, almost like a pant. On and on it went for an hour, her small chest heaving under the lightweight cotton sheet.

Clay dabbed her lips and mouth with a small wet sponge attached to the end of a stick that looked like a grape lollipop. How long could this go on? How long could her heart beat at that pace?

In an instant it changed. She stopped panting and her breathing slowed. She took long gasps of breath and then exhaled them. Then the rhythm changed: a gasp of air, an exhale, and then a pause. Another gasp, another pause. Within a minute or two, the pauses grew longer. A gasp of breath to fill her lungs and then an exhale. They waited five, six, seven seconds, and then another gasp. After each exhale they waited, hovering over her. They willed her to take another gasp of air, holding their breaths as they did, torn between wanting her to inhale and wanting for her suffering to end.

They claimed to know for certain there was life after death—that Jenny would live on, but still there was some doubt. For how could they really know?

Another gasp, another exhale. Then nothing. No words were spoken. They hovered, they wept, they stared, they silently prayed. But they did not speak. After fifteen seconds another sharp gasp, which startled them. An exhale. Then quiet. Deathly quiet. Willing her to breathe. Willing her not to breathe. Fifteen seconds. Twenty. Thirty. Forty-five seconds. One minute. But there would be no more breaths.

Jenny's huge heart, trapped in her tiny sunken torso, had stopped. She was finally free. Still not a sound. No one said a thing. Clay bent down a few inches lower and kissed her pale forehead. Joanne and Rich fell into each other's arms and wept. Still, no one said a thing.

In the stillness of the room, there was a concentrated urge to feel Jenny's spirit, her energy, her essence. Where had she gone? Was she still in the room? Was she watching them, aware of them, trying to communicate with them? If so, her voice was too soft, her whisper too silent. Clay desperately tried to feel her presence. But he felt nothing. She was simply gone. Her body still lay there, but it wasn't Jenny. She looked the same; her color and her facial expression was the same, but she was unmistakably gone. Suddenly and permanently gone.

Two and a half months later Liz gave birth to a beautiful baby girl. Grief and sadness were replaced, at least partially so, by the miracle of rebirth. Another baby girl with big blue eyes.

They named her Jennifer.

PART II

It is stillness to live when to live is torment;
And then have we a prescription to die
When death is our physician.

—William Shakespeare

32

"Blake, please, stop! You're hurting me!"

"I'm doing this for you, Mom. It's for the best."

"What are you *doing*? You're scaring me! Let me go!"

"But, Mom, this is for your own good. Remember, we talked about it?"

"Get off of me!"

"But you said you were in pain. You said you wished you could just die. Can't you see I'm helping you? It's time, Mom."

"Blake!" She was screaming for help, but they were alone. Blake was kneeling over her, pinning her down with his knees on her arms. She was small and frail. Wisps of white hair escaped from the tidy bun at the nape of her neck. He pulled a syringe from his breast pocket and removed the cap with his teeth. There was enough poison to finally, and mercifully, stop her suffering.

"I'm doing this for you, Mom, because I can't bear to see you suffer any longer." She shook her head back and forth on the pillow as he brought the syringe down to her neck. Blake didn't *want* her to die, of course he didn't, but her suffering and the cost of her medical care was crippling.

He hesitated with the syringe just inches from her neck. The crying was louder now. He was confused.

Now someone else was speaking. "It's your turn. You get

her this time." He was nudged on his side. "Please, Blake, I need to get up early. Let me sleep this time."

It was Naomi. He was in their bed. The crying was coming from the other room where his one-year-old daughter slept.

There was that brief delay, like the delay between the lightning and the thunder, when comprehension settled in and the dream became just a dream. He sat up in bed, shaking. It wasn't real. His mother was still very much alive, living in a Scottsdale retirement center a few miles from his home.

He'd had disconcerting dreams before just like everyone else. He could hardly count the times he'd gone to school in his underpants, forgotten to study for a test, or fallen off a cliff. But this? Blake knew he would never hurt his mom, or anyone else. He'd only been in one fight in his life when an eighth-grade bully challenged him (it ended quickly when, blessedly, it'd been broken up by the P.E. teacher). So where had this dream come from? Weren't dreams a perverted extension of subconscious thoughts? He wondered if maybe he'd become too wrapped up in the whole "right to die" business.

Seven years earlier he'd published his human interest story on the aftermath of the accident on Highway 60. Hal Crawford, his surly editor who'd since retired, had given the story prime space. The piece had evolved into a five-part series in the *Arizona Republic* about end of life choices. Blake wrote about Jenny, Gene, and George; the good and the bad. He'd come to believe the issue should command center stage in the social consciousness of all people, young and old. But he wasn't obsessed about it. Not now anyway.

His story had been met with modest success. The *New York Times* picked it up and ran a summary as an extended op-ed piece. He even won a journalism award (but not the biggee). It was a local award for "Excellence in Investigative Journalism" and came with a handsome bronze plaque and a two-thousand-dollar check. Blake was an unpretentious man who wasn't prone to smugness, so he didn't parade around the office with the plaque, but it did help nourish his belief that he was, indeed, a real journalist.

When the story ran, he received mail from friends and foes. He'd struck a nerve. The unintended consequences of his story led him to speak at a few Death with Dignity conferences, the ones which champion legislation to allow for physician-assisted suicide. He wrote a few articles for their magazines, too. For a fleeting time, he thought he might become the spokesman for their cause, but then a world crisis here and a national political scandal there drowned out the conversation and his message disappeared, forgotten by everyone except the desperate.

Blake looked at the clock. It was 2:00 a.m. He got up and walked to his daughter's room. She was standing in her crib, holding onto the bars like an innocent jailbird. Her face was covered with tears and snot. There were teeth marks along the top railing, for Libby would gnaw on anything.

She stopped crying when he came into the room, just a few follow-up intakes that racked her entire twenty-one pounds. He picked her up, changed her diaper, and then held her in the rocking chair next to the crib. There was a Cinderella nightlight; otherwise the room was barely light enough to see it had been painstakingly decorated with princesses. This was all lost on Libby who didn't care—she didn't even know what a princess was. And her closet was jammed with clothes she wore maybe once because Naomi rarely came home without a new "adorable," "precious," or "darling" little outfit for Libby. Libby didn't care about that, either. They both drifted off to more pleasant dreams.

Blake awoke with Libby still in his arms. Light filtered through the partially opened curtain. He didn't move, for he knew she would wake the moment he stood from the chair. So even though his arm was numb, he waited a few more moments with her sweaty face and hair mashed against his chest. From the moment Libby was born, Blake knew that he would die for her. Yes, he would die for her, but he wouldn't kill for her.

The hinge on Libby's door squeaked and he turned to see Naomi. She was holding a cup of coffee up to him and mouthed the words Thank You. She was already dressed in workout clothes, presumably on her way to sunrise yoga. She had usually closed with Namaste and driven home before he got out of bed. She'd urged him to go for a year before she quit asking him. He went to the gym to lift weights, not practice yoga. Besides, he said he was too stiff to stretch.

Blake arrived at this point in a room with a Cinderella nightlight because he couldn't live another day without Naomi. Naomi bucked the cliché, for her beauty penetrated deeper than her skin. She was smart and assured in a way that didn't require her to prove it. Their marriage four years earlier had been the third best day of Blake's life (Alex and Libby's births occupied the top spots). She was still running her private practice in clinical psychology and business was thriving because anxiety, depression, sexual frustration, and messed up childhoods abounded. Her job was good for their marriage too, because she realized that Blake was actually quite functional.

Blake had become assistant editor at the *Republic*. He was on track to take over the top spot within a few years, courtesy of Hal Crawford who'd promoted him before he retired. He'd kept the same cubicle because he didn't want to bother with moving his stuff. Several pairs of running shoes had rotated from the corner of his space, too, because he'd run several marathons in the preceding years. But not with Steve, who'd bailed out of his commitment and had been forced to endure Blake ever since.

The dream about his mom lingered. He fed and dressed Libby and took her to see his mother. The Golden Rest was a retirement center of dubious quality, but it was all they could afford. More than one resident had wandered away from the Reminiscent Wing, where there was precious little reminiscing underway. Blake's mom was down the hall from the Reminiscent Wing, in the independent living section. She enjoyed making crafts and talking over other women there (some of whom could go on for hours, repeating the same stories in a continuous loop).

Blake found her in her room on her hands and knees, surrounded by a disorganized mess of photos, cards, and papers strewn about the floor. There were cardboard boxes stacked against a wall.

"Mom, what are you doing?"

"Oh, Blake dear, I'm so glad you're here. I'm organizing some of my albums."

"Where did you get all this stuff?"

"That cute Roberto brought these boxes up from storage

this morning. He's a darling, bless his heart." Roberto was a twenty-five-year-old CNA who had caught her fancy.

Blake peeked into a box. It was jammed with disorganized memories. There were birthday, Valentine's Day, and Mother's Day cards that she dared not toss, for she felt it would have tarnished the moments. So she kept it all in boxes—all the crayon portraits, cutout drawings of pilgrims, and report cards. There was a dried boutonniere with the rusting pin still in its stem, Polaroid photos, a garter that she'd wrestled away from Myra Stenson fifty years earlier, and a funeral program from a dead uncle.

"Wow, Mom, this is a big project."

"I know it is, and I swear I'm losing my marbles. I can't remember what half this is," she said and dropped her head in frustration, still on her hands and knees.

She wasn't as sharp as she'd used to be and her short term memory was shot. In the previous two weeks, she'd run a stop sign and scraped her Buick against the trunk of a tree. Then she'd banged the car door on the carport post. Then she'd sideswiped a car in the grocery store parking lot. And to top it all off, she'd about taken off the trunk when she'd backed into a garbage dumpster. Later that day she'd described some of the challenges of aging to Blake. "I can hardly remember what to buy at the store anymore," she said. "And for the life of me, I can't remember what day it is, or what I ate for breakfast. But, thank God, at least I can still drive."

He didn't have the heart to take her car keys. He knew that her driver's license was about to expire anyway. With failing eyesight and her hearing starting to go, he figured the problem would take care of itself when she took the test to have it renewed. She passed with flying colors.

Blake put Libby down on the floor and then kneeled next to his mom in the debris. Libby crawled over.

"Blake, hurry and get her. I don't want her to make a mess of this."

33

Steve and Alison's youngest son, Chad, was now a spoiled eight-year-old. This was the collective fault of everyone who knew him because he was so adorable. His parents hoped it wouldn't catch up with him, but so far he'd behaved like a prince. He was enrolled in every sport imaginable, but for the moment it was soccer, and his father was the coach. Regrettably, the coach knew virtually nothing about soccer.

Blake's cell rang. "Hello, this is Blake."

"Hey, um, Uncle Blake, could you, um, come to my soccer game in the morning? We're playing these one guys." He called Blake "uncle" even though there was no familial connection, only the godfather business.

"Sure, Chad, I'd love to. What time does it start?"

"Um, it's in the morning I think."

"Okay, do you know where it is?"

"Um, yeah, it's the one place by my school, but I'm not for sure."

"I'll be there. Can I talk to your mom or dad for a second?"

"Yeah, but they're already going to my game."

The next morning Blake found the school. He took Libby so Naomi could sleep in. This she would rather do than spend Saturday morning at Steve and Alison's son's pee wee soccer game. They had Alex that weekend, too. Alex was fifteen and had grown weary of being had. That's the way it always was, his parents negotiating over who "had" him. He preferred being with Blake over his mom, primarily because his mom tried too hard, both with him and all the other men in her life. Anyway, Alex had no interest in the soccer game of a little kid he hardly knew and he figured he'd be on "Libby duty" if he went. That was another thing his parents did, put him on Libby duty. So he slept in that morning and was still in bed when Blake and Libby returned at eleven.

Blake drove Naomi's minivan that morning (it had the car seat and Blake didn't have the energy to put the damned contraption into his car). He pulled into the elementary school and parked in a row of other minivans, next to Alison's minivan. He knew it was hers because it was the one with a Jesus fish on the hatchback.

The parking lot had once been the asphalt playground and the minivan straddled the remains of an old hopscotch diagram whose paint had chipped and faded. It had been a long time since Blake had been to an elementary school and his mind drifted back to a time when monkey bars spanned the asphalt and kids threw balls at each other without being sued. They ran nowhere in particular just to have fun and not to burn calories. They thought their twenty-five-year old teachers were old and the artwork that wound up on the fridge at home was collectable.

A chain link fence separated the soccer field from the adjacent street. The lower half of the fence was clogged with plastic bags and other random pieces of litter—junk mail and political yard signs, mostly—that had blown into the fence and stuck there. The soccer field was bumpy, and one side had the slope of a beach. The grass field doubled as the school's baseball diamond and there were holes at first, second, and third base. So the kids playing soccer appeared to shrink whenever the soccer scrum intersected a base. But the kids didn't seem to mind.

Blake carried Libby down the slope of grass to the sidelines where parents were congregated. It was a crisp morning and some of the parents sat in folding lawn chairs, wrapped in blankets, while others stood with hands in their pockets hunched in on themselves to stay warm. They said vaguely sincere things to pass the time, like "Now, remind me, which one is yours? Oh, she's darling." The kids scarcely felt the chill. They were so small their soccer socks were pulled nearly to their crotches. Half of them were in the scrum and the others were picking their noses, or clovers from the grass, waiting for the Capri Suns and orange wedges from Alison, the team mom.

The green team was better. They were coached by a spirited woman of about thirty who roamed the sideline yelling encouragement to her team and to one player in particular; a tall blond girl who was delightfully unaware of her talent. Blake assumed she was the coach's daughter because she was getting most of the attention. He noticed a slightly older couple standing a few yards down the sideline yelling encouragement to her, as well.

"Go, Jen! You can do it, Jen!" They were too old to be her parents. Perhaps her grandparents. There was something familiar about them, too. The man was pleasant looking with thin gray hair, and the graying woman wore spandex. She was the most vocal, yelling for both of them. When she called out to "Jen" again, Blake realized they were indeed the grandparents of this blond eight-year-old girl. Rich and Joanne Kimball had aged some, and so had their daughter, Liz, the coach.

"Rich? Joanne? Hi, it's me, Blake Morgan."

"Oh my goodness, Blake. It's so good to see you again." Joanne had softened in the years and had recaptured some of her joy. "What on earth are you doing here?"

"Oh, I'm here to see my friend's son. He's the one over there," Blake pointed, "the one picking dandelions."

"And is she yours?" Joanne said as she stuck out her index finger in front of Libby so she could grab it like most people do. Libby cooperated.

"Yeah, this is Libby."

"She is so precious."

"Thanks. So that is your granddaughter? It's hard to believe it's been nearly eight years."

"We can't believe it either. Those were tough times for us. Sometimes I wonder how we survived."

"How are you doing now?"

"It's been hard, but I think we've come to terms with it all." She looked at her husband.

"Yeah," Rich said, "it tore us apart. But in the end I think maybe it's made us closer as a family."

"When you last saw us we were . . . it was really hard, to say the least." She turned her head toward the soccer field, looking at nothing. "Sometimes I can't believe we made it through all that. But we did. And we want you to know we appreciated the way you treated our Jenny in your articles after she passed away. You showed our family a lot of compassion, and we wanted to thank you. I'm sorry we never did."

"Thanks," Blake said. "What an amazing girl she was. She

inspired me, and a whole lot of other people, too. And I'm sorry I never had the chance to tell you that."

Blake had thought of Jenny and Clay many times in the years after her death. He'd wondered what had become of her family. He thought about contacting them, but just never had. And as more time passed it became easier to procrastinate. But they had survived. And now here they were again, watching an apparition of their daughter just as they had twenty-five years earlier.

"You remember Liz?" Rich said. "She's the coach."

"Of course. She's a beautiful woman. You must be very proud of her."

"You have no idea. She's been a rock. Three kids, too. Can you believe it?"

"Good for her," Blake said. "And Clay? Are you still close to him?"

"Clay was devastated after Jenny died," Joanne said. "He immersed himself into his career—he's a lawyer, you know—and we didn't see much of him. But he's since remarried and we hear he's doing well. Of course, we wish the best for him. He was so good to Jen. He's entitled to some happiness and we hope he's found it."

Jenny came running up to her grandparents. The resemblance to her aunt was unmistakable.

"Did you see!"

"We sure did!" They high-fived her. "Great job!"

"I made one!"

"I know, we were watching."

Blake hoped that one day she would meet her own Clay Lawson. And one day he hoped she'd look through an old photo album and be inspired to write a story about her aunt Jenny.

"K, bye!"

She took off at a dead run for the scrum, her blond hair flying, without a care in the world.

34

Alison informed Steve that he'd like to go to the ballgame. He'd found it usually worked better if the idea was hers in the first place, anyway.

"That was Blake," Steve had said as he hung up the phone. "Apparently he's got some VIP tickets to the Giant's game tomorrow night. He's taking Alex and wondered if I wanted to take Chad. But I don't know; I was going to catch up on some work."

"You'd like to go to the game," she'd said. "Take Chad. It'll be fun."

"Are you sure?"

"You need a break. Go for it."

They sat directly behind the dugout. Alex, who had always taken his mitt to the Diamondback games, was too cool to do that now. To be precise, he said it was "gay." But he practically knocked over the entire row to catch the first pop-up that came their way. And Alex used to be impressed with the fact that everyone at the ballpark knew his dad. Now he just scanned the crowd for girls and wondered why the sixty-five-year-old manager wore a baseball uniform. Shouldn't they change the rule on that? he asked his dad.

"What rule?"

"The one where the coach has to wear a uniform. You

don't see football coaches wearing uniforms."

"I don't know," Blake said. "They just do it." Then Blake saw the pudgy manager waddle out to the pitcher's mound in his uniform where several of his players had gathered. He looked like a bowling ball about to strike five pins.

"So how's it going at work?" Blake asked Steve.

"Ffine I guess."

"Nice job at the soccer game last Saturday. You suck, by the way. But I think it's cool that you're coaching, even though it's obvious you don't know jack about the game."

"I gguess somebody's gggotta do it."

"What in the hell's wrong with you? You sound like you're drunk or something."

"I think I'm jjust ttired."

"Hey, dude, are you okay?"

"Yeah, I'm ookay, I just haven't been ssleeping too well lately." This did not sound like someone who hadn't been sleeping lately—it sounded like somebody who'd had a stroke.

"How long have you been feeling like this?

"Couple ddays."

"Have you seen a doctor?"

"Yeah, and he thinks I'm ookkay, but he wants me to take an MMMRI."

"When's that scheduled?" Blake was alarmed and searched his friend's face for an explanation to this slurring. But Steve didn't seem too worried about it.

"Ttomorrow morning. I'll be ookay. It's nnothing."

He was not okay. He looked and acted normally, but there was obviously something the matter with him. He as-sured Blake he would call him immediately after the brain

MRI. And he did. The results were essentially normal.

"They said mmaybe my thyroid is out of wwhack or ssomething."

Blake was relieved, but he called Alison after he hung up with Steve.

"Can you talk?"

"Sure, what's up?"

"Well, I just talked to Steve. He said they think his *thyroid* is out of whack?"

"Yeah, they think he's just been tired and overworked and something about his thyroid. But they didn't seem too concerned. They're doing more tests next week."

"Is he going to be okay?"

"They seem to think so. And Steve says he feels fine. In fact, he went straight into work after the MRI. We got into a big fight, because I told him he had to go home and go to bed. But you know Steve. He said if the tests were normal, it couldn't be that bad."

There were more tests over the next week. Steve was poked, filmed, and drained. All the tests were unequivocal and there was no diagnosis. He was sleeping well, perhaps more than normal. They took solace that if it was a truly awful thing the doctors would be able to zero in on it quickly.

It was Alison who wasn't sleeping, for while her husband lay snoring beside her, she lay in the dark conjuring up worst case scenarios. Maybe it was cancer. Yes, that must be it. Yes, it was definitely a brain tumor. And then she tried to divine how much time he had. She made lists of questions to ask and wondered who would write the obituary. As soon as it was light outside she'd call her mom, or a friend.

"Hi, it's me. Sorry to call so early."

"What is it, honey?"

"How come they can't find out what this is?"

"You mean about Steve?"

"Yeah, mom. How could it be his thyroid? I've been on-line and I'm sorry, but it isn't his thyroid."

"We'll just have to wait and see. Is he feeling all right?"

"I guess so. You know Steve, though. He just doesn't want me to worry, so he tells me what I want to hear."

"Do you need me to watch the kids?"

"No, they're fine, but they know something's wrong with their dad."

When she hung up with her mom she called a friend and went over it all again.

The next week Blake went to Chad's soccer game again, only this time it was to watch his coach. Blake stood on the opposite sideline and stared across the grass at Steve, who roamed the sideline shouting encouragement once again. He wore his trademark golf shirt tucked into out-of-fashion jeans with the braided belt and white tennis shoes. Was there a slight limp in his stride? Or was Blake just imagining it? It was subtle, but it looked like he had rusty gears. His speech was still slurred, but not appreciably worse.

The soccer game itself was no contest; his team scored one lucky goal when the opposing goalie was distracted by his mom calling out to him. The other team scored at least ten. Steve gathered his kids together in a post game huddle.

"Did we win, coach?" asked one of the dandelion pickers.

"Well, we pplayed ggreat, you all ddid your bbest. You are all winners. I'm vvery pproud of you."

Blake looked at Steve, his lifetime hero, standing in the center of those kids who worshipped him as much as he did. Here was the finest man Blake had ever known; tall, lanky, humble, and out of fashion. Blake loved him in that moment more than he ever had.

"What's the matter, coach? Are you sad? You're talking funny."

"He's okay," said Chad. "He already went to the doctor."

"Yeah, I'm ookay. And I'm ppretty luckky to be your cccoach."

35

Regardless of your opinion about cows, you probably don't wish them ill will or unnecessary suffering. Granted, they aren't man's best friend. You wouldn't let them in your house, into the cab of your pickup truck, or onto your bed. But they aren't rude and they mind their own business. And, to be fair, they make a lot of sacrifices for humans. That's why there was near panic when their brains began disintegrating in England and a few other European countries several years ago.

Bovine Spongiform Encephalopathy. Mad cow disease.

These cows were not "mad" in the traditional sense, but mad as in crazy. And that's because they had a disease that was eating holes in their brains. Under a microscope their brain tissue looked like a sponge, or like Swiss cheese. And that is a condition that would make anyone mad.

This is a burden that would otherwise be borne by cows alone, except for the fact that humans eat cows. Unfortunately, if someone eats a diseased cow, one with a holey brain, that person just might get a holey brain, too. So, this is what happens: a cow gets this neurological abnormality and he passes it on to other cows (assume it was a male cow because males are responsible for most of the havoc that goes on in the world). Soon lots of cows are sick.

Those sick cows are then slaughtered and eaten by humans. They are eaten before the humans realize the cows had holey brains, as there is no particular test to render their pre-slaughtered IQ. The neurological abnormality can then be passed from the diseased cow to the human carnivore. This doesn't happen every time, but it can.

Once the infection occurs in a human being, there is a long incubation period that usually lasts several years. The person who is about to get the holey brains doesn't know he has the disease stalking inside him. Sometimes it does nothing more than lurk, and other times a trigger is pulled and it does more, much more. In the meantime, the human goes about his business, eating hamburgers and enjoying his life. And then, *POW!* he'll get symptoms that would be expected if there are developing holes in his brain.

If a human gets it from a cow, he can pass it on to other humans. But the odds are remote, because there are only a few unlikely ways he might do it. One way is to feed himself to another human. This is rare. Another way to spread it is through transplantation of diseased brain tissue. Fortunately, brain tissue transplants are about as common as cannibalism.

The most common way to spread the disease between humans is through a blood transfusion. Terrible people with criminal records and hearts of stone can still donate blood. However, someone who was in England (or a few other European countries) from 1985 to 1995 for more than six months cannot donate blood. And neither can they donate sperm, because that's another way mad cow disease can spread between humans. The FDA has even banned donor sperm completely from some countries, including the ever-popular Scandinavian sperm.

Steve most likely contracted mad cow on his honeymoon, but no one could be sure. It was a cruel irony that his memorable London trip would have conspired to inflict him.

"We sshould have ggone to Nnniagra Ffalls," he said to Alison.

"This isn't funny," she sobbed as they sat in the doctor's office. "What are we going to do?"

The doctor was a specialist in infectious diseases. He met with several colleagues before pronouncing his diagnosis: Creutzfeldt-Jakob disease, the human variant of mad cow. He had enormous compassion for the couple who sat before him. But there was a sliver of unspoken professional excitement, for he had never seen a case of Creutzfeldt-Jakob before, because there are only a few hundred cases a year diagnosed in the United States. Of course, the doctor felt guilty when he felt the excitement, for it had come at such an appalling cost to this young father. But still, he felt it.

Given the lengthy incubation period, some doctors fear the disease may yet rear its holey head. Vegetarians (some of whom are haughty and act superior to barbaric meat eaters) might be tempted to privately gloat, but transmission of the disease is still not completely understood. It may have been lurking inside Steve as a degenerative jack-in-the-box for fifty years before the weasel popped.

There is no effective treatment and the disease is fatal. Always fatal. Death usually occurs within six months to a year once the symptoms appear. Sometimes the patient can live for two years.

Blake was numb. Why Steve? Why not someone who'd already lived a long life, or someone that didn't have children who needed him? How could a loving God allow this to happen to Steve? It was inexplicable. Maybe it wasn't His call to make, Blake thought. But if not, then what good was He? Or maybe He had reasons that Blake was unworthy to understand.

It was such a random, catastrophic thing. Mad cow disease? There was no use trying to make sense of it, because it was senseless. And, yet, it needed to have meaning; an explanation was required. So, some called it an act of God, by default, and assigned responsibility to Him.

There was so much suffering in the world—so many children with flies in their eyes. Where was He? Blake wondered. Why not show His children some mercy? Blake could never forgive Him for his silence, or His inaction. He had always assumed God existed, but now he wondered. Was all his cursing of the Almighty a matter of vanity, the notion that humans arrogantly believed they were relevant enough to have a God who gave a shit about their cells and DNA? Was it all just wasted bitterness? Maybe there was no God to forgive, or to blame.

When Blake arrived at Steve's home after hearing the monstrous news, he fell into Steve's arms and wept. Steve's arms were not well controlled and his movements were jagged and undisciplined. There was so much Blake wanted to say, but couldn't. So Steve consoled him.

"It will bbbeee ookay, Baalake. I nneed you to beee there ffor my kkids. Will you ppromise mmmee?"

Blake could not respond, and he didn't need to. Steve knew Blake would be there. Steve was irreplaceable, but Blake would do his best. Never had Blake felt more pain, more love, more regret, and more loss than he did at that moment, hanging on to Steve and onto every word he tried to speak.

36

It didn't really matter *why* he got sick because that wasn't going to change anything. And neither did it matter that it was unfair, except to those who wished to wallow in the inequity, as if a certain amount of time had been guaranteed to Steve when he was born and the Almighty had then arbitrarily reneged on the deal.

The months following his diagnosis were remembered now only in general chunks. The first chunk was the hospital where he spent the first two weeks, but there was no remedial treatment given to him because there is no treatment for Creutzfeldt-Jakob disease. The second chunk was the rehabilitation center he'd been transferred to. This was a misnomer because they weren't trying to rehabilitate him. It was simply a less expensive place to be cared for by round-the-clock nurses.

Steve's room at the rehab center was ugly. There were a few flowers and Get Well cards that added some color, and a few balloons hovered near the ceiling, their strings hanging limply like the mood in the room, but it was otherwise dreary. A window halfway up one wall was covered by overgrown shrubs that deprived the room of natural light. Blake was given permission to go outside and chop them down. He and Alex borrowed a pickup truck and went over with clippers and a chainsaw. As they were cutting them out, Blake looked through the dirty window to see Steve inside giving him a clumsy thumbs-up sign.

Blake visited Steve every day. Of course, Alison was there a lot, too, and so were his four kids. They sat on his bed or roamed the depressing halls without knowing what they were supposed to do or say, for it is a difficult thing to watch your father deteriorate like that. His teenage daughter read him a book, but then there was a scene where someone died and she burst into tears.

The moment Blake would never forget, the crucial conversation that he had replayed so many times, occurred after Steve had been in that ugly room for two months. By that time he was hardly able to move. He could still speak, but his speech was progressively slower and more difficult to understand. It would have been easy for Blake to embellish the conversation, to emphasize Steve's role in it, or how lucid and sincere he'd been. But that is mostly irrelevant now.

"Blllake. I wwant to ddie."

"I know you do, Steve. And even though it will kill me, I want you to go as soon as you're ready."

"I'mm rready nnnow."

"What's the latest from the doctors? Do they expect you to pass soon?"

Steve was difficult to understand, but he was able to say that he'd had a great life and now just wanted a "quick kkkilll."

"God, I'm so sorry, Steve. I wish I could help you. You know I would if I could."

Steve sputtered that Blake could help him.

"Steve, you are the strongest person I know. You can do this. It'll be over soon, probably within another six months."

"Bbut I ddon't wwant tthat."

"None of us do."

Blake heard it clearly, even though it stuttered and stopped, and even though it was inarticulate. "I wwant to ddie nnnow."

"What are you saying?"

"Yyou know thaat I'mm ssufferrring, Baalake. And sssoo is my ffammilyy. Ppleese. Yurr the onnnlyy one."

"Steve. Look at me." Blake stared into Steve's eyes. They were still sharp, about the only thing on his body that hadn't failed him. Despite his lack of motor skills, his look was imploring. It scared Blake.

"Pppleeese tthink abouttt it."

"Steve, there's almost nothing I wouldn't do for you. You know that. We talked about this very thing several years ago. Remember? You said you'd never want to end your life."

"I dddinn't haave Crrrushfielld dddiseeease baack then."

"Steve, I'd do anything to help you. I'd maybe even help you with that if that's what you really want. But . . . I just can't do that now. Forgive me, but I don't think there's a way I could. But we can talk about it some other time. Okay? Let's just think about it and hope the doctors can give you more information?"

Steve begged him to think about it and come "bbback sssooon."

The next several days were surreal. Talk had been cheap several years earlier when Blake thought the concept was a reasonable one. However, it had all been hypothetical, something to debate between bottles of chardonnay. But now, when he was asked to actually help his best friend? Blake didn't want to go back to the rehab center. He didn't want to face Steve, but knew he must. Maybe Steve had forgotten about it, or maybe he'd just been testing him. But he knew Steve well enough to know he wasn't. This was for real. Blake would stall him out until it became a moot point.

He returned two days later after work. He hoped Alison would be there so the subject wouldn't come up. Blake knew Steve would never ask her to help him. Alison would be appalled and probably angry. But Steve was alone when Blake arrived. He was staring out the window with no expression on his face. Indeed, his face was incapable of expression, for it sagged on one side, a result of paralysis. This made him look much older than his forty three years. Blake came in and sat on the rolling metal chair next to the bed. He said nothing.

"Have yyou tthhought aabout it? Wwillll yyou hellp mmeee?" Steve didn't turn his head to look at Blake. He knew who'd come in.

Blake reached over and held his hand. He didn't respond because he didn't know what to say.

"Nnoobody wwilll knnow. Ppleeese."

Blake moved the chair to the other side of the bed so he could look at Steve's face and directly into his eyes. His eyes were alert and darted around Blake's face looking for a signal, for a sign.

"This sucks, I know, but I can't do it, Steve. I'd do just about anything for you, buddy. You know I would. But I'm sorry, I just don't think I can."

"Ppleeese."

"Look, Steve, you know how much I love you. But . . . have you really thought it through?"

Steve told him with starts and stops, saliva running down his chin, that it was all he thought about.

"I wouldn't even know what to do, Steve. I'm not a doctor and I wouldn't even know what to give you."

"Pppilllloooow."

Blake hated everything and everyone at this moment. He hated God for allowing this suffering to go on. He hated the government for allowing this suffering to go on. He hated religion for allowing this, no, *requiring* this suffering to go on.

"Come on, Steve. I can't do that. But I'll come back tomorrow, and we'll talk about it again. Maybe you'll change your mind."

"Thhaanks Blllake. I cccaaann counntt on yyou. I'llll ssseee Aaallisssson and the kkkiiddss tooommorrooow annd wwilll ttelll them ggggooodbye bbbutt I doon'ttt wwaant themm too knnnow annythingg. Okaay?"

Blake tossed until three o'clock in the morning and then got up and went to the living room where he retrieved the "Teen Years" scrapbook his mom had made for him. They were so young. Who could have imagined those two pimple-faced boys in the back row of the Churchill Jr. High Flying Eagles basketball team photo would find themselves in this hopeless situation?

"Babe, are you okay?" It was Naomi who'd come to the living room in her bathrobe.

"Yeah, I'm fine. I just couldn't sleep."

She sat down on the sofa next to him and pulled the throw around her. "What're you looking at?"

"I was just thinking about Steve."

"You've been lucky to have each other. You'd do anything you could for each other."

"You really think so?"

"Of course I do."

They thumbed through a few more pages of photos in plastic sleeves and then Naomi said, "Come to bed, babe. You've got a big day tomorrow."

"I'll be in in a minute."

He closed the book and stared at the fireplace. Then he did the most unusual thing, for he hadn't done it in thirty-five years. He knelt down next to the sofa and prayed. At first, he felt foolish. He'd forgotten how you begin such a thing. And he knew it would probably come to nothing because he was praying to a God he didn't even believe in. But if there was a God, He would know Steve, and He would know Steve needed help.

He went back to bed, but still couldn't sleep. He listened to the small sounds of the house. Could he actually do such a thing? He wasn't a violent person. Sure, he'd been desensitized by life and the media, but that was Hollywood. A few nights earlier, he'd been to a movie with Naomi where at least a hundred people were murdered in an avalanche of gunshots. After the movie, Naomi said it was too violent for her taste. He tried to think back to the movie to recall what had been so violent about it. A bunch of people were shot, true, but he hadn't considered it violent. In fact, the only part that disturbed him was when one of the bad guys kicked a helpless dog. That scene caused most of the people in the theatre to recoil. They didn't have the same reaction when the same guy detonated a car bomb, maiming half the police force.

What would he want if the shoe were on the other foot? Would Steve help him if he asked? Probably not, he concluded, for he believed Steve would fear the wrath of God, where Blake did not. Blake didn't fear the law, either, because he figured no one would ever know.

The next day Alison went to the rehab center. There'd been no change. The doctor said his deterioration had slowed some and he might live another six to nine months. She would relish every day. The two of them sat holding hands and then Alison thought she heard Steve humming. She looked at him and saw his mouth begin to move. She leaned down close to hear. It was barely more than a whisper.

"Fffivvve hunndred twwenttty ffivve thoussannd sssix hunndred mmminutes."

The nurses heard her sobbing from their station and hurried to the room. They saw Alison lying on the bed next to him, stroking his hair and singing along with him, so slowly and quietly that it was difficult for them to make out the song. Then they retreated and quietly closed the door.

Blake returned the next evening. He passed the nurses' station about ten yards from Steve's room. He had come to know the nurses, who were pleasant and kind. They were genuinely sad for Steve and his family and told Blake they'd never seen a patient like Steve. Despite all his suffering and despite his hideous fate, he was always appreciative and kind towards them. It had been their privilege to care for him, and they knew it.

Blake slipped into the room.

"Wwilll yyyou dddooo it nnooow? I'mm rreaddy."

"Steve, tell me again. Are you positive about this?"

"Yyesss. I sssaw Alllissson aand mmyy kkiddss. Prromise mmee ttoo bee therrre ffor tthemm."

Blake knelt down beside his bed and held his hand. He looked at him and did not flinch. "Steve, I promise you I will be there for your kids. It will be my *honor* to be there for them. I want you to know that more than anything else. Your kids will be taken care of. I swear it on my life."

"Thhaannk yyou, Blllake."

"Tell me again, Steve. Are you absolutely sure about this?"

"Yyesss. I wwould doo it bbut I caann't."

"Are you ready?"

"Yyesss. Iff I wwiggglle pplleeese dddonn't ssstop. Itt wwilll bee ooverrr ssooon ffforr mmeee."

Blake's favorite book growing up was Huckleberry Finn. Huck wrestled with his own moral dilemma about Jim, the runaway slave. The law required Huck to turn Jim in, and if he failed to do so, he would go to hell for breaking the law. But Huck knew that Jim was a good and decent man, and if he turned him in, then he would go to hell for doing that to Jim. So in a seminal moment of American literature, Huck did what he thought was right. He refused to turn Jim in. If he was to be sentenced to jail, or to hell, then so be it. This was Blake's Huck Finn moment.

He held Steve's hand a few moments longer. There were no more words. His resolve was firm, or at least firm enough. It was not Steve's choice to get the disease and it was not his choice to die from it. He only chose to end his fatal suffering. And Blake would help him do it.

He looked down at Steve one more time. One more long

look. But what he saw wasn't Steve. He lifted the pillow.

"I love you, Steve," he sobbed.

"Llloovve yyoou tooo. Thhannkkk yyyou Blllake."

He brought the pillow down to Steve's face and held it there. Steve was peaceful at first and then began to writhe, but only slightly. For thirty seconds Blake held it down, and then a full minute. He held it down for another two minutes more. He lifted the pillow. Steve's eyes were closed. He was not breathing. Blake felt for a pulse and found none. Steve Olson, his best friend for over forty years, was dead.

And he had killed him.

Blake was suddenly horrified at what he'd done. What had he been *thinking*? My God, he thought, I have just killed a man! It was like a dream, like he'd been in a trance and had suddenly been brought forth by the snap of the hypnotist's fingers. It had happened so fast. What had he done? If he could have unwound the clock he would have. He would have told Steve no! He would have made him stick it out. But it was done, and he had done it. And no one must ever learn the truth.

He slipped out the door without being seen. He walked to his car and sat in the parking lot for half an hour. He didn't feel like driving home. He didn't feel like doing anything, really. He tried to convince himself that he had done the right thing—that it hadn't been his choice, but Steve's. He wanted to reassure himself that he wasn't a monster, that he was only helping a friend. And he'd done it out of love.

He saw Alison pull into the parking lot. She didn't see

him parked there. He watched her walk to the glass doors of the rehab clinic and step inside. Then he reluctantly drove home.

37

Alison's heart still beat, so technically it wasn't broken. But she was on emotional life support. She'd tried to prepare for his death, but how was she supposed to do that? His death had been so sudden. She thought back to her last conversation with him, a few hours before they found him dead. It was almost as if he'd been saying goodbye to her, as if he'd known that he was about to leave. If only she had known she could have held him longer, loved him fiercer for a few more moments.

She stumbled through those first ugly days, not even re-membering who had taken care of her children. She slept in starts and stops with the desperate hope that she could some-how wake from the unimaginable nightmare of losing Steve this way in the prime of their lives. What would happen to her kids without a father? It was too awful to think about, so she tried not to, but unfortunately that was all she did.

She'd been surrounded by friends and family who tried to reassure her it would be all right, but they didn't really mean it, because it wouldn't be all right. Well-meaning neighbors brought casseroles and soup. They alleged that God must have needed Steve on the "other side" because they could think of nothing better to say. Just once she wished someone would have told her the truth; that this was awful and unfair. Just once she wished someone would have publically asked how a loving God could rip her life apart without reason or compassion, that there was no grand scheme at all. Just unholy luck.

Alison tried to be strong for her kids, who understood it less than she did. They could not comprehend the seismic shift, and they might not recognize it until later—until they wanted to play catch in the backyard, or wanted their dad to help them build a fort or a pinewood derby car, or walk them down the aisle.

Alison didn't have the luxury to climb into bed with a Xanax and pull the covers over her head. She held it together as best she could, but she was living directly on the fault line. A few weeks later they found her at the cemetery. Her mother had been watching the children and Alison didn't return for three hours. She didn't answer her phone. They were worried. Her father drove around looking for her when he finally spotted her minivan at the cemetery. He parked and walked up the small grass hill to Steve's grave, where the flowers had begun to wilt. Alison was lying face down on Steve's grave.

"Honey?"

She was startled, as if she'd been completely lost in her thoughts. She stood and her knees and elbows were indented by the blades of grass.

"I'm sorry, Dad, it's just that . . . "

Her father held her. "I understand, sweetheart," he said, when really he didn't. "We'll get through this."

The funeral was tragically sad. Because he'd been taken in his prime it was sadder—the sense that he'd been robbed. There was the JFK phenomenon, the blessing that Steve would always be remembered as a young, vibrant, attractive person, and not old and bent, with milky eyes and saggy skin. This, however, was no consolation to any of them. Indeed, it only made it worse.

Alison did not ask Blake to speak at the funeral as he'd hoped she might. He and Naomi sat directly behind her at the service and he reached forward and touched her on the shoulder, but she pulled away. Blake tried not to take this personally for he knew how miserable she was.

The few speakers had plenty of material. Everyone claimed Steve as their best friend because of the way he made them feel. A close friend spoke first.

"A few minutes with Steve and you would've thought you'd been friends for a lifetime. Steve died at forty-three, yet he crammed a lot into those years. He was not the kind of guy who would have taken his death lightly, either.

"I can see him walking up to the Pearly Gates. He walks right through and St. Peter yells to him, 'Hey, where do you think you're going?' Steve just keeps walking and yells back, 'It's okay; I just need to take care of a little business with God.' He spots the tallest building and assumes God's office must be on the top floor. Stepping out of the elevator he walks past the receptionist and says, 'It's okay, God knows me.' She mumbles, 'That might not be such a good thing.'

"He opens the door and steps into the biggest office he's ever seen. Sure enough, God stands up from His desk.

"I figured you'd be coming by to see me. How are you, Steve?"

"Well, not good, not good at all. I'm dying of a terrible disease as we speak!"

"Yes, I know," God says.

"Well, you need to do something quick, before it's too

late! I've got a beautiful wife and young kids. They need me!"

"It'll be okay," God says. "I've already put some of my best angels on it."

"But what about Chad, my youngest? He's my only son."

"Steve, I understand the love a father has for his only son. And, remember, Chad is my son, too. So don't worry—I'll take it from here. Trust me, Steve, I can handle it."

As the speaker continued, Blake concentrated on Steve. Where was he now? Did he exist? Was he really with God? Would he ever see him again? All the questions everyone wants to know. And because they can't know, they pretend they do because it makes them feel better. But they can't *know*. Of course, some will only grudgingly acknowledge this. Often their frantic need to know is not based in faith, but in doubt. So the more they privately doubt, the more determined they are to be doubly sure they know in public.

Blake was a pallbearer. He lined up on the left side directly behind eight-year-old Chad who was too innocent to be given the task of carrying his dead father's casket. He wore a suit that was too big for him and one of his dad's ties that was tucked into his pants because it was so long. His cowlick stuck up despite the effort Alison made to tame it by licking her hand and plastering it to his head on the drive to the funeral service. There was audible grief when they saw little Chad line up in the row of full grown men.

The casket was heavier than Blake thought it would be. They solemnly hoisted it from the chapel to the parking lot, where a hearse waited. After it was loaded into the back, they milled about on the grass before the hearse pulled away for the cemetery. He saw the funeral speaker, a mutual friend of theirs.

"Nice job."

"Thanks."

"You really believe that?"

"What?"

"That part you were saying about Steve meeting God and all that?"

"Yeah. Maybe. Hell, I don't know what to believe. It sounds good, and I hope it's true. But maybe we're already dead for all I know and this is all just a big dream or something. Who knows?"

"Well, if you're right, it's a shitty dream right now."

"I hear you."

"But, seriously, good job today. I think Steve would've liked it."

Following the service, Blake went to Steve's home. Members of his church had come through with a feast, as they always do. It is unimaginable that the thought of death makes people hungry, but they eat after funerals; it's just the way it is. For Steve's post-funeral meal there were cakes, pies, cookies, and yams. But there was no beef. In fact, for several weeks after Steve's diagnosis, beef consumption in the neighborhood was down.

Blake roamed the house trying to capture the essence of Steve for the final time while others carried paper plates and plastic forks around the kitchen and family room, looking for a spot to sit. They balanced the plates on their laps and somberly recounted memories of Steve. Some brave souls were quietly talking about the Diamondbacks's upcoming season because they were tired of being sad, or because they didn't know what else to talk about.

There were photos of the kids everywhere, but no memorabilia that testified to Steve's greatness, because that could not be measured by plaques and ribbons. Blake stepped into Steve's den. On the wall was a photo of their Little League baseball team. His proud father was in the photo, too, as the assistant coach. Blake remembered the day it had been taken, thirty-five-years earlier. They'd beaten the Giants that day and afterwards his dad had taken them all for ice cream. Blake felt such profound sadness as he calculated the loss of the two most relevant men in his life.

He sat at Steve's desk. There was a small framed photo of him and Steve, arm in arm, on the desk. Blake broke into tears. That meant more to him than a Pulitzer Prize or the major league MVP.

38

"Everyone must die." It's so fundamentally true that it's become a cliché, and sometimes clichés lose their impact because they're just clichés. And then, bang, someone you know dies and it jolts you, as if death were more exceptional than it really is. Sometimes death is random, like the people who get struck by lightning, or the people who get mad cow disease. Death is funny that way; it's unpredictable, but not extraordinary.

"You okay?" Naomi asked.

"Yeah, I'm okay," Blake said as he was bent over tying the laces of his running shoes. "But it's harder than I thought it'd be."

She reached over and combed his hair with her fingers. "You were there with him to the end. He needed you, and you were a good friend."

Blake looked up at Naomi. Did she suspect something? No, that was impossible. And then she said, "It was just his time. I'm glad he passed peacefully. I only wish someone had been with him at the end."

"Yeah."

"You think Alison is going to be all right?"

"She'll figure out a way I guess. She has no choice."

"Just promise me you won't die, Blake. I couldn't take it if you were gone."

He was a mile into the run and his breathing had settled. His running playlist was upbeat. There were the old stand-bys: Rocky theme songs, Push it to the Limit, and We Are the Champions. But Naomi had downloaded some of her songs too, tunes that hardly inspired a sprint to the finish like AC/DC's Back in Black. He rounded the corner by the high school to Lose Yourself by Eminem. He was feeling good; maybe he'd run the bleachers.

Eminem's last beat trailed off, and then there was evidence of Naomi's tampering. *I close my eyes, only for a moment and the moment's gone.*

He stopped and wiped his forehead with his sleeve.

All my dreams pass before my eyes, a curiosity. Dust in the wind, all they are is dust in the wind. Same old song, just a drop of water in an endless sea. All we do crumbles to the ground, though we refuse to see. Dust in the wind, all we are is dust in the wind. Now don't hang on, nothing lasts forever but the earth and sky. It slips away, and all your money won't another minute buy. Dust in the wind. All we are is dust in the wind.

He stood on the street corner and wept.

Blake came home from work Monday, five days after the funeral. The Cardinals were hosting the Packers on Monday Night Football. He grabbed a beer with one hand and Libby with the other and headed for the family room where he plopped down to enjoy the game. He was tired of being sad.

The doorbell rang. *Who comes to the door at seven o'clock in the evening when the Cardinals are playing?* Blake thought.

He pretended not to hear it, hoping Naomi would answer it. But she waited him out. When it rang a second time, he got up and padded over in his stocking feet to the front door. Later, he would remember the slippery feeling of his feet on the smooth hardwood floor. It's funny the things you remember at a time like that.

When Blake opened the door he saw two uniformed police officers on the porch, and neither of them smiling. So this was not a fundraiser. Oh my God, he wondered, what has happened? Who's been hurt? Naomi and Libby were safe. Was it his mom?

"Can I help you?" he asked the officers.

"Are you Blake Morgan?"

"Yes, I am. How can I help you?" He held his breath hoping it wasn't serious.

"Mr. Morgan, I'm sorry, sir, but you will need to come with us. You are under arrest for the murder of Steven Olson."

39

Naomi was dumbfounded. When they led Blake away in handcuffs she thought it was a joke, perhaps something hatched at the office while Blake and some of the other reporters were bored. But, no, this was no joke. And who would joke about Steve's death like this anyway? Blake was charged with *murdering Steve*? How could that possibly be? How, and more importantly, why?

"Naomi," he said as they put him into the back seat of the police car, "it's not what you think. You've got to believe me. I'll explain everything later."

"But . . . why do they think you killed Steve? It makes no sense. Alison can tell them. I'll call her. This is crazy!"

"No, don't call her. Don't call anyone. Wait to hear from me. I'll explain everything later."

What was there to explain, she wondered? She waited fifteen long minutes and then called Alison anyway.

"Alison, thank God you answered. The police were just here and arrested Blake for murder! You need to hurry and call them. There's been a horrible mistake!"

"Naomi, I can't discuss this with you. I'm sorry. I need to hang up. I'm sorry." She hung up.

Naomi called her again and it went to voice mail. She didn't leave a message. The football game was still on in the

334 | WARREN DRIGGS

family room and Libby was dragging the board games out of the cabinet, something she did ten times a day. No cabinet was safe. Naomi called Blake's cell and heard it ring in the other room. She put Libby to bed and then stood in the kitchen. Who could she call? What was she supposed to do? For an instant she thought about calling Steve.

Blake's arrest created only a local stir at first. His own newspaper put it on the second page: "Former MLB Standout Arrested for Mercy Killing." They deliberately failed to acknowledge he was the assistant editor of the paper. And, technically, it wasn't a "mercy killing" anyway, which implies the *unrequested* taking of another person's life to save them from further suffering. But that distinction was mere hair splitting at this point and hardly justified a retraction in the next day's edition.

Blake's first night in jail was awful. At the Maricopa County Correctional Facility, the lights go off at 9:30 p.m. sharp and when they do, it is very dark. There are no windows, for this was an underground cement bunker. Blake slept in a cell with two others whose names he'd long since forgotten. They were veterans of the jail scene and seemed content with the free room and board. But Blake had never been in jail. He had no rap sheet (no formal record had been made when he'd swiped the *Mad Magazine* from 7-Eleven thirty-five years earlier. He'd been sent home with his parents, whose profound disappointment in him had been punishment enough).

Naomi hired a lawyer for Blake, a middle-aged man with a salt and pepper goatee. His thinning hair was combed straight back over his round head and collected into a very short pony tail held in place by a small rubber band, so that, in profile, his head looked like a balloon. He went to the jailhouse the next morning to meet with Blake. They were separated by a thick sheet of Plexiglass with a few small holes to allow the sound of their voices to be heard. The glass was scraped and smudged to the point that it was nearly opaque. These were three-sided partitions to allow for privacy, the functional equivalent to a row of urinals. Inmates on both sides of Blake complained about the system to their dilapidated-looking girlfriends.

Blake was dressed in a one-piece orange jumpsuit. There was stenciled print on the front breast pocket and back that officially made it the property of Maricopa County Corrections, as if the uniform could possibly be mistaken for anything other than a jail costume.

"My name is Francis Bradshaw. Please call me Frank. Your wife called me this morning and asked that I come down as soon as possible."

"Thank God you're here."

A guard stood behind Blake, leaning back against the wall. He was cleaning his fingernails. There was no indication that he was eavesdropping—he seemed too bored for that.

Blake had decided he would tell his lawyer the truth. His lawyer had been around enough times to know this was rare, because inmates rarely speak the complete truth. They feel compelled to dress it up—embellish it to make absolutely certain the listener knows just how wrongly they'd been accused.

Initially Blake spoke in hushed tones, fearful that someone else might overhear his confession. But then he realized no one else cared.

"Should I tell you what happened?"

"Please," the lawyer said as he took a yellow legal pad

from his briefcase, "tell me everything you can remember, even the details that you might not think are important."

"Well, first of all, you should know that Steve and I had been best friends for forty years. I loved him. I would never intentionally do anything to hurt him."

"Mr. Morgan, I . . . "

"Call me Blake."

"Blake, I appreciate that, I really do. And I think that's important. But," he said with a wry smile, "I'm afraid when you say you would never do anything to hurt him . . . well, that is inconsistent with the evidence the prosecutor says he has."

"Yeah, probably so," Blake said. "I guess I can tell you the truth, right? I mean you're my lawyer and all."

"Yes, please do. Anything you tell me is strictly confidential." His pen was poised to write on the blank legal pad.

"I killed him. But it's not the way it sounds. See, he *asked* me to do it. He practically begged me. I'm not sure you know about Steve's condition at the time. He had Creutzfeldt-Jakob disease. That's basically the human mad cow disease. He only had a few months to live and he was in pain. He wanted to die and avoid those last few months of pain, but he couldn't move. He would have done it on his own, but he couldn't. So he asked me to help him. At first I told him no way, I couldn't bring myself to do it. I'm not a violent person. You can check my criminal record if you want to."

"I have already checked and you're clean; you have no record."

"So that's good, isn't it?" Blake asked. "Won't they take that into consideration?"

"The judge will consider that, I'm sure."

"And what about the fact that Steve asked me to do it? Doesn't that change things?"

"Well," he said, "so far there is no evidence of that, other than what you've said. As it turns out, apparently his wife," he began flipping through some notes, "Alison, I think it is. Anyway, she is quite adamant that her husband would never have asked you to do such a thing. In fact, the prosecutor maintains Mr. Olson believed it was morally wrong. Mrs. Olson insists you had all previously discussed this issue a few years ago, before he became sick, and the discussion was quite heated."

"Well, it's true. I mean, it wasn't heated, but, yeah, we discussed it. We just talked about the general concept, hypothetically. I'll admit that. I was writing a newspaper article at the time about assisted suicide and euthanasia and all that, and we talked about whether it might be acceptable under some circumstances. Steve and Alison are pretty religious and their church bans suicide, but Steve changed his mind when he got sick."

"I see."

"Steve's the one who brought it up, not me."

"Uh-huh."

"Come on, what motivation would I have to kill Steve? He was my best friend. I visited him every day."

"Of course we will present evidence to show the totality of the circumstances. There are mitigating or extenuating factors for the judge to consider. But their evidence suggests this was not a spur of the moment act. They will argue this was not a heat of the moment thing—that you clearly intended to kill him."

"Well, they'd be right. It *was* intentional. It wasn't a 'spur of the moment' decision by either one of us. It was thoughtful and it was—what's the legal word?—premeditated. But that makes it sound worse than it was. They act like it was a bad thing that it was premeditated. But I think it shows it was a conscious choice he made. It didn't just happen."

"*He* made? See, that's the problem, Blake. The focus, unfortunately, is not on the choice *he* may have made, because the judge can't know what that was. Instead, it will be on the choice *you* made."

Blake sat on the metal stool on the captive side of the Plexiglass in his orange jumpsuit as the enormity of his predicament began to sink in. He hadn't considered the legal consequences of what he'd done before he did it. Actually, he'd considered it, but he honestly believed no one would find out. And even if he had been caught he assumed people would be sympathetic. He surely didn't consider himself to be a common criminal who should be put in jail.

"Maybe I shouldn't confess, then."

"That is something we need to talk about."

"But I did it, and I did it intentionally. I just don't think what I did was that wrong. I still don't."

"Unfortunately, it is the law that we need to consider, and not what you think the law ought to be."

"Well, what evidence *do* they have so far? How did they know it was me in the first place? How do they know he didn't just die of natural causes?"

"Apparently you were the last visitor to see Mr. Olson before he died."

"So?"

"Shortly after you left, a nurse went to his room to give him his evening medications and she found him dead. His wife arrived a few minutes after that. Naturally she was upset. She'd seen him a few hours earlier and he'd been doing well. When she was told you had been the last one there, she became suspicious."

"But why would she be suspicious of me? I don't understand."

"Apparently she will testify that Mr. Olson mentioned to her a few days earlier that you and he had talked about expediting his death. Mr. Olson had assured his wife that this had been just talk, but she was not completely satisfied. So when he died unexpectedly she demanded to know the cause of death."

The lawyer told Blake that trained medical personnel can usually tell if someone has been asphyxiated. There are small petechial hemorrhages—tiny red or purple spots on the skin—that are caused by bleeding under the skin. Those red blotches are found in the eyes, face, lungs, and neck area when someone is suffocated. There is also foam in the airways as the victim struggles to breathe and mucus from the lungs mixes with the air. These things are the hallmark of asphyxiation, and Steve had all of them.

There was also a small amount of saliva on the pillow. Because of those discoveries, the nursing staff immediately called a doctor to the center who conclusively stated that Mr. Olson had been asphyxiated. "Naturally," the lawyer said to Blake, "you were the primary suspect—the only suspect, really."

Blake felt like an idiot. He hadn't watched all those forensic television shows where the detectives always figure it out because the stupid bad guy leaves clues. Steve had looked normal to him when he left for his car. Of course he hadn't inspected him closely for a bunch of tiny dots or whatever it was. And how was he supposed to know about the whole mucus thing?

"So what am I being charged with? Manslaughter or something?"

"First degree murder."

"*First degree murder?* Are you serious? I'll admit to exactly what I did if they want me to. I'm not going to lie about this. I'm not even sure I feel the need to apologize for what I did. I know that sounds bad, and I'm sorry, but Steve was already dying for God's sake! He was nearly dead already. He was in pain. He *asked* me to do it! Doesn't that mean anything?"

"Obviously I will try to work a deal with the prosecutor, and hopefully I can. But we got stuck with a prosecutor who's a real gung-ho law and order guy. He's a climber in that office and rarely cuts a deal. He'd rather take his chances with a jury, and especially in a high-profile case like this."

"Who's the judge?"

"We don't know yet. We'll find out in a few days who it's been assigned to, and that will make a big difference, because it's the judge that imposes the sentence."

They released him on bail after two more miserable days in the county jail, the misery compounded by the uncertainty of his fate. The *Arizona Republic* placed him on temporary leave without pay. Letters to the editor poured in from both the right and the left; some called Blake a hero and others called for the noose. Most of the others couldn't make up their mind.

He spent the next few weeks talking with his lawyer and

reflecting on the mess he'd made. His mother was heartbroken. "No one has called. I think they're humiliated for me. I had to hear about it from your Aunt Jean, who couldn't wait to tell me. She was your father's least favorite sister, you know. I told her it was a lie. I told her we raised you to be a good boy. I don't know what on earth were you thinking, Blake. I still don't believe you'd do such a thing. And if you did, I have to believe you had a reason, because that's not something our son would do. That's not who we raised."

"Mom, he begged me to do it and I did what I thought was right. Maybe I wasn't thinking clearly, but I really did do what I thought was right."

"Well, what on earth are you going to do? You're in all the papers."

"I have a good lawyer. It'll work out, mom."

"What about me? What am I supposed to do?"

"Mom, it'll work out."

Friends believed they were charitable for giving him the benefit of the doubt and chose their words of criticism carefully for fear of being disloyal. They said things like, "I guess I could see why he'd want to do it, but I sure as hell wouldn't have done it. It wasn't his call to make. I don't care how sick the guy was. He took it way too far." And co-workers spent hours arguing behind his back about whether their former colleague should be elected mayor, or hung. They asked him for interviews even though they knew he couldn't comment on the pending case.

Blake didn't consider himself to be a moral crusader. He didn't wish to be persecuted for his nobleness. In his mind, he was just the guy who'd made a decision to help a friend. He wasn't all Jack Kevorkian about it, publically advocating for the nobility in his position.

After much legal wrangling on both sides, a deal was finally struck wherein Blake would plead guilty to the charge of voluntary manslaughter. A prison term was probable, but the judge would make that call. Blake was now squarely at the mercy of the court.

40

Judge Cynthia Markham pulled up to her house in a typical suburb of Phoenix. The home was well maintained, but ordinary. They could have upgraded to a bigger, nicer home, but they were happy there. She was exhausted after another trying day on the bench; encouraging drug addicts, scolding criminals, listening to divorcing couples argue over who would get the blender, and otherwise dispensing justice the best she could. She walked into the house and dropped her purse and briefcase on the floor with a thud.

"Tough day?" asked her husband, David.

"Let's just say that after ten years on the bench I thought I'd seen it all. Obviously I hadn't."

"Sounds pretty bad. What happened?"

"Well, I had a jury on a criminal case. There were some fairly gruesome photos, but I didn't think they were *that* bad. Maybe I'm just used to seeing mayhem or something. Anyway, one of the jurors on the back row threw up. I mean, she just let 'er go without any warning. Projectile style. It was awful."

"Are you serious?"

"Unfortunately. Of course, that would've been bad enough, but the sight and smell of it all caused another juror to throw up, too. I know one day I'll laugh about it, but I'm not ready to do that just yet."

"Sorry, but that's hilarious."

"No, it wasn't. I mean, you could hear it splash. My God, it was awful. I've never seen people scatter so fast in my life!" She took a sip of wine that David handed to her. "But, yeah, I guess it was pretty funny. It'll make the book I write one day. Where's Sophia, by the way?"

"Oh, she's up sulking in her room," David said. "I told her she couldn't have a sleepover tonight with Paige. So be fore-warned, we are now officially the meanest parents in Arizona. Congrats."

"Let's go out tonight. I can't bear the thought of fixing something."

"Too late. I made your favorite."

"David C. Markham, what have you done wrong?"

"Nothing, I swear. I'm just trying to cozy up to the good judge, just in case."

"Would we be bad parents if we ate alone? I don't feel like doing battle with her right now."

"Me, neither."

They sat companionably over dinner and wine reviewing the day's events, their cruel treatment of Sophia, and junior high carpool. They finished and stood to clear the table and do the dishes.

"By the way, what's happening with that Blake Morgan case?"

"The sentencing hearing is set for tomorrow," she said. "Even though he's already pled guilty, there's absolutely no agreement between the defense and the prosecution on sentencing. So I guess it's up to me."

"Well, Cin, like they say, that's why you get paid the big

bucks."

"Yeah, right. Sometimes I think they could quadruple my pay and it wouldn't be enough. But other times I think I'd do it for free."

"Have you decided what you're going to do?"

"Not yet. I can't remember a case that I was so torn over."

Cynthia P. Markham was one of the finest judges in the state. She was tolerant but no pushover. She had a remarkable blend of temperament and skills: intellect, commitment to the law, compassion, and fair mindedness.

They finished the dishes and then agreed to tackle the sleepover issue with their picked-upon daughter. To Sophia, life and death legal issues were insignificant when compared to Paige's sleepover. Didn't they know that Paige was the most popular girl at Evergreen Junior High? Didn't they care? Did they *want* her to be a complete loser?

Sophia was sitting on her unmade bed talking on her cell phone, presumably to another girlfriend who was also the victim of parental abuse. She was as difficult to deal with as any stubborn lawyer. Clothes were strewn about her room and spilled out of her half-opened dresser drawers like syrup running off a stack of hotcakes. There were clothes on the bottom of the stack that would have every reason to feel as unappreciated as Sophia did now.

A poster of the latest teen idol was pinned to the wall (she'd told her parents who it was at least five times and still they didn't know—they were so out-of-touch it was embarrassing). There were also a few stuffed animals and dolls, as if she were stuck at the crossroads between a little girl and a young woman. She ignored her parents for just the right amount of time and then, with deliberate annoyance, ended the phone call with a promise she'd call back "that is, if my parents ever let me do anything."

"What?"

"We just wanted to talk to you about the sleepover."

"Everybody's going. It's not like her parents aren't going to be there."

Cynthia and David looked at each other and Sophia mistook their hesitation for capitulation.

"So can I?"

"No, but we want to talk about it."

"You always say that! You never let me do anything! Gol, you make it sound like I'm on drugs or something."

"No we don't, Sophia. We just want to talk about our reasons."

"I'm busy." And surely she must have had plenty to do.

After allowing themselves to be thoroughly manipulated, they agreed to allow a sleepover the following week (there was no rational basis for the delay, other than to show strength and resolve). They left Sophia's room exhausted, drained, and beaten, again, by a fourteen-year-old without a proper legal education.

Later that night Cynthia and David lay in bed reading. David, a lawyer himself, was poring over legal papers and Cynthia was doing the same. She took off her reading glasses and put down the brief she'd been reading, most of which was just regurgitated legalese at $425 per hour.

"Like I said, I'm really torn about this Morgan case."

David put down his own reading and turned to face his wife, giving her his full attention. "Is there any dispute about the facts?"

"Yes and no. There's no dispute they were best friends and that Morgan killed him. He'll admit it. But he insists Olson asked him to do it, and Olson's widow maintains he would never have asked for such a thing."

"Do you believe him?"

"Yes, I think I do. I can reconcile it no other way. The initial charge was first degree murder, you know."

"Yeah, I know. It's not my place to weigh in, but I'll tell you that we've been talking about this case around the office for weeks. Everybody has an opinion."

"I'm sure they do. And so do I," said Cynthia.

"So, what are you thinking?" he asked.

"You know, we're all the product of our lives' collective experiences. Remember when my mom was so sick? She wanted to die and I *wanted* her to die, too. It was horrible, absolutely horrible, to watch her suffer. She could have taken her own life; she had the physical capacity to do that. In fact, she even hinted about it—I think as much to see our reaction as anything else."

"But she didn't," David said.

"No, she didn't. And because of that she lived six more months in pain with no quality of life and no hope for recovery. She was just playing out the string."

"That was her call to make."

"I agree. But I wonder how I would have felt if she *had* taken her life."

"Okay, how *would* you have felt?"

"Well, I can tell you this; I wouldn't have been outraged, and it wouldn't have shocked my moral conscience."

"So what if your mom had wanted to die. I mean, let's say

she *really* wanted to die, but she couldn't because she was too disabled—basically the same deal as the Morgan case? Then what?"

"I'm not sure," she said.

"Well, what if your mom asked you to help her? Maybe collect the necessary pills to do the job—something like that? Would you have considered it?"

"I can't say. I mean, I would've wanted to help her. She's my mom. But I'm charged with upholding the law, not writing it."

"I know," he said. "But let's say you weren't a judge, you were just a daughter and your mom had a painful terminal illness?"

"You mean if she asked me to help her?"

"Yeah."

"I have no idea what I'd do," she said. "What would you do?"

"God, that's tough. I'm not sure what I'd do either." He folded the page he'd been reading and closed the binder. "So, let me ask you this. What if the doctors had come to you in confidence and told you they could give her extra morphine, you know, extra 'comfort care' which you knew damned well would kill her. Would you nod and turn your head?"

"Truthfully, I probably would," Cynthia said.

"So what's the difference? Setting aside the issue of the Hippocratic Oath and all that, should the doctor in that hypothetical case be charged with first degree murder?"

"The law is clear. It's illegal to intentionally take the life of another. I am the judge and that is the law."

"Okay."

"I love the law. I'm sworn to uphold it," she continued, as if to justify her position. "Our country is the strongest country on earth because we are a nation governed by laws and we respect them."

"Nice speech."

"Yeah, I know. And I'm not trying to be all noble and high-minded here, but what is the aim of the law? It's justice, right?"

"Yes."

"Well, the 'law' itself isn't sacred," she said. "It can be changed to suit our designs. We do it all the time. The law simply allows for the pursuit of justice. It is 'justice' that is sacred."

"So how do you fashion a sentence in this case that follows the law, but honors your concept of justice?" David asked.

"Well, I guess that's the great challenge, isn't it."

"I suppose so," he said.

"But it's a challenge I take to heart. After all, somebody's gotta do it. I just wish I had the wisdom of King Solomon. But I don't, so all I can do is follow the law as best I can and do what my heart tells me is right. And that, my dear husband, is easier said than done."

"I'm guessing there will be plenty of media at the courthouse for the hearing. I'm amazed by how much national attention this has been getting."

"So am I. And the protestors are already gathering. I'm sure tensions will be running high," said Cynthia.

"Are they prepared with enough security down there? Do you want me to come?" David asked.

"I'm sure they'll be prepared. And yes, I'd love you to come if you have the time. I could use some moral support."

"I'll be there."

There was a lengthy pause in the conversation and both of them eventually put their reading classes back on and tried to generate enough enthusiasm to get back to their papers.

"How many protestors do you think there'll be?" David wondered out loud. This conversation was more interesting than the deposition he'd been reading.

"Well, they're expecting several hundred. I know the National Right to Life group has filed an amicus brief of its own. So they'll be there and I don't need to tell you what they think. Some of them would sentence Morgan to the firing squad if they had their way."

"You know, Cin, anytime you get religion in the mix, you're in for some fireworks. I have no doubt there'll be plenty of Bible thumpers who want to see Old Testament punishment here."

"I suppose so, but they are lining up on *both* sides of this issue," she said.

"But the far right, the ones who demand that God be in the courtroom, they're the ones who seem to scream the loudest. They've become infected by religion, and the only antibiotic for that is a healthy dose of reason."

"But come on, David. Be fair. The far left has infections of its own, and you know it. They have this arrogance and academic superiority about them that's downright offensive. Both sides claim the high ground. And isn't that the way it is? We demonize the other side but give total amnesty to everyone who agrees with us. No matter how hard we try, we only see the issue after it's been funneled through our prism. And that's true for everybody; the priests *and* the professors."

"And that's why the parties here are lucky to have you decide it, because you'll be open-minded and reasonable."

An hour later, after the lights had been turned off, Cynthia leaned over to where her husband slept. "Are you awake?" she whispered.

"Yeah, I'm afraid I can't sleep either."

"I wonder sometimes," Cynthia said, "how history will judge us, and how history will judge me and the decision I make. Will we be more evolved a hundred years from now?"

"I sure hope so," he said.

"Me, too. I think our level of consciousness is rising, but we still have so far to go. Will jurists in the future look at what I've done and say we were naïve? Will they say the judge in this case was a backward uncivilized idiot?"

"Never!"

"No, seriously. What about the Supreme Court justice who wrote the Dred Scott opinion? He was a smart guy in his day but he thought people of color were inferior. A lot of people did. Does he feel a sense of shame now, lying there in his grave? I'll bet he does."

"Who knows," David said. "I'm sure they'll look back on our era and shake their heads about some of the crazy stuff we believed. But I have more confidence in you than anyone else in the world. You'll do the right thing, Cin. I know you will."

She rolled over onto her back and looked up at the dark ceiling. "You want to know something? As I'm lying here trying to sleep I keep thinking about the contrast between 'law' and 'justice.' Tomorrow morning I'll sentence a good man to prison, as the law requires me to do. But I don't think justice will be served."

41

Cynthia arrived at the courthouse about 8:00 a.m. The Morgan case would be called at 9:00. Already a throng had gathered in the expansive grass courtyard of the Maricopa County Courthouse. People milled about civilly on either side of the walk leading to the courthouse steps. It was a peaceful crowd; citizens exercising their constitutional right to protest and complain. Those on the right held banners decrying the cold-blooded loss of innocent life, while those on the left held posters advocating the right to die whenever you felt like it.

There were a few children with homemade posters— posters that boldly declared, "Jesus = Pro Life" and "Euthanasia is Murder." These were citizens too, but not yet old enough to vote, or drive. Indeed, they were too young to attend a full day of school and needed plenty of help spelling euthanasia, and life, and Jesus.

Makeshift wooden soapboxes had been hastily built and portable microphones were being warmed and tested to shout down the idiotic views of the other side. Allow a man to will-fully kill another and walk away scot free? No, he must be im-prisoned! Imprison an enlightened man who had generously assisted another? No, he must go free! Without acknowledg-ing the potential irony, some of the Right to Life protesters had been on those very courthouse steps five months earlier with posters demanding the death sentence for a man who'd been convicted of killing his wife. So the sanctity of life argument was a tricky one.

The media was there in full force, too, with their cables, booms, and reporters at the ready. Back at the studios, the news anchors promised to "Go live to Phoenix for the breaking news" as soon as it broke. Attractive former journalism majors checked their hair and makeup, adjusted their ties, and took sips of bottled water, hoping there would be outrage to report.

Cynthia pulled into the underground parking lot of the courthouse and into her reserved parking stall, one of the perks to offset the pay cut she took when she became a judge. She took the elevator to the fourth floor and walked down a private corridor to her office. Cynthia had presided over a few high profile cases before, but none had the attention of the national media like the Morgan case. She reviewed her notes and then took the small mirror from her purse and re-applied her lipstick and ran her fingers through her hair.

There was a knock on the open door to her office and she looked up to see Reed, her bailiff. Reed was seventy years old, a holdover from the former judge who once occupied her office, and also the judge before that. He was about 5'3" tall and weighed in at 120 pounds. There was nothing menacing about him. Because he was so thin and small, his gun looked oversized in the thick black leather holster strapped between his chest and stomach (he had no hips to hold it in the conventional position). One hoped a criminal would not go berserk on his watch.

"Excuse me, Your Honor," he said in his high-pitched voice.

"Yes, Reed, what is it?"

"I know the courtroom's going be packed, so I asked Judge Dugdale's bailiff to join me this morning. Just thought you should know."

"Thank you, Reed. I don't anticipate any trouble, but I appreciate the extra precaution."

Tensions run high and hot in the courtroom, especially murder cases where the families of the victim and the killer sit side by side on the gallery pews. Cynthia had seen family members of a victim try to hop the short railing that separated them from the killer seated in cuffs just a few feet away, hoping to get in at least one nasty uppercut before they were restrained.

Cynthia buzzed for her clerk. Joyce squeezed into the leather chair across from the judge. Her make-up had been applied with care, but too thickly. She had the look of a woman who took an hour to primp for the day but was not commensurately rewarded for the effort. But there was no more devoted clerk than Joyce, and Cynthia loved her.

"Are we ready to go?" Cynthia asked.

"I believe so, Your Honor." Joyce referred to Cynthia as "Your Honor" at all times, despite the judge's suggestion that the formality was unnecessary in the privacy of her office. "I've cleared the calendar this morning of any other matters, Your Honor. And Reed will be anxious to report that he's asked another bailiff to help this morning."

"Oh, he's already reported in." They both smiled with affection for Reed.

Cynthia spent the next half hour in her office while the courtroom filled. At 9:00 a.m. Joyce pushed a button at her table in the courtroom, one level below the elevated perch where Judge Markham would sit, signaling to Cynthia that they were all assembled and waiting. Cynthia lifted her black judicial robe from the hook on the back of her door and slipped it on over her dress. She checked her hair one more time and then walked a few feet down the hallway and through a hidden door leading to the courtroom.

"ALL RISE!" Reed commanded, like a Chihuahua that you didn't want to mess with. "The Second Judicial Court, in and for the State of Arizona, is now in session, the Honorable Cynthia P. Markham presiding. You may now be seated."

Cynthia scanned the capacity crowd in the courtroom. There was bench seating for sixty spectators in the gallery. The hard wooden benches were rarely filled. Maybe a loving family member or a bored lawyer waiting for another proceeding would wander in. But most justice in America is dispensed in nearly empty courtrooms. That day in Judge Markham's courtroom was different, for the citizens were snugly packed into the seven rows of pews.

Reed stood guard on one side of the courtroom and the temporary bailiff was on the other. He was short and stocky, unlike Reed who was as thin as his plant namesake. Because of his compacted girth, the other bailiff waddled from side to side when he walked, like a penguin, or an old fashioned metronome on top of a piano. His serious scowl suggested he wouldn't put up with any nonsense.

Blake sat at the counsel table next to his lawyer, adjacent to the jury box that held the only empty seats in the house. The prosecutor and two junior lawyers sat at the other table. The junior lawyers adjusted their cuffs and touched their ties.

They hoped Judge Markham would acknowledge them, but assumed she would not, for they were invited by the senior lawyer simply to be his props. There was an open area in the middle of the courtroom—the pit, they call it—where a lonely podium stood.

Judge Markham sat at her perch, perfectly framed between the American flag and the state flag of Arizona.

"This is the matter of the *State of Arizona vs. Blake Morgan*, at the time set for sentencing. Are the parties ready to proceed?"

"Yes, Your Honor," the two attorneys half stood and spoke in unison before sitting once again.

"Mr. Campbell, do you intend to call any witnesses in this proceeding?" she asked the prosecutor.

"No, Your Honor, we do not. We are confident the court is familiar with the unnatural circumstances of this crime."

"Very well. Mr. Bradshaw?" she asked Blake's lawyer.

He stood fully erect this time. "Yes, Your Honor. Both the defendant, Blake Morgan, and his wife, Naomi, wish to speak before the court imposes a sentence here."

"Very well. First I will hear from the State. Mr. Campbell, you may proceed."

Campbell stood, and with a practiced air of solemnity, he gravely made his way to the podium. He paused for affect as he deliberately spread his notes before him. This did not reflect uncertainty as to what he would say. He'd practically memorized his speech in front of his bathroom mirror and was anxious to give it now, for he believed in what he was about to say.

"Your Honor, Counsel," a quick nod to Blake's attorney, "this case raises fundamental societal concerns that extend far beyond the walls of this courtroom. Indeed, there may be no more compelling legal issue before the courts today. The defendant has admitted, under oath, that he intentionally planned and then carried out the killing of Steven Olson, a completely defenseless man.

"Now, he will stand before this court and say, 'But I am no criminal! Steve Olson and I were friends! Why would I want to kill him?'

"Why indeed? The bedrock of our legal system is threatened when a man can take the life of another, believing he can disregard the law with impunity. The defendant knew this killing was wrong, for he was careful to keep it hidden. But he thought his wisdom and dark philosophy about the sanctity of life was greater than the law. He arrogantly thought he could substitute his own perverse taking of innocent life for that of our time-honored laws that forbid it; laws that were authored thousands of years ago, since Biblical times, and have been honored in our courtrooms and our legal system ever since.

"If society, through its law, allows for the killing of another human being because it satisfies one person's abnormally corrupt philosophy, then where does it lead? He will testify that he thought it was appropriate, as if he were the law. But if the defendant can intentionally make a mockery of the law, regardless of his intentions, then what good is the law? And what good is this court whose duty is to uphold it?

"The slope is slippery, indeed. Did the defendant 'mean well,' or is he just disturbed? And does it even matter? The law is clear. The defendant voluntarily, and in devious secrecy, killed Steven Olson. He intentionally suffocated this defenseless man and then sneaked out, hoping to be unseen.

"This court should impose the maximum sentence allowed under the law, the very law the defendant, and this court, is required to keep and to uphold. Thank you, Your Honor."

"Thank you, Mr. Campbell." She then looked at Bradshaw. "Counsel?"

Blake's lawyer stood and called Naomi to the podium. She stood next to the lawyer, one hand gripping the podium to steady herself.

"Mrs. Morgan," said the judge, "you are free to tell me what I should consider before imposing the sentence. Even though you have not been formally sworn to tell the truth, I have every expectation you will do so."

"Yes, thank you, I will." She swallowed hard and unnecessarily smoothed her hair with her free hand. She willed herself to not look over at Blake.

"Mrs. Morgan," Bradshaw said, "please tell the judge about your husband."

"Your Honor," she paused and felt the tears coming, already at the door. She caught them and continued. "Blake is the finest man I know," she turned and looked at him. "Blake loved Steve with all his heart. He isn't a violent person; he's never hurt anyone in his life. He's a loyal and committed husband, father, and friend. Steve Olson had no better friend in the world than Blake. I just know that if Steve could testify today he would implore you to let my husband go free. He would tell you he was suffering and asked Blake to help him. And like the best friend a man could ask for, Blake did. He helped Steve when Steve could not help himself. But Steve can't testify, because he was already dying of a deadly and horrific disease.

"What good would it do to put Blake in prison? He's no threat to the community. He would leave me and our baby daughter. We need him. There has already been enough loss and heartache. I beg you not to create even more with a prison sentence."

"Thank you, Mrs. Morgan," Judge Markham said. "Counsel, would the defendant care to speak?"

"Yes, Your Honor," Bradshaw said and turned to Blake. "Will you please step forward?"

Blake stepped from the table to the podium. He did not look like a criminal. He was dressed in a suit and tie that fit him, and he looked comfortable in it. He was handsome, athletic, and healthy. But even at the apex of this ordeal, he had little adrenaline left. This was no soapbox opportunity, for what did he know? What had he learned? He was not self-righteous about any of it, and it confused him that so many people were.

"Please tell the Court how you feel."

"Your Honor," Blake began, "I have never been in a courtroom before. I listened to what Mr. Campbell said about me flaunting the law and not respecting it. But that just isn't true. I do respect the law. I have followed it my entire life."

Blake then turned around and faced Alison, who was sitting in the front row, directly behind Mr. Campbell. They had not spoken to each other since Steve's funeral. "Alison . . . I am so sorry. For everything. I hope you know that whatever happens, I am sorry for your loss. I think I know how it feels, because I have lost a best friend, too. But I lost him to Creutzfeldt-Jakob's disease."

Blake then faced the judge again. "I don't know what to say. I don't see how sending me to prison will help anything.

Maybe you think I will flaunt a sentence of probation or a lenient prison term. But I wouldn't. I'm not a crusader. But I do believe in a person's right to choose. And Steve chose. He did. I don't question his decision. And I only partially question my own, because my loyalty to Steve is as important to me as my loyalty to the law, a law that in my opinion shouldn't be rigidly enforced under all circumstances."

He sat back down and listened to the lawyers make their final summations. There was nothing said that was different or new; nothing that would stir the hearts and minds of men in a way that would ever compel universal consensus.

"Will the defendant, Blake Morgan, please stand," Judge Markham said.

Blake and his lawyer walked the few paces and stood again at the podium in the pit of the courtroom.

"Mr. Morgan," she began "a great challenge for any court is to balance the interests of the law and justice. Usually that balance is in perfect harmony, or at least near perfect harmony. But sometimes there is friction between the two. Any sentence that honors our legal system must satisfy both the law, which is quite clear in this case, and justice, which is cloudy. If I were to consider only the law, my decision would be an easy one. But jurists from the beginning of time have struggled to fashion fair punishment for a crime that has already been committed, knowing full well their decision would not, could not, undo the past.

"I am sorry for the loss of your friend, Mr. Morgan. I am persuaded you did what you thought was best. You imposed your personal version of justice, but in doing, so you ignored the law. And that is something I cannot do. Perhaps one day our society will come to universally accept physician-assisted suicide, voluntary euthanasia, and other philosophies of those who lobby for different forms of death with dignity legislation. But that day has not yet come.

"I hereby sentence you to three years of incarceration at the Arizona Correctional Center. The term will commence immediately, but I will allow a brief period of time for you to visit with your wife and beautiful daughter. I want you to know that, personally, Mr. Morgan, there is much in me that admires the courage and devotion you showed to your friend. It is not my place to impose my own philosophy on this decision, but neither is it appropriate that I completely ignore it. I do not regard you as a criminal, Mr. Morgan, but only as someone who has violated the law."

PART III

When I find myself in times of trouble
Mother Mary comes to me
Speaking words of wisdom, let it be
And in my hour of darkness
She is standing right in front of me
Speaking words of wisdom, let it be, let it be

—Paul McCartney

42

Blake heard the boots on the painted cement floor of the corridor at 7:00 a.m. sharp. He had not been provided an alarm clock, nor was one needed, because he heard the same boots every single morning. Then he heard the loud click when the guard pulled the electrical power switch. The bright fluorescent lights sputtered and spit on and off, warming up for the day. They illuminated a small desk, twin bed, wall calendar, and the stainless steel toilet. The cinderblock walls had been painted Navajo White so many times they were practically smooth. This was his home.

There'd been protests every morning. "Turn off the goddamned lights!" But the guards never listened, for they were not a cheery lot. They were crude and mean and treated the inmates with contempt. Blake wondered about the fine line that separated some of them from the men they held prisoner.

Blake stared at the ceiling for the final time and listened to the obnoxious sounds of humanity stripped bare. Inmates farted, burped, peed, and bitched about everything that possibly came to mind. And Blake knew there was plenty to bitch about. No one there was innocent, but all declared themselves to be victims of something or another; a crime superseding their own. Their lawyer was in cahoots, the judge was a jerk, their crime was petty, or they hadn't been properly breast-fed. Precious few confessions of personal responsibility were spoken there. Blake was no different—he didn't think he belonged there, either.

"Hey, Morgan, think maybe you could do us all a favor and shut the fuck up with all the snoring?" It was the guy in the next cell, a menacing bald man who had a prominent vein down the middle of his forehead which caused him to look like a head of green cabbage. Blake wasn't sure if he snored or not, and neither was Cabbage Head—he just wanted to hear himself talk.

"Sure, Jose, I'll see what I can do." Was Jose even his name? Blake could never remember what their names were. They were moved, shuffled, transferred, and released all the time. And he had to watch what few possessions he had because they didn't make the friendliest neighbors. He had a comb, a few dollars, three books, and his "soap on a rope," a gift from Hal Crawford, his former editor, meant as a joke. It hadn't been funny. Blake initially thought about forming a Neighborhood Watch Program, but quickly sensed the futility in it.

He lay on his bed and thought about his first days at the Arizona State Penitentiary. As a new fish, he'd been sent to maximum security for one week. This was not a reflection on the severity of his crime—all new fish start there. Twenty-three hours a day in lockdown. He was allowed out of his cell one hour each day, and it was usually at an inconvenient time (like three o'clock in the morning) to shower or walk around the yard. This first week was a period of relative safety because he didn't mingle with other inmates, something he wasn't eager to do in any event.

After a week they released him to general population where all the inmates are housed together. This had been a horrifying experience. He thought he might be raped, or beaten by violent criminals with pent up testosterone and nothing to lose. It was in general pop where one must make his stand, or become someone's bitch. There were fistfights and threats of intimidation. He received his first care package from Naomi: radio, underwear, coffee mugs, and bowls. Within minutes, three tattooed inmates demanded he give it all to them. As soon as he did, he realized he would never have anything of value again in prison, for he had exposed himself as a coward.

Blake was relieved when they transferred him out of general pop two months later to a smaller section of the prison. This was not the country club section (Blake would learn there was no such thing, even for rich tax evaders and politicians). He slowly became accustomed to the routine of prison life and the dank, twice-breathed air inside the joint. The days turned into weeks and then months.

He now lay on his bunk, the scratchy wool army blanket and flat pillow a comfort to him. That's when he heard the familiar footsteps walking down the corridor, and then the loud click when the electrical switch was pulled.

Blake's time was up. He had served his sentence. They would come for him at 9:00 a.m., and that would give him plenty of time to pack his few toiletries and books.

"Hey, Morgan! I'm glad you're leavin',' you lucky goddamned sonofabitch." This heartfelt send-off from Cabbage Head next door was the only one he was given. There were no balloons and neither had the prison cooks baked a special sheet cake with *"Congratulations Morgan On Serving Your*

Time!" written in cursive frosting across the top.

Blake had come to respect some of the inmates, not a single one of whom was actually innocent. But who isn't guilty of something? These were guys who had done really stupid things. Maybe they were partially justified, but probably not. This one was guilty of robbery to support a heroin addiction, and that one broke into a Rite Aid pharmacy wielding a gun to steal pills and money. None of them had attended Princeton. And what about the doctor down the street who'd given a "humanitarian dose" of morphine to stop the heart of the old woman who didn't even know where she was? *He* wasn't in prison, because no one technically knew he'd done it. In fact, the family of the old woman had looked the other way in gratitude rather than make yet another $7,000 monthly payment to the nursing home.

Blake was not a preachy sort. A few weeks earlier, however, he'd written a letter to the editor, which had been published in his old newspaper.

> "My name is Blake Morgan. I am inmate number 6749 at the Arizona State Correctional facility. I have been in prison for two and a half years now and will be released soon. I am in prison because I helped end the life of my friend. No, I killed him. At the time, I thought it was the right thing to do. Now that I've had time to ponder it (you have a lot of time for pondering here), I've come to believe I was wrong. There are procedures to mend a broken law, or to modernize stubborn antiquated thinking. I ignored them, and for that I was correctly punished. I have no bitterness about it, and I sincerely hope others will not judge me too harshly for what I did. I understand if they do.

"I believe laws concerning how some lives end ought to be changed. I don't pretend to know exactly how they should be changed, but there ought to be open discussion without fear of being labeled a godless mercenary. I'll admit that I've grown tired of hearing how Jack Kevorkian was a reckless lunatic, a loose cannon, or a monster. Views of life and death are varied and complicated. I don't know exactly what I believe, other than my belief that death need not come at such a heavy price. There ought to be a humane way to leave this life without undue suffering. I don't advocate death panels for people who reach a certain age, or the mandatory pulling of plugs. But I do believe many people suffer needlessly because they fear for their salvation. We should all agree this is unnecessarily cruel.

"I met a man named Gene who was dying of ALS. He tried to end his life but failed. He lived several more years that he described as the best years of his life. Surely no one had the right to take those years from him. And there was a remarkable young woman named Jenny who chose to end her suffering with grace and dignity. Who should have the right to deprive her of that choice?"

Blake wrote Alison every week. He understood how angry she must have been. But if he could forgive her for insisting that he go to prison, couldn't she forgive him for helping Steve? He received no response to his letters. Then one day, a year later, she came unannounced to see him.

She was still a naturally beautiful woman, but her wheat-colored hair now had streaks of gray. Her eyes were exhausted looking and there were a few more creases at the corners. She noticed Blake was thinner and paler. He also spoke with more deliberation and care. He had no interest in talking about himself or what he'd been through.

"I still miss him so much," she said.

"Me, too."

"Why didn't you tell me, Blake?"

"Steve knew you'd be upset. But he didn't want to be a burden any longer."

"A *burden*? How could he think that? I would trade everything I have to have him back."

"But he couldn't do it, Alison. He was dying and he just couldn't do it."

"Did he suffer? You can tell me the truth, Blake. What was it like in the end?"

"No, he didn't suffer."

"Do you swear?"

Blake hesitated.

"Oh my God," she said and raised her hand to her mouth. "How long?"

"Alison, please don't do this to yourself."

"How long? Tell me."

"Only a few seconds."

She pulled a tissue from her pocket.

"I'm so sorry, Alison."

"Was he afraid?"

"No."

"He's at peace now, isn't he?"

"He is. It's what he wanted, Alison, I swear it on my life."

"I believe you. I know how much he was suffering. Maybe it was me. Maybe I was selfish to have wanted him to hang on as long as possible."

And so it was that Alison had begun to experience a sea change. It was the thought of Steve's suffering at the end that was the most painful for her. The thought that he had to sneak behind everyone's back, and then struggle for breath under a pillow. Maybe there were times when it was appropriate—when God wouldn't condemn a man for his want of refuge. Perhaps modern science could coexist with her belief in the sanctity of life. Indeed, perhaps it should. Not with a gun, or a pillow, but a humane dose of anesthesia administered in the open by a compassionate doctor. For who wants their final moments to be had as a felon in the sticky, dark hiding places of sin?

The guards came for Blake without fanfare. He was just another prisoner whose time was up. He stood by the bars of his cell, holding what few possessions he had, and patiently waited for them to free him from his cage. Moments later, the last door slid open and he walked out. He didn't know what to expect when they freed him. At first he'd been reluctant to step outside, as if there'd been a mistake and he'd be re-arrested for trying to escape. He almost forgot that he'd pictured this moment in his mind a thousand times since his incarceration.

Naomi was standing on the sidewalk. Libby stood next to her. He'd rarely seen Libby standing, and now she came nearly to her mother's waist. They were both waving, and then Naomi ran to him. There was so much to say, so much to cover. But that could wait. Naomi drove home and Blake sat in the passenger seat holding her hand. He opened the window so the air could rip through the car. Naomi said nothing about her hair; she just looked at her husband whose head was leaned back to the headrest with his eyes closed.

Her cell phone rang.

"Oh, hi, Chad. Yes, your Uncle Blake's here with me now. We just picked him up. Sure, I'll let you talk to him," and she handed the phone to Blake.

"Hello, is this Chad?" Blake asked.

"Yeah."

"Hey, thanks for calling me. I can't wait to see you."

"Um, Uncle Blake?"

"Yes?"

"Um, I made the Titans. That's our baseball team."

"Wow, that's terrific! Good for you!"

"I'm a pitcher."

"That's great. Can I come to one of your games?"

"Yeah, but, um, my coach had to quit."

"That's too bad."

"So, um, I was just wondering. Um, could you maybe be our coach? My mom said you'd be good at it 'cause you used to be in the majors."

———

The final bill was an edited version of the original. Concessions had to be made for it to have any hope of passing. It'd been to committee and back several times. Now it was finally ready to be presented for open comment in the House committee chaired by a conservative Republican who was firm in his belief that man should not frolic on God's turf.

"We couldn't have come this far without you," Blake said on the drive to the Arizona statehouse.

"I think it's what she would have wanted," she said.

They parked and walked up the expansive marble staircase, past protestors who didn't know them, or how close to the issue they actually were. These protestors, who hadn't actually faced the issue, believed the bill before the Arizona House of Representatives would launch a torpedo through the iron hull of their faith. She probably would have been one of them a few years earlier.

The two of them walked down a corridor where lobbyists milled about, cajoling representatives about the urgency of their causes. They stepped into a large room overflowing with concerned citizens. Nearly as many stood in the back as there were available chairs. Twelve state representatives occupied seats in the front of the room, facing the audience.

"Ladies and Gentlemen," said the Chairman, "this is the time and place for public comment on House Bill 376 which, among other things, allows for the restricted right to physician-assisted suicide. I admonish all those present that proper decorum is required and I urge everyone to be respectful of the testimony presented here."

She stood on the side of the room next to Blake because there were no available seats. She deliberately slowed her breathing and thought of her. She touched her hair and picked a small piece of lint off her skirt.

"Will the first witness please come forward to be sworn and address the committee?"

She took a few paces to a table that faced the representatives, the crowd of people to her back. She pulled back the chair and sat down. It was completely quiet in the room. She leaned into the microphone that had been placed on the table.

"My name is Joanne Kimball. I am here to testify in favor of this bill on behalf of my beautiful daughter, Jenny Lawson."

Warren Driggs is an attorney. He is married and has four extraordinary children and four heathly, new grandchildren whose years, at least for now, seem endless. Through the years he watched his grandmother lose her cognitive function and spend the final years of her life in an "affordable" rest home. He also lost his parents to drawn-out fatal illnesses, and his friend to the devastating effects of Creutzfeldt-Jakob disease. These loved ones, and their end of life suffering, are the inspiration for *A Tortoise in the Road*.